A Most Dange...

L.M. Jackson lives in London with his partner Joanne and daughter Clara. He has written four books under the name Lee Jackson, the first of which, *London Dust*, was shortlisted for the Ellis Peters Historical Dagger Award. He is fascinated by the social history of nineteenth-century London and maintains the popular website www.victorianlondon.org which is devoted to exploring the minutiae of daily life in the Victorian metropolis. *A Most Dangerous Woman* is the first in a new series of mysteries featuring lady detective Sarah Tanner.

Praise for L.M. Jackson

'Victorian London is brought vividly to life from the very beginning . . . plenty of wry humour . . . and engrossing historical detail' *Time Out*

'Victorian London can be such an evocative place, having captured the imaginations of countless crime writers. To Conan Doyle, Anne Perry, Andrew Martin . . . we must now add Lee Jackson who [with *The Welfare of the Dead*] makes this patch his very own' *Guardian*

'[Jackson] demonstrates quite brilliantly what the genre can do. [*A Metropolitan Murder*] is a rare and succulent piece of work' *Literary Review*

'The smoky, foggy, horse-dung laden atmosphere of the London streets steams off the page' *Spectator*

'Full of power and substance, *London Dust* is an assured debut . . . a compelling and evocative novel that brings the past, and its dead, to life again' *Guardian*

'Victo... ...an atm...

Published by Arrow Books 2008

2 4 6 8 10 9 7 5 3

T   he
pro   ce to
a   l.

This book i   way of trade
or ot   ilated
without   or cover
other   imilar
co   the

First published in Great Britain in 2007 by
William Heinemann

Arrow Books
The Random House Group Limited
20 Vauxhall Bridge Road, London, SW1V 2SA

www.rbooks.co.uk

Addresses for companies within The Random House Group Limited can be
found at: www.randomhouse.co.uk/offices.htm

The Random House Group Limited Reg. No. 954009

A CIP catalogue record for this book
is available from the British Library

ISBN 9780099498391

The Random House Group Limited supports
The Forest Stewardship Council (FSC), the leading international
forest certification organisation. All our titles that are printed on Greenpeace
approved FSC certified paper carry the FSC logo.
Our paper procurement policy can be found at
www.rbooks.co.uk/environment

Typeset in Sabon by Palimpsest Book Production Limited,
Grangemouth, Stirlingshire
Printed and bound in Great Britain by
CPI Antony Rowe, Chippenham, Wiltshire

L. M. Jackson

A Most Dangerous Woman

arrow books

PROLOGUE

Sarah Tanner bought her coffee-house in the spring of eighteen hundred and fifty-two. It was a small, rather dusty premises, situated upon the corner of Leather Lane Market and Liquorpond Street, in the parish of St. Albans, Holborn. The previous owner – a widower who had taken to drink upon the death of his wife – had rather let himself go, and his old business had rather gone with him. Little remained in the way of fixtures and fittings: only a bronze coffee urn, dull and discoloured, that stood upon the counter, and the faint, melancholy aroma of roasted mocha – or, more likely, the scent of some more economical berry, laced with chicory – which had, over the years, permeated the woodwork.

To some, regardless of the interior, it might have seemed an unfortunate location for any commercial undertaking. For the district was mentioned in the *Police News* with disturbing regularity and, if the respectable folk of nearby quarters said anything of their Leather Lane neighbours, it was generally to condemn them as thieves and parasites; or to commend their souls to the care of the local Home Missionary, which amounted to much the same thing. Sarah Tanner, however, had given the matter some thought:

the area was a poor one, but she had known worse; the two little rooms and attic above the shop seemed perfectly adequate for her own comfort; and, most importantly, the proximity of the street market meant there would always be a passing trade. From thirsty costermongers, who set up stall at the break of dawn, to the weary females who scrabbled for bargains at the close of day, the pavement outside was rarely empty. And if the occasional cadger or out-and-out villain should stumble upon Sarah Tanner's new establishment, she did not much mind – as long as they paid their way.

Mrs. Tanner – she had resolved to appropriate that title to herself at an early stage in proceedings, though only twenty-seven years of age and unfamiliar with the married state – proved to have a sound business mind. The little shop, once cleaned and renovated, soon began to prosper. In fact, it was not long before she employed both a waiter – an elderly man by the name of Grundy, reputed to have known better days – and a certain Mrs. Hinchley, who, upon interview, declared herself 'a plain cook and no nonsense', which was precisely what was required.

Mrs. Tanner's greatest commercial asset was that she kept regular hours. For she happened to have that most useful of objects, a little mahogany clock – a rarity in Leather Lane – and a striking one at that. Thus she opened her door at precisely six o'clock in the morning, rain or shine, and closed it again at midnight – in marked contrast to the neighbourhood's more established eating-houses. Her food, too, was both edible and reasonably priced – a rare combination – and provided the costermongers with a breakfast which was, in their own words, 'a proper tightener'. Tea and coffee came by the pint – one penny – or the small cup – a ha'penny – and something hot was always ready on the grill, from eggs and bacon in the morning to sausage and potatoes at night.

Mrs. Tanner also understood the value of advertisement. After two or three weeks in the business, she hired a Frenchman, a self-proclaimed genius with a brush, much down upon his luck, to hand-paint a signboard, which spelt out the words *Dining and Coffee Rooms* in black and gold. Then came tickets, announcing 'A Good Dinner for 8d.' and 'Leg of Beef Soup, 2d. per cup', placed prominently in the window, above the red curtain that concealed diners' lower extremities from passers-by. And, of course, there was the best advertisement of all – the rich smell of sizzling chops, kippers or Yarmouth bloaters that occasionally escaped from the narrow confines of the kitchen. And it was a narrow little room – for the shop was not a large one, by any means. The front, which consisted of a small plate-glass window and a very plain door, set back a little from the street, could not have measured more than twelve feet across. Inside, there was just enough space for four booths against the wall, the serving-counter, and a pair of tables by the window. It was only after purchasing the lease that Mrs. Tanner discovered the room itself was rather irregular and wedge-shaped and, upon close inspection, she found that the walls buckled inwards slightly, as if the victim of monumental tight-lacing. Still, she was not daunted by the discovery and it soon became clear, to anyone who took an interest, that the new coffee-house on the corner was being admirably managed and maintained by its new proprietress.

But what of Sarah Tanner herself? Now, *there* was something of a contradiction. For example, it was said that she had the good manners of a respectable upper servant but was far too young to have been pensioned; that she spoke as if she had received an education, but knew the costers' slang as if she were born-and-bred to it; and that she not only had no husband – which was a commonplace on Leather Lane, where husbands came and went with remarkable ease, generally via the local beer-shop – but seemed never to have possessed one. This latter point was particularly remarkable, since she had a pretty face, with dark brown hair and deep hazel eyes, and a full, graceful figure – a figure which, upon first sight, some of the more impetuous costermongers even remarked upon to their wives. It was, doubtless, these unfortunate remarks that prompted a few of the coster-women to declare Mrs. Tanner a queer character, not quite 'on the square'; and to suggest that she had got her shop and money *somewhere*, and *they* didn't care to inquire where that might be.

One thing was for certain: Sarah Tanner was not going to tell them. And if, upon her arrival, she was the subject of gossip, it was the proverbial nine-days' wonder, soon over-shadowed by more exciting news, like the mysterious theft of old Bill Teach's donkey during the night, or Sal Perkins 'clouting' her rival in love outside the Presbyterian Chapel. Indeed, the streets between Leather Lane and nearby Saffron Hill, whatever the morals of their inhabitants, howsoever poor they might be, were never short of incident. The mystery of Sarah Tanner was soon put to one side and Mrs. Tanner, for her part, was quite content with the outcome. For she went about her business with – well, not shyness by any means, but a certain degree of reserve. And even Ralph Grundy, who saw her every day, would happily testify that his employer was 'a close 'un, and no mistake'. And, if asked to say any more on the subject, Mr. Grundy would merely tap his nose, raise his glass, and refuse to reveal any dark secrets.

To a degree, this was a natural discretion on Ralph Grundy's part; but, principally, it was his own ignorance of Sarah Tanner's history. All the same, relying upon the wisdom of his years – for he was in his sixties, and rather given to solitary speculation – he privately concluded that his employer had 'a past' of one sort or another, one that might well catch up with her.

And, of course, he was quite right.

CHAPTER ONE

It had just gone half-past eleven at night and the little coffee-house on the corner was quite empty of customers. Mrs. Hinchley had long since gone home and Ralph Grundy was busying himself in the kitchen. Sarah Tanner, meanwhile, had moved from her usual seat behind the counter to stand in front of the fireplace and warm her hands. It was just as she stood there that she heard the shop-door creak behind her.

'Sarah? It's never you, is it?'

The interruption startled Mrs. Tanner. It was peculiar for anyone on Leather Lane to address her by her first name. She turned to see a figure at the door, a man two or three years older than herself, dressed in a smart brown suit and hat, with a russet-coloured waistcoat and rather extravagant red cravat.

'Don't say you don't remember George Phelps?' continued the newcomer, an exaggerated look of sorrow on his face. 'Don't say it, old gal!'

The proprietress of the Dining and Coffee Rooms visibly paled at the sight of her visitor.

'I know you all right,' Sarah Tanner replied quietly, stealing a nervous glance over her shoulder, towards the kitchen. The man, in turn, grinned and sat down onto a bench seat in one of the shop's little booths.

'How are things with you, eh?' he inquired. 'How long's it been?'

'Never mind that. What do you want here, Georgie?'

'Me?' said George Phelps, removing his hat with something of a flourish, and setting it down upon the table. 'I don't *want* nothing, old gal. I was going my merry way and just saw you standing there, large as life. Gave me a shock, seeing you in these parts. Last I'd heard, you'd ran off with a certain young gent.'

'Then you heard wrong,' replied Sarah Tanner emphatically. As she spoke, the rattling sound of Ralph Grundy industriously cleaning the gridiron echoed from the kitchen. She softened her voice. 'I mean, I'm sure it's good to see you, Georgie, but, if you don't mind, you can oblige me by leaving.'

'Leaving?' replied George Phelps, scratching his chin. 'That's a fine welcome, when I only just pitched up! Don't an old friend deserve better than that?'

'An old friend might.'

'Come on, Sarah, don't be like that. Now, for one thing, the way I recall it, you still owe me two bob for that last cab we took from Norwood. I weren't planning on calling in my debts, mind you. But, seeing as I've found you here, well, I reckon it's fate we met up. We might do some business, you and me.'

'So it's money you're after.'

'Sarah, I just happened to be passing . . .'

Sarah Tanner dismissed George Phelps's reply with a shake of her head and walked over to the shop-counter. Opening the till-drawer that lay beneath, she retrieved two shillings and placed them on the wooden surface.

'Now we're square,' she said. 'You can go.'

'Square?' he replied, contemplating the money. 'Maybe. You're pretty free and easy with that money-box. Do you work here? Is that it, eh?'

George Phelps sounded incredulous, as if he could not truly conceive of such a thing. But Mrs. Tanner had no chance to reply. For, at that moment, Ralph Grundy's grey head appeared at the kitchen-door. The waiter peered into the shop.

'You all right, missus?'

'Yes, Ralph, thank you. Mr. Phelps here – he's an old acquaintance of mine.'

Ralph Grundy glanced in Phelps's direction, but found the stranger's face inconveniently obscured by the curtains that divided the booths.

'You finish off, Ralph,' continued Mrs. Tanner. 'Then you can help me with the shutters.'

Ralph Grundy nodded and returned to his duties. Sarah Tanner, meanwhile, looked back at George Phelps. Her visitor was chuckling quietly to himself.

'"Missus"?' he said. 'You? Don't tell me you've gone and settled in this queer little rat hole? I'd never have believed it! Not in a million years!'

'I'll have you know, Georgie Phelps,' she replied, a degree of indignation in her voice, 'that I do very nicely here. I don't need the likes of you to spoil things for me.'

'"The likes of me"!' he exclaimed, still visibly amused. 'Oh! Sarah, I never thought—'

'Never thought what?' she said impatiently.

But George Phelps fell silent. Moreover, in an instant, all humour had drained from his face.

'What?' said Mrs. Tanner, puzzled.

8

'Hush, listen!'

George Phelps dropped down into the booth, his back to the window. Hunched up, concealed from the street, he motioned for Sarah Tanner to come and sit opposite him. His expression was so urgent and insistent that she obeyed.

The sound was that of heavy footsteps – sturdy boots, walking at a steady pace, along the street outside, close by the shop-window. Sarah Tanner peered out through the glass. Directly beneath the flare of gas that illuminated the Dining and Coffee Rooms sign-board stood a tall, blue-uniformed figure, a heavy-set man with large side-burns and moustache, and a high glazed hat.

'It's a Peeler, ain't it? Big fellow, whiskers?' said Phelps.

She nodded.

'Don't catch his eye, for God's sake,' said Phelps, pulling her back.

'At least you haven't changed much, Georgie,' she whispered.

George Phelps said nothing. He stayed quite still, a finger to his lips. After what seemed an age, they heard the sound of the policeman moving on.

'He's been dogging us all the way from Covent Garden,' he muttered, mumbling a curse under his breath.

'With good reason, I expect.'

'Maybe,' said Phelps. 'I thought I'd lose him round the alleys.'

'What was it this time?'

'Some hotel work,' he replied. 'Though I don't know how he got fly to it.'

'What if he catches up with you?'

'He won't find a thing on me; I ain't even done the job.'

'Well, perhaps you had better be off, all the same,' she suggested. 'He might come back.'

'Aye, he might at that,' replied George Phelps.

Sarah Tanner said nothing.

'Well, as you like,' said Phelps, getting up from the booth and pocketing the two coins that still lay on the counter. 'I'll remember you to Her Majesty, anyhow.'

'I'd rather you kept it dark, Georgie.'

'Would you now? Well, I suppose it weren't the best parting, now that I come to think about it. Still, you know me, darlin',' he replied with a wink. 'I won't say a word. Word of honour.'

The look upon Sarah Tanner's face rather implied that she knew nothing of the sort. Nonetheless, George Phelps, with a rather satirical bow, proceeded to make his way to the door.

'I'll see you again, *missus*,' he said with a grin, as he stood in the doorway. Then, out upon the street, he turned up his collar and walked quickly away.

Mrs. Tanner returned to her counter, with every intention of counting the day's takings. But her mind was distracted and she continued to gaze out of the window – until her reverie was interrupted by an unexpected sight. For the burly figure of the policeman passed by the shop a second time, doubtless having completed a circuit round the back alley. It was not his presence that unnerved her, nor the grim determined look upon his face as he passed beneath the gas-light. Rather, it was the item he held, partially concealed in his hand, just visible above the curtain that covered the lower portion of the window. It was not the familiar wooden truncheon of the Metropolitan Police. She could see it clearly – the glint of a sharp metal blade.

Sarah Tanner tried to gather her thoughts. After a moment's hestitation, she called out to Ralph Grundy – bidding him to mind the shop – grabbed her shawl from where it lay behind the counter, and hurried outside.

Leather Lane was all but empty. The only exception was a trio of convivial gentlemen, staggering out of the Bottle of Hay, the nearest public-house. Nonetheless, beyond them, she could just make out the policeman, a couple of hundred yards distant. Then the drunken men veered off, towards Saffron Hill, and the policeman took the opposite direction, turning into Baldwin's Gardens.

Mrs. Tanner knew the road. The 'Gardens' were, in fact, a dingy, narrow side-street, quite barren of any flora – like most metropolitan thoroughfares which make historic claims to rusticity. She walked slowly to the junction, her face partly concealed by her shawl, and glanced warily round the corner. To her annoyance, there was nothing to be seen. For the gas-lights above the little row of nearby shops – long since closed – were not illuminated.

She resolved to press on, just a few steps further. And it was then that something drew her attention to a little alley on the right.

What was it?

Was it the choking, spluttering sound that suddenly assailed her ears?

Or the hint of movement in the darkness, the scratching hands, scraping in the dirt?

Both were terrible enough; quite sufficient to cause a chill to run down her spine. In truth, another woman might have screamed and fled.

And that woman – wise, sensible creature – would not have witnessed the death-throes of George Phelps,

11

the bloody twists and turns of his guts spilling out onto the mud.

Nor would she have seen, in the distance, the sight of a blue-clad figure casting a wary glance in her direction, then disappearing into the darkness.

CHAPTER TWO

A t first, Sarah Tanner felt sure that she was dreaming.
For it seemed quite impossible that George Phelps's
ruined body lay before her. To her stunned senses –
even as desperate half-formed sounds issued from the
man's throat – the scene resembled some strange piece
of bloody theatre, staged for her particular benefit.
But, at the same time, there was no doubting the
evidence of her eyes. Nor could there be any doubt
that George Phelps was dying.

George Phelps himself seemingly became aware of
her presence and raised his head. His eyes silently
pleaded; his hand reached out, grasping at thin air in
short convulsive movements. But she found that she
could only stand and watch, like a dreamer; passive;
utterly helpless.

How long was it, before he died? She had not the
slightest conception. It seemed an eternity. It was only
the smell that finally woke her from her daze; it was
like the scent of the slaughterhouse, the stench of the
back-streets of Smithfield Market; it was the blood
pooling at her feet. Instinctively, she stepped back.

She might cry for help, she thought to herself. She
might cry 'Murder!' and raise the alarm.

But what then?

George Phelps was dead.

It was too late. What good would it do?

And it was the policeman that had killed him.

She turned it over in her mind.

The policeman?

It was Georgie's fault, she assured herself – his bad luck. Mixed up in something he oughtn't to be.

Murder.

It was a bad business – terrible – but not *her* business. Plain and simple.

Sarah Tanner made her decision. Quietly, cautiously, she turned round and retraced her steps back to Leather Lane.

She found that the door to the coffee-shop was locked, the gas-light turned off, and the shop's rickety wooden shutters already slid into place. Ralph Grundy, however, kept sentry inside, his face just visible through the gap between the protective boards, his thin features pressed against the plate glass.

'Thank you for locking up,' she said, hurriedly, as he opened the door.

'Them shutters are a blessed trial, for an old man on his own.'

'Then you should have waited for me,' she replied.

The old man shrugged and looked back at her. 'Something up with your pal, was there, missus?'

'Yes,' she said, with only a slight hesitation. 'He forgot his gloves.'

'Oh, gloves, was it?'

Mrs. Tanner merely nodded.

'Ah, well,' said Ralph Grundy, buttoning his coat. 'I'll be off then.'

'Good night.'

'Night, missus.'

Ralph Grundy put on his hat and quit the shop. Sarah Tanner, meanwhile, locked the door behind the old man, though it was more through force of habit than any conscious decision. Then, just as she did every night, she took the oil-lamp that sat upon the counter, and carried it carefully up the back stairs to her bedroom above the shop. It was the privilege of the owner: a small room, overlooking the street. It contained a bed, dressing-table and washstand, all kept clean and tidy, a comfortable armchair beside the window, and a rather grand old wardrobe, only a little scratched here and there.

She sat upon the bed, unlaced her boots, and unbuttoned her dress. There was already a small fire burning in the hearth – a luxury she always carefully prepared a good hour before closing – and, as was her custom, she undressed with her back to the glowing coals, changing into her woollen night-gown.

But she knew in her heart that she would not sleep.

Morning crept stealthily over Leather Lane, a faint and smoky half-light, filtering through the murky metropolitan sky. And with the break of day came news of a terrible discovery in the region of Baldwin's Gardens. The intelligence came neither from the street-patterers, who daily gathered at either end of the market, armed with dubious ballad sheets of bygone murders, outrages and tragedies, nor from the penny papers, who would have to wait a full twenty-four hours for their opportunity; nor even from the Metropolitan Police, although they gave the matter their full attention. Rather it darted spontaneously here and there, communicated in quiet whispers and loud speculation, until at last it came to the notice of a certain respectable old matron, who cooked breakfasts, 'full hot', in a certain coffee-shop upon the corner of Leather Lane and Liquorpond Street. And she, in her turn, had no desire to keep the information to herself.

'Murdered in cold blood,' said Mrs. Hinchley in her most matter-of-fact tone, brutally cracking an egg on the rim of the frying-pan. 'They found him off Baldwin's Gardens not three hours ago.'

It was almost half-past seven in the morning. The kitchen of Mrs. Tanner's Dining and Coffee Rooms, a rather dark and gloomy place at the best of times, seemed particularly dismal as Mrs. Hinchley made her grim pronouncement. Nothing, however, could dampen the curiosity of Ralph Grundy, who stood nearby, in the little corridor that led through to the shop, waiting to serve up the fruits of Mrs. Hinchley's labours.

'Quite certain are they?' inquired Ralph.

'Certain? I'll say,' continued Mrs. Hinchley, rapidly poking a fork into a pork chop, and depositing it upon the gridiron, warming to her theme as the meat began to sizzle. 'Cut up something awful too. Proper gutted he was, too, like a bleedin' mackerel.'

'Gutted?'

'And they reckon dogs had got to him, poor beggar. Margie Bladstow saw it, and she'll swear on it. And now the Peelers are leaving him there 'til the inquest this arternoon. It ain't Christian. Not from round here, neither; Margie would had know'd him if he were.'

Ralph Grundy nodded his head. Finding Mrs. Hinchley preoccupied with a second and third egg, he glanced back into the shop, where Sarah Tanner stood behind the counter.

'The missus don't look too clever, neither,' he remarked.

'Just!' replied Mrs. Hinchley. 'I said to her first thing, I said, "You're sickenin' for something, my gal. Mark my words. Dodd's Pulmonic wafers. One in the mornin'; one at night. I swears by 'em." Looked right through me. She's too proud, that one.'

Ralph Grundy muttered his agreement and turned to look back at his employer for a second time. There was something wrong with her, that much was certain.

What did Mrs. Tanner say for herself? When asked – and Ralph Grundy did make the inquiry – she merely professed that she had not slept well. But that was not the entire truth: for she had not slept at all. She had, rather, lain awake in her bed and contemplated the scene she had witnessed in Baldwin's Gardens. Nothing else had occupied her mind, from the moment the coals in the hearth dwindled into darkness, until the clock upon her mantelpiece chimed six. And the daylight brought no release; for, as soon as she began serving in the shop, the very first words she heard were rumours of an awful murder.

A murder!

Who could imagine such a thing? Sarah Tanner, for her part, feigned astonishment. And when a certain Joe Drummond, a coster, eating his breakfast, contended that the district had 'sunk bleedin' low', she heartily agreed. When another man conjectured it 'were most likely a foreigner', she did not deny it. Indeed, she played along with every conjecture and theory, without contributing anything to the conversation herself. Thus, as the day progressed, no-one entertained the slightest suspicion that she might know a single detail about the circumstances of the tragedy.

The only possible exception was Ralph Grundy. For

17

the waiter had noticed one small fact: that every time a policeman passed by the shop – and a good many did – Mrs. Tanner was inclined to glance rather anxiously in their direction.

In the event, however, the police did not favour Mrs. Tanner's establishment with their presence. Moreover, if Sarah Tanner noticed Ralph Grundy's attention, it was only upon the several occasions he came over to ask after her health. Thus, to all intents and purposes, Mrs. Tanner spent her day much as she had the day before: serving coffee and busying herself at the counter.

The only difference was that when the clock upon her bedroom mantel chimed midnight – by which time she had ushered Ralph Grundy out of the door, locked the shop, and retired – Sarah Tanner had come to a rather important decision.

In the solitude of her room, rather than putting on her night attire, she went to her wardrobe and selected her best silk gown. It was a fine article: the Paris fashion of the previous year, wholly unsuited to the humble proprietress of a mere coffee-shop.

But, strangely enough, it suited Mrs. Tanner rather nicely.

CHAPTER THREE

Sarah Tanner left her home in Leather Lane at a half-past midnight. She stepped hesitantly into the street, cloaked in a long, ordinary-looking brown shawl, which she had carefully arranged to almost completely conceal her dress. As she stood in the cold night air, she paused and assessed her appearance. The gas above the shop-front was already extinguished and only the keenest observer might have noticed the fine lace trimmings just visible beneath her woollen wrap. Nonetheless, she made a final effort to hide every trace of the gown, tugging at the shawl here and there, until she was quite contented. Then, at last, she set off, walking in the direction of Gray's Inn Lane.

It was a swift progress, to Gray's Inn, along Holborn to New Oxford Street, shunning the worst alleys of Seven Dials, past the towering chimney of Meux's great brewery, all the time heading westwards. She did not falter for a moment, keeping her head slightly bowed, deliberately avoiding the gaze of the few nocturnal stragglers who hung about the streets. They were a motley collection: vagrants without money for even the lowest lodgings; unfortunates for whom the hours after midnight were hours of business; a mysterious few, like herself, whose motives could hardly be guessed by any passing stranger. But Sarah Tanner ignored them all; and everything about her own bearing, from her brisk gait to the expression upon her face, told the world that she would not countenance any delay. Consequently, no-one troubled her – neither man nor woman – nor even the solitary, rather bored policeman who stood on fixed point duty, at the corner of Oxford Street and Tottenham Court Road.

Her destination was Regent Street. The object of her quest, however, was not the same broad, respectable thoroughfare that, in the hours of daylight, formed the capital's chief commercial pleasure-ground. It was a more dubious street altogether. True, it looked quite identical: it contained the same grand shops, the same magnificent emporia of linen-drapers and milliners, which were the diurnal resort of the *bon ton*; its neighbours in nearby Mayfair were the same respectable neighbours. But it was Regent Street *by night*: where certain private houses opened their doors to guests; where dice and cards were the only form of entertainment; and where men and women mixed with an easy intimacy – an intimacy that would be quite unacceptable in decent society. And it was to one such town-house, a short distance from the Regent's Circus, that Sarah Tanner repaired. To the passer-by, it must be said, the house's front door gave every indication of respectability, from the solid brass knocker to its smart black paint. But Mrs. Tanner knew better.

She rapped gently upon the door and, in an instant, it opened a couple of inches, a metal chain snapping taut. There was no-one to be seen inside: merely a glimpse of a narrow, tastefully decorated hall, and a man's voice.

'Who is it?'

'Don't you know me, then?' she replied.

'No ladies without a gentleman.'

'A strict rule is it?' she said. 'Well, I'd like to become a member.'

'Who introduces you?'

'I thought I didn't need an introduction, Bert. Forgotten me already?'

There was a pause behind the door, and then the face of the inquisitor, a burly, bull-necked man, in a green liveried footman's outfit, appeared in the gap between the door and its frame.

'Damn me!' he exclaimed.

'Do I have to stand here all night?' asked Sarah Tanner.

Open-mouthed, the footman freed the chain and ushered his unexpected guest into the hall. Mrs. Tanner, in her turn, unwrapped her shabby shawl and placed it discreetly beneath the nearby coat-stand.

'You're the last one I thought I'd see here again,' said the footman, shaking his head, as if trying to solve an insoluble puzzle. 'You got no brains in your head, gal?'

'I'd just like a word with Her Majesty, Bert, that's all,' she replied firmly. 'It's important.'

'That's all? That's all, is it? Don't be a fool. She'll swing for you!'

'Still, if you don't mind.'

The footman shook his head. 'Here,' he continued, taking up the shawl and holding it in his outstretched hand – a rather large, rough-looking hand for a footman – and gesturing towards the door, 'you be a good gal, you get on your way. Then there's no harm's done.'

Sarah Tanner took the shawl and placed it back beneath the stand.

'Please, Bert, you know me. Just tell her I'm here.'
The man frowned. Sarah Tanner touched his arm.
'Go on,' she said.

'I know Her, as well,' muttered the footman. 'I know what she's like.'

'As a favour, then.'

The footman mumbled something inaudible, but finally gave way, with an injunction that his visitor should 'not shift a blessed inch', whilst he went to make the inquiry. Mrs. Tanner agreed. Thus, she watched him as he carefully opened one of the doors that led off from the hall, and slipped quietly – for all his bulk – into the front parlour of the house. It was several minutes before he returned.

'She'll see you,' he said, in a grudging tone.

'You see, I told you she would.'

'That ain't the question, my gal,' replied the footman. 'The question is whether it's a clever Christian what pays a social call on the lion.'

The room to which Sarah Tanner sought admittance was no ordinary drawing-room. For a start, at some juncture it had been knocked through into the room behind, creating an elongated space, more like the lounge of some gentleman's club. It was not altogether dissimilar: lit by a trio of elaborate chandeliers, it had the same scent of musty tobacco; the same grand leather armchairs grouped around the two fire-places; the same air of luxurious seclusion from the outside world. But it differed in several crucial respects. For one, it boasted a bar along one side of the room, tended by a pretty young woman. For another, there was, at its centre, a baccarat table, around which some twenty or so individuals, men and women in evening dress, stood or sat, observing the play. And there were other games of chance, too, at smaller tables, where the rattle of dice could occasionally be heard. It was, in short, the typical West End *hell*; the sort of place where, if so inclined, one might readily gamble one's very life away; the sort of place that was occasionally closed by the Metropolitan Police – but only occasionally.

Sarah Tanner surveyed the players at baccarat, and their partisans grouped around the table. She knew some of the women by sight, and had a good idea of their background. The men, for the most part, seemed a rather smart group. A couple had the moustaches of military gentlemen; another possessed a foreign complexion, perhaps a well-to-do Frenchman or Italian; another had the comfortable port-red cheeks of the English gentry. All appeared, if the counters stacked upon the table were any guide, to have money in abundance. Only one man seemed a little more shabby – his shirt-front not pure white, a collar slightly askew – but he was apart from the others, sunk in conversation with a woman at a corner table, an empty bottle of champagne by his feet.

She made her way towards the baccarat table, intent on circumnavigating it. As she moved forward, however, a figure appeared from the shadows and firmly took her by the arm.

'Good evening, Sarah.'

He was a man of about thirty-five years of age. He wore the same black evening suit as the rest of the *habitués* of the place, and his hair – the very colour of his suit – was meticulously slicked back with Macassar oil. His face, moreover, was quite handsome. But he looked at Sarah Tanner with a fixed, stern expression that lent no charm to his features.

23

She smiled politely.

'Mr. Symes.'

'We didn't expect to see you again,' he said.

'I just want a word, that's all, with Her Majesty.'

'How convenient,' he replied, guiding her along. 'She wants a word with you.'

Mr. Symes led Sarah Tanner towards the very back of the room. There, in a quiet corner by the fire, sat a woman in her sixth decade, quite broad about the waist, in a black cap and crinoline, with a fashionable fringe of hair – most likely not her own – peeking from beneath her headgear. Her only companion was a small dog of the Pekinese variety, which lay in her lap, quite content in the great black folds of her dress. As Mrs. Tanner approached it gave a noisy, aggressive yap.

'Hush,' said Her Majesty, patting the dog's head, a rather pinched sort of smile forming on her face. 'That's no way to treat an old acquaintance, is it? No. Not at all.'

CHAPTER FOUR

Her Majesty smiled at her guest, though her dark brooding eyes, which fixed greedily upon her visitor, somehow did not quite concur with her lips.

'You look well, my dear,' she said, after a moment's reflection, 'prettier than I remember, too.'

'Thank you,' replied Sarah Tanner.

'Please, sit down.'

Mrs. Tanner slowly settled herself in a chair by the fire, with a hesitancy that did not escape her hostess.

'Come now, my dear. Don't be so timid, it really does not suit you. I don't bite, do I, Jap-Jap?'

As she spoke, Her Majesty tickled the chin of the Pekinese, still nestled in her skirts. Obligingly, as if to illustrate her point, the dog made a half-hearted snap at its mistress's finger.

'A spirited little creature, isn't he?' she continued. 'No? You do not have an opinion? What do you say, Mr. Symes?'

'Assuredly, ma'am,' said the gentleman in question, who stood behind Sarah Tanner's chair, rather as if guarding a prisoner.

'Much like a certain female we have before us, eh, Mr. Symes?'

'Spirited?' replied Symes. 'Wilful, if my memory serves me well, ma'am.'

Her Majesty smiled.

'Quite so. You are quite right to correct me. Some might even say – forgive me, is the word too strong, Mr. Symes? – ungrateful. But then, I suppose, the young were ever thus.'

'You are a philosopher, ma'am,' said Symes.

'You are too kind, sir,' replied Her Majesty, graciously. 'But I do wonder – forgive me, but I really do – why the fickle, ungrateful creature has suddenly returned to our bosom? How long has it been?'

'Almost a twelvemonth, ma'am,' said Symes.

'I wonder,' she went on, 'does Miss Sarah Mills crave our forgiveness? Is that it? Has she come crawling?'

'No,' replied Her Majesty's guest, although apparently quite content to be addressed by a surname which – in Leather Lane at least – was not considered her own.

Her Majesty's affable smile dropped abruptly, like the fall of a stage curtain, and settled into a distinct scowl.

'No? Have a care, my dear. It is charming to see you once again, but do have a care.'

'I've got some news,' said Sarah Tanner, bluntly, 'if you care to hear it.'

'News? Now you fascinate me,' replied Her Majesty. 'You know I adore gossip, my dear. Do tell.'

'Georgie's dead.'

There was a distinct pause.

'You mean George Phelps?' said Symes, leaning forward, surprise evident in his voice. Her Majesty, meanwhile, kept perfectly quiet, her features placid and inscrutable.

'He was murdered, last night,' she continued, keeping her voice low, conscious of the chatter of the gamblers not a dozen feet away, 'Holborn way. And I saw the man that did it.'

'And – merely for curiosity's sake – how did you happen to be there, my dear?' asked Her Majesty, with glacial calm.

'I just did. You haven't heard the worst of it – there was a Peeler that was after him, following him. It was the Peeler who killed him.'

Symes laughed. 'If you say so, Sarah.'

'I saw him with my own eyes.'

'Well, then, what of it?' asked Symes, a little more serious. 'Was there a fight?'

Sarah Tanner paused. 'I didn't see it happen. I found him, just after. It wasn't an accident, I can tell you that much. What had you got him doing?'

'Mr. Phelps? Only a little hotel work, my dear,' replied Her Majesty, 'nothing in particular. Nothing to trouble the constabulary.'

'Something that got him killed. He wouldn't have picked a fight, not George. He wasn't a brawler.'

'Again, my dear,' said Her Majesty, 'have a care. I am sure I am grateful – if that is the word – for the sad tidings. And, if what you say is true, I am sorry for poor young Mr. Phelps. He was a charming, agreeable young man. But do have a care.'

'Well, aren't you going to do anything?'

'Do? What can I do?' said Her Majesty. 'A weak and feeble woman, such as I?'

'You could find him; whoever he is, the man that did it, teach him a lesson. You've done it before. I can describe—'

'Please, my dear,' said Her Majesty, 'that is quite enough. I make it my business not to interfere with the police. You know that. If poor Mr. Phelps, rest his soul, had some petty dispute with this officer of the law, and came off the worse, it is none of my affair.'

A look of frustration flashed across Sarah Tanner's face. 'He did not "come off the worse". He was butchered.'

'I can see you still possess a temper, my dear,' said Her Majesty. 'You should attempt to contain it.'

'Perhaps I should,' replied Mrs. Tanner. 'Perhaps I should have known better than to come to you.'

'You used to have a tenderness for the young man, did you not?'

'No!' protested Sarah Tanner. 'Lord! I shouldn't have come. I knew it.'

'Oh, my dear, don't say that.'

Sarah Tanner took a deep breath. She brushed down the folds of her skirt and made to rise from her chair. 'I'm sorry to have troubled you. I'll bid you good night.'

Her Majesty, however, shook her head, and motioned to Mr. Symes, who placed a firm hand on Sarah Tanner's shoulder.

'I think you forget your position, my dear,' said Her Majesty. 'It is a pleasure to renew our acquaintance, but there is the little matter of your past conduct.'

Sarah Tanner sighed. 'I'm sorry for the business at Norwood. I never meant—'

Her Majesty waved her hand, as if to dismiss the words as worthless. 'I spent six months on the Continent because of you, my dear. I could not show my face in London, let alone in Society. All because of your sickly little affair of the heart. All because you took pity on a certain wretched youth.'

'I told you, I am sorry for that. But you would have ruined him.'

'Ruined? He was a pigeon, my dear Miss Mills, like all the others before him. You were content to see them plucked. What was so different in young DeSalle's case, eh? He was a handsome lad, I grant you. Was that it?'

Sarah Tanner shrugged.

'Really, my dear. There might have been a brief spell of incarceration for passing the bank-notes; it would not have done him any harm. It might have toughened him up. The fool would have done it, too, had you asked him.'

'And his reputation? What about that?'

'Tell me,' said Her Majesty, gesturing rather disdainfully to the baccarat table, 'how many of our friends here tonight truly value their "reputation"? My dear girl, they consider it part of the stake; a calculated risk. It adds a little spice to proceedings.'

Mrs. Tanner fell silent, extremely conscious of the weight of Mr. Symes's hand, still resting on her shoulder.

'Besides, where is he now, your young man?' asked Her Majesty, her voice quiet and measured. 'Is he here, by your side? Do forgive me, my eyes are not what they were. I am afraid I do not see him.'

Sarah Tanner merely shook her head. Her Majesty, in turn, chuckled to herself.

'Men of that class do not marry their mistress, my dear, no matter how pretty or clever she may be, especially if they discover she is a liar and a thief. Indeed, in my experience, they are wont to discard even the finest specimens of our sex, whenever it suits their fancy. Maybe it has taught you a lesson. I pray that is the case. Still, I do not care to gloat. I am sure there is another more pressing, practical matter – Mr. Symes?'

Symes removed his hand and took out a small pocket-book from his jacket, which he proceeded to consult.

'Fifty-five guineas, ma'am,' said the gentleman with some satisfaction.

'Fifty-five guineas,' repeated Her Majesty. 'We shall forget the other indiscretions; one can become used to the Continent, during the Season, after all. Do you still have the money, Miss Mills?'

Sarah Tanner shook her head. 'I cannot pay it back.'

'You mean you do not care to?'

'I cannot.'

'Most unfortunate,' said Mr. Symes with relish, placing both hands on Sarah Tanner's shoulders, his thumbs brushing the nape of her bare neck. She shuddered. Mr. Symes's employer, however, motioned for him to stand aside.

'Come back to us, Miss Mills,' said Her Majesty, in low confidential tones. 'You were a valuable little creature; you might be again. I would forget our little disagreement. You have not lost your looks. I am sure there are men here tonight who would appreciate your encouragement at the table.'

'Or elsewhere,' added Mr. Symes.

Sarah Tanner looked round the room. A couple of the men lounging by the table glanced in her direction.

'I'd sooner die,' she said at last.

'Please! Please, my dear,' exclaimed Her Majesty, rubbing the Pekinese's neck as she spoke, 'say nothing you might regret.'

'I can find the money, give me a week.'

'Foolish girl. I will give you twenty-four hours, my dear; twice round the clock. What do you say, Mr. Symes?'

'Ample time, ma'am.'

'Ample. Quite. We are agreed. Miss Mills?'

Reluctantly, Sarah Tanner nodded.

———

'She will not find the money, ma'am,' said Mr. Symes, watching Sarah Tanner quit the salon. 'She has spent it. And even if she had the means, we would be the last to see a penny of it.'

'I know that full well, Symes,' replied Her Majesty, tetchily. 'Send Jones after her. He knows the girl, does he not? I am curious to find out where she has been hiding herself.'

'And then?'

'Tell him he may take fifty-five guineas out of her hide. In whatever manner he chooses.'

CHAPTER FIVE

Sarah Tanner left Her Majesty's establishment and set off briskly towards the Regent's Circus. She found the street quite devoid of life and the night grown colder. Indeed, even as she passed beneath the yellow flame of the ornate gas-lights, planted at intervals along the great thoroughfare, she shivered, and pulled the coarse material of her shawl tight about her shoulders.

From the Circus itself, she turned east, retracing her steps. Oxford Street likewise proved quite deserted. Another woman might have thought twice about walking its length unaccompanied, but she paid little heed to her surroundings. Her mind was preoccupied with George Phelps and the consequences of her expedition to Her Majesty's salon. She was so preoccupied, in fact, that it was several minutes before she even glanced back along the road. It was only then that she noticed a man, no more than two hundred yards behind her, loitering in the shadows.

She was not certain at first. She kept walking, then turned her head again, moving her hand as if to adjust the loose arrangement of her shawl.

The man was still there, lurking in the doorway of a shop.

Sarah Tanner silently cursed. She recognised her

pursuer. But she could go no faster than a brisk walk; not in the fashionable crinolined skirts of her gown.

She had gone no more than a few yards further along the road, when she heard the fast, rattling wheels of a cab. It was a hansom – empty as far as she could discern – being driven swiftly eastwards. She turned her head and could just make out the cloaked, slumping driver perched high on his seat at the back, snapping impatiently at the reins. He was going at full pelt; it was too fast for her purpose, she knew as much. Indeed, the cab was already almost upon her; it would be madness to interrupt its progress.

Impulsively, she gathered up her skirts in one hand and darted into the road, waving her arm, standing directly in the vehicle's path.

The cabman, to his credit, shouted a muffled warning, allowing a clay pipe, which had hung loosely from his lips, to tumble on to the roof of the cab and perform an inelegant pirouette on to the muddy pavement. He tugged violently at the reins with both hands – but it was too late to stop. Rather, the horse, relying on its native intelligence, pulled the cab sharply to the right, wrenching the shafts sideways, the iron-shod wheels passing inches from Sarah Tanner's feet, riding up on to the opposite kerb, then dropping noisily back down on to the road with a jolt. Finally, the vehicle came to a halt, some twenty or thirty yards along the road.

The driver's face – the weather-beaten face of the hardened night cabman – was a picture of exasperation and anger, breathless and flushed.

'Are you mad, woman?!' he shouted. 'You damn near got us both killed!'

Sarah Tanner looked anxiously back along the street, then ran up to the cab. Her shawl had fallen loose

33

about her shoulders, revealing her dress; she pulled it back around her neck.

'I am sorry. Please, it is important . . . take me to Gray's Inn Lane.'

'Take you to Gray's Inn Lane, if you please!' exclaimed the cabman. 'If you wanted a ride, you've a fine way of going about it!'

'I am sorry,' she repeated, urgency in her voice. 'Please – I need your help.'

'Don't give me that. I know your sort, my gal, fancy get-up or not. Don't think I don't. Gray's Inn Lane! Down on your luck tonight, are you? Well, you can bleedin' walk home.'

The cabman raised the reins, ready to move off. But his would-be client grabbed at the side of the vehicle.

'Please,' she said, pleading, 'there is a man following me.'

'Who'd have thought it!' exclaimed the cabman, sarcastically.

'I'll pay double. A half-crown. Look, I swear, I have the money.'

The cabman paused as she reached into her pocket, and pulled out a silver coin. He glanced over his shoulder.

'I don't see no-one,' he said.

'Please.'

'Go on then,' said the cabman, reluctantly. 'Get in. And if you baulk us, I'll bleedin' do for you.'

Sarah Tanner nodded and clambered inside the cab, closing the folding doors over her skirts. The driver, meanwhile, said nothing more, except for some mumbled word of encouragement to the horse which, combined with a touch of his whip, prompted the patient animal to break into a steady trot.

In truth, it was not a very comfortable ride. The macadamised road between Oxford Street and Holborn seemed to grow increasingly irregular and afflicted by pot-holes as it progressed eastwards. The journey through the nocturnal streets, however, took no more than ten minutes. Sarah Tanner kept her face pressed against the glass window of the cab throughout. At last, as the hansom drew to a halt upon Gray's Inn Lane, she swung open the twin doors, and clambered down on to the pavement.

'Oi!' shouted the cabman. 'A half-crown! Do you hear me?'

But his fare did not reply. She was distracted by the sight of a second carriage, pulling round the corner at the end of the lane. The cabman, in turn, looked over his shoulder, following her gaze.

'That your admirer, is it?' said the cabman, with a sneer.

'I don't know,' replied Mrs. Tanner.

'He's been followin', anyhow.'

'For pity's sake! You might have told me.'

'None of my business,' said the cabman. 'Now,' he continued, rudely tapping Sarah Tanner's shoulder with the tip of his whip, 'where's my bleedin' money, eh?'

Mrs. Tanner ruefully pulled a silver coin from her pocket, and flicked it into the air. The moment the cabman reached out to catch it, however, she turned and darted into the nearest side-street, a narrow, unlit alley that led in the direction of Leather Lane and Saffron Hill.

It was only when she had disappeared from view that the cabman realised he held just a shilling between his fingers. Though it was an adequate recompense for the journey, he turned round, scowling, craning his neck to look at the cab which was pulling up behind his own.

'She went that way, my friend,' he muttered, gesturing with his whip hand, then spitting upon the pavement, by way of punctuation. 'And I hope you bleedin' well catches up with her.'

———

Sarah Tanner had no intention of being caught. She chose a circuitous route through the narrowest, dingiest courts of the district, which she intended to thoroughly confuse anyone who might follow her. Twice she accidentally tore the fine silk of her dress, catching it upon odd outcrops of exposed bricks or rusting ironwork. Half a dozen times, she stumbled upon the uneven paving, or slipped upon the rotten cabbage leaves, and worse, which littered the loose cobbles behind the old tumble-down houses. But, at last, she came to Liquorpond Street.

She looked behind her and breathed a sigh of relief. There was no-one to be seen. She was, moreover, only a few yards from the Dining and Coffee Rooms, its hand-painted sign just visible in the darkness.

Then a quiet voice whispered in her ear.

'Lost your way, gal? Or just sick of hide-and-seek?'

Bert Jones, the burly footman – if such was his true calling – stood close at hand, his decorative uniform concealed by a heavy woollen great-coat, his boots spattered with mud. He grabbed her firmly by the arm.

'How . . . ?' she said, barely able to manage a word.

The footman smiled. 'My old man used to have a two pair back behind Ely Rents. Regular rabbit warren, ain't they, these old alleys? I used to play round here when I was a little 'un.'

She turned to face her questioner, consciously trying to avoid looking at the Dining and Coffee Rooms.

'You shouldn't have come back,' he continued. 'I told you, gal. I wish you hadn't. I mean, I always took to you. You were a good 'un.'

'Then leave me be.'

The footman smiled regretfully, and shook his head. 'Let's go somewhere quiet, eh? Just you and me.'

'She told me I had twenty-four hours.'

'What?' said the footman. 'You can pay her back, I suppose?'

'Yes, I swear. Tomorrow.'

Bert Jones shook his head once more. 'I don't believe you. And you know it wouldn't matter one jot, even if I did.'

Sarah Tanner struggled, but the footman kept firm hold of her arm.

'Now, come on, gal, don't cut up rough,' he continued. 'Let's you and me stay pals, eh? I won't leave no marks, nothing that shows, anyhow.'

'Bert, please!'

'I ain't got all night. Have you got a doss round here, is that it?'

Mrs. Tanner paused for a moment. 'I've got lodgings down past Saffron Hill.'

'A quiet place? Your own room?'

'Yes.'

'That's better. Keep it quiet and respectable, eh? Between friends, like. You lead the way. And no nonsense.'

Sarah Tanner reluctantly set off along the lane.

———

In truth, Sarah Tanner had but one thought: to delay the attentions of Bert Jones for as long as possible.

She even hoped that they might come across someone who could help her. But it was too late at night; no-one passed by. And, she realised, anyone who saw them at a distance, if they thought about it at all, most likely mistook them for a pair of lovers. For they walked through the streets arm in arm, at a steady slow pace, as if taking a moonlit stroll. True, Mr. Jones clasped hold of his partner a little too tightly, as if fearful she might escape; and Mrs. Tanner, for her part, gazed at her other half with anything but affection. It was a odd thing, too, for anyone to take the night air along Saffron Hill. Indeed, the medical opinion of the parish doctor, not entirely unfounded, was that the night air in that particular locality – rather miasmatic in nature – was rather more likely to *take* you, and altogether best avoided. But, all the same, no-one interfered with their progress; and Sarah Tanner knew that they could only walk for so long.

'Where are we going now?' said Bert Jones at last, as they skirted the borders of Smithfield Market.

'I told you—'

'Don't give me that gammon. There ain't no lodgings, is there? I told you, my gal, I know Saffron Hill. I don't need the bleedin' grand tour.'

'I'll scream,' replied Mrs. Tanner. 'I'll scream blue murder.'

'Don't be a little fool. Who'll give a damn round here? Come on.'

The footman grabbed his victim by both arms, and flung her bodily into a narrow yard that they had just passed by. It was a dead-end, pitch black, almost invisible from the road, littered with rubbish.

'When did you last see Georgie Phelps?' she said, desperately.

'Phelps?' said Bert Jones, sufficiently puzzled to stop and answer the question. 'A couple of days back. Why?'

'I heard he's in trouble,' she continued, watching Bert Jones closely. 'What's he been doing?'

'Told me he was working an hotel lay, down Covent Garden.'

'Who with?'

The footman laughed. 'The usual. Some little Abigail that's sweet on him, down at the Hummums. Pretty little thing, just like you. Now, hold still.'

'It's just that Georgie's—'

'I said, hold still! Then we can make it short and sweet, eh?'

'But—'

Sarah Tanner's protest was cut short as the footman lunged forward, pinning her against the alley's brick wall, his hand covering her mouth.

'Hush,' he said, his rough, calloused fingers keeping her silent. 'There now. Be a good gal, eh? Least said, soonest mended.'

And, with that, he clenched his hand into a fist.

CHAPTER SIX

The blow seemed to come from nowhere.

It was not, however, quite what Sarah Tanner had expected. For just as Bert Jones raised his arm, someone stepped behind him in the darkness, swinging a wooden cudgel, which made resounding contact with the footman's head. Bert Jones staggered, dizzy under the unexpected assault. He managed to turn towards his assailant, only to be struck a second time, full in the face, blood trickling from a gash in his forehead. It took a third blow for the footman to drop to ground.

The weapon was, in fact, the spoke from an old cart-wheel, whose skeletal remains lay nearby in the dirt. Its owner – to Sarah Tanner's astonishment – was none other than the man to whom she had said good night a couple of hours previously – Ralph Grundy.

'I'm too old for this lark,' muttered the waiter, throwing the piece of wood to one side and tugging at his employer's arm. 'Well, what are you waiting for?'

Quite speechless, Mrs. Tanner edged round the prone form of Bert Jones.

'Lor! I've gone and killed him!' exclaimed the old man, glancing back at his victim.

'It would take more than that,' said Mrs. Tanner, finally finding her voice.

'I hope you're right, missus,' he replied. 'Either way, we'd best shift, eh?'

Sarah Tanner did not presume to disagree. Thus Mrs. Tanner and Ralph Grundy hurried back along Saffron Hill together. They took the first turn that led towards Leather Lane. Neither of them spoke: Ralph Grundy, because, most likely, he took some small pleasure in keeping the explanation for his timely intervention to himself; Sarah Tanner, because she found it nigh impossible to reconcile her former impressions of the waiter with the circumstances of her unlikely salvation. At length, they came to the door of the Dining and Coffee Rooms.

'Any chance of a drop of something?' said the waiter, rather breathlessly. 'I'm awful dry.'

―

Sarah Tanner sat opposite Ralph Grundy, inside the shuttered-up shop, as the waiter took sips from a small glass of brandy.

'Thank you,' she said, at last.

'It weren't nothing,' said the waiter.

Mrs. Tanner shook her head.

'No, it was. But how did you . . . I mean . . .'

Ralph Grundy blushed.

'I've known hard times, missus. A man learns to look after himself – let's say no more about it. Now, I'll grant you, what I did to that fellow weren't the conduct of a gentleman, but, then, I ain't a gentleman – there's no denying it – and nor was he, not by the look of things.'

'It was lucky for me that you came by.'

Sarah Tanner said the words quite plainly, but there

was something slightly quizzical in her expression, something that implied she did not think, upon reflection, that it could be a question of mere chance. Ralph Grundy saw it, blushed once more, and looked down at his feet.

'Ah, well. It weren't luck, neither. I were keeping watch.'

'Keeping watch?'

'On the shop. I got old Margie Bladstow to let me have one of her rooms –' he gestured towards the lodging-house that lay upon the opposite side of Liquorpond Street – 'and I saw you leave; and I saw you come back too.'

Sarah Tanner frowned, perplexed. 'But why?'

Ralph Grundy took another sip from his glass, then paused, as if mulling over his words.

'He was that pal of yours, weren't he? That fellow in Baldwin's Gardens? Phelps – that was his name?'

Mrs. Tanner fell silent.

'There now,' continued Ralph Grundy, waving his hand dismissively, 'I've said it plain. I guessed as much. And I know *you* never did for him, if that's all that's troubling you. I went and had a look at him, before they took him away – that were a man's work, if ever I saw it.'

'A man of sorts.'

'But,' Ralph Grundy continued, 'you never told the Peelers nothing about it. Worse, you looked afear'd to do it. So I said to myself, "Ralph – what's this? What's up with the missus?" and I got to thinking on it; so I got curious-like.'

'So you followed me?'

'I weren't planning on *that*,' replied the waiter. 'But I'd an idea something was brewing. You was all keen to close up; I could tell you'd been thinking on something all day. So I went and saw Margie – she owes me a good turn – and I waited.'

Sarah Tanner raised her eyebrows. 'And what did you see?'

'Well, I never saw such a fine piece of silk,' he said, nodding at the exposed cloth of his interlocutor's dress, 'not in the Lane anyhow; that struck me as queer. So I had a glass or two with Margie and I waited some more. I was almost giving up, then I saw that brute lay hands on you, when you come back. So I says to myself, "Ralph – the missus needs your help." And I reckon you did, right enough.'

'I suppose I did.'

'Another old friend of yours?' asked Ralph Grundy, watching his employer closely. 'Was he the one that did for your pal?'

'No, I don't think so.'

'Ah,' said Ralph Grundy, a look of disappointment upon his face, as if he rather expected more of an explanation.

Sarah Tanner met the waiter's gaze. 'Can I trust you, Ralph?'

'Trust me? I'm an old man, missus. An old man what's seen better days, and been in more scrapes than I care to remember. I ain't no gentleman and I don't have no "word of honour". But – I'll say this much – there's a fellow waking up – please God – down Saffron Hill with a cracked canister, that likely reckons you might do worse in a tight spot. I just bet he does.'

Mrs. Tanner allowed herself a smile.

'Very well,' she replied. 'I owe you that much. You see, I have not always kept company with the best people—'

43

'No shame in that,' interjected the waiter. 'Neither have I. The Lane ain't the place for folk that have.'

Sarah Tanner shook her head, ignoring the interruption. 'Gamesters and swindlers; they used to be my closest friends, family, all rolled into one. Georgie . . . the man who was killed, he was one of them. The man tonight, he was another.'

'Close family were it?' said the waiter.

'There was a disagreement about money, months ago,' said Sarah Tanner, brusquely. 'We parted company. But then Georgie came into the shop last night, quite by chance. At least, I think so.'

Ralph Grundy nodded.

'And, you must understand, Ralph, what happened to him . . . he was a cheat, he stole, but he never harmed a hair on anyone's head.'

'A bad business, then.'

'Bad enough. You see, I know the man who killed him. Or, at least, I saw his face. And I found Georgie too, where he'd left him. When I went after him, when I left the shop last night – I found him.'

'I'm sorry to hear that. No sight for a woman; nor anyone, for that matter.'

Sarah Tanner shook her head. 'I saw him die. He didn't deserve that. No-one deserves to go like that. So, like a fool, I thought . . . well, I suppose I thought some of my old friends might help; that they might take care of it. I went and called on them, tonight.'

'Turned out badly?'

'It could have been worse, if you hadn't been there.'

Ralph Grundy suddenly looked perplexed. 'Hold up,' continued the waiter, 'I ain't fond of the Peelers myself, missus, but ain't they the persons to talk to here?'

'I don't think so.'

'Well, come now, you ain't wanted for nothing, are you? It ain't that bad? Well, anyhow, I could tell 'em about this chap you saw, if you want to keep quiet.'

'No.'

'Why not?'

'It was a policeman that killed him.'

Ralph Grundy fell silent

'Blow me,' he said, at last. 'You're sunk, then, missus. Leave it be.'

'That's what I told myself, last night,' she replied. 'Just afterwards, after I'd found him, when I came back to the shop and saw you. That's what my . . . well, my old friends . . . that's what they told me too.'

Ralph Grundy studied her closely, frowning. 'But you ain't going to, are you?'

'I owe Georgie something,' she replied.

'I thought you said he was a villain?'

'He was a friend, a real friend, once. Last night, he was as close to me as you are now, and he was dying. I could have done something for him.'

'It didn't look like it to me, the state of him,' said Ralph Grundy.

'I could have said something. I don't know. I could have held his hand; given him some comfort.'

'So, what are you going to do, missus?'

'I'm going to find the man who killed him,' she said, succinctly. 'I don't care who or what he is, he deserves to hang for it.'

Ralph Grundy curled his lips into a wry smile. 'Hold up, missus. A detective in petticoats? What will Scotland Yard say to that?'

Sarah Tanner shrugged.

'They can go to the devil.'

CHAPTER SEVEN

The following morning, a murder was announced.

In *The Times*, *Daily News*, *Morning Chronicle* and *The Post*, George Phelps's death merited but a brief paragraph. From the cheap press of St. Giles, on the other hand, there issued quarter-sheets on crown paper, intended for the street-patterer, bearing *authentic particulars* and a distinctly inauthentic woodcut of the corpse. Every writer was unanimous upon one point: the brutality of the act; not one knew the victim's identity. 'The Leather Lane Outrage' was, in short, something of a mystery.

For some, of course, a murder is always of particular interest. Indeed, in the beer-shops and public-houses of Leather Lane and Saffron Hill, there was talk of little else. But for the majority of respectable citizens who read of the crime – whether seated at their breakfast table, or upon an omnibus bound for the Bank – George Phelps's demise was only of passing remark, a sanguinary footnote in the annals of metropolitan vice.

Charles Goggs, the head-porter at the Hummums Hotel, Covent Garden, undoubtedly took such a view. For Mr. Goggs, a naturally dapper, tidy-looking man in his mid-fifties, was not inclined to sully his white gloves with news-print, nor listen to gossip. Indeed, he paid little attention to news of any kind. He had but one purpose in life: to provide guidance to guests of the Hummums, and answer for the safety of their luggage.

And it was Mr. Goggs who, late that very after-noon, was the first to greet a certain female visitor, as she entered the hotel.

'Can I help you, ma'am?' he innocently inquired.

'Mrs. Richards. You received my telegram this morning. I trust my rooms are ready.'

Mr. Goggs was accustomed to stand on duty in the hotel's hall, with his head held high, and was rather conscious of the dignity which his uniformed presence bestowed upon his work-place. He was not accustomed to being addressed in quite so peremptory a fashion – not, at least, by a woman – and appeared rather taken aback.

'Well?' asked the visitor. She was in her late twen-ties or early thirties; she wore a walking dress of black silk, with a black fur-trimmed mantle about her shoul-ders, and a plain, veiled bonnet, partially concealing her face. The head-porter immediately took her – because she had arrived quite unaccompanied – for a travelling governess or upper servant in mourning; the imperious variety of senior domestic, accustomed to having their own way.

'Richards, ma'am?' he replied, at last. 'I will check with our clerk.'

The head-porter retreated to the adjoining small room which served as the hotel office. Then, after a brief discussion with his fellow employee, he returned to the hall.

'I regret no telegram was received, ma'am,' said Mr. Goggs, adding, with a hint of self-congratula-tion, 'and I regret we do not have a vacancy.'

'Really!' exclaimed Mrs. Richards. 'Lady DeVere was most particular as to where I should stay. She told me – I can recall her very words, sir – "The Hummums – the most respectable little hotel in London." Whatever shall I do?'

Mr. Goggs softened a little. He appreciated such praise; it was, he considered, well deserved. In particular, two words struck him quite forcefully.

'Lady DeVere?' he repeated.

'The Hertfordshire DeVeres. *The* family in the county. I expect you have heard of them. Still,' continued Mrs. Richards, looking around her with a rather haughty air, 'I suppose another place might serve just as well.'

Mr. Goggs knitted his brow. He had not, in all honesty, heard of the Hertfordshire DeVeres; he assuredly had not received any telegram; nor did he find the woman who stood before him a particularly agreeable example of either the servant class or her sex. But, he considered, he was rather obliged to consider the interests of the hotel. For the positive recommendation of a member of the aristocracy – in certain circles, at least – was as good as guaranteed income; a negative report was not to be contemplated.

'One moment, ma'am,' he replied. 'I will just go and make sure.'

He disappeared once more, then returned after a short interval with a rather more obliging expression upon his face.

'It seems I was mistaken. There is a lady's apartment upon the third floor – bed, sitting- and dressing-room. How long are you staying, ma'am? I fear one night is the longest we can offer for that room.'

Mrs. Richards smiled at the concession. 'Thank you. That will be quite adequate for my needs.'

The head-porter nodded. 'Any luggage, ma'am?'

'It will follow shortly; I had some difficulties making arrangements at the station.'

Mr. Goggs nodded once more, adopting a rather sage expression of sympathy. He had long since regarded the humble station luggage-handler as markedly inferior to the hotel variety, in every respect. With a polite bow, therefore, he directed Mrs. Richards into the hotel office, then had her enter her name in the register. It was an elegant signature, and came with an address in the county of Hertfordshire.

If Mr. Goggs had been more alert, he might have noticed a slight hesitation as Mrs. Richards took up the pen. He might have considered whether her manner was just a little too theatrical, even for an upper servant. He might have pondered a little more upon the precise difficulties which had detained his new guest's luggage. But Charles Goggs, though an excellent head-porter in a general way, was a man of limited imagination.

He certainly did not imagine Mrs. Richards – for all her faults – capable of owning a coffee-shop, upon the corner of Leather Lane and Liqourpond Street; not for a moment.

———

The apartment secured by Sarah Tanner, in the guise of 'Mrs. Richards', was on the first floor, directly over-looking Covent Garden, and probably vacant for that very reason, being the least desirable room in the establishment. For, although the Hummums was indeed a respectable hotel, the hubbub of the adjoining market – the shouts from its vendors, the wagon wheels clattering over stone – was a constant nuisance. Even during the afternoon, the classical colonnades and arches of the market piazza, emptied of vegetable matter, still served for the sale of flowers. Filled with oceans of violets, ready to be bunched and sold on, the market was the principal resort of a never-ending procession of ragged flower-girls, intent upon haggling over every last petal.

Mrs. Tanner watched the scene from her window. But her thoughts were occupied with the object of her clandestine visit: to find the girl at the hotel whom Bert Jones had mentioned, George Phelps's sweetheart. For – knowing George Phelps of old – Sarah Tanner had concluded that the girl was his accomplice in the *hotel lay*, whether willing or unwilling. The only problem was – even as a gentle knock struck the door to her sitting-room – she was not entirely sure how to go about it.

She steeled herself and sat up straight.

'Come in.'

The newcomer was a chambermaid, bearing a porcelain jug. She was a small, nervous-looking girl, who did not meet Sarah Tanner's gaze.

'You wanted hot water, ma'am?'

'Yes, please. Take it through to the bedroom.'

The maid obliged, and returned within seconds. Sarah Tanner studied the maid's looks; she seemed too young, too naïve, even for George Phelps's taste.

'Is that all, ma'am?'

'One moment. Tell me, what is your name?' asked Mrs. Tanner, maintaining the same, rather firm tone she had taken with the head-porter.

'Jane, ma'am.'

'Have you worked here long, Jane?'

The girl blushed, looking down at her boots. 'No, ma'am, only a day. Sorry, ma'am.'

'Only a day?'

'The last girl left sudden, ma'am.'

'Really?' said Mrs. Tanner, an idea forming in her mind. 'I was told this was a decent hotel.'

'Oh, it is, ma'am!' replied the maid emphatically. She was no more than fifteen years old – Mrs. Tanner was sure of it – and suddenly seemed doubly nervous. 'Oh, I'm sure it is!'

'Well, that is all very well,' said Mrs. Tanner, looking rather pointedly at the girl. 'Why did this other girl take her leave?'

The girl blushed once more. 'I don't care to say, ma'am.'

'I confess, I myself have heard some talk that she was a thief,' hazarded Sarah Tanner, a little more soft and confidential in her tone.

'I don't know, ma'am.'

'I expect you must have heard something.'

'Just that she was dismissed yesterday morning, ma'am. I swear, I don't know nothing about it.'

'I am sure. How terrible! One wonders how young girls can go wrong so easily.'

'Terrible, ma'am,' replied the maid, hurriedly.

'Well, I am sure *you* will be an asset to the hotel, Jane. I can tell, just to look at you.'

'Thank you, ma'am. If that's all, ma'am—'

'One more thing, my dear. It just occurred to me. I wonder if you might inquire below stairs and find out something for me.'

'Ma'am?'

'I should like to know the name of the girl who left yesterday, and where she might have gone.'

'Ma'am?' repeated the maid, surprised at the peculiar request.

'You see,' continued Mrs. Tanner, racking her brain, 'I know of a refuge for friendless young women, who have lost their employment. They might be able to help her, with clothes and money and such; with spiritual guidance too. It is run by a clergyman, an old acquaintance of mine.'

'Yes, ma'am, if you like, ma'am,' replied Jane, visibly relieved at the prospect of the conversation drawing to a close.

Sarah Tanner smiled. 'I should like some tea in half an hour or so; you may come back then.'

The maid agreed.

It was precisely a half-hour later when, patently anxious to please, the girl returned with a tea tray – and the name of her predecessor.

———

The bells of St. Paul's, Covent Garden, struck six as Sarah Tanner slipped quietly from her empty hotel room and walked slowly down the stairs to the ground floor of the hotel. Her plan was straightforward – to leave quietly by the front door. She had waited a decent interval since her arrival and there was, after all, little chance that she might be stopped; and, if questioned, she had decided on her story: that she was going to inquire after her luggage.

It was only after she turned down the last flight of steps that she saw the policeman.

Instinctively, she froze. But, upon closer inspection, it was not the man of two nights previous: George Phelps's assailant – his killer – was taller, more broad. Before her was a short, clean-shaven individual of middling years, holding his hat between his hands, accompanied by an older gentleman dressed in a smart morning-coat and white cravat. Both seemed to be engaged in some kind of debate with the head-porter, who was in the process of ushering them into the hotel office.

Sarah Tanner watched and waited. Had the policeman come for her? No, surely that was quite impossible.

Gathering her courage, she walked directly towards the front door, her veil down over her face. All the same, she could not resist slowing her pace, since the men's voices, within the office, could still be heard quite plainly.

'And I tell you again, my good man,' said one voice, full of indignation, 'that my sister is a rational, respectable creature of sound judgment and acute discrimination; she would not go wandering the streets unaccompanied!'

'Nevertheless, sir,' said the porter, whose voice Mrs. Tanner immediately recognised, 'the lady has vanished. She said she was going for a stroll yesterday evening, to clear her head. We have not seen her since; I even checked with the night-porter. If she does not return, there is the unfortunate question of the bill. Not to mention her luggage.'

'Constable, I beg you,' entreated the first speaker, 'I will swear on my life, some harm has come to her. The whole business is utterly improbable! It is totally out of character.'

'Very well, sir,' replied the constable. 'I suggest we take a look at Miss Ferntower's rooms, if Mr. Goggs here will permit it.'

'Naturally, I would not interfere with a *police* matter,' replied Goggs, 'although I would beg you to be discreet. The hotel's reputation—'

'Damn the hotel's reputation, sir!' exclaimed the first voice.

There was the sound of a slight scuffle. Sarah Tanner hurriedly stepped back, as the three men re-emerged from the office. She had barely time to move away, as the older man flung open the door, red-faced and angry, and strode off towards the stairs. Next came the policeman and finally Mr. Goggs, wringing his hands, sweat beading his brow.

'Ah!' he exclaimed, at the sight of his guest. 'No need to alarm yourself, Mrs. Richards.'

'No, sir, I am sure.'

Mr. Goggs opened his mouth, as if to offer further reassurance, but then thought twice. He bowed hurriedly, then turned to chase after the constable and his companion, who were already ascending the main staircase to the rooms above.

'Mr. Ferntower! Constable!' exclaimed the head-porter. 'Wait! I beg you! You will disturb the guests!'

Mrs. Tanner hesitated. She was half inclined to follow the head-porter and, if nothing else, assuage her own curiosity. In the end, however, she succumbed to her better judgment and stepped outside.

As she walked away, she took stock. She had been successful enough; she had, from the maid, the name of the girl who had been dismissed: one 'Norah Smallwood'. But there was, it seemed, a missing woman, too: a woman who had disappeared from the Hummums the day after George Phelps's death.

It could not be a coincidence, she was quite certain of it.

She wondered what a police detective might do in similar circumstances; and, for a moment, it crossed her mind that she was quite unprepared and unsuited for the task she had set herself.

And then she recalled George Phelps's last moments on earth; and a smouldering anger rekindled inside her.

CHAPTER EIGHT

That same night, after her brief stay at the Hummums, Sarah Tanner closed her business a full two hours early. Passers-by, used to seeing the gaslight burning bright above the shop-door, remarked upon its absence. Several costermongers, who were in the habit of taking a late supper at the Dining and Coffee Rooms, when their finances permitted, declared the closure 'a bloody nuisance'. One gentleman, a journeyman baker by trade, accustomed to take a hearty meal before commencing his night's work, even banged his fist upon the shutters. But all efforts were quite in vain, and neither the proprietress nor any victuals were forthcoming. For Mrs. Tanner was not at home. She was, rather, a mile or so distant, in an ill-lit thoroughfare by the name of Lumber Court, in the parish of St. Giles.

The road itself was little more than an alley, a vacancy between opposing tenements. Paved with cracked stone slabs and plastered with mud, it was littered with obstructions, dung heaps and dark pools of foul-smelling water.

Sarah Tanner kept her hand cupped round her mouth, trying to avoid the stench. Her companion, taking no such precaution, let out a gutteral, choking cough.

'This is hard going for an old 'un,' muttered Ralph Grundy.

'I never asked you to come,' said Mrs. Tanner.

'Reckon you need someone to keep an eye on you, missus. A female don't go creeping round St. Giles of a night, not on her own – not if she's got any sense.'

'I know my way, Ralph.'

'Maybe. And what makes you so certain you'll find her, this blessed girl you're after?'

'I'm not.'

'Well, why are we here, then, traipsing down this blasted gully?'

Sarah Tanner sighed. 'It's where Georgie would go, whenever he was in trouble, if he got in a tight spot. It's as good a place as any.'

'Aye,' murmured Ralph Grundy to himself, 'well, he's in a tight spot now, right enough.'

As Ralph Grundy spoke, the alley opened out to a small courtyard. It was lit by a single exposed flare of gas, a stuttering, meagre light that projected from a battered pipe, which gave every impression of being improvised by some cunning individual, unconnected with the Gas, Light and Coke Company. Sarah Tanner pulled on her companion's coat sleeve, guiding him to the right, beneath an archway of crumbling bricks, where it seemed there could be no possible progress. But there was a narrow passage – no more than two and a half feet wide – and then an open area, in which steps led down to a door. At the entrance stood a pair of young men, dressed in rather shabby-looking suits, laughing at some shared joke.

'What's up here?' said one to the other, watching Sarah Tanner and her companion approach.

'Nice bit of muslin,' replied the second man.

'Ain't she just! Well, what do you want, darlin'?'

'Just a drink.'

'Private crib, my dear,' said the second man. 'Best hook it, eh? You and your old man.'

'It's all right,' she countered. 'George Phelps will stand for us.'

'Will he now? Georgie-boy, eh? How come he ain't with you then?' asked the second man.

'We're waiting for him,' replied Ralph Grundy.

'And we'd like to wait inside,' insisted Mrs. Tanner.

'Is that so? What name?'

'Starlight Sall and Panther Bill,' replied Sarah Tanner sarcastically. 'What's yours?'

The first man smirked and gave an ironic bow. 'All right, *Sall*, go through then. If Georgie will stand for you, that'll do. He better had, mind, or you and me will have words.'

Sarah Tanner nodded and made her way inside, past the young man. Ralph Grundy followed, looking nervously over his shoulder.

The interior of the house – known to its regulars as the Hole-in-the-Wall – was that of a typical public. It was no gin-palace; there was nothing smart or shining, no plate glass or gilding. It was simply a small, old-fashioned pot-house, with a small bar and parlour, in which a few like-minded individuals might comfortably enjoy the hospitality of their host. The tables were painted deal, the paintwork cracked and faded; the room was lit by oil-lamps, turned down low; an open fire roared in the hearth; and the air was heavy with the smell of smoke and beer.

Ralph Grundy surveyed the drinkers, their faces barely visible in the dim light. Most were young men in cheap fustian and cords. The handful of women wore a cheap cotton print – like the dress his employer had herself adopted for the evening – with their hair in fashionable ringlets and fringes, and seemed inclined to hang languidly upon the arms of their men-folk. In fact, Ralph Grundy concluded, it might have been any low beer-shop in London, but for a little more in the way of gold upon the men's fingers, and a little more in the way of paint – rose-red cheeks and ruby lips – upon the younger girls' faces.

'This your den of thieves, then, missus?' said Ralph Grundy quietly.

'If you like,' replied Mrs. Tanner in a whisper, 'and watch your tongue. Now, let's find somewhere to sit.'

She looked around, then led the way to a rather dark corner table which gave a complete view of the smoky parlour, not least the door by which they had entered. Ralph Grundy trailed at her heels.

'What's your plan, then?' he asked, as he removed his coat. 'Stew here all night?'

'Someone will know something, even if they don't know the girl,' she replied, looking round the room. 'I recognise one or two of them.'

'They recognise you too, I reckon,' replied the old man.

Ralph Grundy's gaze was directed towards a white-aproned barman who, even as they took their seats, approached the table. He was in his early twenties, slightly round in face and body, cheeks flushed with the heat of the room. He looked at Sarah Tanner closely as he came up, as if struggling to place her.

'I know you, don't I?' said the barman.

'I'm a pal of Georgie's, Georgie Phelps. I haven't been in for a while.'

''Course you are. I knew it! Lor, Sairey, ain't it? I ain't seen your phiz for – what is it? – a good twelvemonth.'

'More than that. Has Georgie been about?'

'Not for a week or two. You after seeing him? You'll have to wait your turn.'

'I'll say,' muttered Ralph Grundy to himself.

'Why's that?' asked Mrs. Tanner, casting a withering look at her companion.

'Usual. A young gal – pining for him – was here all afternoon, just on the off chance.'

Sarah Tanner gave Ralph Grundy a brief triumphant glance. The old man raised his eyes to the heavens.

'What was she like, this girl?'

The barman laughed. 'You know George's type. Green as grass. She wouldn't take more than a drop of anything strong, neither. His nibs had half a mind to throw her out.'

'Do you think she'll come back?'

'Likely as not,' he replied. 'They always do. Here, Sairey, all that time, you weren't in the jug, were you? George didn't say nothing.'

'No, nothing like that.'

The barman did not press his inquiry any further. 'What's your pleasure, then?'

'Gin-punch,' replied Mrs. Tanner.

'A pint of fourpenny,' added Ralph Grundy.

'Happy to oblige,' replied the barman with a wink.

Sarah Tanner watched the young man walk away before turning to her companion.

'I swear,' she said, 'you don't have to stay here with me, Ralph. I'll be fine on my own.'

'If you say so, then maybe you might be, missus,' replied Ralph Grundy, looking round the room, 'but I ain't so sure as I would be myself, finding my way home. So I'll stick with you, if you don't mind. For the sake of my health.'

'And a drop of fourpenny.'

'Aye, that would help.'

It was half-past eleven when Norah Smallwood arrived at the Hole-in-the-Wall. Sarah Tanner knew her in a moment, though she had never seen her before. Others had come and gone, but none so young and none so agitated in their manner. She was sixteen years old or so, with long brown hair tied back and half hidden under a feathered bonnet, and a colourful shawl draped around her shoulders. She hurried to the bar; spoke briefly to the barman. They talked for a moment, then she took a stool at an empty table and sat with her back against the wall, nursing a small measure of gin, anxiously casting her eyes around the room.

Sarah Tanner whispered a few words to Ralph Grundy, then got up and crossed the room on her own.

'Norah is it?' she asked in a low voice.

The girl in question jumped in surprise, quite startled that anyone should address her by name.

'N-n-no,' she replied.

'It is, though, isn't it? A friend of Georgie's?'

'Georgie?'

'My name's Sarah. I'm a pal of his too; an old pal.'

'Oh, is that right?' said the girl.

Sarah Tanner frowned. She had no idea what to say to Norah Smallwood; the truth seemed too cruel. But now, she realised, Norah Smallwood thought she was a love-rival for George Phelps's affections.

'It's nothing like what you're thinking. Georgie said to give you a message.'

'What was that, then?' asked Norah, with obviously feigned disinterest.

'He said to tell you he . . . well, that he cared for you, and he was sorry for everything.'

'What?'

'Listen, Norah, please, it's hard to know how to tell you. Georgie told me that before he died; he wanted you to know.'

'Died?' said Norah Smallwood, astonished. As she recovered herself, she shook her head in disbelief. 'What are you on about? Who are you anyway?'

'He was killed, two nights ago. A man stabbed him. Down Leather Lane – it's been in the papers, though they don't know Georgie's name, not yet.'

'You're a bloody liar. What right have you got coming here, scaring a gal to death!'

'Hush! I'm telling the truth,' replied Mrs. Tanner, calmly. 'I swear it. I went to the hotel, and they told me you'd left. So I came looking for you; it's what George wanted, or I wouldn't be here.'

'Just leave me alone!' exclaimed Norah Smallwood angrily. 'You better hook it. I'll tell Georgie what you said. I bloody will.'

'What was he up to, at the Hummums?'

'Never you mind! Hook it, I tell you! Or I'll—'

Sarah Tanner grabbed the girl by both arms, looking her straight in the eye.

'I tell you, Norah, he's dead. I saw him and I saw the monster that did for him. So you'd better tell me what's going on, because it's not a game. And George Phelps might have told you it was all clover in his line of work, but George Phelps – God rest his soul – was a liar and a thief. So just tell what you know, or it'll go the worse for you.'

'Let go of me!' exclaimed Norah Smallwood, loud

enough for others in the room to turn and look, as she attempted to wriggle free. 'Don't you bloody touch me!'

'I swear,' said Sarah Tanner, 'I'm telling you the truth. Why would I lie?'

'Well, who was it then?' asked Norah, her voice still heavy with disbelief. 'Who done it?'

'I don't know his name.'

'You said you saw him,' she replied. 'You're making it up, ain't you?'

'It was a Peeler.'

'Now I know you're chaffing me,' replied Norah. 'Though it ain't much of a bloody joke. Ain't you right in the head? Is that it?'

'I saw him, with my own eyes.'

Norah Smallwood shook her head. But, before she could say a word, there was a distinct thump from behind the door to the Hole-in-the-Wall, which swung open abruptly. A man staggered in, falling upon the floor, with blood pouring from his mouth. Sarah Tanner recognised him instantly: one of the two young men who had stood guard outside.

'There's more where that came from, son,' said the burly, uniformed figure who appeared behind him in the doorway. 'You should have legged it along with your pal.' He casually aimed a heavy boot at the young man's midriff. The young man groaned and slumped to the ground.

'Now, all I want,' continued the policeman, who stepped calmly over the young man's prone body as if nothing had happened, and addressed himself to the assembled company, 'is someone who won't give me any lip. Is that too much to ask?'

The clientele of the Hole-in-the-Wall said nothing. At several tables, certain items disappeared into pockets; packets of cards slipped into sleeves; gold watch-chains disappeared from waistcoats.

'A simple matter, ladies and gentlemen, a young woman by the name of Smallwood. Christian name, Norah. Acquaintance of a gentleman – a man, least-ways – named Phelps. I'd like to locate that young lady. Someone speak up, if you please.'

'That's him,' whispered Mrs. Tanner to Norah Smallwood, who sat wide-eyed beside her. 'Now do you believe me? God help us, that's him.'

CHAPTER NINE

The barman was the first to speak.

'I know a chap called, ah, Phillips,' said the young man, with a straight face. 'Holds horses' heads down the Strand. You'll find him there most nights.'

The policeman cast the barman a withering look.

'Now,' said a drinker at a nearby table, taking up the theme, 'I don't know about that, but I know a bloke called Phil, now I come to think of it. Tinker, I think he is. Kips down by the Adelphi, under the arches.'

Several of the drinker's companions laughed. The policeman pursed his lips and walked slowly towards the bar.

'Come here,' he said, addressing the barman.

The young man smirked rather self-confidently, rubbed his hands on his apron and walked along the length of the bar.

'A little closer, son,' said the policeman. 'I want to tell you something, confidential like.'

The young man leant forward. But as he did so, the policeman turned on him, swinging the heavy wooden truncheon he had kept concealed beneath his coat. With astonishing speed he made a swipe at the barman's head, the wood making contact with the young man's jaw; the crack of splintering bone audible to everyone in the public. The barman screamed in pain but the policeman showed no pity. Even before a drop of blood had been spilt, he had his victim by the collar, thrusting his head down upon the counter, trapping his throat with the truncheon, choking the life out of him.

'Now,' said the policeman, 'I'm not fond of chaff, son. Norah Smallwood. That's the girl's name. Have you come across her?'

The barman spluttered, his voice inaudible.

'I can't hear you, son,' said the policeman jauntily. 'Speak up so we can all hear you.'

Several of the Hole-in-the-Wall's customers stirred uneasily in their seats but not one rose up in the young man's defence.

'Cowards,' muttered Sarah Tanner under her breath. She turned to the girl sat beside her. 'Listen to me,' she whispered urgently. 'Does he know you? Have you ever seen him before?'

'No,' replied Norah Smallwood. 'Lor, I'd know it if I had, wouldn't I?'

Sarah Tanner looked again at the policeman; he had already glanced in their direction and said nothing. It had been dark in Baldwin's Gardens that night. Too dark to see her face?

'Stop!' said Mrs. Tanner, rising to her feet.

The policeman turned his head.

'Stop – I'll tell you. She was here last night. I talked to her. I stood her a drink.'

'Did you now?' said the policeman, releasing his grip on the bloodied barman, who stumbled back-wards, clutching his jaw, knocking over several glasses, sending them crashing noisily to the floor.

'She were an hotel skivvy or something like that,' continued Sarah Tanner, 'just been given the push.'

'That's right,' replied the policeman, with a tight thin-lipped smile, walking over to her. 'What's your name?'

'Sally.'

'Is that so, Sally? And what's your line of work?' said the policeman. 'Or needn't I ask?'

'I manage.'

The policeman smiled, raising his gloved hand to flick aside a loose strand of hair from Sarah Tanner's cheek. 'I'll just bet you do. Who's your little friend?'

'That's my sister,' said Mrs. Tanner without hesitation.

'Hmm. Shy little thing, ain't she?'

Norah Smallwood looked away, cowering in her seat.

'You've frightened her, that's all. What do you expect, carrying on like that?'

'Nothing to be scared of, not if you speak up,' said the policeman. 'So you talked to her then, our Miss Smallwood. What did she have to say for herself?'

'She was looking for some fellow called George,' replied Mrs. Tanner. 'But he didn't turn up and I ain't heard of him. So I told her where she could find decent lodgings.'

The policeman's face lit up at the word *lodgings*. Sarah Tanner watched his expression closely. He had dark, coal-black eyes, a flattened boxer's nose, and a sly-looking mouth that turned down at the corner.

'And where was that?' he asked.

'There's a mission-house on Sardinia Street, one that takes young gals. That's where she went.'

'Very Christian of you,' he replied. 'Now, you wouldn't lie to a policeman, would you, Sally?'

Sarah Tanner shook her head.

'Leave her be,' said a voice from behind the policeman.

Mrs. Tanner's eyes darted to one side. It was the voice of the drinker who had spoken earlier. He was a little better dressed, a little more flash than many of his fellows, wearing a silk waistcoat and white cravat, perhaps a year or two younger than herself.

'You heard me,' said the man. 'You've got what you came for. Leave her be.'

'I'll do as I damn well please,' replied the policeman, calmly. 'And you won't be the boy to stop me.'

The man in the silk waistcoat shrugged. He did, indeed, look no match for the policeman.

'No, you're quite right, Constable,' he went on. 'But I'll warrant there's a dozen here with half a mind to try. Now, the only thing that's stopping *them* – I'd lay good odds – is that they don't give tuppence about this girl you're after. That and that nice blue coat that you're wearing. But if you lay your hands on little Sally here, spoil that pretty face, well, they might just forget themselves, eh?'

'Chivalrous lot, are they? Oh, I can see that.'

'Depends on the circumstances,' replied the drinker.

The policeman chuckled.

'Aye, maybe you're right at that, my lad. She is a pretty little thing. Shame to spoil it. But listen here, *Sally*,' he continued, grabbing a rough hold of Sarah Tanner's chin, 'if you're lying to me, I'll come back. And it'll go the worse for you and your little sister; you can count on that.'

Sarah Tanner merely nodded.

'Good girl,' said the policeman, releasing his grip. He paused for a moment, surveying the room. Then, at last, he smiled a brief self-satisfied smile, and edged towards the door. Stepping over the prone body of his first victim, with a final admonitory glance at the clientele of the Hole-in-the-Wall – as if to say, *Follow me? don't you dare!* – he calmly made his exit, closing the door behind him.

With the policeman gone, as the room erupted into confusion and chatter, Norah Smallwood looked up for the first time.

'He . . . killed George?' she said, stunned.

'Yes,' replied Mrs. Tanner, taking a deep breath. 'And I don't think he's got your best interests at heart, neither.'

Norah Smallwood looked back down at the floor, covered her face with her hands and burst into tears. Before Mrs. Tanner could react, however, there appeared a white handkerchief – offered by the young man in the silk waistcoat who had challenged the policeman. Norah eagerly seized it from the young man's fingers.

'Not a bad performance,' said the man in question.

'I beg your pardon?' said Sarah Tanner.

'You're no more her sister than I am,' he replied. 'You're lucky it didn't occur to him.'

'I'm sorry, but you're mistaken.'

'Reckon I'm not,' said the young man. 'I saw you come in; I know a dodge when I sees one. No need to thank me neither.'

'For what?'

'For saving your skin.'

'Thank you,' said Mrs. Tanner, without much grace. 'But I can take care of myself.'

The young man snorted in derision. 'Looked like it. Anyhow, you'd better hook it; Sardinia Street ain't that far.'

'We'll be gone soon enough.'

'I'll walk you home if you like,' said the young man, with a grin. 'Keep you out of harm's way, like.'

Sarah Tanner looked down; the young man's arm was all but wrapped about her waist.

'I have someone,' she replied, deftly moving to one side.

'Lor! Not that bag of bones you came in with?'

'He'll do.'

'You make it hard going, don't you? What did that blue-coat bastard want with her, anyway?'

'Her!' sniffed Norah Smallwood, from behind the tear-stained handkerchief. 'I am sitting here, ain't I!'

'Well, what's he after, then?' asked the young man.

Norah looked up, rubbing her eyes. 'How should I know! Mind your own bleedin' business!'

Sarah Tanner wearily shook her head. 'Norah, come with me. I'll take you somewhere. Somewhere safe. You can stop the night with us.'

'Why?' asked the girl, plaintively.

'It's what George would have wanted.'

Norah Smallwood gazed once more around the room, at the bloody chaos left in the policeman's wake. At last, still dabbing her face, she acquiesced.

'Here, you sure you don't want no company?' persisted the young man.

'Oh, I'm spoken for,' said Mrs. Tanner, nodding at Ralph Grundy as he came cautiously forward to rejoin her.

The young man looked at the old waiter and shook his head in disbelief.

'Suit yourself,' he muttered, turning away. 'Never do an whore a favour, that's what they say, ain't it? A fellow should know better.'

Sarah Tanner let the insult go; she watched the

young man return to his seat, her face quite impassive.

'Come on then,' she said, as the young man sat down and his friends broke into peels of laughter, 'we haven't got all night.'

CHAPTER TEN

'There,' said Sarah Tanner, putting a steaming mug of coffee down upon the table, 'that'll warm you up.'

Norah Smallwood, her eyes puffed and red from her tears, took the mug and sipped. She sat in the lamp-lit warmth of the Dining and Coffee Rooms, opposite Mrs. Tanner and Ralph Grundy, but she still seemed to shiver.

'George, he loved me, you know,' said Norah. 'He did. He said he didn't want me working, and he'd get us a little cottage—'

'Of course he did,' interrupted Mrs. Tanner. 'But, Norah, please, listen. There must be some reason for what happened to him; I don't know why, maybe he'd taken something or—'

'I told you already,' said Norah, 'he didn't have a chance. He was going to go through some of the rooms, that night, when everyone was asleep. He had it all planned out. But then he never come back. I knew there was something wrong, when he didn't come back –' she paused to dab her eyes – ''cos he promised, see? He promised he'd look after us. And look at me now. I ain't got no place or nothing.'

Then, as if struck suddenly by the weight of the realisation, Norah Smallwood dissolved into tears once more.

'Hang on,' said Ralph Grundy, 'why did they give you the push, if your precious George didn't nab anything?'

Norah wiped her eyes with both hands, her face downcast.

'Spoons.'

'Spoons?'

'I just thought I'd show Georgie; he said I weren't cut out for his line of work, teased me. So I told him I'd do it.'

'You pinched some spoons?'

'It was only a couple of bleedin' tea-spoons,' said Norah sullenly. 'Silver-plate. Cook was always down on me, old cow. I didn't know she'd count 'em again. Not before I'd gone.'

'Spoons?' said Mrs. Tanner, a tone of frustration creeping into her voice.

'Look! It ain't my fault. None of it!' exclaimed Norah Smallwood.

'Now then,' interjected Ralph Grundy, gently, 'no-one said it were.'

'Think, Norah,' insisted Sarah Tanner. 'There must be something – something Georgie had done, or said. Maybe something he told you, something he gave you? There's got to be a reason that man came after Georgie, then came after you.'

'What do you care, anyway?' said Norah, despondently.

'You saw him; you saw what he's like. I'm going to make him pay for what he did – I don't know how, but I swear I will, for Georgie's sake. Yours too. But you've got to help me.'

Norah Smallwood sniffed, rubbing her nose on her sleeve. 'I'm sorry.'

Mrs. Tanner put her hands to her temples. Ralph

Grundy, however, tried another tack. 'What about that lady they were talking about, missus, eh? At the hotel?'

'What lady?' asked Norah.

'There was a woman staying at the Hummums, a Miss Ferntower,' explained Sarah Tanner, taking Ralph Grundy's cue. 'When I came to look for you, I heard someone say she'd gone missing. Could it be anything to do with Georgie?'

'Well, I don't know, do I?'

'Well, did you see her – Miss Ferntower?'

Norah Smallwood paused, then nodded. 'Yes, I remember her.'

'Well, what was she like?' asked Mrs. Tanner. 'Young, old?'

'She only came in on Thursday, but I saw her a few times. She was old – about forty or so, I s'pose.'

'What did she look like?'

'I don't know. She weren't bad-looking, though, if she'd have took her hat off.'

'Her hat?'

'Well, she had this veil, even when she was indoors. I thought it was the fashion, but she must have seen me looking, 'cos she said it was the light; something about her eyes. I didn't pay any heed; none of my business. I thought maybe she'd had the pox or something. But she hadn't.'

'How do you know?' asked Mrs. Tanner.

'I caught her when she was dressing, when she didn't have her hat on. That made her jump! I was only bringing her coals up. A right bag of nerves, she was. Wouldn't surprise me if she had run off somewhere and all.'

'You'd know her again, then, if you saw her?'

Norah Smallwood shrugged. 'S'pose.'

'What about George,' persisted Mrs. Tanner. 'Did he have anything to do with her?'

'I don't know. He might have done. I weren't his bleedin' shadow!'

'Norah, there must be—'

But before Mrs. Tanner could say another word, Ralph Grundy raised his hand.

'Missus, you do as you like but it's gone two o'clock in the morning, and I ain't getting any younger. I need my kip. I reckon a couple of hours wouldn't do you no harm neither.'

For a moment, Sarah Tanner seemed inclined to disagree. But, looking at the tear-stained face of Norah Smallwood, she gave way.

'I suppose you're right,' she replied reluctantly.

'About time,' added Norah, under her breath. 'Lor, you'd think you were a bloody Peeler, the way you go on. I've done my best, ain't I?'

Sarah Tanner nodded wearily. 'I've made up a bed in the back parlour upstairs. You can sleep there, if you like. We'll talk in the morning.'

'Thank you,' muttered Norah Smallwood. 'For the lodgings, anyhow.'

'My pleasure,' replied Mrs. Tanner, with a sigh.

Norah Smallwood needed no further prompting but made her way upstairs, taking a candle to light her way. Ralph Grundy, in turn, got up and picked his hat and coat from the nearby stand.

'Been a fine old night, ain't it?' he said, as he unlocked the door to the shop.

'She doesn't know anything, Ralph,' said Mrs. Tanner, in a low voice. 'And what am I going to do with her now? I can't hide her upstairs for ever.'

'If it were down to me, missus,' replied Ralph Grundy, equally quiet, 'I'd point her in the direction of the big house. Let the parish have her; she won't come to any harm there. And if she don't care for that life, then it's her own look-out.'

'Ralph! The workhouse? She's not so bad as all that. I was no better, when I was her age.'

'If you say so, missus, I won't argue,' replied Ralph Grundy. 'But do you reckon she'll be here in the morning? I'd count the silver now, if I was you.'

'Silver? There's no worry on that score.'

Ralph Grundy smiled. But then, even as he opened the door, his face turned suddenly grave.

'I'm sorry, missus. I should have said before.'

'Whatever for?'

'That I weren't no use, when that hulking brute got hold of you. To tell the honest truth, I'm an old man and—'

'Hush,' said Mrs. Tanner. 'I'm glad you kept quiet. I've seen that man's handiwork; you were better off where you were.'

Ralph Grundy shook his head. 'That's kind of you, missus. But I know what's right and what's wrong. And I know I was a coward; and I ain't proud of it. If I could have—'

'Hush, Ralph, please. Besides, I got the devil's number; that's something.'

'His number?' said Ralph, surprised. 'Here, you kept that quiet. His coat was full over his collar, weren't it?'

'Near enough. But I saw some of it. *K1* something. K division. That means he's from down the river – Rotherhithe or Greenwich.'

'You know 'em off by heart, eh?' said Ralph.

'I've had reason to learn.'

'So what's he doing snooping round Covent Garden?'

'That's what I'd like to know,' said Sarah Tanner. 'But at least it means we know his patch; someone will have heard of him. We can make inquiries.'

'Inquiries! Maybe you'd do better not asking questions, missus. Did you ever think of that?'

'You know I've made up my mind on that score, Ralph.'

Ralph Grundy shrugged. 'Well, then, there's nothing more to say on it, is there? Good night, missus. Keep an eye on her upstairs.'

'Good night. I'll see you in the morning.'

Ralph Grundy nodded and walked out into the street. Mrs. Tanner, for her part, closed the door firmly behind him, turning the key in the lock. She took the solitary lamp that stood on the counter, and in her customary fashion used it to light the way upstairs. She only paused when she came to the door to the upstairs parlour, the little room behind her own, in which she had put down a pair of rugs and some blankets, so that Norah Smallwood might have somewhere to sleep for the night. There was a hint of candle-light still showing, the glimmer just visible in the gap beneath the door.

She hesitated for a moment, then knocked and went in. Norah Smallwood sat cross-legged upon the floor, blankets wrapped round her shoulders.

'Are you warm enough?' asked Mrs. Tanner. 'You should try and sleep a little, if you can.'

'Do you think he loved me?' replied Norah, sniffing. 'Georgie? He said he did.'

'Then I am sure he did.'

'No, you don't think so, not really,' replied Norah Smallwood. 'I ain't stupid. I just thought . . . well, I don't know . . .'

At first, Sarah Tanner said nothing. But, as Norah

spoke, she noticed that a small crumpled piece of paper fell from the girl's fingers.

'What's that?'

'See for yourself,' said Norah. 'Proves you're right.'

Sarah Tanner put the lamp to one side and bent down, opening the piece of paper, finding it stained with the girl's tears.

'"Diana. London Bridge. Sunday, two o'clock,"' said Mrs. Tanner, reading out loud. 'What is it? I don't understand.'

'When he didn't come back that night, I went up to his room. There weren't nothing there, mind. He'd cleared out. I told myself he'd come back for me. He promised, see? But then I found that. Probably fell out of his pocket or something. It's another gal, ain't it? He was going to meet her tomorrow. He weren't going to stick with me at all. I told myself it weren't true, but . . . well, it don't matter now anyhow.'

'You looked in the room? Why didn't you say? Was there anything else?'

'Lor!' exclaimed Norah Smallwood. 'Will you stop going on! I told you – I don't know nothing!'

Sarah Tanner woke at half-past five in the morning. For, although she felt quite exhausted, the daily routine of the Dining and Coffee Rooms was not easily broken. She could, at least, hear Norah Smallwood snoring in the room next door and felt a slight sensation of relief that, contrary to Ralph Grundy's prediction, her guest had stayed the night.

With lamp in hand, she went downstairs. But, as she came to the kitchen, she paused and turned back towards the shop itself. Barely awake, she was somehow conscious of a half-formed thought; a memory that seemed just out of reach.

What was it?

She walked over to the portion of the counter where the newspapers accumulated in the shop – abandoned, lost or generously donated by customers – had been neatly arranged into a pile by Ralph Grundy.

Then it struck her. The papers had been there the day before, whilst she was serving in the shop.

She put down the lamp and took a copy of the previous day's *Times* that lay on top of the pile. She recalled it had been left by a junior clerk who frequented the Coffee Rooms for his breakfast. She ran her finger down the first column: the advertisements, 'BOMBAY STEAMER', 'AUSTRALIAN EMIGRATION', then finally she came to one at the bottom of the page:

STEAM to MARGATE, at 2 o'clock precisely, Tuesdays, Thursdays, Saturdays and Sundays, from London-bridge-wharf by the DIANA, the fastest packet to travel direct, no stations between. Diamond Funnel Company. Offices – 113 Fenchurch-street and at wharf.

Sarah Tanner allowed herself a brief, satisfied smile.

CHAPTER ELEVEN

'What's that again?' said Ralph Grundy, incredulous.

It was Sunday morning on Leather Lane, though there was little sign of church-going amongst the market folk outside. The old waiter's face was illuminated by a shaft of sunlight as he spoke, shining through the rather smeared glass of the Coffee Rooms's window.

'I slept on it. I told her she can stay on, work here, earn her keep. We need another pair of hands; you're always saying we could do with someone.'

'Begging your pardon, missus, but I wasn't thinking of—'

'Norah can stay on,' said Sarah Tanner firmly. 'That's settled. If she gives any trouble, well, that's another matter.'

'It's your gaff, missus,' replied Ralph Grundy, 'and you can do what you like. But I can't see the sense in it. Even if she's straight with us, what if she brings company, eh? What if your friend finds her again?'

'He wouldn't even know where to start. Besides, this isn't a bad place for her to lay low. It'll do as well as anywhere else.'

'Is that so?' said Ralph Grundy. 'Ah, well, I was forgetting that, with everything being so quiet round here lately.'

'Ralph, please. Now, I've just told Mrs. Hinchley she's my cousin. I'd be obliged if you didn't tell her otherwise.'

'Hmm. And where is she, then, your little cousin, if she's supposed to be here working?'

'She upstairs, changing.'

'Changing?'

'I've lent her a dress. If she's going to work here, she needs something better than that rag she was wearing.'

Ralph Grundy shook his head at the highly unsatis-factory development. Any further conversation with his employer, however, was cut short by a loud shout from Mrs. Hinchley – a summons which ran along the lines of 'Done! Two eggs and bacon; full hot!' – which drew him back towards the kitchen.

Mrs. Tanner, for her part, waited for the waiter's return; then, leaving him to his work, she went upstairs.

She found Norah Smallwood in the front bedroom, already dressed, examining herself in her employer's dressing-table mirror.

'You look much better already,' said Mrs. Tanner, standing by the door.

'I s'pose.'

'I hope you haven't changed your mind already?'

'No, I ain't,' said Norah. 'I was just thinking on it, that's all. I ain't got nowhere to go, anyhow.'

'Well then. We've got customers waiting.'

'Four bob a week, food and lodgings?' said Norah Smallwood.

'Three and six,' said Sarah Tanner reproachfully, 'like we agreed. Ralph doesn't think you'll suit, mind you.'

'Don't he just!' exclaimed Norah, instantly roused

to rather exaggerated indignation. 'What's he got to say about it?'

'He thinks you'll take off with the money-box, first chance you get.'

'Who does he think he is – bleedin' dried-up piece of old parchment!' exclaimed Norah. 'I ain't—'

Sarah Tanner, however, interrupted, raising her hand. 'Norah, he might not look it, but Ralph's no fool. And I'm not either. You just remember that.'

'I ain't a thief,' said Norah, sullenly.

'I didn't say you were. Listen, George Phelps made me a lot of promises too, a few years ago; but he didn't keep many of them. Trust me, you're better off here, for now at least. As for Ralph, just put in a good day's work and don't give him any chaff; that'll set you straight with him – and me – quicker than anything.'

Norah Smallwood nodded but it was impossible to tell whether she was entirely convinced. 'What about that steamer, then, the one in the paper? I thought you said we was going to go down to the bridge.'

'Not until this afternoon. Go on, go downstairs – Ralph can introduce you to Mrs. Hinchley; she'll find something for you to do.'

'I ain't afraid of hard work, missus – ask anyone.'

'Good. I'm relying on that.'

Norah Smallwood left the room, though, in truth, the young girl's expression was still rather sullen. Mrs. Tanner herself was about to follow when she noticed something out of the corner of her eye: the top drawer of her dressing table was ever so slightly ajar, although the key was still in the lock, where she herself had left it the night before.

She opened the drawer and examined the contents: a little bundle of letters, tied together with a thin red ribbon. As she turned them over in her hands, she noticed that it was a rather clumsy bow and that the knot was not her own handiwork.

Sarah Tanner frowned.

After a moment's thought, she closed the drawer and locked it shut, ready to place the key in the pocket of her dress. But then she hesitated. For there was another locked drawer, beneath the first.

She knelt down, unlocked and opened it.

At first sight, the contents of the drawer were merely bundles of rags. But beneath the cloth lay something far more precious: a small pocket pistol, with a dark walnut stock and rather tarnished barrel. Next to it lay a wooden case, which she opened with caution. Within were a dozen brass percussion caps and bullets, carefully wrapped in cotton.

Sarah Tanner counted each one, until, relieved, she was quite satisfied nothing was missing.

———

With Norah Smallwood occupied in the kitchen, receiving instruction on the art of cleaning a skillet – an art which Mrs. Hinchley was more than happy to pass on to her new apprentice – Mrs. Tanner addressed a few words to Ralph Grundy then quit the Dining and Coffee Rooms.

She found Leather Lane at its busiest, not only packed with costers' barrows, but the pavements cluttered with the impromptu emporia of lesser businessmen. For, upon every corner, threadbare sheets of cloth were laid upon the ground; and upon them lay everything that could be bought for a few pence, from rather battered-looking Dutch dolls to bags of brass nails. She picked her way between the vendors. Her progress was further hindered by the Lane's ambling itinerant merchants, sellers of food and drink. Given to awkward stops and starts, and their shouts filled the market: *A pint o' prawns for a penny! Hot spiced gingerbread, hot as hell-fire! Fine silver mackerel! Almond toffee!* The cacophany of calls merged into a rather bilious-sounding menu.

At last, she came to Holborn. She crossed the broad road, turning eastwards, following the trickle of Sunday-morning traffic for a quarter of a mile or so, until she came to a narrow tributary of the great thoroughfare, a street known as Feathers Court. It was a narrow, rather dingy, sooty road, with its opposing walls oppressively close, interlaced by the washing-lines which residents had strung from one window to another. Sarah Tanner's goal was a particular building: an ancient-looking house with cracked slates and rickety sash windows. It bore a painted sign above its front door that read *Chas. Merryweather & Son, Bookseller and Law Stationer*.

She tried the door and, finding it open, went inside. A man's voice instantly rang out in the hallway.

'Who's that?'

She found the owner of the voice in the front room, a rather small and gloomy parlour. It contained a small smoky fire-place, and a prevailing odour of spilt ink and sealing wax. On either side of the chimney breast were walls lined with shelves, and the shelves, made of dusty, dreary-looking wood, were lined with dusty, dreary-looking volumes to match. The occupant was a middle-aged man, seated at a writing-desk, a bald, whiskered individual with a slight paunch and a rubicund complexion. His face was half hidden by an avalanche of papers and documents, which, to all appearances, had tumbled from some great height, settled upon the desk, and then spilt promiscuously over the floor. Yet, when he finally caught sight of his visitor, he immediately stood up and smiled a broad smile.

'Miss Mills!'

'Mr. Merryweather.'

'Please, my dear! Charles, if you will – no! – Charlie, if you're agreeable,' said Mr. Merryweather, whipping a handkerchief from his waistcoat pocket and ostentatiously dusting off one of the chairs that sat by the hearth. 'Chas, if you've a heart; if you've a mind to please your old acquaintance. And I know you have a heart, my dear. I know it! Heavens! Sit, my dear young woman, sit!'

Sarah Tanner obliged, but did not have a moment to speak, before her host continued.

'Now, this is an occasion!' exclaimed Mr. Merryweather. 'A glass of port is called for, don't you think? You must take a drop!'

Mrs. Tanner politely demurred, but her host did not deny himself the luxury, disappearing for a moment into the back room of the house, and returning with a full glass.

'Charlie—'

'Ah! Please, my dear!'

'Chas, I need a favour.'

'A favour? Anything, my dear creature. Good Lord – how long has it been, eh? I'd quite given you up for lost. Well, until I heard a little something yesterday evening.'

'Yesterday?'

'Mr. Albert Jones,' said Charles Merryweather, rather coyly, sipping at his glass. 'Medical complaint. Nasty headache. Visit to the Dispensary. All very droll.'

'That wasn't me.'

'Really? Well, I'd steer clear of our mutual friend,

my dear, all the same. I gather he's labouring under the impression you were responsible; and I wouldn't care to correct him.'

'Charlie, listen,' said Sarah Tanner. 'George Phelps, he's dead.'

Charles Merryweather's face merely softened a little, adopting a rather conventional expression of sadness.

'Is that so? I heard something about that too. Poor George; a good chap. Very fond of him. Very fond.'

'I know. That's why I came to you. Listen, you must know how things stand between me and, well, certain parties . . .'

Mr. Merryweather waved his hand, as if to brush the matter aside.

'Well, then,' continued Mrs. Tanner, 'can you help me at all – for Georgie's sake?'

'Of course, my dear. Of course. But, forgive me, how might a humble scribe such as myself assist? I am rather busy, even though it is the day of rest. Is it money, my dear? I could do you a nice *Help, or I Perish!* for a discount. Why, I believe I have one here. Suitable for most purposes, you know. Distressed widow; husband, succumbed to drink, four infants, all with fever, at death's door, *et cetera, et cetera*. I can do a lady's hand to a turn, even if I say so myself. None better.'

'No,' said Sarah Tanner, shaking her head, 'I just need to know something about a woman – well, perhaps a family – named Ferntower.'

'Ferntower?'

'It's something to do with George; I don't know quite what, not yet.'

Mr. Merryweather smiled and walked back to his desk, picking a book from the nearest shelves.

'Post Office Directory, my dear. Could you not have just referred to it yourself?'

'If I had one. My circumstances are . . . not quite what they were.'

'Ah. I see. Well, of course, then let us have a look. Ferntower . . . peculiar name, I could almost swear I know it. Ah, here we are. There is only one in the capital, at least. Mr. M. H. Ferntower, 42, Hillmarton Park, Holloway. A most respectable address.'

Sarah Tanner nodded. 'Is there nothing else?'

'The Post Office don't concern themselves with anything else, my dear lady. That is sufficient for the workings of that great institution. However, *I* might be able to oblige you. Now, where did I leave it? Somewhere safe, I am sure.'

Mr. Merryweather began peering at the shelves behind his desk; then in the drawer within the desk; then upon the floor. Sarah Tanner followed his bumbling movements with bemusement.

'What are you looking for?'

'The old bible, my dear. You may recall, before I went wholesale, a couple of years ago,' – Mr. Merryweather gestured at the mountain of papers of his desk – 'I used to make more direct appeals to the generosity of my fellow man. Holloway was familiar ground to me then.'

'You mean when you were on the tramp.'

'No need to be vulgar, Sarah. Ah, here it is. Now, let's see. *Hillmarton Park. 14th December 1849.* New houses, rather grand, I seem to recall; almost in the country. *40. Widow. Adams. No kin. No money. 2 bob for burying dead wife.* No. Ah, now I have it. *42. Ferntower. Gentleman. Widower. Own carriage.* Crossed out. Now why was that? Oh dear. Yes, it's in the margin here. *MS.*'

'MS?' said Mrs. Tanner.

'Member of the Mendicity Society, my dear. One

of those gentlemen who prefers to dole out tickets for soup, rather than spare a couple of coppers, like a decent Christian. Nothing for Charles Merryweather, Esquire, there. Still, one meets all sorts in one's professional life; one must take the rough with the smooth. Now does that assist you, my dear? I can't imagine how. Of course, if I come across anything more, I shall be sure to let you know. If you'd care to leave an address?'

'No. But, thank you, Charlie. It's very good of you. I'm afraid I had best be going.'

Charles Merryweather sipped again from his port. 'So soon? Are you sure I cannot tempt you, my dear lady? Stay and have a little something to eat. I'll send the boy out for pies. We could discuss old times; old friends.'

Sarah Tanner smiled, but shook her head.

'You take care, Charlie. And thank you.'

Charles Merryweather sat quite still, waiting, until his front door closed.

'You can come out now,' he said at last.

For a moment there was no response. Then the besuited figure of Mr. Stephen Symes appeared from the back room.

'I'm surprised you restrained yourself, Mr. Symes,' said Charles Merryweather. 'You were only just telling me you'd like rid of her.'

Mr. Symes smiled.

'There is a time and place, my dear sir. A time and place. Besides, what does she want with old Ferntower? Now that is quite intriguing.'

CHAPTER TWELVE

'So I said to her, I *am* doing it hard – and then some – but she wouldn't have it. But then she couldn't do no better, which made me laugh . . .'

'Laugh?' asked Sarah Tanner.

'Well, almost,' said Norah Smallwood, as she walked beside her new employer. 'I mean, I held my tongue. But she couldn't do no better, no matter how hard she scrubbed at it.'

'Just do what Mrs. Hinchley tells you, that's all I ask.'

'Didn't I just! Look at these hands – red raw, they are! And that's just this morning. She's a bleedin' slave-driver, that woman.'

'Hush. Just hurry up – we'll be late.'

'I didn't mean nothing by it,' said Norah, in a conciliatory fashion, as they crossed King William Street.

'No, I'm sure.'

'Here, have I done something wrong?' asked Norah, a little puzzled. 'Why are you being so quiet? I did just what she told us, didn't I? Ask her yourself.'

'No, it's not that.'

'What then?'

'This morning. You read my letters.'

Norah Smallwood's cheeks grew flushed. 'No I didn't!'

'Please, Norah,' said Sarah Tanner, 'you're an awful liar.'

Norah Smallwood paused to consider her predicament. 'I didn't think you'd mind,' she said, at last. 'I were just looking for a comb, that's all.'

'A comb?'

'I said I was sorry, didn't I?'

'No,' replied Mrs. Tanner, taking Norah Smallwood's arm, and leading her along, 'I don't believe you did.'

'Well, I am . . . sorry, I mean. I was only looking, missus. I didn't take nothing.'

'I suppose I should be grateful for small mercies?'

'I thought . . . well, I thought they might be from Georgie.'

Sarah Tanner sighed.

'I wouldn't have looked otherwise, that's the truth!' protested Norah.

'Norah, do you promise me you won't go anywhere near my things again?'

''Course,' replied Norah. 'Here, there's the Monument. We're almost there.'

'I swear, Norah, if you stay under my roof . . .'

But Sarah Tanner's voice was drowned out by the rattling wheels of a heavily laden waggon that passed them by, trundling down Fish Street Hill. For they were almost at their destination in the heart of the City: the wharves below London Bridge.

In truth, the river itself was barely visible: for the commercial traffic upon the hill – waggons, carts, coaches and cabs – could only progress so far before coming to a halt upon the cobbled quayside, blocking the view, each vehicle bent upon discharging goods and passengers, almost invariably to the disservice of the vehicle behind. Broad-shouldered porters were on hand, eager to earn a penny or two from conveying luggage between quay and boat; but they only added to the chaos of the scene, since they positively laid seige to any traveller bold enough to carry so much as a paper hat-box in their presence.

Sarah Tanner, however, knew her way. She led Norah Smallwood further on, down towards the wharves themselves, opposite the tall warehouses which lined the water-front. Two ha'penny boats were moored in the shadow of the bridge – ready to ply their trade to Westminster and back – but the location of the Margate packet, a larger vessel, fit for sea-going, was a little further along the quay. In fact, the *Diana* was unmistakeable, marked out not only by its size, the twin diamond-checked funnels, and the guttural purr of its engine, but by the crowd of well-wishers who surrounded it, waiting to wave the passengers good-bye.

'I still don't know why we're here, anyhow,' said Norah, surveying the scene.

'I told you, I want to know why Georgie had it written down – if he was going to get that boat, for a start.'

'Well, if that's it, then we'd better look alive,' said Norah, who began, quite unashamedly, to elbow her way forward.

For the most part, as Norah pressed on, the crowd gave way; for it was not uncommon upon the wharves to see a last-minute dash towards the gang-plank of a Margate boat. And, if a couple of ladies or gentlemen objected to the vigour with which Norah Smallwood propelled herself, their complaints were lost in the mêlée. In any case, it was largely thanks to her young companion that Sarah Tanner eventually found herself upon the very end of the wharf, where a wooden gang-plank and iron rail connected the pier with the steam-packet, managed by a uniformed attendant, wearing the checked livery of the Diamond Funnel Company.

'All aboard,' shouted the attendant, as Sarah Tanner stepped forward. 'Passengers for Margate; transfers Antwerp and Ostend. You travelling, ma'am? Ticket please.'

'I'm sorry, I'm here to see off a friend—' said Mrs. Tanner, but the attendant interrupted even as she spoke.

'No friends or followers now, ma'am. Didn't you hear the bell?'

'No, I'm sorry, I'm late . . . you see, it's very important that I know if he's on board; I have some news . . .' – Mrs. Tanner paused, testing her powers of invention – 'his mother's quite ill . . .'

'What's the gentleman's name, ma'am?'

'Phelps.'

The attendent retrieved a sheet of paper. Perusing it for a moment, he shook his head.

'No passenger of that name, ma'am. You must have the wrong boat.'

'You mean he hasn't arrived?'

'Never arrived, ma'am? Never on the list in the first place,' said the attendant.

Sarah Tanner considered her reply, when another thought struck her.

'He was travelling with a companion – a Miss Ferntower . . .'

The attendant eyed his interlocutor rather skeptically but consulted his list nonetheless.

'No, no-one of that name either. Now, if you'll just step back, that *was* the last bell.'

Sarah Tanner, frustrated, stepped back as instructed, watching the attendant pull in the gang-plank.

On board the steamer, the sound of the captain's orders, then the echo of the call-boy's shout to the engineer, could just be heard above the din of the engine. Then, with a twin burst of steam and black smoke, the boat shuddered into motion, its paddle-boxes churning the silt water below.

Mrs. Tanner watched the boat pull off, dejected. It took her a moment to realise that Norah Smallwood stood beside her, tugging at her sleeve.

'Look, there, on the deck!' she said excitedly.

'What?'

'Look! There's a woman there, in black; a mantle and hat. Can't you bleedin' see her?'

'What are you talking about?'

'That's her! That's your Miss Ferntower. She ain't gone missing; she's on that boat.'

Sarah Tanner peered at the deck, unable to make out the woman in question.

'Missus – that's her. I'm sure of it. No veil, neither. I knew that veil business was all gammon.'

'Where?'

'Lor! Now she's gone round the other side! I ain't fibbing, I swear!'

Sarah Tanner sighed. 'I believe you.'

'Ain't you pleased?'

'It doesn't matter.'

'What do you mean?'

'We're too late. Most likely Georgie was coming here; but what was he up to? Was he meeting her? Following her? She's the only one who might tell us.'

'But she's on the boat,' protested Norah Smallwood.

'Which only stops at Margate. We can't catch up with her; and, even if we followed on the next steamer, unless that fellow was lying, she's not even using her own name. That means she doesn't want to be found, Norah. People don't disappear like that unless they have a reason. You may take my word for it.'

'You don't think she's coming back?'

Sarah Tanner merely shook her head, watching the boat pick up steam and disappear from view, obscured by the black bulk of a coal barge turning towards the southern shore.

'No. I fear Miss Ferntower's gone for good.'

It was two days later that Sarah Tanner's prediction was to be proved wrong.

At the time, Mrs. Tanner herself did not know it; she was asleep in her bed. But she was proved wrong – after a fashion, at least – by a sergeant and constable from the Thames Marine Division of the Metropolitan Police, in a row-boat, performing their regular night patrol along Limehouse Reach.

For, in the darkness, their lantern picked out the ungainly, bloated shape floating mid-stream.

And when the sergeant pulled the corpse in with his boat-hook, it became clear their catch was a woman; a decent woman, whose silk dress had once been an unremarkable, but respectable, article – not the sodden shroud which had buoyed up her lifeless frame.

And when they looked over all her clothes – for the indignity of such close examination was mandated in the catechism learnt by every Marine officer – they found her name, on the discreet label sewn into her petticoat, intended only for her laundress.

Ferntower.

CHAPTER THIRTEEN

Ralph Grundy, seated in one of the Dining and Coffee Rooms' little booths, stirred his tea, tapping his spoon noisily against the earthenware mug. Before him lay an empty bowl containing traces of oatmeal porridge, and a plate which bore the faint yellow trails of two poached eggs. It was Ralph Grundy's custom to take a brief, gratuitous breakfast at his place of work, a pleasant perquisite of his employment. Indeed, Sarah Tanner had noticed that Mrs. Hinchley's cooking was liable to lift Ralph Grundy's spirits, even on the dullest of mornings. Thus, she could not help but observe that, upon this one occasion, the waiter seemed to linger over his drink, and appeared not so much lifted as quite flattened. Sarah Tanner, therefore, took it upon herself to quit her seat behind the counter, as the shop was bereft of customers, and sat down facing her employee.

'The eggs weren't off, I hope?'

Ralph Grundy shook his head. 'Don't let Mrs. H. hear you say that, missus, not about her eggs. You'll find yourself short of a cook. Just you say the word. Remember that fellow who complained of 'em? The way she went at him, you'd think she'd gone and laid 'em herself.'

'Well, what is it?' replied Mrs. Tanner with a smile.

Ralph Grundy merely shrugged. Sarah Tanner, in turn, fell silent, a rather deliberate silence that made her employee shift awkwardly in his seat.

'Where is she, then?' said Ralph Grundy, at last.

'Norah? Is that what's troubling you?'

'Ain't no trouble to me, missus, if she ain't been here a week and goes off on a lark whenever it suits her.'

'I sent her to the butcher's, we're running short of bacon.'

Ralph Grundy shrugged once more.

'Mrs. Hinchley says she's coming along in the kitchen,' continued Mrs. Tanner.

'Hmm. There's girls as would come along twice as strong, and twice as quick,' muttered Ralph. 'Plenty of 'em. And not attract followers, neither.'

'Followers?'

'Ain't you see 'em? Coming in here, sniffing round. They don't even want nothing to eat. It ain't good for business.'

'I haven't seen much sign of that.'

'Hmm. Well, maybe you ain't got your eyes peeled, missus. She's already got two of the young 'uns from the market sweet on her, mark my words.'

'She can't help that, Ralph.'

'Hmph!' replied Ralph Grundy, as if to imply that Norah Smallwood, in his opinion, very much could. 'And what about your precious Mr. Phelps, eh? Soon forgotten him, ain't she?'

'She's young,' replied Sarah Tanner, 'but I doubt she's forgotten.'

'She's trouble, missus. I know her sort. Trouble comes to girls like that, natural. Put her back where you landed her; she don't need any help from you. She'll look after herself.'

'If I didn't know better, Ralph, I might think you were jealous. I told you – if she does her share, she can stay.'

Ralph Grundy gave a derisive snort, then took a long swig of tea.

'You do what you think best, missus. And if an old man ain't no use to you no more—'

'A certain "old man" might be a good deal of use,' interrupted Sarah Tanner, quite calmly, 'if he did not sulk like a spoilt child whenever he did not get his own way.'

Ralph Grundy, unaccustomed to quite such a frank rebuff from his employer, fell abruptly silent. But, at length, a hint of a wry smile spread across his lips.

'"Sulk"!' he exclaimed.

'Ralph . . .'

'No, don't take it back, missus,' said Ralph Grundy, chuckling to himself. 'Maybe an old man deserves to hear a hard word now and then; maybe it brings him up sharp. I've said my piece. And if we don't agree on a certain subject – upon which I ain't saying another word – then that's an end on it.'

'Thank you, Ralph.'

'Mind, if you're still playing detective, missus,' continued Ralph, lowering his voice, 'then I reckon you still needs all the help you can lay your hands on.'

'I wish it was that simple.'

'Ain't it?'

'I don't know,' replied Mrs. Tanner. 'What do you suggest? Perhaps I should just go down to the station-house at Greenwich and tell the Superintendent one of his men is a murderer?'

'It'd be the truth.'

Sarah Tanner shook her head. 'You've seen the sort

of people I used to know; the sort of life I lived. What would a magistrate make of that? What would he make of Norah? There's no proof, no evidence but my word – nothing.'

'Maybe if you talked to that gentleman at the hotel,' suggested Ralph Grundy. 'Ferntower, weren't it?'

'And tell him that I saw his sister taking a boat to Margate? That she's hiding from someone or something? That it involves a dead man in Leather Lane?'

'True enough, though, ain't it?'

'Unfortunately, Ralph, the truth won't do.'

'What if that Peeler's after her too?' he suggested.

'I don't know. Why would a respectable woman run away? Why wouldn't she go to her brother?'

'Maybe,' said Ralph, 'she ain't that respectable.'

Sarah Tanner rubbed her forehead. 'I don't know.'

Ralph Grundy did not reply, his gaze directed over Sarah Tanner's shoulder.

'What is it?' asked Mrs. Tanner.

'I ain't saying a word, missus,' said the old man. 'Not a word.'

Sarah Tanner turned round.

Norah Smallwood stood outside the shop-window, a rather tatty wicker shopping basket slung under her arm. Opposite her stood a young man, a bony-faced boy of the coster class, dressed in green corduroys, a white Belcher tied artfully around his neck, clutching Norah's hand and grinning. They stood together for a few moments, then the boy, no more than fifteen or sixteen years of age, spoke a few words and left.

'Who was that?' asked Mrs. Tanner, as Norah Smallwood came inside.

'No-one in particular,' replied Norah.

'Joe Drummond's boy, Harry, off the market,' interjected Ralph Grundy, getting up from his seat and clearing his plate and bowl from the table, before disappearing off to the kitchen.

'Here!' exclaimed Norah Smallwood. 'Who asked you?' But the waiter had already disappeared from view.

'Just be careful who you speak to, that's all,' said Sarah Tanner.

'He spoke to me; I can't help it,' protested Norah. 'Besides, I told him I was your cousin and everything, like you said.'

'Good.'

'He was asking if I wanted to step out, tomorrow night.'

'Norah, in case you've forgotten, you have work to do here,' protested Sarah Tanner.

'I didn't say I'd go with him. I just said I'd ask.'

'Well, then, the answer is no.'

'Even if I know a secret?'

'Don't play games with me, Norah, please. I have enough to think about.'

Norah Smallwood tutted to herself, and rummaged inside the bottom of her shopping basket, pulling out a page of a newspaper, roughly folded and stained. 'I was going to tell you, anyway. Here, look at this. Yesterday's paper. They was wrapping bacon in it; I heard someone talking about it.'

Sarah Tanner followed Norah's hand, reading the small tightly crammed type.

THE DEAD BODY of a respectably dressed woman was found in the Thames yesterday, in the early hours, on Limehouse Reach, between Cuckold's Point and the Queen's Stairs. The deceased was identified as Miss Emma Ferntower, reported missing on Saturday by her brother. A letter was found upon her person, addressed to her brother. It is suspected that the lady, in a state of mental distraction, took her own life. No reason is assigned for the rash act. An inquest will be held on Thursday 8th at the Acorn Inn, Trinity Street.

'I'll be damned,' said Mrs. Tanner.

'I know,' replied Norah Smallwood. 'And it's today, ain't it?'

CHAPTER FOURTEEN

It was ten o'clock in the morning by the time the cab clattered alongside the great stone walls of the Commercial Docks. The cab in question was an old four-wheeled carriage, a member of the 'growler' class that quite lived up to its name, its wheels complaining noisily at every bump in the cobbled lane. The driver came to a halt, at a junction in the road. There was barely a cloud in the sky, but the looming grey walls upon either side of the street, towering some thirty feet high, cast an inescapable shadow that seemed to leave everything below in perpetual twilight.

The driver coughed and leant down from his seat. He addressed a few words to a small gathering of men, deep in conversation upon the street corner. They were rather resigned-looking individuals – casuals who had, doubtless, not caught the dock foreman's eye at the early-morning levée – but nonetheless they answered the cabman in good humour, gesturing towards the end of the road. The cabman followed their gestures, but peered into the distance, as if still quite uncertain of how to progress. At last, he thanked them, adjusted the collar of his coat and drove on.

'We're lost,' said Ralph Grundy, glancing at the men as the cab moved off. 'Sixpence a mile and we're lost.'

'Never mind the cab, I thought you said you knew the docks,' replied Sarah Tanner.

'I reckon I did, twenty year ago,' muttered the old man. 'St. Kats, in the main.'

'That's the other side of the river,' rejoined Mrs. Tanner. 'You distinctly said—'

'Well, you might need my help, all the same,' interrupted Ralph Grundy. 'Besides, no harm in it. Mrs. H. can keep an eye on your little treasure; she won't let her get up to any mischief.'

'And you can keep an eye on me?'

Ralph Grundy shrugged. 'No harm in that either.'

Sarah Tanner looked at the old man, as if she had in mind a further word of reproach, but there was something in his face that made her falter, and almost smile at his gallantry.

'What did you do at St. Katherine's?'

'Nothing much,' he replied, rather evasively. 'It were a long time ago.'

'Ralph, what was it?'

'Dock Police.'

'Police?'

'I weren't a Peeler, missus. It were for the company. I was on the gates – pockets and passes. That's all I did, missus. It weren't much.'

'Still,' said Sarah Tanner, amused, 'a policeman all the same.'

As she spoke, the cab came to a halt once more. 'Looks like we're here, eh?' said Ralph, as he peered outside. 'About time.'

Sarah Tanner and her companion stepped out of the cab, and gave the driver his fare. There was no doubting it was the correct location. For the Acorn Inn was a substantial tavern of three storeys, with its back to the Thames – where it even took deliveries upon its own wharf – and with its front opposite one of the principal entrance gates to the Commercial Docks.

Inside, they found that the public bar affected a maritime air, with a pair of compasses pinned upon each wall, and several copies of the *Shipping and Mercantile Gazette*, casually abandoned upon the tables. But before Sarah Tanner could say a word, the barman – taking a glance at the unfamiliar faces – gestured with weary resignation towards the stairs.

'Crowner's 'quest's upstairs. You're late, mind.'

———

The coroner's inquest upon the body of Miss Emma Ferntower had, in fact, commenced a good hour earlier. The coroner himself had instigated proceedings in the downstairs bar with a small, complimentary glass of port from the landlord, and then proceeded upstairs to the Acorn's function room upon the first floor. The court clerk had already put everything in order: twelve seats for the jury, a dozen or so more for witnesses, and a comfortable chair and table for his master, upon which had been laid a pen, paper and a Bible for administering the oath. The only article lacking was an inkwell, which somehow had been forgotten. A wine-glass, therefore, had been commandeered from the landlord and filled with black ink, in peculiar contrast to the coroner's ruby glass of port.

The coronor had called the room to order at nine o'clock sharp. Twelve good men and true had been sworn to do their duty by the Crown, then immediately despatched to contemplate the body of the deceased, which had been laid in an outbuilding by the river-side, a resting-place normally reserved for the cold storage of bottled stout. The building was sufficiently small, and the interest of the jurors sufficiently large, for the whole procedure to take an inordinate length of time. Consequently, even though Sarah Tanner and Ralph Grundy arrived a full hour late, the inquest was far from over. Moreover, the function room was quite full – not only with jury and witnesses, but an audience who had merely come to observe the coroner at his work, and who were happy to crowd together, at the back of the room, for that particular privilege.

Sarah Tanner glanced at the people around her: most were women, the wives and daughters of dock-workers, who exchanged knowing looks as the coroner spoke; they were, she felt sure, connoisseurs of Thames-side tragedies. The men present appeared a little more disinterested. A couple wore the thick woollen pilot coats of river-going folk; others were dressed more shabbily, like the casuals who had provided the cabman with directions. All carried the distinctive scent of the district: the aroma of creosote and turpentine that marked out the timber docks. All seemed present principally for their own gratuitous amusement. Some had even brought their own provi-sions. Indeed, she watched as the man beside her – a bearded individual, his face half hidden by the collar of his coat – took a small parcel from his pocket, unwrapped it, and proceeded to eat the meat pie contained within.

The testimony of the witnesses had already begun.

'That's how we found her, Your Worship, two nights ago,' said the police constable who stood before the jury, referring to his notebook. 'Me and Constable Whyte were on night-guard along the Reach. We saw something floating in the water – which ain't uncommon – and when we pulled it in, we found it was the body of a respectable female.'

'Respectable, on account of her clothing?' inquired the coroner.

'Yes, Your Worship. And the boots, sir. Proper pair of quality leather.'

'Pray, continue.'

'Well, sir, we pulled in the body; we found the name on her clothes, and the note.'

The coroner nodded. 'Simpkins,' he said, addressing his clerk, 'read the note to the jury.'

The clerk stood up, coughing, as if preparing for a tragic oration.

'"My dearest Michael, I am much delayed. Our captain was an utter fool. I shall take a room at the Brunswick; I prefer to travel in the daylight; expect me in the morning. Your sister, Emma."'

'That is all?'

The clerk bowed.

'I see. Please go on, Constable.'

'Well, that's the long and short of it, Your Worship. We made arrangements here – being the nearest respectable house. Of course, I knew the lady's name, as I'd seen the notice on some route papers at the station-house.'

'You mean to say you knew the name, because Mr. Ferntower had reported his sister missing?'

'Yes, Your Worship.'

'Now, Constable, we have heard from Dr. Matthews that he believes the body had been in the water for some days; is that likely?'

'Well, Your Worship, most cases, the tide carries them out past the Reach within a day or two. But if a body snags, or is covered, it ain't unheard of.'

'And the marks of violence on the poor woman's person? The wounds to the head and upper body?'

'Oh, they can be knocked about something awful,'

replied the constable. 'Begging Your Worship's pardon.'

There was a distinct sob from the front of the room. A couple of the women present in the crowd muttered, 'Shame!' Sarah Tanner peered past them. She could just make out, in profile, the face of Mr. Ferntower himself, familiar from the staircase of the Hummums, and two women, dressed in mourning, who were seated beside him.

'Thank you, Constable, that will be all. Now,' said the coroner, taking a sip of his port, 'I should like to call upon Mr. Michael Ferntower, the deceased's brother.'

Mr. Ferntower took the seat vacated by the young policeman. He was a man in his late fifties, with a rather stern, angular face, and a fine head of silver-grey hair. Before he spoke, however, Sarah Tanner's attention was distracted by the man beside her – who abruptly stopped eating, and noisily stuffed the remains of the pie inside his coat pocket, wiping his mouth with a rather grey and greasy-looking handkerchief.

'Now, my good sir,' said the coroner, 'naturally, we offer the condolences of the court' – Mr. Ferntower nodded his acknowledgement – 'and understand that circumstances such as these are most disagreeable. Nonetheless, I am obliged to ask you – is there any reason why your sister might have been unsettled—'

'Unsettled, sir?' interrupted Mr. Ferntower.

'As to her mental faculties,' suggested the coroner.

'None, sir,' said Mr. Ferntower, emphatically.

'I see. Can you, therefore, account for her sudden change of heart in quitting the Brunswick Hotel, Blackwall, as we have heard, for the Hummums, Covent Garden?'

'I have only the report of the manager, sir,' said Mr. Ferntower, rather haughtily.

'Who,' said the coroner, looking down at his hastily written notes, 'has deposed that Miss Ferntower stayed at the premises for three hours; during which time she was visited by her nephew. Then left abruptly without giving good cause.'

'Then I know nothing more,' replied Mr. Ferntower.

'Miss Ferntower's nephew – your son, indeed . . . I understand from the police that you are not on good terms with the young man?'

Mr. Ferntower, for a moment, looked slightly flustered. 'I do not believe that is a matter for this court.'

'Hmm,' said the coroner. 'And you cannot account for Miss Ferntower failing to post the letter that was found on her person, nor for her removing herself to the Hummums hotel?'

'No.'

'Nor why she did not continue to your residence in Holloway the next morning?'

'I can only re-iterate, sir, what I have told the police. My sister was a woman of sound mind, and not given to whims or fancies.'

'Hmm,' said the coroner. 'And you have nothing more to add?'

'Only, sir, that I believe my sister had no intention of doing away with herself; to be frank, that I suspect foul play.'

'On whose part, my dear sir?'

Mr. Ferntower paused; there was something in his expression that suggested deep unease. He cast his eyes down to the floor. 'I do not care to say.'

The coroner raised his eyebrows. 'If you do not "care to say", sir, then what is the jury to make of it?'

'They may think what they like. I intend to say no more upon the subject.'

The coroner scowled. He appeared to have the distinct feeling that Mr. Michael Ferntower, with his peculiar mixture of accusation and reticence, was making a fool of him; and he seemed determined to end the sensation as quickly as possible.

'Quite so,' said the coroner. 'Quite so. Well, I believe that concludes our witnesses. You may step down, Mr. Ferntower. Now, I must ask all other parties to withdraw, while the jury considers its verdict.'

Sarah Tanner exchanged a quizzical glance with Ralph Grundy. But before she could move aside, the man who had stood beside her pushed violently past them both, and walked hurriedly downstairs.

⬤

Sarah Tanner sat in the public bar of the Acorn Inn. The witnesses for the coroner's inquest had retired to private rooms; but the remainder of the coroner's audience had, by and large, decanted to the tap-room. Speculation upon the jurors' verdict was rife; and yet Mrs. Tanner had heard nothing that suggested any of those talking had much greater knowledge of the case than she herself. Ralph Grundy, meanwhile, seemed to have quite vanished. Indeed, having promised to purchase a gin-and-bitters, it was some ten minutes before he returned, empty-handed, to the table.

'Don't look at me all 'asperated, missus,' said Ralph. 'You'll thank me, I promise you.'

'I gave you a whole shilling.'

'And there never was a shilling better spent,' said Ralph, taking a seat. 'Now do you want to hear about it?'

Sarah Tanner reluctantly nodded.

'Well, I got talking at the bar there, to a young fellow, who it turns out is coachman to your Mr. Ferntower.'

'Go on.'

'Now, there's another fellow up there, with some tobacco, see – so I says to that young man, "Well, I fancy some of that. Now," I says to the coachman, "you're a man what appreciates good baccy, I can tell—"'

'So you bought him some tobacco,' said Mrs. Tanner, cutting off her companion in mid-sentence. 'Just tell me what he said!'

'Lor! Give an old man a chance! Ain't that what I was trying to do?!'

'Well then?' said Sarah Tanner impatiently.

Ralph Grundy frowned, but continued all the same. 'Well, it turns out the coachman knows what his master meant by that remark, that he didn't "care to say". Your Mr. Ferntower, he reckons his own son did for her.'

'His son? The woman's nephew?'

Ralph Grundy nodded sagely. 'It turns out young John Ferntower went to the bad a few months back – gambling, writing notes against his old man's name, the usual way of such things – and his father's cut him off without a penny.'

'I still don't follow; what has that to do with it?'

'Apparently it was her – his aunt – what found him out; the boy swore he'd swing for her. Now your man's sure it's not suicide – reckons the boy went and murdered her, but he can't bring himself to own to it, not of his own son. That's the opinion of the servants, anyhow.'

Sarah Tanner fell silent for a moment, then shook her head.

'No,' she said at last.

'Hold up, missus,' said Ralph Grundy, 'I'm only going off what I was told.'

'If Miss Ferntower was just afraid of her nephew, why didn't she go straight to her brother? Why was she hiding? Why change her hotel to Covent Garden? Why get on that boat to Margate? And how did Georgie get dragged into it?'

'You've got me there, missus.'

'Where's the son now, in any case?' she said, thinking out loud. 'Did you ask him that?'

''Course I did. No-one knows, missus. The old man chucked him out and cut him off; he ain't been seen since; living off his wits, most likely. He won't have any money to speak of. Here – they've turned out . . .'

Ralph Grundy nodded towards the stairs as the coroner's clerk appeared in the bar, and coughed.

'A verdict has been reached, ladies and gentlemen.'

———

'Can the chairman of the jury please stand and deliver the verdict?' asked the clerk.

The chairman stood; he was a short, nervous-looking man who seemed to shrink visibly as the room's collective attention fell upon him. Sarah Tanner looked around the room; the face of Mr. Ferntower seemed quite impassive; the younger of the two women beside him held a handkerchief to her face; the senior remained more composed.

'We, the jury—' said the chairman in a rather quivering voice.

'Speak up, man,' grunted the coroner.

'We, the jury, have concluded that Miss Emma Ferntower was found drowned, but whether she destroyed herself in a moment of temporary derangement, by accidental means, or otherwise, we believe there is no evidence.'

'Very well, an open verdict,' concluded the coroner. '"Found drowned." I thank the witnesses for their patience.'

Sarah Tanner turned back to Ralph Grundy. But, for the second time that day, a man pushed past her – the same bearded man who had stood beside her earlier – and walked hurriedly towards the stairs. On this occasion, however, he chanced to meet her gaze – their eyes connecting for a brief moment.

She stood aside. But, as she turned her head back towards the makeshift court, to take one last look at the witnesses, something occurred to her. She hurriedly glanced back to the bearded man, as he descended the staircase, disappearing from view.

It was the handkerchief, still hanging half out of his coat pocket, the same one with which he had wiped his face; a dirty piece of cloth, but a silk handkerchief, nonetheless, monogrammed in fine black thread.

'What is it?' asked Ralph Grundy, as Mrs. Tanner grabbed his arm and began to lead him away, elbowing through the departing crowd.

'That handkerchief.'

'Missus?'

'His handkerchief! "J.F." Didn't you see it? And there's something about the eyes; I'll swear it. He's got the look of his father.'

'You've still lost me, missus,' protested Ralph, as Sarah Tanner hurried him along.

'That man – that was him, the nephew, Ferntower's son.'

'Because of a handkerchief? You sure about that,

111

missus?' said Ralph Grundy skeptically. 'He could have got that wiper anywhere.'

'That's why he hurried off; he didn't want to be recognised. I'll lay odds on it. Hurry – we can still catch him!'

CHAPTER FIFTEEN

'I ain't got young legs!' protested Ralph Grundy, as Sarah Tanner rushed down the stairs, to the consternation of several of the women who blocked her path.

'Then don't run!' said Mrs. Tanner over her shoulder, darting into the public bar. But then she stopped. There was no sign of the bearded man; the bar seemed as empty as when she first came in. She glanced towards the barman: he was perusing a newspaper and seemed hardly to have noticed her own abrupt entrance. She ran out into the street. A couple of men stood by the dock's great iron gates; another stood by the tavern's door, puffing on a long pipe.

'Did you see anyone just go by?' she asked, turning to the pipe-smoker. 'Shabby-looking . . . your height . . . he had a beard and a brown coat?'

The man in the doorway, however, merely shook his head. The men by the gates exchanged a wry look with each other.

'Lost something, darlin'?' shouted one.

'Sounds like you could do a sight better, my love!' shouted the other, chuckling. 'Come over here, we'll set you right.'

Sarah Tanner shook her head but said nothing.

Ralph Grundy, meanwhile, slightly breathless, tapped at his employer's shoulder.

'Didn't you catch him, then?' asked Ralph.

'No, plainly.'

'He can't have got far.'

'No,' she said, a degree of irritation in her voice.

'I reckon he went the other way,' suggested Ralph Grundy, looking left and right along the road.

'There is no "other way".'

'Well, if you says so, missus. If you ain't counting the river.'

Sarah Tanner muttered something inaudible under her breath, and turned to head back into the tavern. But the motley crowd from the inquest blocked her path for the second time – with one of the women complaining loudly of *some people's dreadful 'pertinence* – such that it took several minutes for her to work her way to the rear of the pub, and out into the tavern's walled yard, overlooking the Thames. The yard was almost as empty as the street outside. A couple of young men stood huddled in close conversation with a third, whom Ralph Grundy recognised as the illicit vendor of tobacco whom he had met at the bar. Mrs. Tanner, meanwhile, hurried towards the outcrop of the Acorn's private wharf, where she found only a solitary row-boat moored by the wharf's wooden steps. The boat was manned by a waterman, a bronze-skinned, muscular individual of middle years, in a dark blue sailor's jacket, who looked up expectantly as she drew near.

'You from the 'quest?'

Sarah Tanner assented.

'Aye, thought as much,' replied the waterman sagely. 'Good day for business. Well, it's sixpence a crossing, or one and six to the Bridge.'

She looked out across the wide expanse of the river. There was no sign of her quarry. 'Has there been a man here . . . a man with a beard, a shabby-looking coat; he would have just come from the inquest?'

The waterman pondered the question for a moment, then nodded. 'Aye, I reckon there was. You missed him. Tom Stone took him up to the Bridge.'

'Could you catch him up, for two bob?'

'I won't catch Tom Stone now, missy. Not even if I were a steamer and had a boiler 'stead of an heart, and two paddlers 'stead of arms. Tom's a good oar, and half my age. But, for two bob, I'll go at it strong, and I suppose we might see Tom by-and-by, when we gets there, if your luck's in.'

'I suppose that will have to do,' said Mrs. Tanner, reluctantly. And, even as she spoke, she began to clamber down to the boat. Ralph Grundy, however, hung back by the edge of the water, gazing at the rather tarry-looking scull and its owner with a distinct show of nerves.

'Come on, Ralph, hurry,' insisted Mrs. Tanner, as she stepped down, and sat on the blanket provided for the comfort of passengers.

'I ain't too fond of water, missus.'

The waterman laughed. 'I ain't lost a man yet, don't you fret.'

Ralph Grundy laughed in return, without much conviction. At last, however, he gingerly descended into the boat.

'And you told me you were a river-man, Ralph,' said Mrs. Tanner, as the waterman heaved at the oars, propelling the little craft away from the safety of the shore.

'I never did,' muttered Ralph, holding tight to the side of the scull. 'Said I worked at the docks.'

'Near enough, but you never told me, why did you give it up?'

'It were a long time ago. Like I said, I ain't that fond of water, missus.'

'You said you were on the gates.'

Ralph Grundy paused, as if lost for a moment in reflection. 'Well, there was two pound of sugar,' he replied ruefully.

'Sugar?'

'It were one pound down each trouser leg; regular thing. They never checked us, see? Well, that's what I thought, anyhow.'

Sarah Tanner looked quizzically at her companion as the boat pulled out into the current. 'Then maybe it's you I should be watching, when it comes to the money-box, not Norah.'

The waterman briefly looked up from his task, but then fell back to his oars, the boat scudding across the rolling silt water with every firm stroke.

'Don't tease us, missus. I learnt my lesson. They had me quodded for six months, hard labour.'

She looked again at Ralph Grundy; there was something severe in his expression, as if he found the recollection particularly painful. She gently put her hand on his.

'You're fine with me, Ralph. I've heard much worse.'

'Aye, but maybe you'll hear worse again,' said Ralph. 'And then what will you make of it, eh?'

'You'll do, Ralph,' replied Mrs. Tanner. 'I can tell.'

Ralph Grundy took a deep breath, as if recalling his self-possession. 'I'm glad to hear that, missus.'

'Except, perhaps, you look a little pale.'

The waiter looked out along the sweep of the river,

just as the churning passage of a steamer on the northern side sent a surging wash of water, which rocked the little boat from side to side. He took a firm grip, and swallowed rather uneasily.

'I'll be fine, missus.'

———

The little scull came at last towards its landing-place, a small wooden jetty and set of steps, squeezed between the grand steam-boat piers by London Bridge and the wharves of Billingsgate Market, where the distinctive salty aroma of the morning's market's trade – the future fish-supper of the metropolis – still hung heavy in the air. As Ralph Grundy climbed eagerly on to dry land, Sarah Tanner paid the oarsman his fare.

'Well, do you see him?' she asked while the man remained seated in his boat. 'Is he here – you said his name was Stone?'

The waterman peered along the jetty, where several little boats, similar to his own, were moored. For the most part, they were empty – their owners either taking refreshment nearby, or touting for trade by the steam wharves – but there was a stocky young man, in an oilskin coat, who leant against one of the jetty's timber supports. The young man in question seemed preoccupied, staring at a small piece of paper he held in his hand.

'Aye, there he is, missy, large as life, that's him, though he looks fair blown out, don't he? Here! Tom Stone, look alive! What's up with yer?'

'Fellow just baulked me of a shillin', that's all,' muttered the young man.

'Well, there's two parties here as wants a word with yer.'

'What about?'

'The man you're talking about,' said Sarah Tanner. 'Did you just take him from the Acorn Inn?'

'Aye,' replied Tom Stone, a trifle suspiciously, walking along the pier, 'that's the one. You a friend of his?'

'No, not a friend exactly. Did he say anything to you – do you know where he was going?'

The young man smiled knowingly. 'Ah, he did you too, did he? I should have knowed it; he was a queer-looking sort. No, he didn't say nothing 'ticular to me, not where he was going, not nothing else neither; and he came up a shilling short. I should have hauled him up to the bloody magistrate, but I took pity, see? I thought, the way he talked and all, maybe he was a gentleman down on his luck.'

'You're too soft-hearted, Tom Stone,' interjected the other waterman.

'Reckon you're right,' replied Tom Stone, glancing again at the paper in his hand. 'I bet this ain't worth nothing neither.'

'What is it?' asked Sarah Tanner.

'A duplicate – he swore it was worth three bob, so, like a right Sam, I went and took it and let him off. I'd be a bigger fool to spend a shilling on his word, though, wouldn't I?'

'He gave you a pawn ticket?'

'A waistcoat. Said it were good for two shillings more if I went and got it back. I'll lay odds it ain't; I should never have took pity. It ain't worth my trouble.'

Sarah Tanner placed a hand inside the pocket of her dress. 'I'll give you sixpence for it.'

Tom Stone pondered the offer for a moment.

'Done,' he said at last, quite cheered up.

'No cab home, then, missus?' said Ralph Grundy, some few minutes later, as he followed his employer along the riverside.

'I'm not made of money, Ralph.'

'As you like,' said the old man. 'Worth your trouble, was it?'

'Read it yourself,' said Sarah Tanner, handing Ralph the scrap of paper.

Ralph Grundy unfolded the paper and read out the contents.

'"Reeves, Little White Lion Street, 29th March 1852. Waistcoat. One shilling, number six hundred and fifty-three." It's a pawner all right. Well then – St. Giles again, ain't it? Seven Dials. You sure this is your man, missus?'

'I'll swear by the eyes, Ralph. He was the spit of his father.'

'Seven Dials ain't no place for a gentleman, if he is living thereabouts.'

'But not a bad place for a murderer,' mused Mrs. Tanner. 'That brute who murdered Georgie – Miss Ferntower – it's all tied up together, I'll swear it. I just can't fathom how, not yet.'

'So now you do think it's the nephew what killed her? And then what – your pal Phelps, he knew about it, so they got rid of him?'

'That's what I intend to find out.'

CHAPTER SIXTEEN

Reeves's pawn-shop was, indeed, to be found in St. Giles, not half a mile distant from the Hole-in-the-Wall public-house. It lay on Little White Lion Street, one of the lesser points of the compass of the Seven Dials, the notorious junction of seven roads, at the very heart of the ill-famed parish. The street itself was a narrow, sloping affair of small shops and ancient hastily erected tenements, buildings rather given to leaning arthritically forward over the pavement. The result was a peculiar dearth of daylight in the cramped little thoroughfare. In consequence, it took Sarah Tanner and her companion several minutes, going back and forth, and several inquiries at sundry dark doorways and entries, until they found in the shadows a small sign above a cracked lintel, bearing the traditional three balls of the pawnbroker, painted red on black, and with the words *Money Advanced, Articles of all Description* stencilled upon the door.

The interior of the pawnbroker's proved equally gloomy, with the predominance of articles on display being clothing – albeit of the greasy-collared and frayed-cuff variety, arranged upon racks and shelves in great abundance. And at the rear of the shop was the counter. There were no discreet partitioned boxes, in which clients might be quietly closeted. Possibly such bashfulness was beyond the inhabitants of Seven Dials: there was merely a table-top, some ledgers, a set of weights and scales, and Mr. Reeves himself: a thin, grey-suited, dusty-looking individual, whose appearance was quite in keeping with his musty, cobwebbed, establishment.

'What's the item?' said Mr. Reeves in a nasal tone, straight to business. He spoke with a rather dismissive air, as if to suggest that – whatever the item might be – he was rather disinclined to pay good money for it.

'I haven't got anything,' said Sarah Tanner. 'I'm trying to find the man who pawned this.'

Mrs. Tanner held out the duplicate. The pawnbroker looked at it for a moment, as if cogitating whether he should proceed with the conversation, then finally plucked it from Sarah Tanner's fingers.

'Are you now?'

'Do you know him?' continued Mrs. Tanner. 'The man who pawned it?'

The pawnbroker looked at the ticket, then opened the ledger that lay beside him, running his finger down the scribbled abbreviated handwriting that documented each transaction.

'Hmm,' he said. 'What if I did?'

'I need to speak with him.'

'How do I know you ain't stole it, my dear?' said the pawnbroker, holding up the ticket.

'I bought it, as it happens.'

'Why would a person need to speak to the man they bought it from either?'

Sarah Tanner sighed. 'I got it from another party. Do you know where I can find him?'

'Maybe I do, my dear. For a consideration.'

'Keep the ticket,' replied Mrs. Tanner. 'If you can tell me where to find the man who pawned the waistcoat.'

The pawnbroker smiled, and tucked the duplicate in his coat pocket.

'I do like a woman with a head for business. I know the man, my dear, well enough for my liking, anyhow. First called in about a month ago. If you must know, he says his name's Smith: which I'll lay odds it ain't. He says he lives in Shepherd's Buildings: which he don't, 'cos I have inquired. But I know him all the same. We don't get many gentlemen in the Dials, even his sort.'

'Gentlemen? What sort?' asked Ralph Grundy.

'The sort that don't change their clothes for a fortnight; the sort that talks dictionary but can't find money for a night's lodging. He's seen better days, has that one; and I don't see his luck improving, neither. I've had to oblige him on half a dozen items this last couple of weeks. Crying shame to see a young fellow like that gone to the bad, ain't it?'

The pawnbroker's broad expression of sympathy was tempered by a rather facetious smile.

'Do you know where he lives or not?' asked Sarah Tanner.

'There's no getting round it with you, is there, my dear? No, I do not, as it happens.'

'I thought we had an arrangement,' said Mrs. Tanner, wearily.

'I said I knowed him. I don't know where he has lodgings, though it won't be anywhere too fancy. But I do know where you'll find him, if you've a mind to look. You see, I know where he spends his money, when he can lay hands on it.'

'Where?'

'He's a betting man. He likes to brag about it – at least, if he wins. But I know the type; he can't stop himself. I reckon that's where his money's gone. Now, from what I hear, he always goes to matches down the Turnspit.'

'I know the place,' replied Sarah Tanner, 'I'm sorry to say.'

'Well, then, that's where you'll find him, my dear. Now, there's a match tonight, if you're so inclined.'

As he spoke, the pawnbroker surreptitiously retrieved a ticket, slightly larger than one of his dupli-cates, from his waistcoat pocket, and passed it across the counter.

'I like a young woman with a head for business, my dear. Tell 'em Reeves sent you.'

'Thank you,' replied Mrs. Tanner, as she scrutinised the ticket.

RATS! RATS! RATS!
On Thursday, the 8th of April, the Canine Fancy may make sure of a treat by dropping in at Billy Bilcher's,
THE TURNSPIT, TOWER COURT, ST. GILES.
Rats in the pit at Half-past Eight precisely.
Previous to the above entertainment, Mr. Roxton will sing his best finch Battler against Beetle Black's celebrated bird, for a pound a side. Cages uncovered at Eight. Plenty of rats on this occasion, with squeakers for youngsters and shy 'uns. After the sports a harmonic meeting, with
THE RENOWNED BILLY HIMSELF IN THE CHAIR.

'Looks like a good night out,' said Ralph Grundy, mordantly, looking over Mrs. Tanner's shoulder.

'Not for the rats,' replied Sarah Tanner, as she turned and left the shop.

———

It was nightfall, a few hours after her visit to the pawnbroker, when Mrs. Tanner descended from her bedroom into the Dining and Coffee Rooms. The air downstairs was heavy with pipe-smoke, and the rich aroma of burnt – or, in deference to Mrs. Hinchley, well-cooked – pork sausages. Upon each table was a solitary candle and the shop's brass oil-lamp cast its warm, muted glow over Ralph Grundy's naturally glum face, as he stood, wiping down the counter with his cloth.

As she walked by the booths, one of the shop's customers, a certain coster, a young man by the name of Harry Drummond, seated by himself, looked up and caught Sarah Tanner's eye.

'Evening, missus.'

She smiled, recognising the young man – little more than a boy, in truth – as the individual whom Ralph Grundy had pointed out to her earlier in the day.

'Good evening. Harry, isn't it, Joe Drummond's boy? I trust you're well.'

'Thank'ee, ma'am,' said the young coster. 'I bob along all right.'

'I hope you'll take good care of my cousin tonight?'

'We'll make a jolly trot of it, missus, mark my words.'

'I'm glad to hear it. She'll be down in a moment.'

The boy nodded, and confirmed that he was *much obliged*. Sarah Tanner, for her part, went behind the counter and took her shawl from the hook upon which it hung.

'Going out, then, missus?' said Ralph Grundy. 'Anywhere particular?'

'I expect you can guess, Ralph,' replied Mrs. Tanner as she wrapped the shawl about her shoulders.

'I'll be with you in two shakes, missus. Just you hold up.'

'No, Ralph. You stay here. I need someone to run the shop.'

'Well, I don't like leavin' a certain party on her own, missus. I'm glad you're seeing the sense in that. But I reckon you'll have to lump it, on this particular occasion.'

'No, Ralph, you're not listening,' replied Sarah Tanner, in a low voice. 'You stay here. I'll be safe enough. Besides,' she went on, nodding towards Harry Drummond, 'I changed my mind. I told Norah she could go out. So I do need someone here. I can't keep closing the shop; it's bad for business.'

'So that girl's free to come and go, as she pleases?' said Ralph Grundy, instantly indignant. 'She ain't been here a week! Not a week! And here's me, an old man, who's slaving his fingers to the bone, and never asks for nothing—'

'Hush, Ralph, please. Remember what we agreed. Besides, if you want a night's leisure, you only have to ask. You know full well.'

'It's you I'm worried about, missus. Sometimes I wonder what's going on in your head.'

'Believe me, Ralph, you're better off not knowing.'

'But St. Giles – it ain't safe at night for a woman! Why, it ain't precious safe for a man! None of it – least of all some blasted yard in Tower Court!'

'Please, Ralph, I've told you before, I can look after myself. I have my reasons. Now, please, just keep an eye on things here for me, eh?'

Ralph Grundy fell quiet. Sarah Tanner, for her part, chose to take his sullen silence as acquiescence. Consequently, she turned her back on her waiter, and quit the Dining and Coffee Rooms, walking out into the street.

It was only when she was clear out of sight of her own establishment that she carefully felt inside the pocket of her dress, and nervously ran her fingers over the wooden stock of her pistol.

CHAPTER SEVENTEEN

There was no sign to mark the location of Tower Court: for the ragged population of St. Giles knew the place well enough, and the wider world was, by and large, perfectly content to be ignorant. Admittedly, a few outsiders did occasionally seek out the Turnspit, but they came, by and large, by invitation of *those-in-the-know*, members of the *fancy*, dedicated gamblers to a man. Indeed, the public-house, despite the squalor of its surroundings, was a particular resort for a certain class of sporting gentleman, young men from a respectable background, for whom a night at the 'Spit, as they were wont to call it, was something of a rite of passage. Perhaps it was in honour of those individuals that the 'Spit did, at least, have a small signboard, pinned by its narrow wooden door, bearing a rough picture of a tethered, mangy-looking cur, the house's eponymous, rather doleful-looking, guardian spirit.

Sarah Tanner glanced at the mournful creature as she tentatively opened the door and stepped into the parlour.

The interior had the familiar scent of stale tobacco and beer-soaked sawdust that permeated many an establishment in the Seven Dials. Sarah Tanner knew the place of old; for it was an occasional haunt of George Phelps and seemed quite unchanged from her memory of it, except perhaps for a thicker layer of dust that had settled upon the bottles behind the bar. There were only a couple of solitary drinkers in the little parlour, but already the noise of the assembled gamesters could be heard, towards the rear of the building. She made her way, therefore, quite familiar with the territory, through an open door and into the muddy skittle-ground that occupied the back yard. There, walking cautiously along the narrow track, she approached a separate timber building that resembled an old stable. And, with every step, the hubbub of men's voices grew louder; the complaints of several barking dogs grew more abrupt, and the distinct high-pitched chirrup of a solitary chaffinch could be heard above the chatter of the crowd.

Sarah Tanner advanced her ticket to the pot-boy who stood by the stable door. She could see the first bout of the night was under way: the celebrated Battler, perched in a wicker cage, pitted against a far less vocal opponent, held tight in the hands of his master, wrapped in a parti-coloured silk handker-chief. But amongst the general gathering of shabby sportsmen – and they were men in most part, with only a handful of women in the room – there seemed little interest in the match. Possibly the mighty lungs of the famous Battler were odds-on to sustain his claim to pre-eminence; and certainly little money seemed to change hands as the two birds competed in song. More likely, however, most had come for a different sport altogether.

'You here for the match, darlin'?' said the pot-boy, a relatively handsome youth, with sleek brown hair and square jaw.

'I like a good scrap,' replied Mrs. Tanner, resolutely avoiding his appraising glance.

'Is that right?' replied the young man, only a little daunted. 'I'll bet you do an' all.'

Sarah Tanner surveyed the room; the man she had seen at the inquest was not present, as far as she could tell. There was a faint cheer from some of the crowd, and several of the dogs present joined in chorus; the Battler had already been declared winner.

'No sport in that,' murmured the young man. 'Just you wait 'til they brings on the basket. Billy B. never stints, I'll give him that. Here, how'd you like to step round the old yard, take a little stroll with us?'

'And see the sights?'

'Maybe. I could show you a thing or two.'

'I doubt that.'

The young man stood quite dumb-struck at the rejection; but whatever curse followed, it fell too late from his lips. For Mrs. Tanner had already pushed her way forwards through the gamblers. There was still no sign of her quarry. She tried an older man who loitered by the stable wall, beneath one of the half-dozen paraffin lamps that hung from the rafters.

'Beg your pardon, I'm looking for a friend of mine. Do you know him? Name of Smith? He has a beard, he's about so high; dark. He comes here regular.'

'Smith! A friend, is he?' replied the old man, chuckling to himself. 'How much does he owe you, eh? Cop a free ride, did he?'

'Something like that,' replied Sarah Tanner, but her voice was suddenly drowned out by a roar from the assembled audience.

'I ain't got time for you, darlin',' said the old man. 'Too old for that lark. Now let me pass – I've tebbed two bob on Old Charlie to take two dozen straight, and I'm damned if I don't want to see him do it.'

The old man was gone before Sarah Tanner could say another word. For Billy Bilcher, the proprietor of the 'Spit, had arrived. A broad, red-haired man, with extravagant side-whiskers and a voice that commanded the room, he magnetised his customers, drawing them to a circular enclosure in the corner of the building, made up of upright planks of timber, like a giant barrel sawn in half and embedded into the ground.

'Good evening, ladies' – a loud ironic cheer at this – 'and gentlemen. Tonight, for one night only, the game laws, they is suspended' – another cheer – 'and we have a fine bit of sport. Draw up close now, don't be afeard – they don't bite!'

There was another collective guffaw from the crowd, as they pressed towards the enclosure. Bilcher, meanwhile, dramatically pulled away a cloth which had hung over a large box by his side. It was a wooden crate, with a carefully constructed hinged lid; and, although its contents could hardly be seen through the gaps in the slats, there was little doubt on the matter. For the rats inside sensed their fate. The spectators closest to the front of the little arena could just make out the occasional glimpse of dark fathomless eyes, as each rodent scrabbled for an illusory position of safety; and all could hear the awful incessant, desperate sound of their claws scratching the wood.

'Step up, Mr. Cripps,' exclaimed Billy Bilcher. 'Show us that mongrel of yours, won't you?'

A man in the crowd wearing a rather crushed-looking low-crowned glazed hat, stepped forward and raised the dog in question above his head. It was no mongrel, but a black battle-scarred bull terrier, which struggled in its owner's grip, growling, its eyes firmly upon the lively crate that lay only a few feet away.

'How many, Mr. Cripps?' inquired the host, in the blandest of tones, as if taking an order for oysters or penny ices.

'A dozen,' replied the dog's owner.

'Are you sure, sir? These are biters, sir. No teeth drawed at Bilcher's; not unless requested.'

'Certain.'

Billy Bilcher grinned and, with a perverse dexterity, lifted the cage's trap and reached inside. In a blur of movement, the rats were flung into the pit. Only one was quick enough to sink its teeth into Bilcher's wrist; and, for its pains, its head was dashed in pieces upon the wooden boards that enclosed the makeshift arena. The bull terrier, in turn, caught the scent of blood, and barked for all its might.

'Drop him in, Mr. Cripps. Drop him in!'

The dog was lowered into the pit. For a moment, it stood stock-still, its eyes darting this way and that, as if unable to decide which way to turn. Then it began.

The terrier was quite up to its task; the crowd roared its encouragement. But Sarah Tanner did not watch the slaughter. The scraps of bloody fur and scuffles in the soaking red sawdust held no fascination. Moreover, something else caught her attention, causing her to stand back from the rest of the gamblers and withdraw into the shadows.

It was the man she had come to find.

CHAPTER EIGHTEEN

He crept silently into the stable, wearing the same shabby great-coat which Sarah Tanner had seen at the inquest. He seemed restrained and nervous in his movements, unlike many of the men present, who mostly affected a confident strutting bonhomie, and whose jollity was doubtless fuelled by liberal consumption of beer and porter. To Mrs. Tanner's surprise, however, the man did not hang back, even as Mr. Cripps's dog disposed of its last victim, accompanied by raucous applause. Rather, he went over to the individual who stood by the ring holding the wicker bird-cage containing the champion Battler, and exchanged a few words. Then, after some form of agreement between the two of them – for Mrs. Tanner could only make out their faces and little else – he proceeded to Mr. Bilcher himself.

Sarah Tanner manoeuvred herself through the crowd to observe the exchange. Although unfamiliar with Billy Bilcher, and quite unable to hear the conversation above the excited chatter of her neighbours, she could tell it was an argument of sorts. Bilcher's ruddy complexion turned redder still, his chubby finger pointing aggressively at his interlocutor to punctuate his speech. The newcomer, on the other hand, seemed conciliatory, pleading, a look of grim desperation upon his rather unkempt features. Then at last something was decided, the two men shook hands, and the proprietor of the Turnspit returned to the fray.

'Weren't that a match!' proclaimed Bilcher, with a glance at the bloodied bull terrier, being carefully removed from the ring by its owner. 'I'd never have said a dozen, Mr. Cripps – never! Now, as it happens, at this here interval in proceedings, we have a late arrival. A challenge to Mr. Roxton's Battler! A fresh country bird courtesy of our friend Smith!'

Sarah Tanner frowned; she was certain she heard a few of the men snigger at the name. She wondered if his fellow gamesters shared the pawnbroker's low opinion of Mr. Smith.

'A prime little beauty, bran' new to competition, will sing its heart out! Heard him myself only this morning; thought it were a feathery little angel. Come on, don't be shy. I'll give any man here ten to one; you never know, do you, gentlemen? Try your luck against the Battler! Hold him up, Smith – hold him up!'

Mr. Smith followed instruction, and reached inside his coat pocket, retrieving a handkerchief, from which poked the grey-crowned head of a chaffinch. Whether prompted or unrehearsed, the bird gave out a loud trilling call, to which the caged Battler instantly responded.

'A fighting bird!' exclaimed Bilcher. 'Is no-one giving him a chance?'

There was a hint of movement towards the front of the crowd; two or three men approached their host, others exchanged sly glances; money changed hands.

'Step up, then, Smith, bring him here,' demanded Bilcher. 'Look lively! Make a match of it!'

Smith obliged. But Sarah Tanner observed the same nervous posture, a peculiar shy reluctance. And, as he stepped forward, Mr. Smith stumbled upon the trailing hem of his over-sized great-coat. The handkerchief he clutched in his outstretched hands dropped to the floor. For a moment, Mrs. Tanner expected the little bird to fly away into the stable's rafters; but the bird's wings were clipped. It fell, wrapped in the cloth, on to the straw-filled floor, beneath the nose of an inquisitive, jowly grey bull-dog, which waited its turn in the ring. Before either the dog or the bird's master could prevail, a wave of laughter rippled across the drunken audience. For the unlucky little bird had been torn in two, and the look of despair on its master's countenance was somehow quite comical.

'What odds now, Billy?' shouted one good-humoured fellow.

Smith's face seemed stuck in disbelief at his ill fortune. However, it was the look upon Billy Bilcher's face that struck Sarah Tanner most forcefully – for the proprietor of the Turnspit was not laughing at all, and glared at the unfortunate Smith with unconcealed malice. Smith himself, meanwhile, finally gathering his thoughts, turned on his heels and ran, pursued by the laughter of the gamblers.

Mrs. Tanner was ready to follow as best she could. But before she could negotiate a path through the crowd, there was already a man ahead of her – the lumbering form of Billy Bilcher.

'He's for it, now,' muttered a man beside her. 'Billy'll have his guts.'

———

Sarah Tanner, as it happened, found herself rather grateful for Billy Bilcher's pursuit. For he was a substantial, thick-set individual whose breathing was somewhat laboured. Thus, as he ran out of the 'Spit, through the narrow streets and dark lanes of St. Giles, thanks to his heavy footsteps and the wheezing sound of his chest, even a blind man might have followed his progress. In truth, she was not convinced that Bilcher was quick enough to catch the fugitive, and felt sure his bulk would tell against him. But, upon turning a corner, not far from the pawnbroker's on Little White Lion Street, she could make Bilcher out, some fifty yards distant, standing over the huddled body of his prey. Smith himself seemed to have slipped and fallen on the muddy cobbles, and was clutching his leg. Smith's pursuer, meanwhile, grabbed him by the arm, and, despite his protests, dragged him bodily into the nearest alley.

She crept close enough to the corner to hear what passed between the two men.

'So here we are again,' said Billy Bilcher, in a low menacing voice, quite different from his blustering public-house persona.

'I'll find the money, my dear Bilcher,' said Smith, pathetically. 'You have my word, as a man of honour.'

Sarah Tanner listened intently. It was, as the pawn-broker had suggested, the voice of a gentleman, a voice that seemed quite ill-suited to its owner's circumstances.

'Your word, sir,' replied Bilcher, 'ain't worth a blind bit of notice. I had your word on that bird. Damn me, all you had to do was bleedin' hold on to it. All the bets were against it; Roxton would have kept the Battler down, and you could have swung the lot. It were a prize pegger, too. Cost me two bob to have the borrowin' of it.'

'My dear Bilcher, it was an accident,' said Smith plaintively.

'Well, then so is this,' replied Bilcher, his words punctuated by a dull thud and a pronounced groan; the sound, Sarah Tanner guessed, of a well-placed boot meeting Smith's gut. Involuntarily, she closed her eyes as a vivid image of George Phelps's last moments flashed before her.

'Lor!' exclaimed Bilcher, 'I ain't seen a more pathetic human spectacle. Damn you to hell! They should exhibit you as a lesson to young 'uns.'

Another thud; another cry of pain.

'I mean to say,' went on the publican, warming to his theme, 'what's a man worth if he can't pay his debts?'

Another thud; another groan.

'I'd say . . .'

Bilcher halted. His attention was distracted by the sound of Sarah Tanner stepping behind him, standing at the entrance of the ill-lit alley.

'Who's this?' said the publican, turning and squinting. 'Your missus, is it? You can have him when I'm done, my dear.'

Bilcher smiled, and moved his foot as if to place another kick into the crumpled body of his victim. But Sarah Tanner's reply pulled him up short.

'I'd say you've done enough.'

'Begging your pardon, darlin',' said Bilcher with a minatory glance, 'but unless you want some of the same, you had best hook it now, before I get proper baity.'

'Just leave him be,' she said firmly.

'Now why should I do that?'

'Because otherwise, I may shoot.'

Sarah Tanner raised her hand, quite steady, in front of her, the muzzle of the small pistol just visible in the darkness.

'Shoot?' said Bilcher, incredulously. 'Who the blazes are you?'

'It is loaded and capped, I assure you.'

'You mad bitch. You wouldn't dare.'

Sarah Tanner took a step forward, keeping the pistol dead ahead of her, putting only half a dozen feet between herself and the publican.

'I can come closer, if you like. Although I'm told I'm a good shot.'

Bilcher paused, looking closely at the gun. At last, he stepped backwards, slowly, retreating further along the alley, behind the prone body of his victim.

'He ain't worth it, darlin', whatever he's told you.'

'I'll be the judge of that.'

The publican, his face a peculiar mixture of incredulity and fear, backed further away, until certain of his distance.

'To hell with the both of you!'

Mr. Smith, lying upon the muddy cobbles, turned over, coughing violently. Wiping his mouth with his sleeve, he watched his tormentor disappear into the darkness, then turned to look at his unexpected bene-factor in disbelief.

'Whoever you are, my thanks,' he said, raising himself to his knees. 'I believe you may have saved my life.'

'I wouldn't count on it,' said Mrs. Tanner, once more raising her pistol.

CHAPTER NINETEEN

'Good God!' said Smith, dumbfounded. 'Do you intend to shoot *me* now?'

'That depends,' replied Sarah Tanner, warily, as Smith got to his feet. 'But I suggest you keep your distance.'

'Keep my distance? I swear,' said Smith, looking carefully at her face, as if trying to fathom her intentions, 'I thought the female Jack Shephard was the stuff of penny bloods. Perhaps I had better just follow my friend's example and run.'

'Perhaps I had better just shoot.'

Smith smiled, rather uneasily. 'You have a gift for persuasion.'

'What is your name?'

'Smith. John Smith.'

'Not Ferntower?'

Smith paused, as if struck by a sudden realisation. 'I have it! You were there this morning, at the blessed inquest. I remember you now; standing at the back. Good lord! Whatever do you want with me? How did you come here?'

'You admit you are John Ferntower?'

'Why? Is that sufficient cause to blow my brains out?'

'No,' replied Sarah Tanner. 'Not in itself.'

'Then, if I must, I readily confess it to the world. Or, perhaps, I am more like his wretched shadow. But who the devil are you?'

Mrs. Tanner, however, ignored the question.

'You were lucky with the verdict,' she said.

'How do you mean?'

'I hear you killed your aunt.'

'My aunt? Is that why you are doing this? Forgive me, I am a little confused. Did you know my aunt? You do not strike me as one of her circle.'

The man's tone was gently mocking, but there was also a hint of trepidation in his voice, his eyes still fixed upon the gun.

'I never met her in my life. But I would like to know why you killed her; or had her killed.'

A look of puzzlement crept over Ferntower's face.

'I will not pretend we were on good terms, but to imagine that I killed her – what, that I drowned her? that I threw her in the river? – no, it is preposterous!'

'No more preposterous than a gentleman skulking round the Dials, pawning his every possession, keeping company with the likes of Bilcher.'

'That is my private misfortune,' said Ferntower, his pride seemingly stung by Sarah Tanner's words, falling silent for a moment. 'But it does not make me a murderer. I confess, I half expected the attention of the police; I said some rash things to my father, though he deserved to hear them. But I did not expect this.'

'Your father thinks you killed her.'

'My father is an old fool. Still, if you will persist with his foolishness, do you require proof?'

'If you can provide it,' replied Sarah Tanner skeptically.

Ferntower wearily shook his head, but nonetheless

reached inside his coat, rummaging through one of the pockets until he retrieved a crumpled piece of paper.

'Here,' he said, holding out the paper. 'My misfortune and shame. I trust you are quite satisfied.'

'What is it?'

'My release from Clerkenwell gaol. I was detained at Her Majesty's pleasure, last Friday; until yesterday morning in fact.'

'The House of Detention? But you saw your aunt the day before she disappeared. They said as much at the inquest.'

'I don't deny it, much good it did me. And that night, there was a little dispute outside my lodgings; not my affair, in fact, but the police are not always so scrupulous. I went before the magistrate the next day. See for yourself.'

'You know I cannot read a thing in this darkness.'

'Then take it and read it elsewhere. I'm afraid I do not have any lucifers,' he continued, his voice tinged with sarcasm, 'you will have to forgive me.'

Sarah Tanner frowned. 'Then you had her killed. Her and George Phelps.'

Ferntower rubbed his side, wincing in pain. 'I am afraid, whoever you are, you are quite deluded.'

'Did Georgie find you out, is that it? You had to keep him quiet?'

'My dear woman, I have never even heard of anyone by that name. And, forgive me, what concern is it of yours who killed my aunt?'

'You admit she was murdered then?'

'Well, of course. The coroner was a buffoon. And I know the man who did it.'

Sarah Tanner faltered. She was not sure about John Ferntower; and it was not quite the admission she had expected. 'Who?' she said at last. But there was too much eagerness in her voice; and it seemed to give her prisoner renewed confidence.

'Stand me a drink, and I might tell you.'

'I still have the pistol Mr. Ferntower.'

Ferntower shrugged. 'If you meant to shoot me, you would have done so by now.'

Sarah Tanner started to protest, but her words failed her as John Ferntower came forward and gently brushed past her, out into the street. He turned round to face her.

'There's a good ginnery on the corner,' he said, coughing, and simultaneously grimacing, holding his stomach. 'Lord, that man's a brute. Still, I suppose I should thank you, all the same, even if you did mean to murder me. Perhaps you might put that away now?'

Sarah Tanner hestitated for a moment, but finally lowered the gun.

'Very well, for the moment,' she said. 'Lead the way.'

———

The air inside the gin-palace was moist and hot; the glittering ornamental gas-lights that hung from the ceiling, painted gold and silver, a stark contrast to the shabby fustian and cheap cotton clothes of the drinkers. They stood close-huddled in small groups – for there were no seats nor anything else to impede the collective drowning of sorrows – and it took Sarah Tanner and John Ferntower a few minutes to reach the bar, acquire a drink, then find a spot where they might talk. As Ferntower spoke, Mrs. Tanner sipped her gin-punch and looked closely at his features. Beneath the unkempt beard and dirty upturned collar was still a young man; a handsome one at that.

'Let me tell you a story, Miss . . .'

'Richards.'

'Really? Well then, let me tell you, Miss Richards, a story about a man. A poor wretch of a man.'

'I do not need to hear the story of your life.'

'Do you wish to hear about my aunt?'

'Yes.'

'Then, Miss Richards, pray let me proceed. Now, where shall I begin? Well, picture, if you will, a fellow who comes to our great metropolis, a callow youth, but with a head for business. Now this fellow – let us call him Ferntower; it is a good name – this Ferntower, he is no fool. He looks around himself and he sees the world in its true light.'

John Ferntower paused, and took a gulp of the East India pale ale which Sarah Tanner had procured him.

'Now, Miss Richards, come, come – play your part, ask me the question.'

'"Its true light"?'

'Pounds, shilling and pence, Miss Richards. Pounds, shilling and pence. He looks around our great city and he knows it for a fact: every man; every woman; every child; all of it – all merely pounds, shillings and pence. Magic stuff, money, you see, Miss Richards. Turn it into anything you like; nothing and no-one you can't buy. Money is the thing.'

'If you say so.'

'I beg your pardon. I say nothing of the sort. But young Ferntower – he sees it; and he knows what he has to do about it. So he works himself hard; learns a trade – linen-draper, as it happens – finds it's a good living. So good, in fact, he takes premises in Regent Street.'

John Ferntower took another gulp of liquor.

'The premises grow bigger. He grows bigger; pennies

142

into pounds. He marries; and he does that well too. Money marries money; always the way. A child is born; poor thing, the boy has prospects.'

'Wait, you're talking about your father? The child is you?'

'If you like. Now, the child learns its lesson on its father's knee; nothing should trouble him but pounds, shilling and pence. And when Mama dies – well, that is unfortunate, but it is not money. It is not business – except, that is, for the wretched undertaker.'

'Is your father such an ogre, then?'

'An ogre? In the world's eyes, no. Indeed, he gives a good deal to charity; did you know that? He's a governor of half a dozen of them. But it is just a sober calculation upon his part – an account upon the Creator's balance-sheet. His heart is all brass and copper; nothing more, nothing less.'

'Yes, I can see how his riches must have made things difficult for you.'

'You mock me, Miss Richards. But I am the creation of that wretched man. I was educated – well educated, mind you – with an eye to commerce. Other men might have been given leave to contemplate the finer things – art, beauty, love –' he drew breath, as if suddenly reminded of something unwelcome – 'but I was turned to business, and business alone. He could have made me a gentleman, but instead he made me a counting-clerk.'

'I thought you were going to tell me about your aunt,' said Sarah Tanner.

'True. A pious woman; a woman of firm principle. She always despised me.'

'Why?'

'She knew I did not have my father's zeal for the

143

trade; she was the sort of woman who saw through you.'

'Is that all?'

'Please. You have interrupted the story. Now, by the age of twenty-one, the young man with prospects has had his fill of business. He has been in his father's firm for six years, like some wretched apprentice. He seeks out other amusements; the sort of thing that suits a young fellow. He meets sporting gents; he enjoys himself for the first time in his pitiful life, cultivates a love of play. But then he has a run of bad luck; money is owed. He is obliged to draw against his father's name. His aunt, God rest her soul, finds him out. Lord knows how, but she does.'

'And your aunt told your father. And he cut you off. I have heard as much myself; it is common gossip. But you said you knew who killed her?'

Ferntower sighed. 'Miss Richards, you have no patience; you have quite spoilt my little tale.'

'I have not got all night,' said Mrs. Tanner.

'No? Well, let me put it quite simply. My aunt not only told my father about my indiscretions; she told him what to do about it. She was his touchstone upon moral matters; in fact, he deferred to her judgment in all but matters of business. I suppose it saved him the trouble of thinking for himself. And that is why she is dead. She would have prevented all this in an instant.'

'All what?'

'Why, the engagement. She intended to do so. Indeed, she came back to England, as soon as she heard of it.'

'The engagement?' echoed Sarah Tanner, quite lost.

'Ah, I see you are not entirely familiar with all my family's affairs, as you profess. My father has a ward,

Miss Richards, named Elizabeth – a distant cousin of mine; orphaned only last year; the sweetest girl in the world. You might have seen her at the inquest. You see, when I went to see my aunt that night, to plead with her to show me some mercy –'

'To give you some money?' suggested Sarah Tanner.

Ferntower's face darkened. 'When I went to see her, she told me all about it. My cousin Elizabeth is recently engaged to be married to one Cedric Hawkes. It is a rushed affair – the wedding is set for next month.'

'And what am I supposed to make of that?'

'Nothing. Except Cedric Hawkes is the greatest gamester, felon, villain, swindler and scoundrel in London. A plausible gentleman, though; claims to be a broker on the 'Change. My father is too blinded by gold to see it. The man will stop at nothing . . . if anyone killed my wretched aunt, Mr. Hawkes is your man. I am quite sure of that.'

John Ferntower paused and drained his glass.

'Poor sweet Elizabeth,' he said at last. 'She hasn't the slightest conception.'

Sarah Tanner frowned. 'Even if it is true, how do you know all this about this man Hawkes?'

'How? Why, I introduced them.'

CHAPTER TWENTY

'I am beneath her now, of course,' continued Ferntower, 'but I had thought at one time that perhaps myself and Elizabeth might . . . well, that time has passed. Now I could only ruin her.'

'Tell me, I saw another woman at the inquest, with your cousin and your father,' said Mrs. Tanner. 'Who was she?'

'Ah, I expect that was the redoubtable Miss Payne. My cousin's governess. Now, there you have another female with firm opinions upon my character.'

'Really? You seem to make enemies with remarkable ease, Mr. Ferntower.'

'I have made mistakes, Miss Richards. No man is perfect. But I am a veritable saint compared to Cedric Hawkes, rest assured.'

'Very well, tell me more about this man Hawkes. How did you meet him?'

'Hawkes? At a night-house on the Haymarket; we played a few hands of baccarat. We got on quite familiar terms; I even lent him money. Of course, then,' said Ferntower, looking rather wistfully into the dregs of his beer, 'I had money to lend.'

'And so, naturally, you introduced him to your family?' said Sarah Tanner skeptically.

'He passed for a respectable gentleman, Miss Richards. More than respectable, in fact. Besides, it was amusing to parade him before my father, talking about his business affairs, when I had seen him lose twenty guineas on the wheel the night before.'

'A taste for gaming, even one that extravagant, does not make a man a villain.'

'No, that would be a fine thing, would it not? But what would you make of a man who changes residence every month; who lets his creditors go hang, whilst he begins his business again under another name?'

'A fraudster, perhaps. But a murderer?'

'And yet you would readily believe I am capable of such a thing?'

'I do not know what to believe, Mr. *Smith*.'

'Listen,' said Ferntower. 'One night, shortly before my own fall from grace, I caught a hansom with Mr. Hawkes. The cab took us from Regent Street to the City, where he had rooms. There was a disagreement about the fare. A matter of pennies, but the cabman spoke crudely to him. He laughed about it; told the cab to take us on further; that he had forgotten that he wished to call upon a friend. He waited until he found a quiet lane; a dead-end near the Minories, and told the cab to stop. He pulled the man down from his seat and thrashed him with his own whip, until he could barely draw breath.'

'Even a cruel temper is no guarantee—'

'Wait. You asked for my opinion, Miss Richards. You may as well hear it. That cabman was seventy years old if he was a day; but Hawkes showed no mercy. He split the handle of the blasted whip in two, he had struck him so many times. Even then, he did not stop. If I had not pulled him back . . . well, in all honesty, I do not know to this day if the old fellow survived it.'

'You might have told the police.'

'You did not see Hawkes's face. There was no emotion, no anger; just concentration. He was . . . how can I put it? . . . methodical. I have never seen a man so completely in control of himself. He made my friend Bilcher look like a milksop. I did not dare. I had to think of my own skin.'

Sarah Tanner looked Ferntower in the eye.

'How do I even know this man exists?'

Ferntower shrugged. 'I cannot produce his card, if that is your question. Nor can I magic him up from the aether.'

'Then where can I find him?'

'I have no idea. But I wish the happy couple all the best. Good luck to them both.'

'And what about your cousin?' said Mrs. Tanner, thoughtfully. 'Will he make her a good husband?'

'Oh, but she will make him an excellent wife. You see, she is an heiress, Miss Richards; worth ten thousand a year on her majority. That is why she is under my father's wing. And that will do my friend Hawkes nicely. Yes, that's where you'll find him, I imagine. He'll stick to Elizabeth like glue; mark my words.'

Sarah Tanner looked at John Ferntower. He spoke with deliberate world-weary irony. But there seemed something beneath the detached and debased tone of amusement, not least when he mentioned his cousin: a peculiar sadness in his voice when he spoke of her. She almost felt sorry for him.

'Suppose what you say is true,' she said, after a moment's reflection. 'If I wanted to be introduced to your father and cousin, how should I go about it?'

'Introduced? I fear, Miss Richards, you draw the

wrong inference from my unfortunate circumstances and apparel. I hardly think—'

'Please,' she interjected. 'You may assume that I can dress myself in a fashion more suited to their society.'

'You are a queer creature,' said Ferntower, rather surprised. 'Very queer indeed.'

'Just tell me how should I go about it.'

'There is only one way into my father's good graces, Miss Richards, and that is money. Do you have money?'

'I might.'

Ferntower laughed derisively. 'If you say so. Very well, if I were you, I should make a donation to one of his little schemes. He likes to play the philanthropist, my father. He has quite a little collection, the old hyprocrite. An almshouse; a dispensary; even a juvenile reformatory. Why, that is quite amusing, is it not? I expect he wishes he had sent me there.'

'Perhaps he ought to have done.'

'Well, perhaps you should put me out of my misery, Miss Richards. There is still time.'

'No, not tonight.'

'No?' said Ferntower, with a wry smile. 'That is something. Is my interrogation finished?'

'No,' replied Sarah Tanner, pensive. 'How should I go about making a donation, so that your father knows about it?'

'Do you truly intend to go through with the idea? I was not serious.'

'But I am, Mr. Ferntower. I intend to put your story to the test.'

It was nearly midnight when Sarah Tanner arrived back at the Dining and Coffee Rooms. There was a hint of fog in the air, and she had to pick her way carefully along the rather inadequate paving and faltering gas-lights of Leather Lane. Upon arrival, she found Ralph Grundy in the process of ejecting a rather lethargic young man from the premises, whose breath stank of cheap brandy, and who seemed determined to spend the night in one of the coffee-shop's little booths, having mistaken it for his bed. Between them, they levered the young man into the street, setting him in the direction of the Bottle of Hay, the public-house being the only local landmark with which he seemed familiar.

With no further customers, Ralph Grundy dragged the shop's wooden shutters out on to the street, and Sarah Tanner set to helping him lift them into place.

'Glad to see you came back, missus,' said Ralph Grundy, as they lifted the last board on to the slat beneath the window.

'Where else would I go?'

'It's more that you got back in one piece, that's all.'

'I'm sorry, Ralph. I didn't mean to be rude.'

'I don't take offence, missus. It ain't in my nature. So did you find him? Mr. Smith?'

'I did, as it happens.'

'And was it him, the son?'

'Yes, I was right on that score. But he says there's a man named Hawkes who's wooing his cousin; apparently he's an out-and-out villain. Ferntower thinks Hawkes killed his aunt, to prevent any objections to the match.'

'That's convenient, ain't it? And what do you reckon? Do you trust him to set you right?'

'I've no idea. The man's . . . well, you've seen the state of him.'

'What about this Hawkes, then? Could it be your policeman? Maybe that's his name.'

'No, not by the sound of it. Hawkes is a gentleman or passes for one. I can't see our friend managing that.'

'Maybe this Hawkes gets other fellows to do his dirty work.'

'If he even exists, I . . .'

Sarah Tanner paused since, as she bent down to fix the padlock upon the last of the shutters, something fell from her dress and clattered on to the paving stones. The pistol, undamaged by the fall, lay at her feet. Hastily, she grabbed it and replaced it in her pocket. Ralph Grundy, however, saw the gun; and his brow creased into anxious ridges.

'You shouldn't be carrying that thing, missus. What if it goes off?'

'It's not capped, you have my word.'

'But it's loaded?'

'Never mind.'

'Only takes a spark,' muttered the old man. 'And what was you planning to do with that barker, anyhow?'

'You said yourself; the Dials aren't safe.'

'Well, as long as that's all it was,' said Ralph Grundy, looking closely at his mistress's face. But Sarah Tanner turned away, and opened the shop-door.

'I suppose we had better lock up,' she said, stepping inside.

'Ain't you forgetting something?' he said.

'What?'

'Your little cousin, Norah,' said Ralph, glumly.

'Hasn't she come back?'

'No, missus,' replied Ralph Grundy, with a rather significant look. 'She ain't.'

Harry Drummond had thought long and hard upon where to take his companion for the evening. In the end, he had settled upon Evans's Dancing Academy, on the corner of Saffron Hill and Charles Street, not far from Leather Lane. Situated above the Green Man public-house, the Academy was little more than an open assembly room, given over twice weekly to the delights of the terpsichorean arts. How much in the way of instruction went on was, perhaps, debatable; but there was dancing aplenty, of the *hop* variety – jigs and reels, varied by the occasional rather unlikely polka – depending principally upon the tireless musical exertion of a single fiddler, and the vigorous stamping of several dozen hob-nailed boots. As Harry's father had suggested, it was the place for a *good trot and no mistake about it.*

As for Norah Smallwood, she seemed to enjoy herself. Indeed, as the night wore on, and the consumption of beer and porter, by all parties, increased commensurately, Harry Drummond was inclined to harbour various romantic notions, largely incompatible with his notion of himself as one of nature's gentlemen. Having briefly descended to the bar of the Green Man to acquire more liquid refreshment, he returned shortly after the stroke of eleven o'clock.

He was surprised to find Norah Smallwood had utterly vanished.

Norah Smallwood had, in fact, not gone far. She stood in the doorway of a nearby shop, sheltering from the cold night air, together with another gentleman of a different ilk from Harry Drummond.

'He said that?' exclaimed Norah Smallwood, angrily.

'I swear he did. What kind of fellow leaves an out-and-outer like you all alone, anyhow? You're better off with me, gal. Here, come a bit closer.'

'Why should I?'

'Pretty gal like you . . . you know why. What's your name again?'

'Norah. And I ain't so fast as all that.'

'Pretty name, though.'

'What's yours then?'

'Mine? Albert.'

'I s'pose I'm pleased to meet you, Albert.'

'Likewise,' replied Bert Jones.

CHAPTER TWENTY-ONE

'Have you seen him?' said Ralph Grundy, as he squeezed past the counter, nodding in the direction of the window. It was lunch-time in Leather Lane, the day after Sarah Tanner's encounter with John Ferntower, and the coffee-shop was busy with men from the market, leaving the waiter little room to manoeuvre.

'Who?'

'He'll be back – just you watch.'

Mrs. Tanner stood behind the Dining and Coffee Rooms' great bronze coffee-urn. Three costers, meanwhile, stood nearby, waiting to be served. The urn's brass tap had somehow grown too hot, an unfortunate eccentricity to which it was rather prone. She cursed it as she wrapped a cloth round the metal and struggled to pour each man their drink.

Ralph Grundy tutted. 'That burner's slipped again.'

'Really?' she replied, with more than a hint of sarcasm.

'I was only saying. Here, I'll do it.'

As the men paid for their coffee, Ralph Grundy leant down, took a bread-knife, and poked at the burner's charcoal. Sarah Tanner, meanwhile, finally took the waiter's advice and glanced towards the shop-window.

'Who am I supposed to be looking for?'

'Any second now,' replied Ralph Grundy, with a wry smile. 'Ah, there he is.'

The object of Ralph Grundy's uncannily accurate prediction was Harry Drummond. For the youth had been pacing the corner of Liquorpond Street and Leather Lane, at five-minute intervals, for a good half-hour, sauntering past, with thumbs placed jauntily in the pockets of his waistcoat. There was, however, something far too deliberate in his perambulation. Moreover, a forlorn look upon his face, and his brief hopeless glance through the glass, argued against an altogether casual demeanour. It was only when he accidentally caught Sarah Tanner's eye, that he turned his head away, and hurried off.

'Been lurking there all morning,' said Ralph Grundy, with a slight degree of exaggeration. 'Did you see the state of him? And then there's Her Ladyship—'

'If you mean Norah—'

'Aye, I do. Grinning like the cat that got the cream, not sparing him a look. Now, you tell me what's going on there.'

'If I am any judge, I expect she met another young man last night.'

'Yes,' muttered the waiter. 'Well, I expect you're right there. So much for mourning your pal Phelps.'

'Ralph, please, not again. I've other things to worry about. I'm not the girl's mother. She can do as she likes. In any case, it's better she forgets George Phelps. Now, there's people seated that want serving.'

'Well, if you told me what you're planning,' he said, lowering his voice, 'maybe I'd have more to think about and all.'

'Planning? Who said I'm planning anything?'

'I ain't such a fool, missus. If you don't want my help, well, that's another matter. I saw you looking through the papers all morning. And I saw you tidy one away, too.'

'You'd do better at Scotland Yard, Ralph, I swear.'

'Well then?'

Reluctantly, Sarah Tanner retrieved a copy of the previous day's *Times* from behind the counter. Running her finger down the first column of advertisements, she pointed to a particular notice, which Ralph Grundy read to himself.

FANCY SALE FOR THE BENEFIT OF
FINSBURY JUVENILE SCHOOLS

A fancy sale will be held at Radley's Hotel, Bridge-street, Blackfriars, on Monday 12th April, in aid of the maintenance fund of the above schools. Under the patronage of Her Grace, the Duchess of Beaufort. Tickets from the Secretary, 10 Waterloo Place.

'It's one of Mr. Ferntower's charities,' said Mrs. Tanner. 'Most likely he'll be attending; at least, that's what his son told me.'

'So you're thinking of going and all?'

'I think so. The business with his sister – it's all to do with what happened to Georgie, I'm sure of it.'

'You'll need a ticket, missus. How are you going to manage that? I ain't much up on these things, but if it's dukes and duchesses, then . . . I mean to say, I know you can talk proper as you like but—'

'They won't give a ticket to just anyone. I know that.'

'Well then?'

'I fear I will have to call upon an old friend.'

'Lor! That didn't work last time, missus – or have you forgotten?'

'A different friend,' said Sarah Tanner with a rather thin smile. 'Very different. Tell me, Ralph, have you ever driven a carriage?'

'A carriage?'

'Have you? The truth, now, if you do want to help me.'

'Well, I worked second-fiddle to a carman, once. I did a fair bit of the driving. I reckon I'm all right with horses.'

'Better than boats?'

'Aye, I should hope so, missus. What are you thinking off, anyhow?'

'I'll tell you later. Mind the shop. I'm going out.'

'Where?'

'Never you mind.'

Ralph Grundy murmured something inaudible under his breath.

'Where's she off to?' asked Norah Smallwood, coming out from the kitchen.

'Never you mind,' said Ralph Grundy.

In fact, Sarah Tanner's journey took her down to Fleet Street, then west along the Strand. But her destination was one which Ralph Grundy would have been unlikely to have guessed: namely, a bench in St. James's Park, facing the grand ornamental lake, the great iron gates of the Queen's own residence visible in the distance.

The weather was quite temperate for a spring day in the metropolis and it would not have been an unpleasant place for anyone to take a brief rest. But Sarah Tanner seemed to sit more in expectation than repose, and anyone who passed her by – if they thought about the matter at all – was probably inclined to imagine her a servant on an afternoon's liberty, whether sanctioned or illicit, awaiting a romantic tryst with an off-duty guardsman, or junior clerk. Certainly, that was the opinion of several nursemaids who cast knowing glances in her direction, as they guided their infant charges away from the lake's shore. Even the policeman on duty, who circled the lake twice on Sarah Tanner's account, concluded as much. For, although he was obliged to keep an eye out for unfortunates, who might importune unwary gentlemen, it seemed plain that the object of his observation was waiting for someone in particular.

The man in question appeared at ten minutes past two o'clock, a young individual of about twenty-two years of age, strolling along the gravel path that ran by the lake. He was, beyond dispute, rather handsome, with boyish features and a rather unworldly, abstracted expression. That he was a gentleman was not in doubt. From the silk of his hat, to the fashionable winged collar of his shirt, the gold of his watch-chain, and the black lustrous sheen of his boots, every detail was quite in order. So much so, in fact, that the police constable, from the other side of the lake, briefly doubted his own judgment; for it seemed unlikely that such a person could have any social connection – decent or indecent – with the merely presentable female who sat upon the bench. And yet, remarkably, it was the young man who spoke first. The constable looked across at the mismatched couple. Whatever it signified, he reasoned, resuming his round of the park, it was not police business.

'Good Lord!' exclaimed the young man at the sight of Sarah Tanner, rising from her seat.

'Mr. DeSalle.'

'What are you doing here?'

'Waiting for you. Shall we walk?' said Sarah Tanner calmly.

Arthur DeSalle looked cautiously along the lake-side in either direction.

'You needn't take my arm,' she continued.

Arthur DeSalle looked quite flustered. 'I hardly think—'

'Must I make a scene?'

'Sarah – please!' exclaimed DeSalle in hushed tones. 'What is this?'

'You always were such a creature of habit. I knew you always come this way after lunch at the club. I didn't mean to startle you. I suppose I could have gone to the Reform—'

'God forbid!' exclaimed the young man.

'Then just walk with me a little. No-one will think anything of it. Or must I follow you home?'

'Sarah, really, I don't know what to say.'

'Or I suppose,' she went on, with a backward glance at the policeman, who still could be seen across the water, 'you might have me arrested.'

Arthur DeSalle hestitated for a moment, then fell in step as Sarah Tanner began to stroll along the path. After a moment or two, he offered her his arm.

'Sarah,' said the young man, finally collecting himself, 'please, don't trifle with me like this. It's been six months. I'd quite given you up.'

'Seven,' she corrected him.

'Seven, then. When we parted, you made your sentiments quite clear. You swore I would never see you again. It has been so long. I never dared imagine you might reconsider—'

Sarah Tanner shook her head, deliberately interrupting. 'No.'

'No?'

'I've come to ask a favour, Arthur, nothing more.'

'A favour?'

'For the sake of our friendship.'

DeSalle paused and freed his arm from his companion; there was a look of pained frustration upon his face.

'"Friendship"? Good God, woman! What is this? You tell me to go to blazes, disappear off the face of the earth – heavens, I spent weeks looking for you – and now, you spring up like some jack-in-the-box and you want a "favour"?'

'An indulgence then, for old times' sake.'

'I already gave you everything, Sarah,' said DeSalle in a hoarse whisper, 'and, if I recall, you threw it back in my face. Damn me, why did you do it? You know I adored you. You could have had a home, an income—'

'And you could have had a mistress in Jermyn Street; like any self-respecting young gentleman. But Jermyn Street didn't suit me.'

'I would have taken care of you.'

'No,' replied Sarah Tanner. 'Not on those terms. Now do take my arm; people are staring.'

Reluctantly Arthur DeSalle complied.

'So where the devil did you run off to?' said DeSalle, after a few moments' silence. 'How do you live?'

'I had some money put aside. I've taken on a coffee-house, Holborn way. Quite respectable.'

'A coffee-house? Good Lord.'

'Is it so strange as all that?'

'I thought it would be some other . . .'

'Another man? No.'

Arthur DeSalle fell silent again.

'I suppose it cannot be long now, until the wedding,' said Mrs. Tanner.

DeSalle stopped walking for the second time. They stood, not far from the lake, in the shadow of one of the old oak trees that lined the paths.

'July.'

'You should really try and look more cheerful,' she added.

Arthur DeSalle's frown did not waver.

'Sarah, I could make arrangements; there need never be any awkwardness or misunderstanding. You know I worship you – and as for Arabella, I swear, her only concern is that she be in London for the Season. I am quite superfluous.'

Sarah Tanner merely shook her head.

'I won't change my mind, Arthur. I'm sorry – that's not why I came.'

'What then? Is it money?'

'No, not that.'

'Well?'

'I need a letter of introduction.'

Arthur DeSalle laughed out loud. 'Good God! What can I say about your character?'

'My character is my own affair. I need a letter to the Secretary of the Finsbury Juvenile Schools, on behalf of Mrs. Sarah Richards.'

'And do I know Mrs. Richards?' said Arthur DeSalle, facetiously. 'I certainly do not know the Secretary of the Finsbury Juvenile Schools.'

'She's a distant relative of yours, from Hertfordshire, staying in London as your guest. A widow, with a considerable fortune to dispose of. She intends to use it in aid of the metropolitan poor. As for the Secretary, I suspect your name will be quite enough.'

'What makes you think I can countenance such a deception?'

'Arthur, you have my word, it's not a trick—'

'Sarah, please, credit me with some intelligence.'

'I am trying to put something right, for once. I swear it.'

'Very well, then, explain yourself.'

'I think it might be safest if I did not.'

Arthur DeSalle shook his head. 'Sarah, you presume a good deal on our "friendship". Even if I believe you, it would hardly be prudent, in my position . . . with the wedding . . .'

Sarah Tanner looked away.

'I still have the letters, you know,' she said, almost in a whisper.

'Lord! Do you intend to blackmail me?'

'No,' she replied. 'But if you help me this once, I swear, I will burn them.'

Arthur DeSalle hesitated. He reached out his hand and took hold of Sarah Tanner's arm.

'You know, I once thought you loved me, Sarah. I would have bet my life upon it.'

Sarah Tanner blushed, gently pulling her hand away.

'And I once thought much the same about you. So, will you do it? For an old friend?'

Arthur DeSalle sighed.

'Very well, what is their address?'

CHAPTER TWENTY-TWO

Some three days after Sarah Tanner's meeting in the park with Arthur DeSalle, she found herself in the vicinity of Blackfriars Bridge. A short distance from the river lay Radley's Hotel – a decent, large establishment – and it was there she alighted from her hired carriage, dressed in a manner suited to the occasion.

Inside, the ball-room had been decked out in fine fashion by the Lady Patronesses of the Finsbury Juvenile Schools. For the prospect of a fancy sale, which the Duchess of Beaufort herself *might* condescend to attend, had driven the worthy matrons in question to new heights of invention, creating a patriotic spectacle – *Albion* being selected as the theme – which threatened to surpass the highest expectations of all involved. Thus several grand Union flags had been draped from the ceiling; garlands of red and white flowers burst forth from every nook of the wainscoting; and a backdrop entitled 'Trafalgar' – the work of Drury Lane's most eminent scene-painter – filled an entire wall. Nor was the scene entirely inanimate, since two juvenile representatives of the Finsbury institution – a boy and girl of thirteen years of age – had been press-ganged into service as St. George and Britannia respectively, guarding the sea-battle with red faces that reflected both the radiance of the nearby gas-lights and, most likely, a degree of personal embarrassment.

As Sarah Tanner entered the room, she could not help but ponder why such an elaborate display was quite necessary. Her companion, who had greeted her at the door – the Secretary of the Finsbury Juvenile Schools, a Mr. Tebbins – noticed her expression, even if he did not succeed in interpreting her sentiments.

'Marvellous, is it not, Mrs. Richards?' said the man in question, who was a wiry individual, about fifty years old, prone to nervous wringing of his hands. 'The Ladies have done such marvellous work!'

Sarah Tanner surveyed the ball-room. She had never had the pleasure of visiting a fancy sale, but understood the principle. Female supporters of the Schools – highly respectable wives and mothers, under normal circumstances – stood behind a series of trestle tables, whilst other charitable individuals sauntered between them, placing bids upon the various 'elegant nothings' which the respectable *marchandes*, shop-girls for a day, had brought with them. There was, all in all, quite a crowd.

'What is for sale?' she asked.

'Oh, everything and anything, Mrs. Richards,' said Mr. Tebbins, with admirable exaggeration, leading the way to the first table, where several guests picked over half a dozen pairs of ladies' Turkish slippers. 'Why, whatever takes your fancy. All profits to the Schools – such a worthy cause.'

'And this?' said Sarah Tanner, picking up a cardboard token from the table, bearing a picture of a hand with extended finger.

'I do not know, ma'am – let me find out,' said Tebbins, pausing to interrupt the conversation of the table's supervisor, who stood near at hand. 'Ah, I gather a gratuitous lesson on the operation of the electric telegraph.'

'Quite remarkable.'

'Pray, tell me, Mrs. Richards,' continued Mr. Tebbins, as they strolled on, 'if it is not an impertinence, may I ask how the Schools came to your attention? I wonder – forgive me – was it perhaps the advertisement placed in the *Christian Mercury* last month? I only inquire, since it was placed upon my recommendation – I should be most gratified to know.'

'Yes, you're right,' she replied. 'That was it. It struck a chord. I mentioned it to my dear friend, Mr. DeSalle – he has such a sound knowledge of the world, you see – and he suggested that if I was minded to subscribe an annual sum, I might come up to London, to see things for myself. It was so good of you to invite me today.'

'Not at all, ma'am. Indeed . . .'

Mr. Tebbins continued, but Sarah Tanner's attention wandered. For, amongst the crowd by the next table, she suddenly recognised the face she had been looking for: Michael Ferntower, who appeared to be engaged in the charitable purchase of some lacework of dubious merits. As the Secretary pointedly praised the annual benevolence of his subscribers, Sarah Tanner edged closer to the table in question.

'And tell me,' she said, close enough that Mr. Ferntower might overhear, 'what are the terms to become a governor? Mr. DeSalle suggested I might inquire on his behalf. I believe I have rather piqued his interest in the subject.'

'Fifty pounds a year, ma'am, and, of course, the annual privilege of nominating one deserving juvenile to the Schools.'

Sarah Tanner nodded; she felt sure that Mr. Ferntower had heard her. 'I expect many of the gentlemen here are governors?'

'Indeed, ma'am,' said Tebbins who, impressed by the spontaneity of his own intellect, suddenly saw the opportunity that lay before him. 'Why, if I may, ma'am, let me introduce you to one of our greatest benefactors. Sir – Mr. Ferntower – if I may . . .' he continued, catching Ferntower's eye, 'this is Mrs. Richards. She saw the advertisement in the *Mercury*. She was only just inquiring after our governors.'

Mr. Ferntower, affecting to have heard none of the preceding conversation, turned and bowed. Sarah Tanner nodded politely, looking at his face. It was certainly a stern expression, with a hard mouth, framed by neatly trimmed mutton-chop whiskers, exaggerated by the austerity of his black mourning. She wondered, nonetheless, whether he was quite the man his son had described.

'I have the honour of being a governor, I confess,' said Mr. Ferntower, folding the lace in his hands, and placing it inside his jacket pocket.

'Mrs. Richards, sir,' continued the Secretary, 'is considering taking out an annual subscription. She has come down especially from the country. Oh! Now, one moment! Mrs. Richards, will you forgive me?'

'Sir?' said Sarah Tanner, following the Secretary's gaze to another part of the room, where a manservant waved discreetly in Mr. Tebbins's direction.

'I do believe my attention is required outside – it may be the Duchess! I am sure Mr. Ferntower will

tell you more about the Schools, if he might condescend . . .'

Mr. Ferntower nodded; the Secretary positively
dashed across the room.

'What part of the country, ma'am?' said Mr.
Ferntower, rather awkwardly making conversation.

'Hertfordshire.'

'You are to be commended for your generosity,
ma'am,' continued Mr. Ferntower, after a slight hesitation.

'Have you been a governor for many years, Mr.
Ferntower?'

'More than I care to recall,' replied Ferntower,
warming a little to the subject of his own beneficence.
'Still, I consider it my Christian duty.'

'Quite. I gather the school takes both boys and
girls?'

'From the ages of five to fifteen, ma'am. Takes
them from the lowest estates of humanity. A good
general education, then the girls learn feminine and
domestic disciplines; the boys are fitted out for the
mercantile marine. There is a training-ship for
the older ones, moored off Greenwich Reach; a
marvellous institution.'

'Really? It all sounds quite fascinating. I should so
like to see it.'

'Would you, ma'am? Well, I am sure I could make
arrangements; a tour perhaps.'

'Oh, that would be delightful.'

'Ah!' said Mr. Ferntower, distracted by the approach
of a young girl and another woman, nearer to Sarah
Tanner's age. 'Now here is my ward. Allow me to
introduce you. Miss Elizabeth Fulbrook, and her
governess Miss Payne.'

Mrs. Tanner looked at the two new arrivals, as

introductions were made. Both were dressed in mourning and were the same two women she had glimpsed at the inquest. Mr. Ferntower's ward was a pretty, rosy-cheeked girl, with dark brown hair in ringlets, rather quiet in her manner, no more than eighteen years of age. It was not hard to imagine, she thought to herself, John Ferntower in love with such a girl – at least, before his fall into St. Giles. Miss Payne, upon the other hand, was a slim, rather mousy creature, quite plain, with hair pulled tightly back from her scalp, constrained by several substantial pins.

'I was just telling Mrs. Richards,' continued Mr. Ferntower to his ward, 'that we might arrange a tour of the Schools for her. Perhaps you might care to come too, Elizabeth?'

Miss Elizabeth Fulbrook demurely agreed. Sarah Tanner, meanwhile, glanced at the young woman's hand, observing a gold ring.

'I see you are engaged, Miss Fulbrook?'

Elizabeth Fulbrook blushed. 'Yes, thank you.'

'A handsome young man, I hope.'

Miss Fulbrook seemed to redden further. Her guardian, however, merely laughed.

'You should not tease my ward, Mrs. Richards. However, I expect you can judge for yourself. Speak of the devil! Here's the fellow now – Hawkes! Over here, sir!'

Sarah Tanner, gratified that John Ferntower's story had proved true to some degree, turned to look at Cedric Hawkes. She steeled herself against displaying any trace of emotion in the encounter, recalling Ferntower's description of his erstwhile acquaintance. But there was some slight hint of dismay – a gasp of surprise – when she found herself face to face with a countenance that was already terribly familiar to her, a face she had last seen in a darkened room in Regent Street.

Mr. Stephen Symes.

CHAPTER TWENTY-THREE

Sarah Tanner's confusion was brief, but impossible to mask.

'Are you quite all right, Mrs. Richards?' inquired Mr. Ferntower.

'Forgive me, sir. For a moment I felt a little light-headed; please don't concern yourself. It has passed.'

'Are you sure, ma'am?'

'Quite.'

'Well, then let me introduce my ward's fiancé. Mr. Hawkes – Mrs. Richards, a new subscriber to the Schools. We were just talking of you.'

Stephen Symes bowed politely.

'I fear I startled you, ma'am,' said Symes, drily.

'No, not at all,' replied Mrs. Tanner, regaining her self-possession.

'Well, I am charmed to make your acquaintance, ma'am, in any case.'

'Thank you. I gather I must congratulate you, sir, on your engagement.'

Symes bowed once more. Sarah Tanner, for her part, as she mentioned the subject, glanced at the bride-to-be who stood nearby. There was no change in Elizabeth Fulbrook's shy and diffident manner; if anything, the topic only seemed to increase her awkward reticence, and she did not even look at her fiancé. Whatever reason existed for the match, she felt certain, it was not love.

'Tell me, Mrs. Richards,' said Symes, 'what drew you to the Schools in particular? I myself have been convinced of their merit by Mr. Ferntower's ardent advocacy – but what brought you here? I am rather curious to know.'

'I saw an advertisement, sir. It was most affecting.'

'I'm sure,' continued Symes, rather pointedly. 'It is certainly a marvellous undertaking. In fact, I myself have seen the most wretched little creatures improve, when placed in the appropriate hands. It is amazing what a change can be effected.'

'Quite right,' murmured Mr. Ferntower, oblivious to the telling glance that passed between Mr. Hawkes and his new acquaintance.

Sarah Tanner resolved not to linger.

'Well, I am sure I have monopolised your company long enough, Mr. Ferntower. So charming to meet you and your charming family.'

'And you, ma'am.'

'Must you leave us so soon, ma'am?' added Symes.

'I am afraid I must,' replied Mrs. Tanner, perhaps a little too severely. 'Oh, but, Mr. Ferntower,' she continued, 'I quite forgot – our tour of the Schools.'

'Allow me to give you my card, ma'am. I am sure something might be arranged.'

Sarah Tanner silently cursed to herself. The prospect of entering into correspondence was not something for which she had prepared herself. An address upon Leather Lane would not do.

'Oh, but I am only in town until tomorrow evening. I do not suppose, sir, you could spare me a little time tomorrow afternoon? It would be an awful imposition, I know.'

Mr. Ferntower visibly hesitated.

'I suppose,' she continued, 'I might speak to Mr. Tebbins, but, confidentially, I confess I find him, well, rather poor company. Perhaps I should give the matter more thought, in any case.'

'Well, I believe I could spare an hour or two in the afternoon, ma'am,' replied Mr. Ferntower, unwilling to contemplate losing a new subscriber. 'If it would be no inconvenience to yourself, shall I send my carriage, say at two o'clock?'

'A carriage? Oh, please, do not go to such trouble.'

'I am sure it is no trouble at all, ma'am.'

'No, there is no need,' said Sarah Tanner. 'I have a few errands to run myself and I think it might be better if we might meet at the Schools? I already have the address from Mr. Tebbins.'

Mr. Ferntower bowed. 'I look forward to it, ma'am. Two o'clock.'

'A pleasure to make your acquaintance, *Mrs. Richards*,' said Stephen Symes.

Sarah Tanner walked briskly through the decorated ball-room, past the assorted guests of the Finsbury Juvenile Schools. Her only intention was to quit the hotel, but she found herself thwarted by the return of Mr. Tebbins, who inadvertently blocked her path, peering into the room from the hall.

'Ah, Mrs. Richards!'

'Sir, you must forgive me. I am a little fatigued. Could you possibly send for my carriage?'

'Of course, ma'am. I trust Mr. Ferntower was able to provide some insight into our work.'

'Yes, he was most helpful. We have arranged a tour of the Schools tomorrow.'

'Now, ma'am, that is an excellent idea! Ah, now, is that Mr. Hawkes?'

Mrs. Tanner frowned, turning to look back into the room. 'Yes, indeed. We were just introduced.'

'Ma'am, my apologies. I will find a boy to run for your carriage. Then I must just inform Mr. Hawkes his mother has arrived.'

'His mother?'

'Yes – do you know Mrs. Hawkes?'

Sarah Tanner hesitated.

'No, forgive me. As I say I am a little fatigued, sir. Please – do not let me detain you.'

Mr. Tebbins, with suitably polite words of obligation, hastened in the direction of the hotel office. Mrs. Tanner, meanwhile, once the Secretary disappeared from view, slipped out on to the street, standing beneath the hotel's stone portico.

In truth, she had a fair idea of whom she might find there – and she was not proved wrong. For, in front of a rather grand landau, painted in dark green livery, was another all too familiar face: a woman in her fifties, being seated in a three-wheeled bath-chair, by a manservant from the hotel; a woman known in certain purlieus of the metropolis simply as 'Her Majesty'.

For a moment, Sarah Tanner held back. It was, after all, still possible to slip away unseen, as the footman fussed over his charge. But something made her stay and step out on to the pavement. If she had hoped to cause astonishment, however, she was disappointed. On catching sight of the new arrival, Her Majesty's regal countenance remained calm as ever.

'My dear! Fancy!' exclaimed Her Majesty. 'Why, this is quite marvellous.'

'*Mrs. Hawkes.*'

'You know, my dear, I fear an old woman's mind plays tricks . . . why, I quite forget . . .'

'Mrs. Richards.'

'Of course. Mrs. Richards. What else! How lovely to see you again!'

'A delightful coincidence.'

'Indeed, isn't it? Why, let us talk – push me, my dear.'

'I beg your pardon?'

'Along the road. Why not down to the bridge? It is such a delightful clear morning, and I would so enjoy taking the air, and seeing the dear old river. Boy! Tell Mr. Tebbins I have met an old acquaintance, and she insisted upon taking me on a little stroll, so we might exchange a few womanly confidences. Come, my dear Mrs. Richards – push!'

Sarah Tanner surveyed the wicker invalid chair. Reluctantly, she took the handles, and pushed.

'Now, my dear Miss Mills,' continued Her Majesty, as she trundled along the pavement, towards Blackfriars Bridge, 'you must tell me all your news.'

'My news? I have none.'

'Then what brings you to Radley's Hotel, my dear? I confess, I cannot imagine.'

'Oh, I think you can.'

'I fear I'm not one for guessing games, my dear. It's my age; unnecessary cogitation becomes rather troublesome. It is so pleasant to see you again, my dear, but do humour an old woman and speak plainly.'

'Very well. I know what you're planning, and why you didn't want to hear about Georgie. Because it was your man who did for him.'

Her Majesty sighed, rather theatrically.

'Is this your policeman friend again, my dear? I do not know who fed you this nonsense, Miss Mills. It is quite ridiculous.'

'Nonsense? So there isn't a certain young girl in that hotel, engaged to be married to *Cedric Hawkes*?' said Sarah Tanner.

'Ah. Well, Mr. Symes has a range of interests which occupy his time, my dear. You know that better than anyone.'

'But not many worth ten thousand a year. That's why you had Miss Ferntower killed, because she would have objected; she tried to run away but she couldn't manage it. Was your man on the boat?'

'Miss Ferntower? Ah yes, lately deceased. A sad incident. But, forgive me, I had gathered the poor woman killed herself.'

'I doubt that,' replied Sarah Tanner. 'And that's why your man did for Georgie, isn't it? He wouldn't have stood for murder, not a defenceless woman. What was it? Did he try to warn her at the hotel?'

'Why, this is quite fabulous! But, again, forgive me if I don't share your high opinion of poor Mr. Phelps's high morals.'

Sarah Tanner stopped pushing the chair; they were already at the beginning of the bridge, the wharves beneath St. Paul's to the left, the grimy cylinders of the City Gas Works to the right. A few fellow pedestrians – City clerks, in the main; black-suited and hats tall as chimneys – tutted at the obstruction.

'I'll hazard they imagine us mother and daughter,' said Her Majesty, with a chuckle. 'Now, isn't that amusing?'

'Not particularly.'

'Really, Miss Mills. You used to be such a merry

little creature,' continued Her Majesty. 'How did you come to be so serious, my dear?'

'Perhaps it was when you set Bert Jones to kill me.'

'Now, Sarah, please,' said Her Majesty, with infinite condescension, 'hold your temper and do not exaggerate. I am sure Mr. Jones would not have broken any bones; well, no more than necessary, and then all would be fair and square. As things are, well, I really can't tell where we stand. Poor Mr. Jones is quite beside himself, and there is still the matter of my fifty-five guineas.'

Sarah Tanner glanced over the stone parapet of the bridge, down at the dark silt waters of the river.

'I should just tip you over.'

'Miss Mills, you surprise me. Why, I declare, you set my heart a-flutter.'

'I did not know you possessed one.'

Her Majesty smiled. 'Do have a care, my dear, I beg you.'

'You forget, I am not one of your little girls any more.'

'And you, my dear,' said Her Majesty, 'should look behind you.'

Sarah Tanner turned swiftly, to find Stephen Symes standing only inches away.

'Are you quite well, *Mother*?' inquired Mr. Symes, with a degree of detached amusement in his voice. 'I see you have met *Mrs. Richards*.'

'Indeed,' replied Her Majesty. 'We had such a lovely little talk – so full of chatter and nonsense. Such a remarkable young woman. But perhaps you had best take me back; I should not care to catch a chill.'

Sarah Tanner willingly stepped to one side as Symes took hold of the bath-chair.

'Goodbye, my dear,' said Her Majesty, turning her head. 'I do hope we meet again, under better circumstances.'

'For your sake, I swear,' said Sarah Tanner, 'pray we do not.'

Her Majesty merely laughed. Stephen Symes, however, let go of the chair and turned to face Mrs. Tanner, his eyes narrow and black as coal. He leant forward, his voice a whisper.

'If you meddle in this business, Sarah, it will be the end of you. Now, learn your lesson.'

Sarah Tanner opened her mouth to speak, but, too late, she saw Stephen Symes's hand dart towards her cheek, the sharpened blade, a small pocket-knife, just visible. The movement was astonishingly fast, and it took her a second or two to register that she felt no pain; that there was no blood – only a lock of hair, cut from the curl beside her cheek, which Symes held between his fingers.

'A keep-sake,' said Symes, as he put the lock inside his waistcoat pocket. 'Something to remember you by.'

And with that, Stephen Symes smiled and walked away, pushing Her Majesty back along the bridge.

CHAPTER TWENTY-FOUR

The carriage which drew up on to the bridge, close by Sarah Tanner's side, was a hackney coach. Painted in a rather rusty brown, the sides showed some marks of wear and tear, a scratch here and a dent there, suggestive of a long history upon metropolitan streets. It was, nonetheless, a fairly respectable-looking vehicle of the rented variety, and its driver, an old man, dressed in heavy overcoat, looked like a long-suffering example of the coach-driving class, as he nodded politely to Mrs. Tanner, then clambered down from his seat, and opened the carriage door.

In fact, his principal employment was that of waiter, in a coffee-shop upon the corner of Leather Lane.

'Who was that, then?' said Ralph Grundy, as he closed the door behind his passenger.

'Never mind for now,' said Sarah Tanner. 'Just drive until I tell you to stop.'

'Very good, ma'am,' said Ralph Grundy with mock gravity. 'Anywhere in particular?'

Sarah Tanner thought for a moment.

'St. Giles.'

'Missus—'

'Drive.'

Ralph Grundy sighed to himself but nonetheless obeyed, climbing up to the driver's seat, taking the reins and whip, waiting for a good moment to pull the horses round, and head back towards Ludgate Circus.

It was as the coach approached New Oxford Street that Mrs. Tanner untied the leather straps on the vehicle's window blinds and peered out on to the road. She herself had undergone something of a transformation, with the smart silk day-dress she had worn to Radley's Hotel safely stowed away in a capacious carpet-bag that lay by her side, and replaced by one of plain cotton. She pulled on the check-string and waited for Ralph Grundy to draw the carriage to a halt. It took a few moments. When the waiter finally did descend and opened the coach's door, he proceeded to step inside.

'Lor!' he exclaimed, as he sat heavily on the cushioned bench. 'That seat weren't made for an old man's bones, mark my words.'

'Ralph, I don't believe that it's customary for coachmen to come and sit with their passenger.'

'Don't fret, missus. Besides, I don't believe it's custom for their passenger to be changing their get-up on the fly, neither,' replied Ralph Grundy, with a nod to the carpet-bag, 'clattering about like nobody's business, though I ain't complaining of it. And who's to care, anyhow? You've got this bone-setter jobbed all decent and above board, ain't you?'

'Of course.'

'Then we're all right; there can't be no objection from any quarter. There's a young 'un holding the horses' heads, and he'll keep 'til he gets his penny. So, I reckon I can rest up.'

'I'll need you again tomorrow, and the coach. I've arranged to meet Mr. Ferntower at the Juvenile Schools.'

'You met him, then?' asked Ralph Grundy.

'Him and his ward. And "Cedric Hawkes".'

'So he ain't just your pal's imagination?'

'If only he was. You saw him on the bridge.'

'Was that him? Well, I'm blowed. Respectable-looking gent, ain't he? Here, missus, who was the woman in the chair?'

Sarah Tanner sighed.

'That, Ralph, is the very woman who raised me up; who taught me how to make my way in life; how to lie and steal, and make a living by it. They call her "Her Majesty". "Mr. Hawkes" is a man named Symes; her right hand.'

'Your old friends?'

Sarah Tanner nodded. 'They want the girl's money; Symes is supposed to marry her. That's why Georgie was killed; he must have been against what they were planning – he wouldn't have stood for murder.'

'So that Peeler's one of 'em too? How come you didn't know him?'

Mrs. Tanner sighed. 'They call her "Her Majesty", Ralph, because she has her own little empire. A dozen or more hells in Regent Street; three night-houses on the Haymarket; enough fashionable bawdy-houses to satisfy a regiment. She would put any man to any use that might suit her, if he were willing. I wouldn't be surprised if she had bought out a whole division of policemen all together.'

'Well then, all you have to do is tell old Ferntower what's going on; tell him the truth.'

'And if he doesn't believe me? What then? I would just be a self-confessed fraud. Most likely the Schools' Secretary would have me locked up.'

'You could write him a letter, anonymous.'

'No, that's too uncertain. Besides, Symes will have covered his tracks; he's no fool. There will be nothing I can prove.'

Ralph Grundy shrugged. 'It seems to me, missus, you're stuck.'

'No, not quite. Listen, take the carriage back and talk to the job-master. Then you'd best get back to the shop – take my bag with you.'

'And where are you off to?'

'To find John Ferntower. I need to have another talk with him.'

'Listen, missus,' said Ralph Grundy, 'it ain't my place to say one way or another, but are you sure about this?'

'Please, Ralph, not again.'

'No, missus, you hear me out this once. The way I reckon it, you've already got two parties six feet in the ground, on account of your old friends; you've gone and got a girl skivvying for you who I wouldn't trust with a penny loaf; and now you're palling up with this Ferntower, whose own father reckons he's a murderer. And, even if he's not, well, he's a bloody wreck.'

'Are you trying to cheer me, Ralph?'

'I'm just saying, think on. If your pal Phelps hadn't gone down Leather Lane that night, and took some other road, I reckon you'd be better off for it. Maybe the game ain't worth the candle, missus – that's all.'

'For the last time, I can take care of myself, Ralph.'

'No offence, missus, but I bet your pal Phelps said

the same. And I don't want to find myself out of a job and at a bleedin' funeral; I've seen enough of them occasions to last me a lifetime.'

Sarah Tanner smiled. 'I'll do my best to avoid it. But you're wrong about Norah.'

'Maybe,' said Ralph Grundy, skeptically. 'Well, I ain't saying a word.'

———

Norah Smallwood stepped back from the booth, and craned her neck, peering down the little corridor that led to the rear of the coffee-shop. Mrs. Hinchley, she could tell, was quite preoccupied; for several frying-pans had just clattered noisily to the floor, followed by a loud, despairing shout, its precise nature not quite clear, but most likely a curse upon mankind in general, and ruined pork sausages in particular. Norah Smallwood, therefore, quietly slipped out the front door.

'What are you doing here?' she said, addressing herself to the man who leant casually against the wall of the adjoining shop.

'Blow me, gal, you took your time. I ain't doing nothing in particular. I thought you might be happy to see me. What's wrong, then? Is your missus about?'

'No, just the cook,' said Norah. 'How did you know where I was? I never said.'

'Just asked around, didn't I? Asked where I'd find the prettiest gal what I ever set eyes on.'

Norah Smallwood blushed. 'You never!'

'Give us a kiss, then. You can't be my gal if won't give us a kiss.'

'Not in the street!'

'Go on.'

'And who said I wanted to be your girl?'

'Go on.'

Norah Smallwood, her cheeks still rosy, leant forward, half reluctant, half willing.

'That's better,' said Bert Jones. 'That's my gal.'

CHAPTER TWENTY-FIVE

Sarah Tanner skirted the edge of Seven Dials, taking particular care in her route, to avoid the vicinity of Tower Court and the Turnspit. But the address she had memorised – the address vouchsafed to her by John Ferntower three days previously – was still rather close to the location of her encounter with Billy Bilcher, and she was rather glad of the peaked bonnet she had brought to protect herself against any turn in the weather, which also served to partly obscure her face.

At length, after making inquiries upon several street corners, she found the building in question, located on Prince's Row, Newport Market. In another part of the metropolis, John Ferntower's address might have passed for a rather elegant little town-house. Three storeys high, part of a narrow terrace, with small but neat sash windows, guarded by iron rails – it doubt-less once had been the home of a respectable minor tradesman. But the terrace had long since been divided and subdivided, with many of its homes turned into warrens of separate apartments, let out to undiscerning young gentlemen, and impecunious young families. It was one such house, a short walk from the nearby Horse and Carriage Repository – whose distinctive aroma rather permeated the narrow street – that was Mrs. Tanner's destination.

She tried the door-bell, but no-one came in reply, nor could she even hear a bell. Finding the front door open, she went inside.

The hall was predictably shabby: the carpet dusty and threadbare, the walls covered with a yellow paper that had faded in the rays of sunlight that occasionally shone through the fan-light of the street door. She cautiously climbed the stairs. As she ascended the final flight, in search of the three-pair front to which John Ferntower had given directions at the end of their last meeting, she heard the sound of a door closing. Turning on to the landing, she found herself face to face with a man, about forty years of age, dressed in a smart black suit, an extravagant red waistcoat and a white muslin cravat. Upon first sight, his face, marked by a meticulously groomed moustache and side-whiskers, flared up into an exuberant smile.

'My dear young woman! Stop! Hold still!'

'Sir?' said Sarah Tanner, involuntarily obeying the injunction, as her interlocutor blocked her path.

'What a chin! What bones! What beauty! Tell me that they are not wasted on some wretch of a man who keeps you locked away in this Stygian gloom! Tell me, I beg you, there is not some petty clerk who has made you his wife and mistress of his wretched rooms, to keep you from the world, a-dusting and a-sweeping!'

'I think you must have me confused with someone else, sir. In any case, I do not live here, I am looking for the front apartment.'

'No confusion, my dear. Allow me to introduce myself. Theobald Stamp – dramatist, actor, manager – at present, of the Adelphi, Strand.'

Mr. Stamp paused for effect, as if to emphasise how deep *the drama* ran in his character.

'Forgive me, sir,' said Sarah Tanner, 'if I might just pass you.'

'Pass, my dear? No, wait, you have not heard my proposition! Ten nights – the company woefully depleted – all congenial souls – small speaking part – you would be perfect! I swear, I know an actress when I see one, my dear lady. Perfect! Such beauty! Such poise! You cannot tell me you have never trod the boards?'

Despite herself, Sarah Tanner smiled politely. 'No, I have not, nor do I intend to. I would like to pass if I may—'

'Wait,' said Stamp, 'pass? You must mean to my dear friend Smith! You are visiting Smith? A woman of your charms! And he said nothing! I should have him hung, drawn and quartered, my dear lady, if the hanging weren't too good for him.'

'You know Mr. Smith?'

'Know him? I pay the fellow's bills. He copies my scripts – he has a fine hand for it. And I said to him, "I need an actress, Smith – find me an actress! Mine vanish, whenever it suits them!" And he says to me, "Don't know of such a creature!" Why, the man is a fraud!'

Mrs. Tanner, if inclined to express any opinion on the matter, fell silent – for the door behind Theobald Stamp opened, revealing John Ferntower.

'Ah, here is the wretched villain! Smith!' exclaimed Stamp cheerily.

'For pity's sake, sir, please,' exclaimed Ferntower, 'what is it? I thought you had left. I can hardly get started, if you insist upon an impromptu performance on my doorstep.'

'You have a visitor, sir,' replied Stamp, moving to one side.

John Ferntower peered along the landing.

'Ah, Miss Richards. I was not expecting you this afternoon.'

'My apologies,' replied Sarah Tanner.

'Well, I suppose you had best come in. Goodbye, Stamp; I'll have the work for you tomorrow.'

'Oh, I'm obliged, my dear sir,' replied Mr. Stamp, calling out as John Ferntower shut the door behind his guest. 'Miss Richards – delightful name – my offer remains open!'

John Ferntower's rooms were little better than the hall in terms of decoration: the walls dingy, the paper the colour of tobacco; the curtains a grim, dark-glazed calico; a crack in the wood of the mantel-piece; and the grate below seemingly quite unfamiliar with black-leading. Admittedly, the room was not quite dirty, but neither was it quite clean. Sarah Tanner looked around, and noted the small mahogany corner-table where sheets of paper were piled high, beside a quart-pot, half empty, of beer or porter.

'You did not tell me you had an occupation,' she said, as John Ferntower offered her a seat.

'Did I not? Did you imagine I lived solely off Bilcher's good-will? Well, I was not aware you required such fulsome particulars, Miss Richards. I would not call it an occupation. I hardly think it does me great credit, but a man must eat.'

'You might try law-writing. The stationers always need copyists. It would pay better.'

John Ferntower smiled. 'No, I do not have the

temperament. I am not quite so dry and dusty as that, not yet. I rather prefer the theatre. Mr. Stamp is free with tickets; it offers some small opportunity for recreation. But come, Miss Richards, I hardly imagine you came here to discuss my fascinating career. And I see you do not have your pistol.'

'No. I came because I met your father, at the fancy-sale this afternoon, like you suggested.'

'Really? Good Lord, I did not imagine you would do it. Does he send his regards?'

'I did not give him the opportunity. Your friend Mr. Hawkes was there too, and your cousin, Miss Fulbrook, and her governess.'

'Is Miss Fulbrook well?'

Sarah Tanner shrugged. 'Well enough, I suppose. In any case, you were right about Cedric Hawkes.'

John Ferntower paused, visibly perplexed.

'Indeed?'

'You seem surprised.'

'Well, I am surprised to hear you say it, if you have only seen him in decent society. He is the most convincing fraud I have ever met.'

'Unfortunately, I have seen much more of him. His real name is Stephen Symes; he is the agent, the deputy, of a woman whose real name I do not even know, who likes to be called "Her Majesty". She appeared at the sale, claiming to be his mother. They are both the worst pair of conniving villains you are ever likely to meet. I fear it is likely they murdered your aunt, and had my friend killed too.'

'How on earth do you know all this?'

'I used to work for them.'

John Ferntower's world-weary demeanour slipped a little, as open astonishment fell across his face. It took him a moment to recover his faculties.

'You are a queer creature indeed, Miss Richards. I was right about that.'

'Never mind what I am. The question is whether you wish to see your cousin married to such a man.'

'Of course not. But what on earth do you propose I can do about it? My father already believes me capable of every deception. Unless you have some proof . . .'

Sarah Tanner shook her head.

'Then what do you suggest?'

'Do you believe your cousin has any romantic attachment to Symes?'

'I doubt it. It is most likely my father's doing.'

'Good. That is something. That was my impression at the sale. And what about you? You said there was once something between you.'

'I do not know about that. I have fallen so far—'

'Listen to me,' insisted Sarah Tanner. 'The marriage can be prevented, if you will only help me do it. If the girl cares for you, then it can be done.'

'But why would you help me?'

'Your cousin is worth ten thousand a year on her majority, is that so?'

'Yes, but I can hardly promise you—'

'I don't want charity,' Mr. Ferntower. 'I want to see the look on their faces, when it slips through their fingers. That will do, I assure you. Now, I need you to write a little note.'

CHAPTER TWENTY-SIX

The next day, Sarah Tanner's carriage – the same carriage, rented from a job-master near Euston Square – pulled up outside the Finsbury Juvenile Schools. Not far distant from Clerkenwell Green, the Schools were housed in a small two-storey converted warehouse, formerly the business premises of one of the governors. Little concession had been made to the building's change in circumstances: a winch and pulley still projected above the street, as if ready to pluck unwary unreformed juveniles from the road-side, and in large painted letters, indelibly inscribed upon the brick-work, the words 'Wholesale: Tea, Coffee, Spices' were plainly visible. Sarah Tanner noted that a rather hand-some black landau was already parked outside.

Ralph Grundy climbed down from his seat, and opened the carriage door.

'Are you sure you know what you're doing, missus?' he said in a low voice.

'As long as you made the arrangement at the receiving-house.'

'They're expecting letters for the name of Richards.'

'Good. Then we're settled.'

Ralph Grundy reluctantly agreed. As he helped his employer to step down on to the pavement, the warehouse doors opened, and Mr. Michael Ferntower strode purposefully forward.

'Ah, Mrs. Richards. I thought I heard a carriage. I trust you found the Schools with no difficulty.'

'Yes, thank you, sir,' said Mrs. Tanner. 'It is very good of you to spare me your time.'

'Please, come inside. I am sure you will be impressed.'

Sarah Tanner nodded and followed, walking underneath words recently etched into the stone lintel above the warehouse doors. *Create in me a clean heart.*

<hr/>

The interior of the warehouse had been long since stripped of its crates and boxes, weights and measures, although there was still a lingering aroma, a hint of mocha, that rather reminded Sarah Tanner of her own establishment on Leather Lane. In one corner, iron stairs led to the upper storey, whilst the ground floor was dominated by twin rows of plain wooden benches, made of the cheapest unvarnished deal. Scattered amongst the wooden forms were three large groups of children, none of them more than ten years of age, taking instruction from their school-masters. One group consisted of girls, the other two of boys. Few of those being taught could lay claim to a clean face or unmatted hair; and none possessed an article of clothing that was not either torn, mended, or patched. Moreover, from the smocks of the girls to the ill-fitting jackets and trousers of the little boys – mostly too small, occasionally too large – all the garments on display seemed to have acquired an indeterminate hue, the colour of London brick, which rather matched the dull complexion of their owners.

'Poor little wretches, are they not, Mrs. Richards?' said Mr. Ferntower.

'They seem quite attentive, all the same,' remarked Sarah Tanner.

'The power of kindness and Christian love, Mrs. Richards. The first lessons here are in the Scriptures; duty to one's neighbours and duty to God. Now, where is Mr. Bournelle? He is the principal master. He can tell you much more than I. Ah! I see him . . .'

Mrs. Tanner followed Mr. Ferntower to one side of the room, where a table lay prepared for the next class, stacked with Bibles. Beside it was the school-master in question – a balding man in his mid-fifties, in a rather old-fashioned frock-coat and white cravat. He was engaged in animated conversation with Elizabeth Fulbrook and her governess. There was, however, another gentleman, who stood slightly apart from the group. Sarah Tanner had rather anticipated his presence, albeit not with any pleasure.

'You recall Mr. Hawkes, Mrs. Richards?' said Mr. Ferntower, nodding towards Stephen Symes. 'He happened to call, and I suggested he come with us.'

'Of course.'

Sarah Tanner smiled politely as introductions were effected. Avoiding Symes's gaze, she addressed herself to Mr. Bournelle.

'It was good of you to allow our visit at such short notice, sir.'

'Not at all, ma'am,' effused the teacher. 'I welcome it. Indeed, Mr. Ferntower is one of our most dis-tinguished governors. I was only telling Miss Fulbrook and Miss Payne here, how we are so grateful to her guardian.'

Mr. Ferntower nodded his head in discreet acknow-ledgement.

'Tell me about the children, sir,' said Sarah Tanner. 'They are all quite young?'

'Ah, only because the infant school is the day-time school, ma'am,' replied Mr. Bournelle. 'The older children require night-schooling; they "work" during the day, if that is the word for it.'

'Street Arabs, for the most part,' interjected Mr. Ferntower.

'Quite,' continued the school-master. 'You will see them everywhere in our metropolis, ma'am, if you spend any time in London. A terrible indictment against a Christian country, but there you have it. Many of them beg; a few sell lucifers, or make some other excuse for importuning members of the public.'

'In short, sir, you reclaim the wretched creatures from the gutter,' added Stephen Symes. 'It is so worthwhile, Mrs. Richards, is it not?'

'Absolutely,' replied Sarah Tanner, as flatly as possible.

'Yes, it is astonishing, Mr. Bournelle, what can be done with the proper instruction and guidance,' continued Symes. 'Although upon occasion I suppose you find one of your charges proves ungrateful?'

Mrs. Tanner watched Stephen Symes. The remark was directed at herself; she knew as much.

'A very rare occurrence, my dear sir,' protested Mr. Bournelle. 'But even the most vicious and criminal may be redeemed by sound moral influence, in our experience.'

'Oh, I imagine so,' added Sarah Tanner, with a glance back at Symes. 'In most cases. Tell me, do their parents pay for the privilege of attending?'

Mr. Bournelle smiled rather indulgently at his guest's naïveté. 'In half these cases, ma'am, you would be hard pressed to find one parent who would claim

193

them as their own, let alone two; as for the remainder, even a penny a week would have a heavy burden. No, the Schools are quite gratuitous, solely for the benefit of the destitute poor; we rely entirely on our subscribers. Perhaps you might care to see upstairs? We are in the process of converting it into a night refuge.'

'So the children do not sleep here?'

'That is our intention, ma'am, when the work is done – for some thirty of them, at least. At the moment, we are obliged to return them to the streets. We have a training-ship for any of the boys who are inclined to the mercantile marine, but that is only the older ones. If you would care to come this way?'

'Please, lead the way,' replied Sarah Tanner.

The school-master bowed and directed his tour party towards the staircase.

'Do watch your footing, Mrs. Richards,' said Stephen Symes. 'These iron steps can be treacherous.'

Mrs. Tanner smiled politely. 'Thank you, sir. Please, don't trouble yourself on my account.'

❦

Sarah Tanner absent-mindedly inspected the wooden truckle-beds, under construction upon the second floor. Her thoughts were elsewhere. Meanwhile, Mr. Bournelle waxed lyrical.

'Indeed, ma'am,' continued Mr. Bournelle, 'what was it Lord Ashley said? "We must seek to reclaim a wild and lawless race!" I often feel one's work here is as much missionary as anything upon the dark continent itself.'

'Quite. Do you have any difficulties with discipline?'

'Ah, well,' replied Mr. Bournelle, 'I must confess, in the early days, in our old building upon Saffron

Hill, there were insults and "larks" aplenty. We once had such a "row", as they call it, that the gas-pipes were torn off the ceiling, and we had to call the police. But things are much improved; the poor understand they need the benefits of civilisation, and, dare I say it, the masters have a greater sympathy with their charges.'

'How long have the Schools existed, sir?' asked Elizabeth Fulbrook, meekly joining the conversation.

'Some twenty years, Miss Fulbrook. I could not count the hundreds who have passed through our doors, and obtained a Christian independence in mind and spirit.'

'Well, I am sure we have taken enough of your valuable time, my dear Mr. Bournelle,' said Mrs. Tanner. 'I am so grateful.'

'You are most welcome, ma'am,' insisted the schoolmaster. 'Perhaps you might care to listen to a lesson in progress? I am sure none of the masters would object.'

Sarah Tanner agreed to the idea. But, as Mr. Bournelle gestured towards the stairs, she insisted he lead the way. At the bottom of the steps, moreover, as Mr. Bournelle politely extended his arm to aid her progress, she suddenly paused, and put her hand to her neck.

'Oh dear!' exclaimed Mrs. Tanner. 'Such a nuisance!'

'Ma'am?' inquired Mr. Ferntower.

'A little silver locket,' she continued. 'A tiny thing. The clasp is always slipping; I fear I may have lost it upstairs. Oh, Mr. Hawkes, I expect you have excellent eye-sight – could you possibly oblige me . . . ?'

Stephen Symes scowled, just long enough for Sarah Tanner to take some satisfaction in his discomfort.

'Of course,' he replied, after a slight pause, with perfect politeness.

'We'll both look, ma'am,' added Mr. Ferntower. 'Bournelle – do take the ladies to observe a class.'

Mr. Bournelle followed his instructions, as the two men climbed the staircase for a second time. Meanwhile Sarah Tanner soon found herself seated on one of the benches, beside a ragged group of girls, listening to the story of the Good Samaritan.

And it was there, just as Mr. Bournelle turned away – with Stephen Symes still occupied upstairs – that she expertly opened the small reticule that Elizabeth Fulbrook had brought with her, and surreptitiously added an additional item to its contents.

———

'I regret there is no sign of the locket, ma'am,' said Mr. Ferntower, as he returned to the ground floor.

'No?' replied Mrs. Tanner. 'Oh dear! Well, perhaps I lost it before I arrived here; I can't now recall whether I had it when I came in. How foolish of me! Never mind; it is really just a trinket. Mr. Ferntower, you have been so kind, but I have inconvenienced you long enough. I had best take my leave.'

'Of course, ma'am. I trust you found the visit instructive?'

'Most valuable, sir. I shall be in touch with Mr. Tebbins presently.'

'Indeed? I am pleased to hear it. You must allow me to walk you to your carriage, ma'am.'

Sarah Tanner did not demur. In consequence, after making appropriate farewells, she found herself outside the Juvenile Schools, upon Mr. Ferntower's arm. The announcement of an intention to subscribe money – or, at least, the hint she had offered – seemed to raise Michael Ferntower's spirits, and, as her host ushered her to the coach, he adopted a rather confiding, slightly self-satisfied tone.

'May I ask, ma'am,' said Mr. Ferntower, 'what you make of Miss Payne?'

Mrs. Tanner paused. In truth, she had given the governess little thought, since she had remained quite unobtrusive, offering no opinion or comment throughout the tour.

'Miss Payne, sir? Why, she seems very pleasant.'

'Indeed, she is, ma'am. I am glad to hear you say it. Of course, I would not entrust my ward to a woman whose discretion and sound judgment I did not prize; a woman of good education and possessing the social graces.'

'Quite,' she replied, somewhat mystified.

'Ah, well, here we are. You have my card, ma'am – if you should pass through Holloway on your journey, by all means pay us a call.'

Sarah Tanner expressed her thanks. Once settled in her carriage, as Ralph Grundy snapped the whip, she looked back at the Schools. The visitors stood at the door, bidding Mr. Bournelle goodbye. Stephen Symes was too preoccupied with attending to his fiancée to watch the carriage depart – for which she was grateful. But Michael Ferntower seemed to look neither at Mr. Bournelle, his ward or his departing guest. His gaze lingered upon the rather plain countenance of Miss Payne; it lingered rather too long, and Miss Payne looked demurely away.

Mr. Ferntower, Sarah Tanner realised, had made a confession of sorts, seeking the approval of a stranger for something he dared not admit. Mr. Ferntower was enamoured of his ward's governess.

CHAPTER TWENTY-SEVEN

That night, Sarah Tanner sat in front of the fire-
place in her bedroom. There was no other illumin-
ation save the flickering light of the coals, and she sat
close enough to the hearth for the fire to bring a red
glow to her cheeks. For a moment, she was distracted
by the noise of the street: the sound of a barrow being
pushed over the uneven cobbles; then the distant shrill
piping of a cornopean carried on the breeze, most
likely accompanying a free-and-easy at the Bottle of
Hay. But her attention soon returned to the bundle
of letters which she held in her hands: the correspondence of Arthur DeSalle. Her fingers toyed with
the string; she held them in one hand, as if ready to
throw them into the fire; then her hand dropped back
to her lap, as a knock at the door interrupted her
reverie.

'Missus?'

Sarah Tanner turned her head. Norah Smallwood
stood in the doorway.

'What is it, Norah?'

'Mrs. H. says she's off home, and the beef-tea's gone
but she'll make up some more tomorrow.'

'Tell her that's fine.'

'Ain't you coming down?' asked Norah, looking

round the darkened room. 'I'll bring you a couple of candles up, if you like.'

'No, there's no need.'

Norah Smallwood nodded, and made to leave. But her employer called out to her, just as she turned away.

'That's a new bow, isn't it?'

Norah blushed, involuntarily touching the rich russet-coloured ribbon that tied back her long brown locks.

'It might be,' she replied coyly.

'A gift?'

'How did you know?' asked Norah, surprised.

'Because you couldn't leave it alone all morning. If you weren't tying it up again, you were looking in the mirror.'

'That don't mean nothing,' said Norah Smallwood, rather put out.

'Who's this fellow, then? I don't suppose it was Harry Drummond? Last time I saw him, his face still looked like you'd flattened him with an iron.'

'I didn't do nothing,' protested Norah.

'I expect that's what he's unhappy about.'

'He's just a boy.'

Sarah Tanner raised her eyebrows. 'So this is a *man*, is it?'

'If you must know, his name's Albert and he works down Smithfield.'

'I expect it's none of my business,' said Mrs. Tanner, rather enjoying teasing her employee.

'I expect that's right,' replied Norah firmly. 'So are you doing your disappearing trick again tomorrow?'

'How do you mean?'

'I ain't stupid, you know. That's two days you ain't

hardly been here, gone all afternoon, and you're thick as thieves with old bag-o-bones . . .'

'Ralph?'

'Yeah, and don't think I mind, 'cos I don't, you're welcome to him. But I reckon I've a right to hear about it, if it's about Georgie . . .'

Norah Smallwood's voice trailed off, as if she herself was slightly surprised by the force of her own outburst.

'I suppose you do,' said Mrs. Tanner, after a moment's reflection. 'Listen, Norah, did Georgie ever talk to you about a woman he called "Her Majesty"? Or a man called Symes?'

Norah Smallwood shook her head.

'Well then,' she continued with a sigh, 'sit down, and I'll tell you.'

Not long after Norah had quit her room, Sarah Tanner once more heard the sound of footsteps on the stairs.

'You wanted to see us, missus?' said Ralph Grundy.

'Sit down, Ralph,' said Mrs. Tanner, offering him the seat opposite her own, in front of the fire.

'I'm obliged, missus.'

'I've been thinking about tomorrow. If the girl replies to the letter, I'll need the coach again. I'll need *you* again.'

'That's what I reckoned,' said the waiter.

'Please, Ralph, wait a moment. If this all goes wrong . . . well, they've had two people killed already. Symes wouldn't hesitate to make it three; he'd probably do it himself, if he thought it would help him get his way. There's no reason why you should risk your neck for my sake.'

Ralph Grundy hesitated.

'Them's strong words, missus,' he said at last. 'Brings a fellow up short, does a speech like that. The thing is, you says I'm risking my neck, if it goes wrong. But – and I may be a fool to think it – I'm inclined to matters going right, 'cos I reckon if anyone can square this business, you're the one to do it. Here's a thought, though, now I come to think on it – what if things *do* go right? Am I risking my neck then and all?'

'I don't follow, Ralph.'

'Well, missus – let's say you put a stop to this here wedding – that's your idea, ain't it? That still leaves the Peeler what did for your friend Phelps, and the parties what got him to do it. And they ain't going to be full of the milk of human kindness, are they?'

'No,' replied Sarah Tanner with a rueful smile, 'they're not. That's just what I've just been thinking. But I know them, Ralph. I know how they think. They plan it out like a game of chess; the trick is to make us more trouble to them dead than alive. They won't trouble us, not if it means they lose by it.'

'Well, you've lost me, anyhow, missus,' said Ralph Grundy, scratching his forehead.

Sarah Tanner reached down to the floor and picked up Arthur DeSalle's letters, which lay by the side of her chair.

'These are letters, between the son of a certain peer of the realm, and certain other parties; I've had them for a while. Give them to the police – at least, God help us, if there is an honest policeman to be had – and mention a certain minor scandal last Season, and they could mean ten years hard labour for all concerned.'

'Your old pals?'

'Yes. They don't know I have them, not yet. But if I tell them I do, and that I'll make sure they'll come out if anything happens to me—'

'Hold up, missus – why don't you just show 'em to Scotland Yard and have done?'

'Because you could add me to the list of "other parties", Ralph. And I don't fancy spending my days picking oakum.'

Ralph Grundy smirked. 'You're a rare 'un, missus. And I'll stick by you, if you'll have me.'

'Are you sure, Ralph?'

'Let's just hope that letter does the trick, eh?'

'If Miss Fulbrook has just an ounce of curiosity,' said Sarah Tanner, 'it will.'

———

In the privacy of her room, Elizabeth Fulbrook looked at the piece of paper. The envelope in which it came, bearing the words *Private and Confidential* written in an elegant script, lay on the table beside it.

My Dear Miss Fulbrook,

Please forgive the peculiar method by which this letter has come into your hands. I would not practise such intrigue were it not of the utmost importance, both in relation to my own conscience and your future happiness, that these words reach you without any prospect of interference by a third party.

It is difficult to know where to begin. I hope it is sufficient to say that I have your very best interests at heart, and very particular reasons for wishing that neither your guardian, nor Mr. Cedric Hawkes, is made aware of this letter.

In short, I happen to possess information concerning Mr. Hawkes, and his history, which, having learnt that you are to marry the gentleman, has caused me considerable mental anguish. It is my duty to say more, but I dare not in this letter. I implore you, favour me with a private audience, at a time of your choosing, and I will reveal the truth.

I beg you, secrecy is all. I am only in London for the week – I am delaying my return home – but you may write to me at the Post Office, 125 Holborn.

Your most sincere friend,
Sarah Richards

Elizabeth Fulbrook read the letter again. Hesitantly, she picked out a new sheet of notepaper from her desk drawer, and dipped the nib of her pen in the inkwell.

CHAPTER TWENTY-EIGHT

The day after her visit to the Schools, Sarah Tanner once more took her hired carriage and directed Ralph Grundy towards Hillmarton Park, Holloway. For she had received a brief note from Elizabeth Fulbrook and had an appointment to keep.

Looking out of the window, Mrs. Tanner was certain the road was a new one. For a start, every house had a clean, newly minted appearance, seemingly barely touched by the soot and grime of the metropolis. Indeed, from the paint upon the front doors to the young saplings that lined the gently sloping road, there was something almost unsettling in the scene's pristine perfection. The vista was only marred by the occasional remaining open plot of ground, marked out by boards, twine and bricks, ready to be built upon.

As for the houses themselves, they seemed to grow larger and more grandiose according to their eminence upon the slope. None, however, were insignificant: being three- or four-storey villas, rather gloomy and Gothic in appearance. Most were in pairs, seamlessly twinned, each a mirror image of the other, so as to present a grand façade to the outside world. She looked at the tall respectable windows and wondered for a moment whether she herself would be happy in such symmetrical isolation; on balance, she concluded she would not.

The Ferntower residence stood detached, surrounded on all sides by a neatly tended lawn and spear-tipped railings. From the front gate, a gravel path led to a stone bridge of steps above the basement area, and a heavy panelled front door, painted black, with a brass bell-pull.

Sarah Tanner paused to collect her thoughts, then rang the bell.

'Mrs. Richards,' she announced to the maid who answered the door.

'Yes, ma'am. Miss Fulbrook is expecting you.'

She followed the maid indoors. The drawing-room of the Ferntower home, upon the first floor, was a rather grand place for welcoming guests. She wondered whether, in consequence of its size, a rather excessive effort had been made to fill it. Certianly, the walls were covered in framed prints and paintings, such that only the smallest strip of the ornate trellis-work paper behind was visible. Meanwhile, two large chiffoniers dominated two of the walls, displaying porcelain and coloured glass in superabundance, whilst even the floor was decorated: a carpet whose twists and turns would have been worthy of an Ottoman sultan. The ostentation, however, seemed in peculiar contrast to the young woman who stood to greet her visitor. For Elizabeth Fulbrook, her hands clasped nervously together, looked quite lost in the great drawing-room, as if she hardly belonged there at all.

'Mrs. Richards.'

'Miss Fulbrook. It is a pleasure to see you again.'

Miss Fulbrook nodded rather awkwardly in reply. 'Would you care for some tea?'

'Why, yes, thank you.'

'Please, do sit down,' replied Miss Fulbrook, ringing the servants' bell.

Sarah Tanner obliged, taking the proffered seat before the fire-place, as her hostess sat opposite.

'Mrs. Richards,' said Miss Fulbrook, visibly steeling herself to speak, 'you must forgive me if I forego the niceties required by society. I think it is fair to say you have already presumed to do so yourself, in the peculiar manner in which you chose to communicate with me. I trust, therefore, I do not offend you, by saying as much.'

'No, not at all,' replied Mrs. Tanner. It struck her that Elizabeth Fulbrook, despite her youth, perhaps had more spirit than she had thought.

'You can hardly imagine the sentiments your letter occasioned in me, Mrs. Richards. What on earth can you have to say to me, that could justify such an interference in my affairs?'

'I will tell you, Miss Fulbrook, I swear; but first, please, I must know, have you kept my calling here a secret?'

Elizabeth Fulbrook hesitated. 'Yes, of course, as you asked.'

'Are you quite sure?'

'Very well,' replied Miss Fulbrook with a hint of agitation, 'I consulted my governess, Miss Payne. But I hardly think that matters.'

Sarah Tanner frowned. 'Miss Fulbrook, please—'

'It was she who advised that I invite you here and hear you out,' continued Miss Fulbrook. 'But now it appears not only am I to be imposed upon with secret letters, and clandestine meetings, I am to be interrogated in my own home!'

'I'm sorry,' replied Mrs. Tanner, placidly. 'Please,

do not distress yourself. But your guardian is not here?'

'No; he has business in the City. Although, again, I can hardly see why that should—'

Elizabeth Fulbrook fell silent, as a knock at the door heralded the appearance of the maid and a silver tea service. Both women waited until the tray had been set down, and the maid had been dismissed. Sarah Tanner, however, was first to break the silence.

'You do not trust me, Miss Fulbrook. I realise that. You would be a fool to trust a complete stranger under such circumstances, and I don't blame you for it. But I swear to you, upon my life, if you marry the man you call Cedric Hawkes, he will make your life utterly wretched.'

'The man "I call" Cedric Hawkes?' said Miss Fulbrook, incredulously. 'Does he have another name?'

'Yes, several. But his real name is Stephen Symes. Tell me, do you know your fiancé's occupation?'

'He is a broker on the Exchange.'

'Perhaps, when it suits him. In truth, he is a fraudster, Miss Fulbrook, a villain whose only interest is in your inheritance. I could name a dozen women whom he has ruined; a dozen companies whose shareholders have lost everything, upon his account.'

'Really?' said Miss Fulbrook, disbelief etched in her voice. 'And you have proof of these charges?'

'Not here; not now. But, if you give me time, I could take you—'

'Mrs. Richards,' interrupted Miss Fulbrook, with a sigh, 'honestly, I have done you the courtesy of giving you a hearing, in private, as you requested. But I cannot believe these wild accusations against a gentleman whom my guardian respects and admires, a man who has treated me with the utmost civility and consideration. I cannot conceive what might have possessed you to come here and slander Mr. Hawkes in this way. Indeed, it can only be pure malice or some form of madness; I suppose I must be charitable and assume the latter.'

'There is no love between you, I am sure of that,' said Sarah Tanner.

Elizabeth Fulbrook blushed.

'Mr. Hawkes paid his addresses to me like a gentleman,' she said quietly. 'I will not pretend it is a love-match, Mrs. Richards, but I will come to love him, in time, I am certain. Now I think you had best leave; I was foolish to invite you here. Forgive me, I would be grateful if you did not trouble myself, or my guardian, again.'

'Did Miss Ferntower approve of the marriage?' said Mrs. Tanner, regardless.

'Miss Ferntower?'

'I attended the inquest, Miss Fulbrook. I am sorry to say it, but I do not believe she drowned. I know your guardian thinks the same, except he blames his son. But I believe Stephen Symes, your Mr. Hawkes, arranged it all.'

'Good Lord, you really are quite mad.'

'The marriage is quite soon, is it not? It is a rather short engagement?'

'Mr. Hawkes has business abroad; it is more convenient. Heavens! I do not have to explain myself to you, ma'am!'

Elizabeth Fulbrook reached towards the servants' bell. But her guest reached forward and intercepted her arm, placing in her hand a folded piece of paper.

'Please, I know it must sound quite incredible, but, I beg you, read this first, before you dismiss me.'

Baffled, Elizabeth Fulbrook's curiosity overcame her anxiety to terminate the interview. Upon opening the paper, she visibly recognised the hand, before she had even read a word.

'John,' she whispered to herself.

Sarah Tanner watched as Elizabeth Fulbrook glanced at her in confusion, then turned back to read the letter. There was a look in Miss Fulbrook's eyes, a look of sadness and dormant affection, that gave her some cause to hope.

'Well?' said Mrs. Tanner, as Miss Fulbrook finished reading and folded the note.

Miss Fulbrook straightened her posture. 'My cousin repeats everything you have told me, ma'am, in so many words. He begs me to listen to your counsel.'

Mrs. Tanner said nothing; she was not at all certain the letter had had the intended effect.

'At least, now I understand why you have come here, Mrs. Richards. And I am very sorry my cousin has made you his unwitting agent. I fear these accusations can only be the product of some terrible form of nervous derangement. I only wish . . .' Miss Fulbrook broke off, her voice failing her. 'I am sorry, Mrs. Richards, I really must ask you to leave. I am expecting another visitor.'

Reluctantly, Sarah Tanner nodded and rose from her seat. But there was something in the way Miss Fulbrook spoke that made her ask one more question.

'May I ask whom you are expecting?' she said.

'Mr. Hawkes will be here at half-past the hour,' said Elizabeth Fulbrook with a sigh. 'He often takes a walk over the fields and pays a visit. I had thought, if there was any substance to your letter . . . in any case, if you think that I intend to lay my cousin's charges before him, you are quite mistaken.'

Mrs. Tanner thought for a moment. 'But if I could prove to you that Mr. Hawkes is not at all the man you imagine, would you agree to putting it to the test?'

'I do not believe you could possibly do such a thing.'

Sarah Tanner looked directly into Elizabeth Fulbrook's eyes. 'If I am wrong about Cedric Hawkes, Miss Fulbrook, then what I propose will occasion you no embarrassment. But if I am right, it may spare you a lifetime of misery.'

Elizabeth Fulbrook said nothing for what seemed like an eternity.

'Very well, if first you tell me what would you have me do?'

'Do you have someone in the household, whose word you trust? Whose discretion can be absolutely relied upon, without question?'

'My governess, Miss Payne. I would trust her with my life. She is upstairs, in her room.'

'You can take her into your confidence?'

'Absolutely.'

'Then I suggest you ring the bell, and have her come down.'

~

Sarah Tanner watched Stephen Symes walk up Hillmarton Park. He arrived precisely at the hour he was expected; and she noticed him glance up at the Ferntower residence as he walked, doubtless catching sight of Elizabeth Fulbrook at the drawing-room window above. The look upon his face suggested he was gratified to know the object of his affection – or, at least, attentions – was at home. But the look faded, as Sarah Tanner herself stepped out on to the front steps and walked down to the road. They met at the gate, just as Mrs. Tanner's carriage pulled up in front of the house.

'Why, Mr. Hawkes, is it not?'

Stephen Symes glanced up towards the drawing-room window, and back at the carriage.

'You risk a good deal coming here, Sarah,' said Symes in a low voice. 'I warned you on the bridge. Any sensible woman would have heeded my words.'

Mrs. Tanner merely smiled. Her silence only seemed to infuriate Stephen Symes.

'What have you told her?' he demanded.

'Miss Fulbrook? Only that marriage is an honourable estate. What does the Church say upon the subject? "Not taken in hand lightly, to satisfy men's carnal lusts and appetites"? You can hardly object to that, Mr. Symes?'

Stephen Symes looked nervously back towards the house, where Elizabeth Fulbrook still stood at the drawing-room window, his anger barely contained. He carefully angled himself so that his back was turned towards the house.

'I swear, Sarah, I do not know what you are playing at, but I will break every bone in your wretched body, if I so much as see you near this house again. And if you have interfered in my business here, that will be the end of you—'

'Your fiancée is waiting, Mr. Symes,' said Sarah Tanner, calmly.

Stephen Symes grimaced, but, with a rather stilted bow, brushed abruptly past, walking briskly up the path to the house.

Mrs. Tanner, for her part, opened the door to her

carriage and stepped inside, not waiting for Ralph Grundy to descend and offer his assistance. Nor did she pull up the blind which had rendered the interior invisible to the outside world. Instead, she merely turned to address the woman already seated within.

'Did you hear, Miss Payne?'

'I'm afraid I did,' replied Elizabeth Fulbrook's governess. 'Good Lord, I would never have believed it.'

'Just be sure to tell Miss Fulbrook every word.'

'I shall not forget any of it, ma'am, be sure of that,' replied Miss Payne, although she looked at the woman seated opposite her with a rather curious expression.

'You don't trust me, Miss Payne? I gathered it was you who advised Miss Fulbrook to see me.'

'I only want the best for the girl, ma'am,' replied the governess, warily. 'But you seem on quite familiar terms with Mr. Hawkes.'

'I was at one time, Miss Payne,' replied Sarah Tanner. 'But I am trying hard to make amends.'

CHAPTER TWENTY-NINE

The following day, Sarah Tanner left the Dining and Coffee Rooms in the early afternoon, and walked down Leather Lane to Holborn. The receiving-house where Ralph Grundy had arranged for her letters to be kept was situated in the establishment of Sheel & Hardman, Dealers in Fancy Goods. And it was there, between a display of fine china, and shelves of Parian philosophers, rows of miniature busts of worthy Greeks, guaranteed to enliven any mantel-piece, that she inquired at the counter discreetly labelled 'General Post Office' for anything under the name of 'Richards' – and was rewarded with a single envelope.

She quit the shop and walked for a few yards along the busy street. But if she ever intended to return home before reading the letter, she did not keep to her resolution, and, stepping into a side-street not far from Leather Lane, she opened the envelope and read the contents.

Hillmarton Park, 14th April

Dear Mrs. Richards,
Miss Fulbrook has entreated me to put pen to paper upon her behalf, and I cannot refuse her.

In truth, I do so with a heavy heart, since I cannot conceive that any further correspondence between us concerning upon this painful subject is either wise or proper. Nonetheless, Miss Fulbrook has taken me into her confidence. I am, therefore, willing to subordinate my own sentiments and act as her agent, in the hope that I may further her best interests.

The reason Miss Fulbrook does not write on her own behalf is one which, I trust, can readily be surmised. The account which I gave of your conversation with Mr. Hawkes has affected her deeply, throwing her into a state of distress and confusion which it pains me to witness. It is fortunate that Mr. Ferntower is content to ascribe her condition to the fickle humours of our sex.

In short, Miss Fulbrook, having received the gloomy intelligence which I provided her, now entertains every doubt regarding the character of her fiancé.

What is to be done? The answer is quite plain to me: that we must reveal all to Mr. Ferntower, in whose power it is to prevent this marriage, and that Mr. Hawkes must explain his conduct in full. If there is an explanation of his words and manner, then so be it; if not, then the matter is settled. Miss Fulbrook, for her part, seems incapable of decision; she is fearful of taking action. She has requested that I write to you, with this purpose: to say that she is grateful for your advice; that she is, at present, incapable of any sensible thought or deed, but that in due course she will write both to yourself *and one other*. Upon that point, I quote her very words.

Mrs. Richards, I beg you, if you act from honourable motives in this matter, you must counsel Miss Fulbrook to follow *my* advice. I fear that I know precisely whom Miss Fulbrook means when she declares 'and one other' and I have no confidence in *that* party. That 'one other' – Mr. John Ferntower – there! I have 'spoke the truth and shamed the Devil!' – has proved himself an unaccountable villain, time and again, in word and deed. I will not ask under what circumstances *you* made his acquaintance – Miss Fulbrook has informed me you are an intimate of that unfortunate gentleman – but you must know he would be her ruin.

No! She *must* speak to her guardian. Surely no other course of action is permitted to her? If, as you claim, you value this young woman's honour and happiness, I beg you to commend this course of action, by return of post.

Yours respectfully,
Lydia Payne

Sarah Tanner finished the letter. After a few moments' thought, she put it in her pocket and turned her steps westwards.

—

It was some half an hour later that she reached her intended destination – Prince's Row, Newport Market. The street door was unlocked, just as it had been upon her previous visit, and she climbed the stairs to the third floor unmolested by any of the building's residents. She found, however, that no-one answered her knock upon John Ferntower's door and, after waiting several minutes, she reluctantly resolved to return homewards. As she quit the building, however, she caught sight of a garish parti-coloured play-bill, one of a multitude pasted upon the wall opposite. It reminded her of John Ferntower's occupation, and, upon a whim, she turned south, in the direction of St. Martin's Lane, and Trafalgar Square.

When she came to a halt a second time, it was not outside a private dwelling, but rather a quarter of a mile distant from John Ferntower's lodgings, in front of the Adelphi Theatre, upon the Strand. The theatre's exterior was a rather narrow, unprepossessing one, with plate glass and twin folding doors that could easily be mistaken for the front of a minor gin-palace. Indeed, sandwiched between the Hampshire Hog public-house and Batt & Rutley, Seed Merchants, with no matinée to make it blossom into life, the theatre seemed positively gloomy, its only mark of distinction being several additional street-lamps upon the pave-ment outside, lined up together in a neat row, ready to illuminate evening crowds.

Sarah Tanner hestitated, wondering whether the building might be entirely empty during daylight hours. But before she could even try the door, a voice called out from the doorway of the adjoining public-house.

'Mrs. Richards!'

It took her a moment to place the voice's owner: Theobald Stamp.

'Mrs. Richards! How charming to see you!' exclaimed Mr. Stamp, striding out on to the street. 'Now, say you have reconsidered my offer, my dear young woman! Say it is so, my dear, and gladden this old man's heart! For it would gladden it, ma'am; it would, I assure you. A shilling a night!'

'No, sir, I can't say the stage appeals.'

'No? Then it is the bill? You have seen the bill, my dear woman, and you seek amusement. You and the rest of the great metropolis, ma'am! A full house every night: "Stamp is the genius of the comic burletta"; "one of the most creditable productions of the day"; "Miss Woolgar knows no equal"! Have you seen the bill, my dear lady? It must be so.'

Sarah Tanner shook her head. 'No, sir. I was looking for Mr. Smith.'

'Smith? Again! Always Mr. Smith. Why, a creature like yourself could do far better than Smith, my dear. Still, you have found him; he is with the company,' said Mr. Stamp, nodding towards the Hampshire Hog, 'working on some minor changes to the text. Come, come inside. I shall procure you a seat and a little refreshment.'

'No, please, sir, there is no need. If you might ask Mr. Smith to step outside for a moment, that will suffice.'

'You ain't of the temperance persuasion, ma'am?' said Mr. Stamp, in serio-comic manner. 'Because, of course, if you were, I'd never touch another drop, you have my word of honour.'

Sarah Tanner smiled politely. 'No, sir, I am not. But if you might just—'

'Of course, my dear lady,' replied Mr. Stamp, with a flamboyant bow, terminating in a flourish wave of his hand. 'Of course!'

Mrs. Tanner sighed to herself, rather relieved, as the theatrical impresario retreated into the public-house. It was a minute or two before John Ferntower emerged from the Hampshire Hog; and, although he was not quite drunk, she could not help but notice the strong aroma of gin about him.

'Mrs. Richards, you have a positive talent for

discovering my whereabouts,' said John Ferntower, in a fashion that sounded not entirely complimentary.

'I was just fortunate to see Mr. Stamp.'

'I take it there is news?'

'I saw your cousin Elizabeth. I think I may have persuaded her to, well, at least reconsider her choice of husband.'

John Ferntower's face grew more serious; and, indeed, as Sarah Tanner recounted the events of the previous day, he seemed to lose some of his customary cynicism.

'You gave her my note?' said Ferntower.

'I did. Here, this is the letter Miss Payne sent this morning.'

John Ferntower cast his eyes over the governess's letter, reading it at speed.

'She intends to write to us both, I think,' said Mrs. Tanner. 'But Miss Payne already seems against you.'

'Miss Payne?' replied Ferntower, glumly. 'She was a favourite of my aunt's; she knows a good deal about my circumstances; it is not altogether surprising. I doubt she can be persuaded of my virtue as a suitor.'

'For pity's sake, sir,' exclaimed Mrs. Tanner, exasperated, 'do you love her?'

John Ferntower seemed to flinch at the directness of the question. 'Elizabeth? If she could bring herself to love me.'

'Then write to her again, before she writes to you. Tell her she is everything to you, that you would marry her tomorrow, if it would save her from a man like Symes. Tell her what you like, but give her some hope.'

'Will that be enough?'

Sarah Tanner sighed. 'I do not know.'

'What if she follows Miss Payne's advice and talks to my father?'

'If your father believes her, and calls off the marriage, then I would be quite content with that.'

'And if she tells him, and he does not believe it? I swear, he thinks Hawkes – Symes, whatever we must call him – can do no wrong, I am sure of it.'

'Then, if I know Mr. Symes,' replied Sarah Tanner, 'you may expect a wedding even sooner.'

John Ferntower shook his head, though it was hard for Mrs. Tanner to judge whether in mute pessimism or defiance.

'Tell me,' she continued, 'does Miss Payne have much influence with your father?'

'That is a peculiar question,' replied Ferntower, puzzled.

'Not if she can persuade him against Symes.'

'Why should she be able to do that?'

'Because I rather think he might have formed an attachment to her. He asked me my opinion of her, when I saw them at the Schools.'

'I hardly think that signifies much,' said John Ferntower.

'You did not see how he looked at her.'

Ferntower shrugged. 'Nothing would surprise me about that man. But I should be surprised if Miss Payne reciprocates his sentiments.'

'Is your father such a monster?'

'They hardly share the same station in life, Mrs. Richards. And I think my father has had his fill of scandal.'

Sarah Tanner did not debate the point. 'But you will write to Miss Fulbrook?'

'Yes, I suppose I will. But I hardly . . .'

John Ferntower's voice trailed off, as he noticed the re-appearance of Theobald Stamp from the Hampshire Hog.

'Dear lady,' exclaimed Stamp, in full voice, waving a couple of pieces of paper in the air, 'you are still here! I was just talking to my fellow players, ma'am, and it struck me. I said to myself, "Sir! Are you a blackguard? Are you a rogue?" Why – it is the least I can do for a friend of Mr. Smith!'

'Sir?'

'Two complimentary tickets for tomorrow night's performance, ma'am,' effused Mr. Stamp. '*The Queen of the Market* – translated from the French – followed by *Bloomerism, or The Follies of the Day.*'

'Thank you,' said Mrs. Tanner, as politely as possible.

'I am sure Mrs. Richards has better uses for her time,' added John Ferntower.

'In any case, sir,' said Mrs. Tanner, 'I had best be going. I trust you will keep up to date with your correspondence, Mr. Smith?'

'I'll do my best,' replied John Ferntower. 'I assure you.'

'Goodbye, then, my dear lady,' said Theobald Stamp, with another of his patented bows. 'I look forward to seeing you at our performance. And if you might care to see behind-the-scenes, you need but ask at the Stage Door.'

'Goodbye,' said Sarah Tanner, quite determined to do nothing of the sort.

～

Sarah Tanner walked slowly homewards. When at last she came to Leather Lane, she was surprised to hear someone call after her.

'Here, missus!'

It was, she realised, Joe Drummond, a burly individual in his late forties, a regular at the Dining and Coffee Rooms, and father of Norah Smallwood's would-be suitor.

'Here, missus,' repeated the coster, stepping out from behind his barrow, rather shyly, for all his bulk. 'What do you say to this – Yarmouth bloaters, three a penny? Best that grow in the sea.'

Sarah Tanner cast her eye over the fish, laid out in neat rows, which, all the same, looked for the most part rather the worse for wear.

'I think we're fine for fish today, Joe.'

'They're only a little touched, missus – no harm in it.'

'No, thank you, Joe, not today.'

'I'll have some halibut at the weekend,' persisted the coster, after a moment's hesitation. Sarah Tanner looked back at him; there was something rather anxious about his expression.

'Well, perhaps I will have those when they come.'

'Or haddock. I might have some haddock, prime 'uns.'

'Was there something else you wanted, Joe?' she asked, feeling certain of it.

'Ah,' replied the coster, as if a weight had rather been lifted from his shoulders. 'Well, it's the barrow, missus.'

'The barrow? What's wrong with it?'

'Ah,' said the coster, as if feeling his way round a particularly difficult subject. 'It ain't that there's anything wrong of it. But it's a heavy article, and takes a fellow a long while to load up, see?'

Sarah Tanner nodded, though rather uncertain where the conversation was heading.

'Well, an heavy article needs two hands, missus. I mean, I *can* work on my own hook, but two hands is what's needed, or I'm last in and last out; and that won't do.'

'Last out?'

'Down Billingsgate. And that's my point.'

'I am sorry, Joe, but I don't understand.'

'My Harry!' exclaimed Joe Drummond, as if stating the utterly obvious. 'I mean, he comes with us, missus, but he ain't with us,' continued the coster, tapping his head with his finger, 'if you take my drift. And where is he now?'

Sarah Tanner denied any knowledge of Harry Drummond's whereabouts, although she began to understand the broad nature of his father's complaint.

'He's outside your gaff, missus, mooning over that gal of yours, Norah. I've told him, but he don't listen. That gal's dealt him a proper facer, and he don't know what to do with himself.'

'I'm sorry, Joe, but I think there's another young man.'

'Well, then maybe you could say something, missus. An hard word or two in his ear wouldn't do no harm; he needs to hear it.'

'I'll do my best.'

'Thank 'ee, missus,' replied the coster, gratefully. 'Thank 'ee! Here – take a bloater, gratis!'

'No, thank you, Joe,' replied Mrs. Tanner

❧

'Harry! Harry Drummond!'

Sarah Tanner found the young man, as predicted, loitering a short distance from the corner of Liquorpond Street. Upon hearing his name, he walked over rather reluctantly, a somewhat guilty-looking expression upon his face.

'Missus?'

'Who are you waiting for?'

'No-one particular,' replied the young man, sullenly.

'Your father thinks I should have a word with you.'

Harry Drummond blushed. 'Well, it ain't none of his business.'

'If it's Norah you're after, I think she's spoken for.'

'Just!' exclaimed the young coster with much emotion. 'And ain't that fine, when a fellow cribs another fellow's gal when he ain't even there to set to!'

'Well, I don't think you should fight for her,' she said, struggling to conceal a degree of amusement at the young man's vehemence.

'Well, what can I do?'

Sarah Tanner looked at the young man's face; there was something so deeply sincere in his devotion that, despite it being comical, she felt rather moved by it. An idea struck her.

'Do you have a suit, I mean a good one?'

Puzzled, the young man nodded.

She reached into her pocket and pulled out the twin tickets to the Adelphi.

'I'll lay odds she's never been to anything half better than a penny gaff,' said Mrs. Tanner, handing over the tickets to Harry Drummond. 'I got these for nothing. You're welcome to them, if you like. Why don't you ask her to the theatre?'

The young coster's face lit up.

⬦

'What was that in aid of?' said Ralph Grundy, as his employer entered the shop, staring at the departing figure of Harry Drummond.

'You won't approve, Ralph,' said Sarah Tanner. 'I'll tell you later.'

Ralph Grundy frowned, but tried another tack. 'Did she write, then, Miss Fulbrook?'

'After a fashion,' she replied, as she reached into her pocket, and handed over Miss Payne's note.

'What next?' said Ralph Grundy, having finished reading. 'Are you going to write back, like she asks?'

'No; we've done enough. We just wait.'

CHAPTER THIRTY

A second letter from Holloway came the following morning, written in a different hand.

Hillmarton Park, 15th April

My Dear Mrs. Richards,

I will be brief. I have turned this matter over in my mind a thousand times, and I am no nearer a course of action. I know Miss Payne has informed you of that much. I also have received a letter from a certain party – a gentleman with whom you are familiar – which has caused me great consternation. I fear I must speak with you again, at the earliest opportunity.

Forgive me, but I have therefore taken the liberty of making an arrangement whereby we might meet. Mr. Ferntower is holding a small dinner party tomorrow evening. We have just received apologies from one of our guests. I have told my guardian that I shall write to you, since you are still in town.

Will you come? Please send an answer. We dine at eight. If the evening affords no chance for private intercourse, then at least we may make some future engagement.

Yours sincerely,
Elizabeth Fulbrook

P.S. Mr. Hawkes has business in the country; you need have no fear on his account.

'Seems to me like you've swung it, missus,' said Ralph Grundy, reading the letter. 'She ain't marrying him.'

'It sounds like Ferntower has done his part, at least,' replied Sarah Tanner. '"Great consternation"!'

'Either way, you don't sound too happy about it,' remarked the waiter.

'Stephen Symes can be quite persuasive, when it suits him. Even if I stop the match now, nothing is certain. I think there is only one thing that will do it; and that is up to John Ferntower.'

'What's that, then?'

'He not only needs to sweetheart her; he has to marry her.'

Ralph Grundy raised his eyebrows. 'That's a tall order, missus, from what you tells me.'

'I think she may love him; he may even love her.'

'Ah, well, there's no accounting for what *that* does to a party,' muttered Ralph, as if referring to some obscure ailment. 'So you'll be going back to Holloway – what, tonight is it?'

'I had better.'

'And you'll need a driver.'

Sarah Tanner hesitated.

'No,' she said at last, 'not this time. I'll hire one, or take a cab. I need you here.'

'Here? Hold up, missus – you ain't let Her Ladyship go out—'

'Oh, but I have to – Norah's got tickets for the Adelphi. I think she's developing a taste for the drama.'

Ralph Grundy was speechless.

'You should watch that mouth, Ralph,' said Mrs. Tanner, 'you'll catch flies.'

———

That evening, at about seven o'clock, the inhabitants of Leather Lane were treated to two unusual spectacles. The first was the appearance of a new hackney cab, a rather smart, well-equipped carriage, which negotiated the length of Liquorpond Street and parked in front of Sarah Tanner's Dining and Coffee Rooms. It was not so much the carriage itself that was considered remarkable – although such vehicles were rare in the narrow lanes between Gray's Inn and Saffron Hill – but the sudden departure of Sarah Tanner herself, for whom the cab seemed to have been ordered. Cloaked in her long shawl, she walked briskly from her shop and climbed inside, with barely a word to the driver.

The costers, in the process of closing their day's business, only remarked that the cab was a *fine rig*, since, in the way of street-traders, they considered themselves connoisseurs of the horse-and-carriage, even if they themselves were restricted to practical experience of the donkey-and-barrow. The few coster-women who saw the vehicle's departure were more inclined to draw inferences as to Sarah Tanner's destination, none of them overly complimentary to her character or morals.

In fact, the self-same gaggle of females might have speculated all night upon the hackney cab, were it not for a second prodigy that occurred a half-hour later: the appearance of Norah Smallwood dressed in silk (borrowed, in fact, from her employer), upon the arm of Harry Drummond (who wore a suit belonging to his father, normally reserved for the mourning of close relatives). The opinion of said females upon Norah Smallwood had hitherto been divided; some taking the view that the girl in question had treated Harry Drummond, in his own words, *awful rotten*, others, less charitably, that Harry Drummond probably deserved no better. But, upon seeing Norah Smallwood in a fashionable silk, no matter how unassuming the dress, the debate was settled; like her cousin, Norah Smallwood was *no better than she ought to be*, and that was plain fact.

Sarah Tanner, for her part, put all thoughts of her employee behind her, as her cab drove on, passed the Islington toll-gate and headed northwards. Instead she mused over Elizabeth Fulbrook's letter and whether John Ferntower might be relied upon. And if she had any compunction that a marriage to John Ferntower might not be the best fate for the young heiress, she thought about the character of Stephen Symes, and resolved to put it firmly to one side.

'Hillmarton Park, weren't it?' shouted the driver, as the cab began to slow.

'Yes, thank you.'

———

It was a half-hour later after her departure from Leather Lane that Norah Smallwood looked around the small theatre. The unchecked admiration which Theobald Stamp held for Sarah Tanner had only run to seats in the front row of the gallery, but the performance had not yet begun and, from the gallery's lofty heights, there was ample opportunity to observe the playhouse, and its audience. For the most part the crowds in the stalls were clerks and their women-folk. Illuminated by the flaring lights of the grand crystal gasolier above, a fixture that seemed far too large for public safety, Norah Smallwood could see that the men boasted modest silk hats, and the women, in many cases, wore smart fur-trimmed mantles, instead of mere shawls. The gallery crowd, though respectable enough to afford a shilling seat, were more working men, the better class of labourers and mechanics, distinguished not only by a cheaper cut of cloth, but by the privilege of the gallery – food and drink in abundance. Thus, to the right and left, the liberal consumption of smuggled bottled porter and steaming meat pies, and the crunch of dry biscuits.

'This is prime, ain't it?' exclaimed Harry Drummond enthusiastically.

Norah agreed, looking wistfully at the stalls, and thinking how much nicer to be down there, with a man – a man like her Albert – not a mere boy.

———

Sarah Tanner rang the bell at 42, Hillmarton Park. Ushered inside by the same maid she had encountered on her previous visit, she followed the girl up the stairs to the drawing-room, as the rich odour of roasting pork wafted up from the kitchen below.

'I expect Mr. Ferntower has an excellent cook,' she said to the maid.

'Yes, ma'am.'

'Yes, quite excellent, Mrs. Richards,' added a third voice.

Sarah Tanner peered up the stairs. She recognised the voice immediately. It was Miss Payne, already descending the steps from the landing above.

'I trust you are well, Mrs. Richards?'

'Quite. Thank you, Miss Payne. Yourself?'

'Indeed, ma'am, thank you.'

She looked carefully at the governess; there was something slightly anxious, almost urgent, in her manner of speech, not least the fact she had spoken so readily, without any prelude or introduction.

'Although the aroma from downstairs is a little over-powering, I fear,' said Miss Payne. 'I will go and ask Cook to make sure she airs the kitchen. She assures me she leaves the door open, but I rather wonder. In any case, I hope you enjoy your evening.'

Sarah Tanner nodded politely. Inwardly, however, she was puzzled as to the governess's peculiar frank-ness about the workings of the household kitchen. There was a point to it; she was sure; she had said it quite deliberately.

'Here we are, ma'am,' said the maid, holding open the drawing-room door. Mrs. Tanner stepped inside. To her surprise, she found only Mr. Ferntower and his ward seemed to be present.

'Ah, Mrs. Richards,' said Mr. Ferntower, with his customary rather cool reserve. 'How good to see you again. My ward assured me that you would still be in London, but I confess, I rather doubted her. Please, have a seat.'

'Thank you, sir. It was good of you to invite me. Am I the first to arrive?'

'The first and almost the last, ma'am. I'm afraid nearly all my friends and acquaintances seem to have been beset by ill health or misfortune. We are just waiting for one gentleman. It will just be the four of us; I told Elizabeth we should cancel the whole affair, but she insisted upon it.'

Elizabeth Fulbrook blushed, snatching a glance in Sarah Tanner's direction. The sound of the door-bell could be heard in the hall.

'Now,' continued Mr. Ferntower, 'that is the man,

I'll warrant. Forgive me, Mrs. Richards, I must just have a word in private – a business matter.'

Sarah Tanner smiled politely, denying the necessity of forgiveness. As soon as Mr. Ferntower quit the room, his ward turned to her guest, speaking quickly and nervously.

'You do not know what you have done! I had thought my life comfortable and settled. I had thought I should marry a decent man.'

'I am sorry for that. Would you prefer I had said nothing?'

'No. I would not. But there are questions . . . we cannot talk now. We can retire together after dinner. Mr. Ferntower always shares his best cigars with his guests.'

'Who is the gentleman he's expecting?'

'I do not know—'

Before Elizabeth Fulbrook could continue, there was the sound of footsteps upon the stairs, and Mr. Ferntower returned, in the company of a gentleman a few years his junior, dressed in tweed, with dark brown hair and neatly clipped whiskers.

'Elizabeth, Mrs. Richards, may I introduce Mr. Murdoch.'

Sarah Tanner nodded. But there was something about the new arrival that struck her as peculiar. She had the same intuitive sense of confusion she had experienced when meeting Lydia Payne upon the stairs, even before the man uttered a word. His suit was not quite suitable for evening wear; his manner strangely self-contained.

'Elizabeth,' added Mr. Ferntower, 'could you come here for a moment?'

To all appearances equally perplexed, Elizabeth Fulbrook complied, walking over to her guardian.

The hairs upon the back of Sarah Tanner's neck stood on end.

'Now, ma'am,' continued Mr. Ferntower, turning back to address his guest in a voice which suddenly turned rather grave, 'perhaps you can explain your unaccountable interference in my affairs?'

'Sir? Forgive me, I do not understand you.'

'She's convincing, sir, I'll give you that,' said Mr. Murdoch, addressing his host. 'Sounds the part.'

'Sir?' said Elizabeth Fulbrook. 'What is going on?'

'Mr. Murdoch is from Scotland Yard, my dear. It appears Mrs. Richards here is some peculiar sort of imposter, though I cannot yet account for her actions.'

'Scotland Yard?' said Sarah Tanner, rising from her seat.

'At your service, ma'am,' replied the policeman, with a rather impish grin. 'It is a pleasure to make your acquaintance. Now, I'm rather afraid I must place you under arrest.'

CHAPTER THIRTY-ONE

There was, Sarah Tanner realised, little doubt of Mr. Murdoch's profession. He had the air of self-satisfied omniscience cultivated by the Detective Police; even the way he held himself, the angle of his head, seemed to express a degree of self-conceit.

'This is quite ridiculous,' protested Mrs. Tanner.

'What is ridiculous, *ma'am*,' said Mr. Ferntower, laying rather sarcastic stress on the last word, 'is that you should attempt to impose upon a decent family in such a despicable manner.'

'Sir?' said Elizabeth Fulbrook. 'Whatever is the matter?'

Sarah Tanner followed Elizabeth Fulbrook's gaze. The girl was genuinely surprised by the policeman's arrival, she was sure of that much.

'Do you dare to deny that you have deceived us?' continued Mr. Ferntower.

'Why, in what way?' asked Sarah Tanner, doing her level best to maintain an air of innocence. She wondered who had betrayed her. Was it Lydia Payne, not keeping her charge's secret, surrendering to her conscience? Or was it Symes? In truth, she had not thought Stephen Symes would risk the police.

'Allow me, sir,' interjected the detective. 'We need

not prolong proceedings. The answer to your question, my dear, is that you have fraudulently represented yourself to come from a respectable background in the county of Hertfordshire; that you have forged documents to that effect; and, I firmly believe, that you do so with every intention to impose upon this young lady here present, no doubt with a mind to some form of pecuniary advancement. Now, I'm afraid I require your presence at the Islington station-house.'

'Forged? That is utter nonsense,' said Mrs. Tanner, quickly glancing round the room even as she spoke, looking for some means of escape; and finding none. 'Mr. Arthur DeSalle is a relative—'

'None of that gammon,' replied the policeman, stepping forward. 'Save that for the magistrate.'

'I took the advice of a friend and wrote to Mr. DeSalle,' added Mr. Ferntower. 'It was good advice. He denied all knowledge of you. So, if you think you can still make a fool of us, ma'am, you are quite mistaken.'

Sarah Tanner stood silent for a moment; for the thought that Arthur DeSalle might take such a step quite shocked her. Was the 'friend' Symes?

'Come along,' said the policeman. 'We're done here.'

The sound of the policeman's voice brought Mrs. Tanner to her senses. She performed a dispiriting mental calculation. There was nowhere to run; no weapon to hand. There was little that could be said.

'Very well,' she replied, letting the policeman guide her towards the door. 'But I am sure we can resolve this misunderstanding.'

'Gammon,' said the policeman, bluntly. 'I don't have a taste for gammon, ma'am. Let's keep things simple; you come with me, and no fuss, eh?'

'But—' protested Elizabeth Fulbrook.

'Hush, my dear,' said Mr. Ferntower. 'Let the man go about his business.'

'Thank you, sir,' replied the policeman, with studied politeness. 'And if you come to the police-court on Upper Street tomorrow first thing, we'll see what the magistrate makes of the matter.'

Sarah Tanner listened to Mr. Ferntower and the detective make arrangements; but, as the detective began to lead her from the room, her mind was elsewhere. For the station-house led directly to the police-court; the police-court to gaol. If there was any hope, she had to escape; there was nothing to be gained by waiting. But where and how? Upon the stairs? At the door? In whatever carriage was waiting for her?

A rising sense of panic welled up deep within her stomach.

'One moment, sir, I must tell you something,' said Sarah Tanner, maintaining her haughtiest tone.

The detective sighed a self-consciously world-weary sigh, the reply of *gammon* already upon his lips. But he had no opportunity to express the sentiment. For, as she spoke, Mrs. Tanner twisted her body, swinging booted foot into the policeman's shin. And as Mr. Murdoch yelped in pain – and it was a yelp, she noted with approval, one that rather undermined the detective's air of self-confidence – she nimbly dodged his outstretched hands, grabbed her skirts, and ran towards the stairs.

It was, of course, quite hopeless. Although the evening dress she wore was not of the crinolined variety, she could not hope to out-run a man in it. At best, a few yards; at least, she reasoned, if she made it as far as the stairs, Murdoch might tumble down them; a small hope, but better that than nothing.

However, even as she ran, she became dimly awares of footsteps, and then confusion behind her; not merely the policeman's pursuit. As she turned down the stairs, she saw the source of the chaos. For the detective, in his haste to pursue his quarry, had somehow collided with another party – Lydia Payne. As a result, the two lay entangled in a heap on the landing outside the drawing-room, the policeman trying desperately to free himself from the folds of the governess's dress without any accidental impropriety.

Mrs. Tanner did not pause to appreciate her luck; she merely ran.

It was only as she reached the downstairs hall, her rapid footsteps echoing throughout the house, that she was struck by the incongruity of the governess suddenly appearing upon the landing. It was a peculiar coincidence, at least, that she should arrive at that precise moment, and interrupt the policeman's pursuit.

Was it just pure luck? What was it Miss Payne had told her?

She leaves the kitchen-door open.

She hesitated; then, decisively, she ignored the front door, by which she had entered the house, and ran towards the back stairs, rushing down them as fast as her legs could carry her.

In truth, she still half expected to run into the arms of a waiting police constable. But the kitchen seemed quite unprepared for her arrival, containing only a kitchen-maid and cook, the former of whom screamed as Sarah Tanner barged past her, upsetting a row of plates and dishes laid out in preparation for the evening meal. Mrs. Tanner, meanwhile, ignoring the sound of breaking crockery, rushed through the kitchen-door, left ajar upon Lydia Payne's instruction.

The back garden was long, some hundred feet or more, turfed, with a handful of shrubs about its borders, dimly visible in the darkness. But there was a low wall at its rear, no more than three feet high, and behind the wall – nothing. For Hillmarton Park lay upon the very border of the metropolis; and the rear of number 42 was bordered by empty plots of land in the process of being dug for clay. Sarah Tanner stopped to catch her breath. But the sound of voices raised in the house, and the glimpse of a lantern-light flashing in the kitchen, drove her onwards across the uneven ground, into the brick-fields.

She ran as fast as she was able, although the sky was pitch black, with no sign of moon or stars; though the ground beneath her feet, half exposed clay, half mud, seemed to stick to her boots like glue. And she did not stop, though her lungs felt raw with effort, and her legs as heavy as lead.

She did not stop, in fact, until she fell, tumbling headlong down the side of a gaping clay-pit, all but invisible in the blackness. It occurred to her, as she plunged into the pit, involuntarily swallowing particles of the wet earth, that she might as well be falling into an open grave.

CHAPTER THIRTY-TWO

Sarah Tanner opened her eyes, conscious only at first of a dull ache around her ribs. It took her a minute or more, in the pitch black, to focus her mind, and identify where she lay. It was the pit; the porous soil was all about her, the clay soaked into her dress, stuck to her cheeks. Instinctively, she moved her arm, to wipe some of the dirt from her face. But then she heard the sound of footsteps tramping upon the soft ground above, and saw the glint of a lantern, its light swinging round in a broad arc.

'She's not here, sir,' said a voice, which she recognised as Murdoch's.

'I cannot credit that you allowed her to escape,' replied Michael Ferntower, angrily.

'I had a man out the front, sir. I just didn't reckon on having to surround the premises. Regular little hell-cat, weren't she?'

'Yes, well, clearly the woman is an out-and-out criminal, a vicious one at that; there can be little doubt of it.'

'Not much,' replied the detective, dourly. 'I've never yet met a respectable female that could out-run the police.'

Michael Ferntower sighed.

'Very well, call off your man. I only hope that we have seen the last of her.'

'She won't come back, sir. You gave her a proper scare tonight, upon my word you did.'

Sarah Tanner listened from the bottom of the clay-pit, as the two men walked slowly back towards the house, and allowed herself a sigh of relief. She pondered how long she should remain still; she resolved to remain hidden for a few minutes, at least.

Wearily, she closed her eyes, and wondered whether Norah Smallwood's evening had progressed any better than her own.

———

Norah Smallwood, in fact, was not at all sure about her night at the theatre. For, although the first play, *The Queen of the Market*, contained a variety of remarkable incidents, a love affair, and a live horse, she was distracted by Harry Drummond's habit of slipping his right arm around her waist at regular intervals, a habit which she felt obliged to discourage. Moreover, although the gallery were vociferous in booing every comic disaster and applauding every triumph of the play's titular heroine, she felt certain she herself had lost all sense of the plot after the first quarter of an hour. She was rather grateful, therefore, when the Queen took her last bow, and the gas was turned back up, in anticipation of being dimmed once more that night, for the performance of *Bloomerism*.

'Lor, weren't that a proper stunner!' exclaimed Harry Drummond, who had joined in the gallery's commentary with gusto.

'Weren't it, though?' agreed Norah Smallwood,

trying to summon a semblance of enthusiasm. 'Here, fetch us something to eat, won't you?'

'I thought you didn't want nothing?' replied Harry Drummond, with a pang of regret, having already turned down an itinerant pie-seller earlier in the evening, upon account of his companion's disinterest.

'Well, I do now. I don't mind what; even an orange would do; a girl can be hungry, can't she?'

'There'll be someone coming around,' muttered the young man. But as he looked both ways along the gallery's benches, there was no sign of any refreshment.

'Go on, please,' insisted Norah, 'I'm starving.'

'You'll still be here when I come back?'

''Course I will. I swear.'

Upon receiving a promise, Harry Drummond grudgingly agreed, a degree of chivalry being a natural facet of his youthful character.

Norah, for her part, watched him push past the rest of the row, and – if truth be told – hoped rather wistfully that another gentleman entirely might appear, and take the empty space beside her.

When, however, that materialisation did not occur, she turned her gaze to the scene below. She could just see the orchestra – partly sunk beneath the stage – and, if she craned her neck, the comings and goings in the stalls below. It was as she watched that she noticed something out of the corner of her eye; the face of a woman in the crowd, visible for just a moment.

Norah Smallwood turned rather pale.

'Lor!' exclaimed Harry Drummond, who reappeared at her side, the proud owner of two oranges. 'You seen a ghost?'

She frowned, and shook her head. 'Nah, it weren't nothing. I was just day-dreaming, that's all.'

After all, Norah Smallwood thought to herself, Miss Emma Ferntower was dead. No, it was not her; it was quite impossible.

A bell rang. The theatre lights began to dim.

Sarah Tanner's journey from Upper Holloway was an exhausting and weary affair. It was several hours after her departure – at about half-past midnight – when she finally returned to the Dining and Coffee Rooms. She presented quite a different spectacle to that of her departure, and if any of the same coster-women had seen her, they might have remarked upon it with a degree of smug satisfaction. For the fine silk dress she had worn had been turned into the dirtiest, mud-soaked excuse for a garment that had ever graced the cobbles of Leather Lane. Ruined by the trek through the brick-fields, the fabric seemed to have been torn in every conceivable location, with scraps of material loose, dangling like tatty ribbons from rents in the material. Her face, too, still bore smudges of clay, though she had made a vain attempt to improve matters at a water trough in the vicinity of King's Cross. Ralph Grundy – a self-appointed sentry, his watchful eyes ranging between the shutters – hastened to let his employer inside.

'Lor! Are you alright, missus?'

'Never better,' said Mrs. Tanner, sitting down heavily on one of the shop's benches.

'Do you want a drink?'

She shook her head. 'Is Norah back?'

'A good hour. She's probably asleep,' replied Ralph

Grundy, foregoing his customary commentary upon Norah Smallwood's character. 'Should I get her?'

'No, I just wanted to know if she had a good night. It will keep.'

'Never mind that!' exclaimed the waiter indignantly. 'What's happened, for pity's sake?'

'Ferntower knows about me. Or, at least, that I'm not who I claimed to be. The dinner was a trap; he had a detective waiting.'

'A detective? Who told him?'

'Symes, I'm sure of it,' replied Sarah Tanner.

'Symes? Not the governess?'

'No, I rather think she helped me to get away.'

Ralph Grundy listened as Mrs. Tanner recounted the story of the evening, not least the trek from the clay-pit, through the outskirts of London, back to Leather Lane. At the end of her narrative, he sighed.

'I ain't saying nothing, missus, but I reckon none of this is worth your trouble. It ain't your business.'

'You don't think a man losing his life is worth my trouble?'

'That depends on the man. But it strikes me, missus, that you care more about squaring up to this Symes fellow than the man what properly did for your pal. Of course, if you wants to settle old scores, that's your business.'

'It's not like that, Ralph.'

'You don't have to explain yourself to me, missus.'

'No,' replied Sarah Tanner. 'I don't.'

Ralph Grundy shrugged. 'Well, I'll be off then. You'd best get some rest, I reckon.'

Sarah Tanner nodded, and silently watched him depart. Her ribs still sore, she forced herself upright and locked the door behind the old man, in her customary fashion. Taking the lamp upstairs, she repaired to her bedroom, where no fire had been lit. Too exhausted and cold to undress, she merely removed her boots, and wrapped the blankets around herself.

In a matter of moments, she was asleep.

For the second time in the same night, she awoke dazed, uncertain of her surroundings.

It struck her as odd: she was in her bedroom, and the lamp, which she had snuffed out, had been lit once more.

But it wasn't her lamp at all; more like a lantern. And the sound she could hear was something like a muffled scream.

There was somebody there, in the room.

Was she dreaming?

She peered into the semi-darkness, until the figure of a man revealed itself.

Her stomach sank.

'Hello, Sarah,' said Stephen Symes, seated at her dressing-table, a cruel smile upon his lips. 'I thought you'd never wake up.'

CHAPTER THIRTY-THREE

Sarah Tanner levered herself up against the wooden head-board of the bed. Stephen Symes, for his part, remained seated, his hand propping up his chin as if engaged in some abstract philosophical contemplation.

'You are a sorry sight, you know,' said Symes at last. 'The Sarah Mills of my acquaintance had higher standards. She would not have got herself into such a condition. And in Leather Lane! Still, I suppose it was inevitable that you should return to the gutter, eh, my dear?'

'It is still a cut above the sewers of Regent Street,' replied Sarah Tanner.

'Really?' said Symes. 'I took you for many things, Sarah, but never a hypocrite.'

'At least I've never killed a man in cold blood.'

'And you think I have? Surely you know me better than that.'

'No, that's right. You let others do the work.'

Stephen Symes sighed, shaking his head.

'This won't do, Sarah, not at all. You're not a fool – what the devil possessed you to go back to Ferntower's? I gave you fair warning, twice over.'

'I saw Georgie die, remember? I know your game. I won't let you profit by it, I swear.'

'Sarah, please, you are hardly best placed to make threats,' said Symes, a hint of amusement in his voice. 'You think I killed poor Phelps?'

'One of you gave the word; don't deny it.'

'You think so?' said Symes, standing up. 'Ah, Sarah, at one time we had such hopes for you. It is such a waste; all this for nothing.'

'Do you mean to kill me?' said Mrs. Tanner.

'You could have done the decent thing and yielded to Inspector Murdoch,' replied Symes, utterly avoiding the question. 'But I suppose I should have given you more credit. You always were rather resourceful, I'll confess that much.'

'So you arranged it all, at the house?'

'I pointed my friend Ferntower in the direction of the Detective Police, that is all. I doubt it took much doing to uncover Mrs. Richards – or, rather, should I say, Mrs. Tanner?'

The sound of her name on Stephen Symes's lips – or, at least, the name by which she was known in Leather Lane – made Sarah Tanner pause for thought.

'How did you find me?'

Stephen Symes smiled a particularly serpentine smile, nodding towards the open bedroom door. She turned her head, following his gaze, to see the hulking figure of Bert Jones standing there, a look of smug satisfaction upon his face. She noted his face was still scarred from Ralph Grundy's assault, where the cartwheel had met his forehead.

'I ain't such a Jack Adams as all that, my gal,' said Jones, his voice full of self-congratulation. 'I saw you stop here in the road that night, and I says to myself afterwards, "Her lodgings can't be that far." So I made inquiries, on the quiet, like. Told you I used to doss hereabouts, didn't I?'

'You did,' replied Sarah Tanner, biting her lip.

'Oh, but Mr. Jones is too modest, Sarah,' said Stephen Symes. 'Come, sir, show Miss Mills your little sweetheart.'

Bert Jones smirked and reached back into the corridor outside the room, pulling something – someone – roughly forward. Even before Sarah Tanner could see for herself, she knew who would be standing before her.

His name's Albert.

Involuntarily, she closed her eyes for a moment, as if still not persuaded she had woken into a bad dream. When she opened them again, she gazed into the tear-soaked visage of Norah Smallwood, who stood shivering and helpless, in the cotton shift she wore as her night-dress, the right side of her face swollen with bruising, and a trickle of dried blood running from her nose to her chin.

'I'm sorry,' she said, her voice quivering, 'I didn't know nothing—'

The back of Bert Jones's hand interrupted Norah Smallwood's protestation of innocence. It was the merest flick of the big man's arm, done with casual disdain, as if swatting a fly. But the impact was enough to send the girl's body reeling against the jamb of the door, and stain the cotton shift with a fresh spray of blood.

'You'll speak when I say, gal. Have you got that?'

Norah, curled into a ball upon the floor, shuddered, nodding her head in mute despair.

Mrs. Tanner glanced back at Stephen Symes. He tutted in a rather mannered fashion, but his disapproval was of the most perfunctory kind. Indeed, she could not help but think there was something almost gleeful in his expression.

'There is no need for this,' said Sarah Tanner. 'I'll leave it alone, I swear. Just let her be.'

'Do you hear that, Mr. Jones?' said Symes contemptuously. 'Our Miss Mills has discovered sentiment. "Just let her be."'

'Oh, begging your pardon, sir,' replied Jones, with a guffaw. 'Well, if Miss Mills says so, that's another matter, that is.'

'No, Sarah,' continued Stephen Symes, turning back to Mrs. Tanner, 'I can find a good use for your little cousin. She'll scrub up well enough, once the bruising goes down. There's a pleasant little room put aside for her in the Row. I'd do the same for you, upon my honour, if you'd kept yourself in better trim; but I'm afraid you've had your day.'

'I still have the letters from the Norwood business,' said Sarah Tanner hurriedly. 'If you kill me, I've made sure they'll come out. Everything you wrote about DeSalle; everything he wrote to me. You'll be ruined.'

Stephen Symes paused, as if considering the argument.

'The letters? You still have them?'

'Yes.'

'Hmm. Well, I rather fear, my dear Sarah, you ought to have taken better care of them.'

Sarah Tanner frowned. For, as Symes spoke, Bert Jones pulled a sheaf of papers from inside his coat pocket, tied with red ribbon.

'You should really teach your little cousin to keep her mouth shut,' continued Symes, cheerfully. 'Although Mr. Jones is doing a decent job of that now, is he not? Mr. Jones – if you please?'

Stephen Symes motioned for the letters, turned them over in his hands, then placed them on the table, picking out one at random, and reading out loud.

'"My dearest sweet love, Sarah . . ."' recited Symes, then broke into a chuckle. 'Oh, it is too amusing. But you are quite right, something must be done.'

And, without another word, Stephen Symes reached inside his jacket and pulled out a box of congreves, taking one of the matches out and striking it – then carefully applying it to the end of the letter he had held in his hand.

Sarah Tanner watched in silence. Symes took the lit paper and simply dropped it upon her dressing-table. For a second she could not understand his motive, until the entire surface sprung into flames. Only then did she see the remains of her own oil-lamp, the glass smashed and its viscous contents now alight. In an instant the fire was already licking at the blue check curtains which covered the bedroom window. Symes, meanwhile, stepped nimbly back towards the door, his own light now in his hand.

She noticed that Norah Smallwood opened her mouth to scream; but nothing came out.

'There is an object lesson here, Sarah, is there not?' said Symes. 'I am sorry to be the teacher, I truly am.'

Instinctively, Sarah Tanner tried to get to her feet. But she could not manage it before Symes flung his lantern forcefully into the room, pausing only to watch it shatter as it hit the side of the bed, the sheets splattered with burning oil.

Symes, followed by Bert Jones, stepped back on to the landing. And with a polite nod, as if bidding good afternoon to an acquaintance, he closed the bedroom door.

And turned the key in the lock.

CHAPTER THIRTY-FOUR

The small room began to fill with acrid smoke. The flames trailed up the curtains, which themselves turned black and began to tumble in loose charred tatters on to the fire which had engulfed the table. The bed, meanwhile, took the appearance of a makeshift funeral pyre. Even as Sarah Tanner jumped back from the blaze, she could not quite conceive how she had escaped its embrace. For the material of her dress was quite untouched where it ought to have been scorched or set alight. Then she realised that the residue of the brick-fields, the damp clay soil, was still heavy in the fabric. And yet, as she inwardly gave thanks for her luck, her chest convulsed. The thick smoke seeped into her mouth and stung her eyes; the whole room turned shades of angry black and red.

Dropping down to the floor, she laid hold of the empty jug that sat upon her wash-stand. She had one idea in mind, albeit with no good notion of escape. Breathless and choking, she hurled the jug in the direction of the bedroom window, swinging her arm in a wide arc, throwing with all her might. At first, it seemed to disappear, as if gathered up by invisible demons of the smoke, and, for what seemed an age, she imagined it had fallen, quite useless, upon the floor. Then came an almighty crash, the breaking of glass, which somehow, even amidst the crackling flames, seemed as loud as an explosion.

As the glass broke, she could hear shouts from the street outside. The noise itself calmed her; the fire had not gone unnoticed. Yet, even as some of the smoke escaped, the fresh air seemed to fan the flames, making them roar higher, spreading up to the ceiling, generating a furnace-like heat that all but overpowered her.

She looked around the burning room. There was a gap between bed and window not yet aflame, a path across to the hearth. She darted through, her head low, hand over her mouth, and grabbed the iron poker that leant against the grate. With the metal hot to the touch, she ran back to the bedroom door and jabbed it violently at the lock.

The ceiling groaned, the flames spreading along the joists.

Sarah Tanner's efforts became manic as she tasted her lungs filling with the poison, burning inside her. Her legs seemed to buckle beneath her, as she made one last desperate lunge at the lock.

Then the wood gave way. The door sprung open. But, as the smoke billowed out on to the landing, a burly figure stood there, blocking her way.

She swung wildly with the poker, and fell headlong to the floor.

———◆———

Falling, falling, falling.

Sarah Tanner landed upon a feather bed, stretched upon a quilt of coloured goose down in a cotton cover.

The man stood by the window, looking down upon Jermyn Street, his back turned.

She knew it was Jermyn Street; she was quite sure

of it. The room was decorated after the fashion; the wall-paper repeating an endless pattern of twisting briars and leaves. The fire roared in the grate, even though sunlight shone into the room.

The man told her that she was ready for the magistrate.

She raised herself up to object; but she could barely raise her head.

He slapped her face; her cheek stinging.

Again. He hit her again. Harder, this time.

And all the time the room around her grew hotter.

—

'Water, for pity's sake get her some water.'

'I thought she was dead.'

'She's the luck of the Devil, that one.'

'Born to be hung, if you ask me.'

—

Regent Street. They took her to Regent Street; a hansom cab. Up the steps to a private room; a salon; a game of cards.

George Phelps put more money in the pot.

'Ain't you playing, Sairey?'

'What's the game?'

'"Wilful murder". I'll teach you.'

Wait. No, that made no sense at all.

George Phelps was dead.

—

'Water, get her some water.'

Sarah Tanner woke up, coughing, her throat parched. It was daylight, but the curtains were half drawn, the room in shadow. She squinted in the semi-darkness.

'Where am I?'

'Go easy, missus. Have a sip.'

She was in bed, her back propped up on pillows. She turned her head. It was Ralph Grundy who spoke. The old man sat beside the bed; he held out a chipped china mug towards her. Gingerly, she raised her hands and cradled the china, raising it to her lips.

'Where am I?' she repeated.

'Margie Bladstow's, missus,' replied Ralph. 'Took the liberty of getting you a room, seeing as you needed it. The doctor, he saw you this morning; said you'd want a good rest, though any fool could see that.'

Sarah Tanner let her arms drop to her lap, rolling her head back, wearily closing her eyes.

'It was Symes. The fire – he meant to kill me.'

Ralph Grundy fell silent for a moment. 'I reckoned as much.'

'Not a word to the police. Promise me.'

'The police? Everyone's saying it was an accident with that old lamp; I've only seen the local fellow sniffing around, and he weren't too interested. What about your Norah, though? She weren't in there. They didn't find nothing.'

'Symes took her. He still thinks she's my cousin.'

'How do you mean, he took her?'

'He mentioned a house-of-accommodation, one of Her Majesty's little dens; most likely he'll put her to work. It will probably amuse him.'

The old man fell silent for a second time. It was a minute or more before he summoned the will to speak, changing the subject entirely.

'The shop needs a lick of paint; new sign, maybe.'

'I expect so. Is it all gone?'

'They had four parish engines here, you know. All of 'em fighting over the street-plug. Never seen so much water go through an hose.'

'Is it all gone, Ralph?'

'There's enough to build it up again. Could be done, if you had the heart for it.'

Sarah Tanner coughed, propping herself upright. 'Since when did you become the optimist?'

'Thought I'd cheer you up,' said the old man, sounding utterly grim – so despairing, in fact, that Sarah Tanner almost raised a smile.

'Joe Drummond and his boy will want to see you,' continued Ralph Grundy. 'It was Harry who went for the brigade.'

'Harry Drummond? I knew he was good for something,' remarked Mrs. Tanner.

'And it was Joe who went inside, after you, afore they got here.'

'I think I nearly hit him with a poker.'

'He's a good man,' said Ralph Grundy. 'Maybe saved your life.'

'Tell him "thank you", I can't . . . I don't want to see anyone.'

'If you like.'

Sarah Tanner made to reply but, instead, began to cough; it took a minute or more for the fit to subside.

'I'll close them curtains again,' said Ralph Grundy. 'You get some rest.'

'You don't have to nurse-maid me, Ralph. What time is it?'

'Two o'clock in the afternoon. I don't have to do anything, missus; and you don't need to do nothing but be grateful, if you can manage it. Now you go back to sleep, eh?'

She nodded, and watched as Ralph Grundy got up and closed the curtains. As he reached the door, however, Sarah Tanner spoke out.

'They'll beat her, Ralph. Norah – they'll beat her

and they'll starve her until she'll do anything they want. I'm damned if I'll let it happen. I won't let Symes get away with it – not this, not Georgie – none of it.'

'Have you seen the state you're in, missus?'

'I've been worse. Will you help me?'

Ralph Grundy looked down at the floor, as if contemplating his boots. Finally, he seemed to come to a decision.

'I reckon you knows the answer to that question, missus. I ain't denying that I'm not over-fond of that girl, but you knows the answer.'

Sarah Tanner, content with Ralph Grundy's reply, nodded and shut her eyes.

CHAPTER THIRTY-FIVE

The day after the fire upon Leather Lane, a police constable walked at a leisurely pace up the wide flight of stone steps that led from the Mall and St. James's Park, up to Waterloo Place. Even though it had begun to rain, he felt it rather at odds with the dignity of his office to hurry. Moreover, the waterproof cape tied around his neck provided a degree of protection against the elements. Indeed, as he approached the top of the steps, directly beneath the tall granite column dedicated to the memory of the Duke of York, he actually came to a halt. The keeper of the Duke's monument, whose task it was to take the occasional sixpence for the privilege of ascending the spiral steps within, nodded in the policeman's direction, as was his custom. He even glanced heavenwards, as if to signify the futility of expecting much of the English climate. But the constable did not respond, his attention distracted by a figure standing by the railed gardens some fifty yards distant.

It was a woman, in her late twenties, in a rather dirty-looking dress of faded brown cotton, with long unruly brown hair loosely tied by a single ribbon, half concealed by a battered poke bonnet. Upon seeing the policeman, she turned and walked in the opposite direction. However, if the policeman had half a mind to follow, he did not yield to the dictates of his conscience. For he had finished his duty in the park, and, he reasoned to himself, he could not pursue every unfortunate in the capital.

Besides, it was raining.

It was only as he reached the top of Waterloo Place that his memory stirred; he had seen the woman before, waiting for a gentleman in the park, dressed quite decently.

As he walked on, he idly wondered precisely what misfortune had befallen her, to leave her in such a sorry state.

———

Sarah Tanner waited until the policeman had passed and returned to the corner of the gardens. It was a half-hour more before she moved from the spot. For it was then that she saw the figure of Arthur DeSalle, wrapped beneath a woollen great-coat, clutching a black umbrella, walk briskly past, entirely unaware of her presence.

'Why did you do it?' she exclaimed, deliberately loud, as she stepped out on to the pavement, trailing behind him.

Arthur DeSalle stopped in his tracks. As he turned and faced his interlocutor, the look of astonishment upon his face was unmistakeable.

'Are you surprised?' she continued. 'Did you think you were rid of me?'

Arthur DeSalle regained – if not his composure – then at least his voice.

'Rid of you? What are you doing here? Good Lord, Sarah, I thought we had made an agreement?'

'So did I.'

'For pity's sake,' said DeSalle, 'if you must accost me in the street, must you speak in riddles? And the state of you . . .'

'This?' replied Sarah Tanner, glancing down at the careworn material of her dress. 'Unfortunately, I can do no better at present.'

'Sarah, I swear, I cannot talk to you like this. If anyone from the club were to see us together—'

'Then I would tell them I was your mistress you had abandoned; and I would enjoy the look upon your face. That might be some compensation, at least. In fact, I might invent a child; would that be better still? I think it might.'

'Good Lord, woman, I do believe you are raving mad. Whatever do you imagine I have done to you?'

'You wrote to Ferntower, Arthur. You told him you had never heard of me.'

Arthur DeSalle fell silent, as if struck by a sudden revelation. When at last he spoke, his voice was calm and composed.

'I had no choice, I'm afraid. It was a matter of necessity.'

'I find that very hard to believe.'

'Sarah, do you really imagine that I wished – what? – to spite you? Listen, I beg you, I cannot talk here; anyone might see us. In any case, the rain is only getting worse; you will catch your death. I will take a cab at the rank and have him wait on Panton Street; meet me there. Will you trust me that far?'

Sarah Tanner scowled. 'I am not sure I trust anyone.'

'I am sorry to hear it. Here, take my umbrella. I will go and get the cab.'

And before she could reply, Arthur DeSalle thrust

the umbrella into her hands, and walked briskly back along Waterloo Place.

———

There was no doubting the rather knowing expression adopted by the cab-driver, as Sarah Tanner climbed inside the waiting hackney. Nonetheless, as she sat down inside, facing Arthur DeSalle, the vehicle pulled off into the Haymarket traffic.

'I'm sorry to make you walk any further through the rain,' said DeSalle.

'Where are we going?'

'I told him to go down Piccadilly and back, until I give the word.'

'Very obliging of him.'

'I gave him five shillings. Now will you hear me out?'

'I'm here, aren't I?'

'Very well. Four days ago I received a letter from a gentleman by the name of Ferntower inquiring after a "Mrs. Richards", a supposed acquaintance of mine—'

'You promised you would not give me away,' interrupted Sarah Tanner.

'Wait, I am not done. The letter came to my secretary. He did not know the name – and the terms Mr. Ferntower used were calculated to excite the greatest suspicion – and so he came and asked me directly if I knew the *lady* in question.'

'You could have told him you did; or that you would reply.'

'No, I could not. Arabella was there. She knows all my family's acquaintances. In fact, she is so intimate with my mother she knows them all better than I do. I could not lie; Arabella would have found me out in an instant.'

'I see. And so you sacrificed me instead.'

'I am engaged to be married,' said DeSalle, exasperated. 'Good Lord! I would have written to warn you, if you had deigned to give me an address!'

Sarah Tanner sighed, taking in the information. Her anger seemed visibly to subside. Leaning forward, elbows propped upon her knees, she rubbed her temples.

'Yes, I suppose you would,' she said at last, a rather weary note in her voice.

'Sarah, will you tell me what's going on? I have never seen you like this, so . . .'

'Wretched?'

'If you like.'

'Let me tell you then,' said Sarah Tanner. 'What money I had is gone; the coffee-house, the one I told you about, is gone. I have seen one friend murdered, and have other "friends" who would gladly see me dead. And a girl whom I promised I would protect has been kidnapped by a brute who will take great pleasure in destroying her, in body and spirit. Is that enough?'

'More than enough, I should suppose,' said Arthur DeSalle, rather taken aback. 'But you have not told me anything. What has happened? How did all this begin?'

Sarah Tanner looked back at him.

'If I told you, would you help me?'

'I might, if you can be honest with me. I am sure I can spare something.'

'I do not need money,' she replied. 'I mean, I do, of course I do, but that is not the thing. I need your help. The girl I spoke about – her name is Norah – I must save her. If it was not for me . . . well, they mean to ruin her. Arthur – will you help me? There's no-one else.'

Arthur DeSalle hesitated for a moment.

'Tell me one thing first,' he said. 'The letters?'

Sarah Tanner blinked, then looked her erstwhile lover in the eye.

'Yes, I burned them.'

CHAPTER THIRTY-SIX

It was midnight, that very evening, when a rather smart carriage came to a halt upon the cobbles of Avery Row. The Row itself was a narrow affair, comprised of rather hum-drum private residences, no more than three storeys high, some with a front of exposed brick, others faced in white-washed stucco. The houses might have been rather desirable, if located elsewhere in the metropolis; but, although situated in Mayfair, a short distance from Bond Street, the cramped confines of Avery Row lent its modest buildings an unwholesome air of confinement. Indeed, the carriage almost filled the width of the street, leaving barely enough room for Arthur DeSalle and Sarah Tanner to open the door and step down on to the pavement. The former, dressed in a black evening suit beneath a woollen great-coat, held out his arm to help his companion.

'Are you quite certain about this?' asked DeSalle, somewhat nervously.

'Quite,' replied Mrs. Tanner, who had undergone something of a transformation in the course of the day. For her tattered dress had been replaced by a gown of purple moiré silk; her hair washed and tied back into a tight knot; and her bonnet replaced by a broad-brimmed hat, ornamented by a single feather, with a heavy Maltese veil hanging from its rim.

'They will suspect the veil,' muttered DeSalle.

'They will think some gent has blacked an eye, that's all. Now, tell your man to drive on, and come back around . . . he can wait by the mews, the one we just passed.'

Arthur DeSalle did as his companion suggested, and the carriage set off down the narrow street.

'Is he your usual man?' asked Sarah Tanner, as the vehicle disappeared from view.

'God forbid!' exclaimed DeSalle. 'I got him jobbed with the coach.'

'I'd have preferred someone we might rely upon.'

'And I would prefer that I do not become the talk of Belgravia; so you will have to forgive me for not inviting my entire household to watch this adventure.'

Sarah Tanner did not respond to Arthur DeSalle's complaint. Rather, she turned and looked at the unexceptional property which was their destination.

'This is the place, I am sure of it.'

'Have you been here before?'

'No, not here,' replied Sarah Tanner. 'But I know its reputation. Go on, ring the bell.'

Arthur DeSalle hesitated but a moment, then leant forward and rang the bell. There were no protective railings nor any basement area to cross, the green front door merely set back a few inches, two steps up from the street.

There was the sound of a bolt being released. The door opened.

'Good evening, sir,' said a manservant who stood to one side. 'Do come in.'

———

The hall was little different from any private house: a gilt mirror upon the wall; a rug laid over polished boards; a mahogany coat-stand. The only difference was in the house-of-accommodation's distinctive welcome to strangers. No card was required, nor any name expected. Unfamiliar faces were simply ushered quietly into the front parlour, where the *grande dame* of the house – a substantial woman in her forties, dressed quite plainly, but with a good deal of rouge about her cheeks – sat by the hearth and rose to greet her visitors.

'Good evening, sir,' said the woman, with an appraising glance at Sarah Tanner. Her voice, though well-mannered, had a distinct cockney tinge.

'Good evening,' said Arthur DeSalle, sounding rather formal.

'Please, do have a seat.'

Arthur DeSalle sat down rather awkwardly in one of several armchairs placed around the walls of the parlour, in the manner of a railway station waiting-room. Mrs. Tanner sat down beside him.

'I can see you are new to our establishment, sir,' said the woman, with a broad smile, 'and I don't believe I know your lady friend,' – Sarah Tanner shook her head – 'but we keep a decent house. And we do our best to oblige our guests, so – let me say it plainly, sir – now that you've found us, there's no need to be shy. There! I've said it; we keep things all frank and natural, here, sir; that's our way.'

'Indeed?' said DeSalle, a slight quaver in his voice.

'Of course. Now, how can we oblige you this evening? A glass of something, perhaps?'

'No, thank you, I don't think so.'

'Well then, what *can* we do, sir?'

Arthur DeSalle hesitated.

'Well,' he said at last, 'I should like to see a girl . . .'

'Of course, sir.'

'A girl who does not object to . . .'

Arthur DeSalle's words failed him, but he glanced rather deliberately at Sarah Tanner as he spoke, and the intimation was not lost on his hostess.

'Mixed company?' said the woman. 'Of course, sir; nothing could be easier. Now, are you sure you wouldn't fancy a glass of fizz, while you wait, sir? Or perhaps for your friend?'

'Well, perhaps I might,' replied DeSalle.

'There, sir! That's nice; that's natural. I won't be a moment, sir,' said the woman, as she quit the room. 'Do make yourself comfortable. I'll bring down a couple of our girls; you can choose who's the most agreeable.'

Mrs. Tanner waited until the woman was out of ear-shot, before whispering to her companion.

'"Oh, I should like a girl who would not object terribly to . . . to . . . to . . ."' she said, teasing.

'Sarah, please, I am doing my best,' replied Arthur DeSalle, blushing scarlet. 'It is not my custom to frequent such places.'

'And the champagne will cost you double,' she added.

'I think,' said Arthur DeSalle, 'that is the least of our worries.'

—

The bedroom, upon the second floor at the rear of the house, was small, no more than ten square feet, decorated in dark, rather plain fashion: an oak wainscoting around the walls, and plain red paper above, the floor merely the polished boards. An iron bed, with pristine white sheets, dominated the room, and a large mirror, set in an ornate gold frame, was fixed upon the wall directly facing the bed. The girl who led Sarah Tanner and Arthur DeSalle inside was about eighteen years or so, wearing a dress of red cotton.

'Here we are then,' she said.

'Here we are then . . .' echoed Arthur DeSalle.

The girl chuckled at her client's patent discomfort. 'Louisa, sir. You forgotten already? Can I get anything? Are you hungry? How about some more fizz, or some oysters? We can have 'em sent up.'

'No, thank you.'

'How about you?' added the girl, turning to Sarah Tanner. 'You can take your hat off, can't you?'

'Yes,' she replied. 'I suppose I can, now.'

The girl glanced at Sarah Tanner's face, as she removed the veil. She had expected bruises, or the scars of smallpox; but there was nothing out of the ordinary. Sarah Tanner, for her part, cast a telling glance in Arthur DeSalle's direction.

'She's pretty, your friend,' said the girl, addressing DeSalle once more. 'You'd better tell us what you fancy then.'

'If you could take off your dress, ah, Louisa . . .' said Arthur DeSalle, hesitantly.

The girl said, immediately turning her back, 'That's more like it, sir. You undo me, then, eh?'

DeSalle coughed. Nonetheless, he undid the dozen buttons that ran the length of the girl's back. Unembarrassed, she shuffled her arms free from the sleeves, revealing a white chemise and the outline of her stays beneath. She sat down on the bed, briskly pulled down the flannel petticoat that the waist of the dress had held in place, and finally took off the dress itself.

'Now, ah, if you would just stand up . . . facing my . . . facing my friend,' said Arthur DeSalle.

'Stand up?' said the girl with a coquettish smile, 'I hope this ain't nothing too peculiar.'

'I'm sorry, my dear,' said Sarah Tanner, 'but I'm afraid it is.'

The girl frowned. But before she could reply, she felt Arthur DeSalle grab her hands, pulling them behind her back, and looping a length of cord around her wrists.

'Here!' she protested. 'That ain't what I—'

Her protests were cut short, however, by Sarah Tanner bringing the blade of a pocket-knife close to the girl's confused face.

'If you scream,' she said, her voice stone cold, 'I will have to use this on your tongue. If you help us, and give me no reason, we'll be on our way, and no harm done.'

Warily, the girl nodded her head.

'Good girl. Now, I am looking for a friend of mine, by the name of Norah. They brought her here last night.'

—

'I cannot believe that I allowed myself to be drawn into this wretched business,' said Arthur DeSalle in a whisper, as he ascended the narrow gas-lit stairs.

'Why?' murmured Sarah Tanner.

'We are burgling a bawdy-house, for heaven's sake,' whispered DeSalle. 'And I have just left a young woman downstairs bound and gagged. I should think my reasons were quite plain.'

'I know some who would pay for the privilege.'

DeSalle blushed once more. 'I hardly think it amusing.'

'Nor do I. And I hardly think you needed to apologise to her so fulsomely. But I am sure she will remember you kindly when they untie her. In any case, hush, we are there.'

The stairs had come to an end upon a narrow landing, in the attic of the house. There was a solitary door, with a bolt drawn shut. Sarah Tanner opened it slowly, and cautiously crept inside.

It was an attic room, the roof sloping at a sharp angle upon one side. There was no light, save that which came in from the landing. Nonetheless, even in the semi-darkness, it was possible to make out a bare mattress laid on the floor, and the figure of a girl curled upon it.

'Is that her?' asked Arthur DeSalle.

'God help us, yes,' muttered Sarah Tanner. 'You wait outside. Keep watch.'

Arthur DeSalle nodded, whilst Sarah Tanner crept into the room.

'Norah . . . Norah, wake up.'

'Please,' mumbled Norah Smallwood, wearily, 'please, have pity, won't you? I ain't done nothing. Just let me be.'

Mrs. Tanner crouched down beside the mattress.

'Norah, it's me.'

Norah Smallwood opened her eyes wide. For a second she seemed uncertain as to whether she might still be in the depths of a dream.

Then she threw her arms around Sarah Tanner's neck and burst into tears.

'I'm a sight, ain't I?' exclaimed Norah Smallwood, as her sobs finally subsided.

Sarah Tanner peered at the girl's face. It was bruised and puffed, its natural symmetry distorted by swollen flesh.

'It'll heal up, don't worry. We'll take care of you.'

Norah bowed her head.

'Too late for that, I reckon. I swear, missus, I didn't know who he was. I swear I didn't know nothing.'

'I know, Norah. You don't have to explain.'

'No, but I thought you were done for, missus. Honest. And then they brought us here. So I told 'em everything, about Georgie and you and all. I'm sorry; I know it weren't right, but I thought you was dead. And he kept thumping me, and the other one, he watched, all the while, like he was at a play or something. So I told 'em. And that other one, he just watched, even when he . . .'

Norah's voice broke, as she rubbed her tear-stained cheeks.

'I hadn't never done it before, missus,' she said, almost inaudible, her voice trembling. 'But I couldn't stop him, could I? And the other one, he watched us all the while.'

'Hush,' said Sarah Tanner. 'Come on, get up, unless you want to stay here?'

Norah shook her head. Unsteadily, she scrambled to her feet.

'Now,' said Mrs. Tanner, forcefully. 'Help me out of this dress.'

'The dress?' said Norah.

'My friend Arthur's on the landing. You can trust him. If you put on the dress, and the veil, he can take you back out; just keep quiet and stand up straight and they'll think you're me – or, at least, the same girl he came in with. There's a carriage waiting; he'll take you somewhere safe.'

'I don't understand,' said Norah Smallwood. 'What about you?'

'I've borrowed a dress,' said Mrs. Tanner, putting down Louisa's red cotton frock which she carried with her, bundled under her arm.

'I mean, how will you get out?'

'I'll manage.'

CHAPTER THIRTY-SEVEN

Sarah Tanner waited on the attic landing, listening to the footsteps of Arthur DeSalle and Norah Smallwood descending the stairs. The house, despite its warren of corridors and rooms, was remarkably quiet, its business admirably conducted. The only noise to be heard was the occasional discreet opening or closing of the panelled oak doors that led to individual rooms, doors which were heavy enough to muffle any sound that might come from within. And if there was an occasional lapse – if a single scream or guttural moan escaped – the noise was so quickly stifled by the muted respectability of the establishment, that it was impossible to distinguish its origin, or, indeed, tell whether it signified pleasure or pain.

Sarah Tanner shuddered; the thought of Norah Smallwood at the mercy of Bert Jones, an object of Stephen Symes's amusement, made her stomach turn.

The footsteps diminished. She peered down the gaslit stairs but could see nothing. She guessed they had reached the ground floor.

She pictured the *grande dame* bidding her new client good night; then, no doubt, the doorman would hold out his hand, in expectation of sixpence or a shilling.

She should have mentioned that to Arthur. Could Norah hold her nerve?

The seconds seemed to turn into minutes.

What if Arthur let something slip? It would not take much.

Then it came, the sound of the door opening; the distant click of the bolts being loosed; then the door slamming shut.

Had they done it?

The house seemed eerily quiet.

They had.

She smiled to herself. Now, she pondered, there was just the small matter of her own departure.

In fact, she had a plan. She had foreseen that there would be, at the very least, one man guarding the street door. And, more than likely, there were others, not far distant, who would come running, in the event of any trouble. For that reason, she had ruled out the possibility of simply fleeing the building and forcing an exit: there was no telling where that might lead, even if she were armed with a pistol. She had foreseen, too, that all the windows would be bolted; for it was not unknown for certain young gentlemen to attempt an ungentlemanly exit after taking their pleasure. The one remaining possibility, therefore, was to escape through the front door, unnoticed. She knew as much before she had set foot inside the house.

She held her breath, and waited.

———

Ralph Grundy, standing in the shadows, upon the corner of Avery Row, watched Arthur DeSalle's carriage roll by, its window blinds drawn up. Beside him, a boy lolled against the nearby wall, a street Arab no more than ten years of age, dressed in a fustian suit that appeared not so much tattered as all but shredded, his hair thick and matted, his feet unshod.

'You saw the house he came out of?' said Ralph Grundy.

'I saw it, guv'nor,' replied the boy. 'I knows it and all.'

'And you know what you're a-doing?'

'I ain't fresh from the farm,' replied the boy, mildly indignant. 'I knows it; I'll do it, I told you. Long as you pay up.'

'You'll get your two bob. Go on then,' urged Ralph Grundy. 'And remember, you run like the Devil and say nothing to no-one.'

The boy tilted his head in a rather cock-sure fashion, as if to suggest that *his* abilities in the running department were not in question. Glancing over his shoulder, he sloped off along the street. He allowed himself another glance, upon reaching the middle of the road, a short distance from the house, doubtless accustomed to watching out for Her Majesty's Police, even at the best of times. Then, without any further ado, he picked out a handful of sharp stones from his jacket pocket, and, one by one, flung them in swift succession at the brothel's upstairs windows.

The boy was a good shot, and the glass shattered in every pane it struck. For the most part it simply left a jagged hole where it flew inside, although in one instance the window smashed entirely.

The sound of splintering glass echoed along the street.

'Peelers!' shouted the boy, at the top of his voice. 'Hook it! It's the Peelers!'

And, with that, he ran like the Devil.

———

Sarah Tanner struggled to contain a smile. For the quiet which had reigned upon the stairs was suddenly overthrown by a hubbub of confused voices, doors opening and closing, exclamations and curses.

Hurrying down to join the chaos, she found that a crowd seemed instantly to have formed upon each landing. It comprised a mix of both men and women, equally eager to quit the building – or, at least, not be discovered inside it in a state of deshabille. The men seemed bent upon making hasty adjustments to their dress, tugging at collar-less shirts whilst attempting to put on a jacket; fiddling with trouser buttons whilst running down the stairs. The women, on the other hand, seemed worse afflicted as to their dress, most of them wearing little more than a cotton shift and petticoats. She threw herself into the confusion, and ran down the stairs with the rest.

The doorman, it turned out, had already yielded the front door. For the *grande dame* needed his help in coralling the girls, or, at least, providing the re-assurance that *they* need not rush out on to the street, or to the back door. The clients seemed to accept no reassurance whatsoever and, whether silently scurrying from the house, or bombastically protesting at being so heinously *imposed upon*, they all seemed of a mind to depart. Sarah Tanner fell in amongst them, idly wondering how many had excused themselves from paying.

She was almost at the door, when a young man in a lounge suit barged past, pushing her back. Then, before she could move, she found her way suddenly blocked, by a man coming in the opposite direction, entering the house from the street.

'Well, I'll be blowed,' he said, staring Sarah Tanner full in the face.

It was Bert Jones.

Mrs. Tanner cursed, as a smile spread over the big

man's face. Doubtless the footman had returned to torment Norah Smallwood. For a second, she contemplated flying at him with her pocket-knife. But it was only a small blade, and Jones, she was sure, was too fast and too strong for her. If nothing else, she would be caught in the struggle. She stepped backwards into the hall. There was still sufficient confusion for her to push through the mêlée and so she ran towards the back of the house.

With no basement, the kitchen was simply down a few steps at the rear of the building. She had already passed the cook in the hall; the room was empty, with only a couple of pots left simmering on the stove, and the pervasive salty aroma of oysters. For the second time in as many days, she prayed that the back door might be open.

Instead, she found it locked.

Keys?

She saw them in an instant; hanging from a hook by the door through which she had entered. And right beside them stood Bert Jones.

'They always said you had nine lives, gal,' said Jones. 'Lor! I would have sworn you was a dead 'un and here you are again. Wait 'til Her Majesty hears about this. I reckon she'll give me a bleedin' medal.'

Sarah Tanner pulled out the knife from her pocket, brandishing it. The big man, however, merely laughed.

'You want to play that game, gal? With that little pig-sticker?'

Bert Jones shook his head. There was a carving knife lying on the table beside the door. He picked it up and wiped the greasy blade upon his sleeve.

'Well, do you then?' he said.

She looked about her. Bert, she was sure, would

stay by the door, in case she attempted to run past him. But there would soon be others behind him; and then she'd be done.

What else was there?

The footman had taken the knife that lay upon the table; the pots of water – no, too heavy to lift; not as a weapon, at least. Nothing upon the polished flags of the floor, a hint of disinfectant mixing with the scent of the oysters.

There. A narrow door to her right.

Sarah Tanner ran across the room, pulled the door open and dashed through, slamming it behind her.

Bert Jones chuckled to himself. He sauntered casually across the room, and stood by the door.

'Now, that weren't too clever, was it, my gal?'

Mrs. Tanner caught her breath. She understood Bert Jones's crowing, as the door led nowhere; or, to be more particular, it led to the pantry. The only light was that which seeped under the door from the gas-lit kitchen, and, around her, in the darkness, lay the household's cleaning stuff, mops and buckets, and rags and bottles.

'Now, why don't you come out, like a good gal, eh?' said Bert Jones, his voice booming.

Sarah Tanner coughed. The air in the pantry had a peculiar scent. What was the smell? The same as on the floor.

'Or shall I come and get you? How'd you like that? Is that what you fancy, gal? Some rough-and-tumble?'

Bert Jones, apparently unprepared to wait for an answer, swung the door open with considerable force. He stood silhouetted in the doorway, the knife poised in his hand, a self-satisfied grin upon his face.

'Now, that won't get you nowhere, will it?' he said, finding her crouched, her back to the wall, her blade raised. 'Drop the chiv and maybe I'll go a bit easy on you, eh?'

She slowly stood upright. Her eyes fixed on Bert Jones, and she let the pocket-knife drop from her fingers, and clatter to the ground. Jones, in turn, visibly relaxed, lowering the kitchen knife.

'Now,' said the footman, 'I reckon we might have some fun, you and me, at least before we call it a day.'

'No. I don't think so.'

'I never said you had a choice, gal.'

If Sarah Tanner had any riposte, she did not make it. For Bert reached forward, to grab hold of her. She, in turn, twisted to one side, and swung her left arm in an arc towards Jones's face. He laughed, at first, as she lashed out. There seemed no chance she might even scratch him as he made to grab her hand. But Bert Jones did not see the unstoppered bottle which she had kept concealed in the folds of her dress – not, at least, until its contents splashed his face, by which time it was far too late.

The liquid set the big man's skin burning, as hot as if it were actually aflame; his eyes suddenly turned raw and bloody, transfixed by a thousand burning needles.

Bert Jones screamed, clutching his face, tottering backwards.

Sarah Tanner saw her chance, and ran.

'Damn you, you bitch,' screamed Bert Jones, his voice hysterical with pain. 'I'll gut you alive.'

In a trice, she had the keys off the hook. Bert Jones staggered towards her, blinded, swiping wildly with the knife. She ran for the door; the keys seemed to tumble through her fingers. There was a bolt; she pulled it back.

There would only be one chance at the lock.

There was an audible click as the key turned.

'I'm damned if you will,' said Sarah Tanner, slamming the door behind her, and turning the lock.

———

'Lor, I thought you was done for, missus,' exclaimed Ralph Grundy, as Mrs. Tanner climbed into the waiting hansom.

'Near enough,' she replied, breathless. 'Lord! Have the man drive, won't you?'

Ralph Grundy pulled the check-string, and the cab set off in the direction of Bond Street.

'What's that on your dress?'

Mrs. Tanner looked down. The purple silk was bleached almost white, splashed down the front.

'Chloride of lime,' she replied. 'Look at it! Ruined. Arthur will kill me.'

Ralph Grundy frowned, perplexed. He could not fathom why Sarah Tanner's expression broke into a sly smile.

CHAPTER THIRTY-EIGHT

Some two days after Norah Smallwood's liberation, Arthur DeSalle strolled through a region of the great metropolis with which he was unfamiliar. The sky was a rather leaden grey and the road – by the name of Guildford Street – seemed to grow worse as he progressed eastwards, the surface uneven and marred by pot-holes, collecting the morning's rainfall in pools of murky water. As he walked, the houses changed too. In the west, upon the fringes of Bloomsbury, they were the abodes of middling to well-to-do families, where the windows sparkled and the steps were polished. Past the Foundling Hospital, as he drew nearer the Gray's Inn Road, the buildings gave way to lodging-houses with dull somnolent casements and dreary sooted bricks, that looked as if no-one much cared for them, nor for their inhabitants. Finally he came to his destination, a narrow artery by the name of Calthorpe Street, which terminated in an unpaved patch of ground, surrounded on one side by builders' yards, and upon the other by the high wall of the Middlesex House of Correction. It was outside the final property that he paused, checked the address he had written down, and then rang the second of three bells.

A sash window slid open above; he stepped back and peered up.

'The door's not locked,' said Sarah Tanner, looking down on to the street. 'Come up.'

—❦—

'When I said I would help you, Sarah,' said Arthur DeSalle, glancing round the little room, 'I had something better in mind.'

'Jermyn Street?'

'No,' replied DeSalle. 'But the place is so terribly bare – so out-of-the-way.'

'If you recall, Arthur, I did not have much to bring with me. Besides, it's clean; there is room for us both; it will do for now.'

'It is hardly a decent district,' muttered DeSalle, gazing out of the window where the grim prison's buildings dominated the view. 'What on earth made you choose it? Surely the money was sufficient for something better?'

'No-one will find us here, Arthur, not by chance, at least. In any case, we won't impose upon your generosity for long, you have my word.'

'I am glad to hear it. Good God, if Arabella were to find out, my life would not be worth living.'

Sarah Tanner said nothing.

'Well, how is the girl?' asked Arthur DeSalle.

'Norah? She's well enough. I didn't want to wake her.'

Arthur DeSalle nodded. 'I am glad she is safe, at least. I cannot believe that born Englishmen can be such savages. Sarah, I am sure if you were to explain matters to the police—'

'No,' said Sarah Tanner, firmly, 'I cannot risk that. Her Majesty has too many friends. And I have taken too many chances already.'

'Then, if you truly believe that, forgive me, Sarah, I wonder if you should let this wretched affair rest.'

'I swear, Arthur, you sound like Ralph.'

'The old man?'

'Job's comforter. Still, he brought me a letter this morning. Perhaps you might care to read it.'

As she spoke she reached down to a rather scratched walnut card-table that sat beside her chair, and handed Arthur DeSalle a single sheet of paper.

Hillmarton Park, 21st April

Dear Mrs. Richards,

It will surprise you, I am sure, to receive this letter. In truth, it astonishes me that I must, by constraint of circumstances, appeal to a woman about whose character, company and morals I harbour the gravest misgivings. Nonetheless, I place some hope in the belief that you have, hitherto, acted in the best interests of my Miss Fulbrook. Your true motives are your own affair. But if your desire is to thwart the schemes of Mr. Cedric Hawkes, then know this – we are of like mind!

It was Mr. Hawkes who persuaded Mr. Ferntower that you were a fraud. I expect you surmised as much. But it was I who prevented the Scotland Yard detective from effecting your capture – I wonder, did you guess that? An hour before you arrived, I heard Mr. Ferntower arranging the business with Mr. Murdoch; I said nothing to Miss Fulbrook; I thought it best not to alarm her. Instead, I made sure that we collided upon the stairs and I made certain that you had a means of escape. Had you chosen the front door, you would have been apprehended.

I wonder, did you contemplate why I should act in such a reckless fashion? Did you ask yourself why I should assist *you*?

In short, because I believe Cedric Hawkes to be an out-and-out villain *who must not be allowed to marry Miss Fulbrook*. My certainty is not founded simply upon the conversation to which you made me party, though that gave me good cause for concern. Nor, indeed, the manner in which he attempted to lay a trap for you, an act quite unworthy of a gentleman. There were – there are – two further proofs. First, since the day you spoke to Mr. Hawkes, *we have been watched*. There is a young man, who passes along the road, in the dress of a common labourer, and I am certain he is Hawkes's creature. He even follows me to the receiving-house; I am thankful the clerk can be trusted, or I could not write. Second – this is the most telling – *the wedding has been brought forward*. Mr. Hawkes and Miss Fulbrook are to be married *in four days*. There will be no banns; there will be no guests, save Mr. Ferntower, myself, and Mrs. Hawkes, his mother. A licence has been obtained; a church in the country has been reserved for the purpose – though its location has not been vouchsafed to the bride-to-be – and I am to be dismissed as soon as a honeymoon commences, albeit with a gratuity. The shameful pretext is some foreign business which will entail Hawkes's prolonged absence, and 'it is easier to have it done sooner rather than later' – as if a wedding at short notice might be considered convenient, let alone proper!

I write to you again, therefore, because I do

not know where else to turn. Mr. Hawkes is in such favour with my employer; there is nothing I can say against him. Moreover, the termination of my employment will give any complaint the appearance of mere spite. The police? I fear Mr. Murdoch has his suspicions of my action upon that fateful night; I cannot risk my own disgrace. Miss Fulbrook herself? She lies beside me in such a condition that I do not believe she can resist her guardian's will. Of one thing, I am quite certain. Nothing good can come of this wretched 'marriage' which now resembles, to my mind, a species of abduction.

What can be done? I do not know. But I have observed you, Mrs. Richards, and I have seen reserves of ingenuity and courage which are uncommon in our sex. I beg you, therefore, if there *is* anything to be done then, for pity's sake, you must do it. I fear there is no-one else who can save Miss Fulbrook from ruin.

Yours respectfully,
Lydia Payne

P.S. The address for your reply is Murray's Furniture Warehouse, Upper Holloway; I trust the clerk. *Do not* write to the house.

'She has a dramatic turn of phrase,' said Arthur DeSalle. 'It seems Symes is determined to marry the wretched girl.'

'Unless someone prevents it,' replied Sarah Tanner.

'Perhaps if her guardian can be made to see sense about Symes,' remarked DeSalle.

Sarah Tanner smiled. 'I knew you'd help, Arthur. I knew it.'

Arthur DeSalle frowned. 'One moment, I never said that. I only came here to see how your friend Norah was faring.'

'You know Symes. If you told Ferntower the truth about him, he would listen to you.'

'Why on earth should he?'

'Because he's a linen-draper – a successful one, but a tradesman all the same – and you come from one of the most respected families in London. You could tell him the moon was made of cheese, he'd still be grateful to make your acquaintance.'

'That does not mean I can tell the fellow who should marry his ward.'

'If you told him what you know about Symes, it might.'

'If I do that, Sarah, I risk my own reputation. Have you forgotten that we met at a baccarat table?'

'I thought you were done with gaming?' said Sarah Tanner.

'I am, I assure you. But this is a man who disowned his own son! Can I trust him to respect my confidence?'

'You saw what Symes did to Norah. Do you think his wife would fare much better?'

'Surely there is another way?'

Sarah Tanner paused. 'Symes only wants her money; there is nothing more to it. I suppose if she were to marry another man . . .'

'I do not propose to forego my wedding to Arabella, Sarah, even for a good cause.'

'I meant John Ferntower. I think she might be sweet on him. In fact, I am almost sure of it.'

'I thought you told me he was a destitute wastrel; that he drinks and has a mania for gaming.'

'Well, the lesser of two evils, perhaps? I pity her, in either case.'

Arthur DeSalle shook his head, as if conceding defeat. 'Very well,' he said. 'Good Lord! I will try.'

CHAPTER THIRTY-NINE

That evening, for the second time in as many days, a carriage containing Arthur DeSalle and Sarah Tanner drove through the streets of the metropolis. There were, however, some differences in the nature of the expedition: namely that it was barely dusk as the coach set off from the Gray's Inn Road; that the coachman was none other than Ralph Grundy; and that the direction was not towards the heart of Mayfair, but outwards into the suburbs, through the back-streets of Islington, at last coming towards the prosperous avenues of Upper Holloway.

Arthur DeSalle looked rather uneasy, as Ralph Grundy made the final turn on to Hillmarton Park.

'You are sure this Grundy fellow has a steady hand?' he asked, anxiously. 'I swear, he nearly sent us over on that last corner. I should never have let you persuade me; I could easily have jobbed a man with the carriage.'

Sarah Tanner smiled. 'Ralph's safe enough.'

'Is my neck safe enough, Sarah? That is the question. Good Lord! I still do not know what I can say to the man about Symes.'

'That he's a fraud, a procurer of women, the most repulsive foulest ruffian you have ever encountered—'

'I am sure he speaks well of you, too. You are not planning to come in with me, I hope? I doubt I can persuade Mr. Ferntower of your virtue as well.'

'No, I don't suppose you can work miracles.'

Arthur DeSalle smiled, relaxing a little. 'There are times I miss your company, Sarah.'

Mrs. Tanner ignored the comment, peering through the side of the window blind.

'I won't come in,' she said. 'I'll wait outside, in case there is any—'

Sarah Tanner suddenly fell silent, as she looked out on to the darkened street. The carriage was now no more than a couple of hundred yards distant from Mr. Ferntower's residence, and, from the carriage window, she could just make out two figures standing upon the front step, shaking hands. One was Mr. Ferntower himself, his face illuminated by the gas-light. The second stood in silhouette, as he bid the owner of the house farewell. He was a substantial individual, whose broad body and roughly hewn features were unmistakeable, even in shadow. In fact, even if his uniform had not given him away, she would have known him in an instant: it was the policeman – the very man who killed George Phelps.

'In case there is any what?' said Arthur DeSalle.

'Hush!' replied Sarah Tanner, banging on the roof of the carriage with her fist. 'Ralph, for pity's sake, don't stop – drive past!'

'Missus?' came the reply, muffled.

'Drive past! Can't you see who's there? Use your eyes!'

'Perhaps his eye-sight is not what it was,' suggested DeSalle. 'But whatever is it?'

'The Devil himself,' replied Mrs. Tanner, as the

carriage sped past 42, Hillmarton Park. She waited until the house was no longer visible, then pulled the check-string and called out for Ralph Grundy to stop. Once the carriage drew to a halt, she opened the door. Ralph Grundy, meanwhile, clambered down from his perch.

'You may as well stay in there, missus,' said the old man. 'Let me tie 'em up.'

It was only a matter of seconds before the carriage door opened wide and Ralph Grundy himself, wrapped in a heavy coachman's coat, climbed inside.

'Room for one more, Your Lordship?' said Ralph, squeezing beside Arthur DeSalle, to the latter's astonishment. Sarah Tanner could not help but smile to herself, watching her companion's discomfort.

'Did you see him?' asked Mrs. Tanner.

'Aye, I saw him.'

'And did he see you?'

'Reckon not, missus,' replied the old man. 'At least, I don't reckon he saw my face, which amounts to the same thing. Probably wouldn't know me if he did, seeing as how it was you who squared up to him that night.'

'For pity's sake, who on earth was it that you saw?' exclaimed Arthur DeSalle.

'The Peeler,' said Ralph Grundy.

'The man who killed your friend Phelps?'

'But that ain't all,' continued Ralph, 'not by a long chalk. He was coming down the steps of that there house, and your Mr. Ferntower was there, shaking his hand, waving him goodbye, friendly as you like. What does it mean, missus?'

'It means we've had a wasted journey,' replied Sarah Tanner gloomily. 'There's no point pleading with Mr. Ferntower; none whatsoever.'

'You think Ferntower is in league with this fellow?' said Arthur DeSalle. 'What then? That he had his own sister killed?'

'Well, I reckon that blue-bottle weren't collecting for no benevolent fund, eh?' muttered Ralph Grundy, with a rather cynical glance at the man beside him.

'Ralph, hush,' said Sarah Tanner, frowning. 'Let me think.'

Ralph Grundy reluctantly fell silent, whilst Arthur DeSalle glared back at him.

'It must mean one of two things,' said Mrs. Tanner. 'The first is bad enough – that Michael Ferntower is in league with Symes; that they arranged together to have his sister killed, to remove any obstacle to the marriage, and the policeman is their agent.'

'What is the second possibility, then?' asked DeSalle.

'Worse,' said Sarah Tanner, a hint of despair in her voice.

'How can it be?'

'Because it means all I've done in this affair is to make things worse for myself; to lose the shop, to make Norah suffer, all for nothing.'

'You ain't making sense, missus,' interjected Ralph Grundy.

'What if,' she continued, 'Symes told me the truth. What if he knows nothing about the policeman or Emma Ferntower's death? What if her own brother had her killed, to ensure the marriage, and that is what Georgie saw – and why he died?'

'Do you truly think Symes could be innocent?' asked DeSalle. 'You were only just telling me—'

'Never mind that,' said Sarah Tanner. 'It is too soon for conjecture. Ralph, he wasn't coming this way, I take it?'

'No, missus. I reckon he was going back to the Holloway Road.'

'Then turn round. If he keeps walking, we'll catch up with him. When you see him, go past a good distance, and turn off a short way on the nearest road, so I can get out unnoticed.'

'Sarah,' said DeSalle, anxiously, 'what are you proposing?'

'I shall follow him; that is what any respectable detective would do, don't you think?'

'I'll come with you,' said DeSalle. 'We can expose him; challenge the brute!'

'With what, precisely? In any case, that is precisely what I want to avoid. No, I want to see what he's up to. And there are some places I can go, in this plain get-up, Arthur, that you can't.'

Arthur DeSalle shrugged, involuntarily fingering the fine material of his suit. 'I could still—'

'No,' she said emphatically. 'You've done enough, Arthur. I don't want to drag you in deeper, I really don't, I swear.'

'But he has seen your face afore, missus, or are you forgetting?' said Ralph Grundy.

'I haven't forgotten a thing, Ralph,' said Sarah Tanner. 'Not a damn thing. Now do as I say.'

CHAPTER FORTY

It did not take long for Ralph Grundy to spy his quarry, and drive past, according to his mistress's instructions.

Sarah Tanner, for her part, let Ralph Grundy drive off with a reluctant Arthur DeSalle, then cautiously began her pursuit along the Holloway Road, walking along the broad gas-lit pavement, some couple of hundred yards distant from the policeman, upon the opposite side of the thoroughfare.

Even though night had fallen, the road itself – one of the principal routes leading out of the metropolis – was still busy with the hubbub of evening traffic. From omnibuses laden with tired clerks, to the occasional solitary broker, riding his own steed homewards, much of the traffic was of the City variety, leavened only by the occasional cart or wagon. The pavements, too, were still largely the province of City men, men confined by day in gloomy offices, walking with the determination engendered by the promise of an evening meal and warm hearth. The policeman, however, was not difficult to make out in the crowd; his uniform gave him away at every turn, as he kept walking, against the tide of workers.

Sarah Tanner wondered where he might be bound.

But all her thoughts kept returning to the night George Phelps was killed. In her mind she involuntarily pictured George Phelps's face.

What was it about his face? Not merely the pain she had seen in his eyes; it was the dreadful fear; fear of what was to come.

She peered at the policeman, pushing past a pair of women upon the opposite pavement, and contemplated – not for the first time – whether she could truly bring herself to kill a man.

It was almost an hour later that the policeman chose to halt his progress, just past the Angel toll-gate, where every carriage and waggon in London seemed to wait upon the toll-house's elderly gate-keeper. It was not the toll, however, which caused the policeman to slow down – the pavement being mercifully free of any form of taxation – but what lay beyond. For the Angel public-house formed the terminus for more than half a dozen omnibuses, stationed upon the road, outside the old coach-stables. And it was beside one such vehicle, a green 'Favourite' bound towards the City Road, that the policeman paused. He spoke briefly to the conductor, then climbed aboard, just as the driver started the bus moving.

Sarah Tanner hurriedly looked about the busy junction; she could not catch up, nor, in fact, could she risk climbing inside the bus, even if she were able – there was little doubt in her mind that the policeman would remember her. She began to regret dismissing Arthur DeSalle and Ralph Grundy. There was only one option left open to her: a hansom waiting at the nearby cab-stand, and a rather shabby-looking waterman half-heartedly scrubbing the coat of the bay mare to which it was attached. Sarah Tanner dashed across the road.

'Where's the driver?' she said, with considerable urgency.

'He'll be along soon, missus,' said the waterman, glancing back at the public-house. 'Just having a little refreshment, if you get my drift.'

'Bring him out now, and tell him he can have a shilling on top of his fare, if he comes directly. And sixpence for you.'

The waterman raised his eyebrows, but ran off at a trot. Sarah Tanner, meanwhile, hastily counted the coins in her pocket and silently thanked the heavens for Arthur DeSalle's financial generosity.

The cabman arrived with remarkable rapidity.

'Where to then, missus?' he asked, as Mrs. Tanner climbed inside and closed the hansom's folding doors.

'There's a green Favourite going down the City Road. I need to catch up with it; then you can just follow on until I tell you.'

The cabman grinned. 'What's your game, then?'

Sarah Tanner pushed two shillings into the cabman's hand.

'I don't have time for your chaff. Will you drive or won't you?'

The cabman quietly pocketed the coins and drove off.

━━◆━━

The omnibus followed its pre-appointed route through the metropolis: along the City Road, then Old Street, London Wall, the Bank of England, and finally towards the Tower. The cabman, in fairness, showed considerable skill at keeping his distance without ostentatious stops or starts. But Sarah Tanner, for her part, grew increasingly nervous that the policeman had already disembarked, in the brief interval before the cab had caught up with the bus. It was only when the omnibus reached the Tower, and the last passengers climbed out, that she was relieved to see the blue uniform amongst them.

'Lor, is it the copper?' asked the cabman, with the familiarity common to certain members of his class.

'My old man,' she replied. 'He said he was on fixed point, but I knew he'd done the hours. He's keeping company with a bloody kitchen-maid; thinks I don't know it.'

'Awful shame,' said the cabman. 'If I had one like you at home, I wouldn't go looking, I tell you.'

Sarah Tanner merely smiled politely at the compliment, as she pulled open the hansom's doors and stepped into the street. The policeman had already set off into the narrow lanes that lay towards Fenchurch Street.

'If you ever fancy a reliable sort of chap . . .' said the cabman. But his fare was already out of ear-shot. For she had some idea of the alleys and yards that lay in the vicinity of the Tower and the Blackwall Railway, and feared her pursuit could come to nothing.

The streets themselves were of the commercial type particular to the City of London – bustling during the day, but utterly lifeless by night. At first, the only figures Sarah Tanner could make out were a man with a cart in the distance, and a couple of drunken sailors from the nearby docks – identifiable as sea-faring men by the distinctive broad-brimmed hats and flared canvas trousers of their trade; visibly drunk by the irregularity of their gait, and reliance upon each other's shoulders. She hurried on to the next junction in the road, and cautiously turned the corner. After a few anxious seconds, she saw the policeman's distinctive figure. He had only gone so far as a small public-house, no more than a hundred yards distant, by the name of the Lord Nelson. At that very moment, he stepped inside.

The place was too small to follow him; she would be seen in an instant.

There was, however, an alley almost opposite, into which the public's gas-lamp, projecting above the door, cast no light.

She resolved to wait.

After an hour or so, Sarah Tanner's will-power began to flag. For the alley smelt of beer and more unsavoury fluids; the ground was muddy under her feet; and the night air had begun to turn cold. Moreover, the Lord Nelson was an old house, its windows made up of bullion glass panels, impenetrable to the eye. In truth, she had almost resolved to abandon her vigil, when the door to the public opened and the policeman came out, accompanied by a woman. Sarah Tanner wondered whether her company had been paid for. She was a good-looking creature in her early forties, with full features and curled brown hair, tied back by ribbons. But there was something about her manner, the way in which she held the policeman's arm, that seemed too easy and relaxed. She knew the man well, whatever her trade; Mrs. Tanner was sure of it.

Letting the pair walk on a good way, she stepped out from the alley, minded to follow the policeman once more, hopeful that she might, at least, find his name or lodgings. But two men stepped out of the public at the same moment, the two sailors she had seen before, quite unaware that they blocked the rest of the road from her view.

'Halloa, my lovely,' said the first man, slurring every syllable.

'Ain't she a peach?' said the second, slapping his friend upon the back. The smell of liquor wafted through the air.

'What'll you do for a half-crown, gal?' continued the first. 'There's me and my pal here, eh?'

Sarah Tanner stepped back, pulling out the knife she kept in her pocket.

'Get out of my way, you fools, or, so help me, I'll gut the pair of you where you stand.'

The first man stood open-mouthed. The second merely laughed. Nonetheless, they both staggered to one side, awake enough to be wary of the blade, as she pushed past.

It was too late. There was no sign of the policeman or the woman.

Sarah Tanner swore.

And if she had looked behind her, she would have seen two members of the merchant marine blush.

It was midnight when John Ferntower rose from his bed to answer a knock at his door. He was astonished to find Sarah Tanner standing upon the landing outside his rooms.

'Do you know what hour it is?' he said.

'Will you invite me in?' asked Mrs. Tanner.

'If I must.'

'Yes, you must.'

John Ferntower gave way, and ushered his unexpected guest inside.

'I presume you have some news? I have heard nothing from Elizabeth.'

'Most likely because she is scared out of her wits.

Symes is having the house watched; and your father is determined to have her married to him within the week.'

'Within the week?' echoed Ferntower. 'God forbid. My father's an utter fool.'

'No, he's far worse than that,' said Sarah Tanner, with a sigh. 'But let us put that to one side for the moment.'

'Whatever do you mean? Forgive me, but why have you come at this ridiculous hour?'

'Do you love her?' asked Mrs. Tanner, ignoring the question. 'Your cousin – will you tell me at least that you love her?'

'Yes, you know it. I have told you before.'

'And she may love you?' continued Mrs. Tanner.

'In her last letter, she said as much . . . if circumstances were different . . .'

'Then, God forgive me, that will have to do. Get a pen and ink, Mr. Ferntower. We do not have much time.'

'To do what, may I ask?'

'To plan your cousin's elopement.'

CHAPTER FORTY-ONE

It was two o'clock in the morning when Sarah Tanner finally returned to the house in Calthorpe Street. She crept quietly up the hall steps to the first-floor landing, and turned her key in the lock with great care, anxious not to rouse any of her fellow tenants. But, upon entering the front parlour, she found Norah Smallwood was still awake, seated in front of the fire. As she opened the door, Norah jumped in surprise and reached out to grasp a solitary object that lay upon the nearby table. It was a kitchen knife, the metal dull and discoloured, but the blade sharp.

'It's me,' said Mrs. Tanner, as Norah turned hurriedly towards the door. 'You're safe enough. Put that away, won't you? I'll bolt the door.'

Norah Smallwood sighed in relief and replaced the knife on the table.

'You startled me, missus.'

'Only Arthur and Ralph know we're here, Norah, I promise you. Didn't Ralph tell you I'd be late back?'

'He was here until an hour ago, waiting for you,' replied Norah. 'Worried sick and all. Said he'd be back first thing in the morning. Never mind old bag-o'-bones – ain't you going to tell us what happened with the Peeler?'

'Nothing,' replied Mrs. Tanner in a rather dejected tone, sitting down opposite her. 'I followed him down to the river. He met a woman in a public near the Tower; a friend; someone he knew. Then I lost him.'

'But he's a pal of your Mr. Ferntower?'

'It would seem like it.'

Norah Smallwood fell silent. Sarah Tanner, meanwhile, seemed to grow thoughtful, before speaking once more.

'Norah – there's something I must ask you, if you're strong enough.'

Norah frowned, but nodded.

'That night at the Row,' continued Mrs. Tanner, 'you said something. You said that when they were . . . when they were hurting you, you told them everything, about Georgie—'

'I couldn't help it,' interjected Norah, her eyes immediately growing tearful. 'I swear I couldn't, missus!'

'Lord Almighty!' exclaimed Sarah Tanner, reaching forward and grasping Norah Smallwood's trembling hand in her own. 'If you think for a moment – for a second – I'd blame you for that! But there's something I need to know, all the same. Did you tell them that you weren't my cousin – that you met Georgie at the hotel?'

'I s'pose I must have,' said Norah. 'I reckon I did. I don't remember everything . . .'

'Hush,' said Mrs. Tanner, quietly, releasing Norah's hand from her own. 'I don't want you to remember. That's all I need to know. In any case, I'm here now. Why don't you go and get some sleep?'

Norah Smallwood rubbed her eyes. 'What about you?'

'I have to think things through,' said Sarah Tanner with a wry smile. 'A wedding takes some planning.'

'A wedding?'

'Miss Fulbrook and Mr. Ferntower. Although it won't be a society affair, rest assured.'

———

An hour or so after her conversation with Norah Smallwood, sleep crept over Sarah Tanner's weary body. Still seated before the fire, she closed her eyes.

Her mind wandered.

She dreamt of Jermyn Street.

She knew it was a dream; for she did not belong there, not any more. But Arthur DeSalle lay beside her, nonetheless, stretched out upon the bed they had shared; he lay there sound asleep. She watched him for what seemed like an eternity and an awful sense of longing began to creep over her; it was a dream – she knew it – but she would have it otherwise; she would make it real. She touched the loose fabric of his night-shirt, stroking his back. But he did not stir. Outside, the sounds of the street; the peel of distant bells.

What time was it?

She got up from the downy bed, and walked to the window. The faintest hint of the morning's early light shone through the gap between the trailing velvet curtains. Arthur DeSalle's old jacket lay casually draped over the chair, abandoned in haste the previous night; her dress lay beside it, a tear in the back where a hook had caught the fabric.

She took up the jacket and the paper fell loose from the pocket; a letter in a woman's hand.

She froze.

That moment was the end of her happiness.

———

Sarah Tanner awoke.

What time was it?

The room in Calthorpe Street had grown cold and dark, the fire extinguished.

The dream was still fresh in her mind's eye, the details of the room in Jermyn Street; those first days and nights she had spent with Arthur DeSalle. She knew that they had had moments of pleasure; joyful hours spent in each other's company; but there was something else, which tinged every memory with bitterness.

What was it?

Ah, yes.

She still recalled the words in the letter perfectly:

My Dear Mr. DeSalle,

Forgive the delay in my reply; I had to consult my heart, and the matters of the heart cannot be hurried. Last night, I was so pleased at being the object of your preference, I could hardly contain my emotions. Now, after calm and rational consideration, I can say truly that I feel much flattered by our proposal, and if my father makes no objection to our union – which he surely cannot – I shall esteem myself happy to have secured the affections of such a good and gentle man.

If you come tomorrow, make it at seven, and you may talk to Papa.

Your own,
Arabella

Sarah Tanner closed her eyes once more. But she did not sleep; and merely sat in the cold room, waiting for day-break.

At first light, she rekindled the fire; then she sat down at the table, took up paper, pen and ink, and began to compose a letter. When it was done, she addressed the envelope – to a certain Miss Lydia Payne, care of Murray's Furniture Warehouse, Upper Holloway.

Then she commenced writing another note entirely.

CHAPTER FORTY-TWO

The following day, as the noon-tide traffic queued on either side of the Islington toll-gate, Sarah Tanner sat in a private room on the upper floor of the Angel public-house. Arthur DeSalle sat beside her, sipping from a pot of porter; but it was not long before he rose from his seat and looked nervously out of the window.

'Do you think she will come?'

'I am certain of it,' replied Sarah Tanner. 'Do stop fretting.'

Arthur DeSalle scowled. 'It is not a case of "fretting". Good Lord, Sarah, I am only here because you begged me to help.'

'Of course. I'm sorry, truly.'

Arthur DeSalle's reply was pre-empted by a knock at the door.

'Come in,' said Mrs. Tanner, firmly.

The door opened to reveal Lydia Payne, dressed in the same plain mourning dress which Sarah Tanner had first seen at the coroner's inquest. She wondered idly whether her governess's salary permitted much of a wardrobe.

'Miss Payne, how good to see you,' said Mrs. Tanner.

'Mrs. Richards,' replied Miss Payne, with stiff formality, 'I must tell you, I cannot stay long. I have absented myself on the grounds of buying some lace for Miss Fulbrook's trousseau. If I am gone much more than a couple of hours . . .'

'I understand. Please, let me introduce Mr. Arthur DeSalle.'

Lydia Payne raised her eye-brows in surprise. 'Sir. Forgive me, Mr. DeSalle, but I had thought that . . .'

'An awkward misunderstanding, ma'am,' replied Arthur DeSalle. 'There were circumstances that did not permit me to assure your employer, Mr. Ferntower, of my . . . connection to Mrs. Richards . . . it is of a rather informal, confidential nature . . .'

'Really?' said Miss Payne, with a hint of superiority in her voice. 'I see. Well, I know something of the ways of the world, sir. There is no need to elucidate any further. My only concern is for Miss Fulbrook; I would not be here otherwise.'

'And that is why Mr. DeSalle is present, ma'am,' replied Sarah Tanner. 'He knows Stephen Symes – Cedric Hawkes – call him what you will – of old, and he is as anxious to see Miss Fulbrook spared the misery of matrimony with that man, as you or I.'

'Well, that is gratifying, at least,' replied Miss Payne. 'But our wretched "wedding-party" travels tomorrow. If Mr. Hawkes is to be unmasked – if Mr. Ferntower is to be persuaded of his duplicity – it must be done at once. Your letter said you have a plan – tell me, what do you intend to do?'

'First, you must tell me, ma'am,' said Sarah Tanner, 'do you trust your employer? Do you trust his intentions towards his ward?'

'Mr. Ferntower? I do not understand your question.'

'The night before last,' responded Sarah Tanner, 'Mr. DeSalle and I went up to Holloway. My intention was that Mr. DeSalle might talk to Mr. Ferntower; to explain what he knew of Stephen Symes. But we chanced to see your employer from our carriage: he was talking, on friendly terms, to a man whom I know to be an utter brute. A man whom I suspect played a part in Miss Emma Ferntower's death.'

A look of surprise passed across Lydia Payne's face.

'I cannot believe that,' she said at last. 'Besides – Mr. Ferntower was alone all evening.'

'Mr. DeSalle will vouch for what I saw. Did no-one call?'

'No-one. Well, only a police constable.'

'Only a constable?'

'I assumed, after the unfortunate evening with Mr. Murdoch, that it was some communication from Scotland Yard.'

Sarah Tanner shook her head. 'I know that very man – that officer of the law – to be the worst villain you can imagine, Miss Payne. In truth, I have seen him murder a man in cold blood. I suspect he killed your employer's sister.'

'He is a member of Her Majesty's Police, Mrs. Richards!'

'A uniform does not make a man virtuous,' said Sarah Tanner. 'Believe me.'

'Well, what then? Are you suggesting that Mr. Ferntower is conniving in this sham of a marriage?' exclaimed Lydia Payne. 'That he already knows Mr. Hawkes's true character?'

'I think it most likely. We cannot look for help in that quarter.'

'I cannot believe it!' declared Miss Payne.

'I assure you, ma'am,' interjected Arthur DeSalle, 'it seems quite probable. Are you sure you cannot credit it? Is Mr. Ferntower above all suspicion?'

'You render me speechless,' replied Miss Payne. 'Lord! Let us imagine you are correct – where does that leave Miss Fulbrook? All hope is lost!'

'Not quite,' countered Mrs. Tanner. 'I believe, if you are willing, if you can persuade your charge, there is one possibility remaining, something that would thwart Stephen Symes utterly.'

'What can you mean?'

'I suggest an elopement, Miss Payne. I suggest Miss Elizabeth Fulbrook marries John Ferntower.'

Lydia Payne looked blankly at Sarah Tanner.

'You are joking, of course, ma'am?'

'They were sweethearts, were they not? I know letters have passed between them – intimate correspondence – over this last week or so; would it be so great a step?'

Lydia Payne sighed. 'You are a friend of that gentleman—'

Sarah Tanner protested the point, but Lydia Payne proceeded.

'You declared yourself a friend to that gentleman, Mrs. Richards, when you met Miss Fulbrook,' continued Miss Payne, with determination, 'and – let me be frank – it is an acquaintance that does neither party any great credit. You may look at me askance, Mr. DeSalle, but I speak as I find. Still, I fail to see how even you can urge John Ferntower as a candidate for Miss Fulbrook's affections.'

'Symes would never trouble her again,' replied Sarah Tanner. 'And I believe John Ferntower is fond of her.'

'He is fond of dice, cards and liquor,' said Lydia Payne. 'You know the cause of his fall, I trust? He squandered his money in night-houses and at gaming tables, and left his father liable for his debts. Is that the man worthy of Miss Fulbrook?'

'He might yet be reformed. Mr. DeSalle here might even be able to find him some honest employment. I have spoken to him; he says he will attempt it – if Miss Fulbrook will have him.'

'So this is your plan – this is the only hope you offer me?' said Lydia Payne, in tones of rebuke.

'Consider this,' said Sarah Tanner. 'Consider the possibility that your employer is content to see the destruction of his ward for the sake of her inheritance; that he intends to give her over to the worst rogue in all London, for that very purpose – a man who, I assure you, will treat her with the utmost disdain and cruelty. Then tell me if marriage to John Ferntower – a young man still, for all his faults, with a fresh start ahead of him; a man who loves her – tell me if that is worse?'

'You have my word as a gentleman, Miss Payne,' added Arthur DeSalle. 'I will do what I can to aid them, if marriage is what Miss Fulbrook wants.'

'Well?' persisted Sarah Tanner. 'What is your answer?'

Lydia Payne fell silent. When at last she spoke, it was quietly, and reluctantly.

'Very well. I will put it to Miss Fulbrook. But there is every difficulty, even if she agrees. Mr. Hawkes still keeps a watch on the house.'

'Do you still not know where the marriage will take place?' asked Mrs. Tanner.

'Only that we are to take a train from Euston, tomorrow, at eleven.'

'That will do, Miss Payne,' said Sarah Tanner. 'That will do.'

CHAPTER FORTY-THREE

It was a little before eleven o'clock on the following morning that Sarah Tanner and Arthur DeSalle stood side by side in the spacious gallery above the Great Hall of the Euston Station, some forty feet above the milling crowd below. Even Arthur DeSalle, accustomed to comfortable surroundings, marvelled at the ambition of the London and North-Western Railway's directors. The vast hall, decorated in the classical style, built from the finest stone, crafted and coloured in imitation of ancient granite and marble, with its mosaic floor and Ionic pillars, resembled more some corner of imperial Rome than the work of a railway company.

'You did not have to come today, Arthur,' said Mrs. Tanner.

'It is worth it, to see Mr. Symes come a-cropper. Though he deserves something more tangible than mere embarrassment.'

'Don't even think of it, Arthur. If it came to it, he would cut your throat in an instant.'

'And yet you are quite content to cross him?'

'Well,' said Sarah Tanner, 'perhaps I have less to lose.'

'I hope you still value your life, at least.'

'I only hope,' said Mrs. Tanner, changing tack, 'that

Ferntower plays his part. And Miss Payne, for that matter.'

'Tell me, Sarah, what you said yesterday – to Miss Payne – does Ferntower truly love this girl?' asked Arthur DeSalle.

'He does not despise her at least; I know many a decent marriage that has been built upon worse foundations.'

'Sarah . . .'

'I meant nothing by it, rest assured. You said you would make inquiries on his behalf; did you have the chance?'

'I went to Baring's. There might be a place for him; a junior clerk's post in the West Indies. They would be happy to oblige me, I am sure; my account is worth the favour. The question is whether your friend Ferntower will take up the offer.'

'He is no friend, Arthur. And, if they wed, he knows full well what he will get when his cousin reaches her majority. I cannot change that.'

'And yet you would still have him marry the girl?' said Arthur DeSalle.

'Better him than Symes. Perhaps he may do the right thing and accept your generosity. Besides, a decent wife may improve a young man, isn't that what they say?'

'Sarah, please, there is no need for these incessant barbs.'

Before he could continue, however, Sarah Tanner tugged Arthur DeSalle's sleeve, pulling him back from the balustrade.

'They're here,' she said.

━

The wedding-party arrived in the Great Hall without any fanfare. It was a small group consisting of Mr.

Michael Ferntower, his ward and her governess, Stephen Symes – in the capacity of Mr. Cedric Hawkes – and a certain aged female purporting to be his mother, propelled in her bath-chair by a footman. If they had luggage, it had already been despatched by the attentions of the station-porters.

'A magnificent building,' remarked Mr. Ferntower.

'A privilege to visit it, sir,' said Her Majesty. 'Such a clever idea of yours for us to travel by train.'

'It is, after all, in keeping with the spirit of the age,' said Mr. Ferntower, rather sententiously, 'and more expeditious than coaching.'

'I fear I show my age, sir,' replied Her Majesty, 'in being more familiar with the humble coach.'

'Nonsense, ma'am,' replied Mr. Ferntower, politely. But his attention was distracted. For he suddenly glimpsed a familiar face approaching through the crowd, negotiating the chaos of heavily laden porters and scurrying passengers, men and women with eyes glued to the station clock, insensible to the world around them. It was a face he recognised all too well.

'Good day, Father,' said John Ferntower.

Michael Ferntower stood stock-still, as if faced with a ghost.

'What do you mean by coming here, sir?' he exclaimed.

'That's a fine welcome for a prodigal, Pa,' said John Ferntower. 'I mean, I knew I was *non grata* at home; I didn't think I was banished from the London and North-Western.'

'I say again,' repeated Michael Ferntower, 'what do you mean by it?'

'To tell the truth, old man, I heard my favourite cousin's tying the knot. I thought I'd come to wish her all the best.'

'You may do nothing of the sort, sir,' replied Mr. Ferntower. 'You forfeited any right to Miss Fulbrook's company long ago.'

'And who's the lucky man?' persisted John Ferntower.

'I expect you know full well,' interjected Stephen Symes.

'Not you, Hawkes? Or is it Symes? How did you swing that, my dear fellow? Did you promise the old man a share of the bingo?'

'You impertinent whelp!' exclaimed Michael Ferntower, raising a hand as if to strike his son. Stephen Symes, however, stepped forward, placing an restraining arm upon his prospective wife's guardian. Faces nearby turned towards them; a dogged-looking luggage-porter pushed past, edging Her Majesty's footman to one side.

'Do not rise to his jibes, sir,' said Symes, in a low voice. 'He only wishes to provoke.'

'And what would it take to offend you, Mr. Hawkes?' continued John Ferntower, stepping close enough to feel Stephen Symes's breath upon his face. 'I am curious to know what a vile rogue like yourself might find objectionable.'

'I fear you have been drinking, sir,' said Stephen Symes, with a rather theatrical sniff, and a degree of equanimity. 'I suppose that may account for your behaviour. I have to say, it is only the memory of our former acquaintance that prevents me from striking you down.'

'Be gone, sir,' added Michael Ferntower. 'The very sight of you disgusts me, and I can assure you that Miss Fulbrook has no interest in hearing your wretched slanders. We have a train to catch.'

'I think that is rather besides the point, old man,' said John Ferntower.

It took a moment for his father to understand John Ferntower's words. But, as Michael Ferntower turned round, he discovered to his astonishment that neither Elizabeth Fulbrook nor her governess were anywhere to be seen. And when he turned back, his son merely smiled, bowed politely, turned his back, and walked away.

Stephen Symes made to follow him, but he felt the tip of a cane prod his leg.

'Leave him. Find the girl, you fool,' said Her Majesty in an angry whisper. 'Find the girl!'

'Mrs. Richards,' protested Elizabeth Fulbrook, as Sarah Tanner ushered her into a waiting carriage, that stood ready at the entrance to the station, 'I am not sure that I can do this. Mr. Ferntower has been kind to me.'

'This is not the time nor the place for second thoughts, Miss Fulbrook,' insisted Sarah Tanner. 'It is not my place to force you to do anything, but please, let us just put a little distance between ourselves and Mr. Hawkes. If you change your mind within the hour, so be it. I will return you to Holloway, you have my word.'

Elizabeth Fulbrook hesitated. 'There are rooms engaged?'

'In a respectable boarding-house, for yourself and Miss Payne.'

'And there will be no deception, I mean, as to the marriage?'

'The banns will be read in the nearest church. We will just not advertise them to your guardian or Mr. Hawkes. Please – if you have made your mind up – can we go?'

Elizabeth Fulbrook took a deep breath and assented. Sarah Tanner, with a sigh of relief, turned to the nearby luggage-porter, handing him a folded piece of paper.

'Have a boy take this over to the old woman.'

The man nodded, and Mrs. Tanner climbed inside the coach.

———

It was no more than a minute later that Stephen Symes appeared under the giant awning that protected customers of the London and North-Western from the elements, as they waited for their carriage or cab. He was, nonetheless, too late to see Sarah Tanner depart, nor did he notice the presence of an elderly luggage-porter, who lurked behind a cart full of luggage at the station's doors.

It was the same porter, in fact, who had passed by the wedding-party in the station – a man with a remarkable resemblance to Ralph Grundy. And it was the same man who, a minute or two later, passed on a slip of paper to a messenger boy who, in turn, presented it to Her Majesty, as she sat in her bath-chair.

Her Majesty unfolded it and found only two words.

For Georgie.
S.

Her Majesty scowled and tore the paper in two.

CHAPTER FORTY-FOUR

Sarah Tanner sat in the parlour of her rented rooms in Calthorpe Street, gazing from the window across to the Middlesex House of Correction. Three peaceful days had passed since Miss Elizabeth Fulbrook's unexpected elopement from Euston Station; three days since she had left the young heiress and her governess safely accommodated in a small but decent boarding-house in Pimlico. An arrangement had been entered into with the priest of the local church; and banns would be read at the earliest opportunity; John Ferntower had offered to contemplate the life of a junior clerk and Elizabeth Fulbrook herself had written her two earnest letters that confirmed her ardent affection for her future husband, despite the reservations she had as to the manner of their alliance. And yet, despite it all, Sarah Tanner felt desperately uneasy.

'Penny for your thoughts,' said Norah Smallwood, entering the room.

'I was thinking about Arthur, if you must know.'

'You're still spooney on him, ain't you?' said Norah.

'No,' protested Mrs. Tanner, with perhaps a little too much vehemence. 'I was thinking about the rent.

It's only paid for a month. I can't ask Arthur for any more favours; I won't.'

'What then?'

'For a start, if I had any sense, I'd leave London. Symes will hate me now more than he did already.'

'Maybe you should, missus,' agreed Norah Smallwood glumly.

'No, not yet. I want to see this business through. I'll go when Miss Fulbrook's married, not before. Besides, there's still Georgie. This wedding doesn't make that right, not by a long chalk. And Symes; I'd like to pay him back, I swear I would.'

At the mention of George Phelps's and Stephen Symes's names, Norah Smallwood frowned.

'I'm sorry, Norah,' said Mrs. Tanner.

Norah Smallwood shook her head. 'T'ain't your fault, missus. So you won't be opening up the shop again?'

'You haven't seen it. It needs pulling down and putting back up.'

'I thought your Arthur might oblige.'

Sarah Tanner shook her head. 'He's not "mine" and he's done enough. I don't want to be in his debt.'

Norah Smallwood hesitated before speaking once more.

'I'll go with you, if you like,' she said at last.

'Where?'

'Wherever you're going. Look, missus, I ain't got no family, and there ain't never been no-one kinder to me. I'm just saying, I'll go with you – I mean, if you wanted company.'

'I nearly got you killed, Norah.'

'It weren't your doing.'

'Perhaps.'

Norah Smallwood looked a little deflated at Sarah Tanner's rather non-committal response. Nonetheless, she walked over to her beside the window.

'The weather's nice today, ain't it?'

'I suppose so.'

'I reckon I fancy a walk,' said Norah, peering into the street.

'Are you sure you're well enough?'

'I'll be all right,' replied Norah Smallwood. 'Here, is that the post?'

The sound of a letter falling in the hall below was unmistakeable. Without waiting for an answer, Norah Smallwood quit the room and hurried downstairs. She returned moments later with an envelope addressed to Sarah Tanner.

'That's *his* writing, ain't it?' she said, as Sarah Tanner opened the envelope and read the contents.

'Yes,' she replied, a little tetchily. 'It's Arthur.'

'Well then, what is it?' she asked impatiently.

'John Ferntower did not turn up for his interview at the bank.'

'You said he weren't too keen.'

'I thought he might at least attempt it,' said Sarah Tanner with a sigh. 'He is a fool to himself – if he has no prospects at all, she may decide against the marriage.'

'Not if she really loves him, though.'

Mrs. Tanner bit her lip, deep in thought.

'I'm going out,' she said at last.

'You're going to see Ferntower, ain't you?' said Norah.

'Someone should talk some sense into him.'

'Can I come with you?'

'Norah, I don't know if it's best.'

'If I stay indoors another day, I'll go mad – I will. I've got to go out sometime, ain't I? Please.'

'Very well,' said Sarah Tanner. 'Get your shawl.'

———

'What are you going to say to him?' said Norah, as the two women approached the house on Prince's Row.

'I'm not sure. I can hardly force him into becoming a bank clerk, whatever his circumstances. Here, this is the place.'

Sarah Tanner led the way. Once inside the house, as they turned on to the final landing, she spied a familiar figure, pacing the floorboards outside John Ferntower's rooms.

'Mrs. Richards!' exclaimed Theobald Stamp, as if greeting a principal actress for the benefit of those in the gods. 'Why, this is a most diverting surprise. May I kiss your hand, ma'am?'

'No, sir,' said Mrs. Tanner, pointedly not raising her arm to meet the indefatigable theatrical's outstretched hand. 'You must forgive me, this is my cousin. We're here to see Mr. Smith. A confidential matter.'

'Smith? You'll be lucky, ma'am. You'd have to be more than lucky, or I'm a Dutchman. And Theobald Stamp, ma'am, is an Englishman, born-and-bred.'

'I gather he's not at home?'

'More than that, ma'am. I don't expect he'll be at home again. I have not had the pleasure of his company for three days or more. Twenty sheets to be copied three times over, and no sign of him; money has been paid in advance. So I ask questions, ma'am. I ask the landlord; no sign of him. I ask the neighbours – last seen departing yesterday morning, ma'am, *with a trunk*. With a trunk! The fellow's thrown my generosity back in my face, my dear lady. He's bolted, 'pon my honour!'

'Bolted?' said Sarah Tanner, surprised. 'No, he would have confided in me.'

'Did he owe you money, my dear?' said Stamp. 'I would not put it past the fellow.'

Mrs. Tanner seemed dumb-struck for a moment. 'Is the door locked?' she said at last.

'I believe so,' replied Stamp.

'Could you force it open?'

'Whyever should I do such a thing, ma'am?' said Theobald Stamp who, despite his considerable bulk, did not seem accustomed to the idea of doing violence to anything.

'Because I fear, sir, that a respectable young woman's honour may be at stake. And because,' said Sarah Tanner, trying to sound convincing, 'I believe you to be a gentleman.'

Theobald Stamp visibly puffed up, like a prize peacock, at the word *gentleman*.

'A young woman's honour, you say?'

'Precisely.'

'Then say no more, Mrs. Richards. No man will speak of Theobald Stamp and say he did not rise to the occasion. Stand back!'

And, with that exclamation, Theobald Stamp ran at the door. He was a large man and the door rattled as he shoved his shoulder against the wood. But it did not yield, and left him rather breathless.

'Again, sir,' said Sarah Tanner.

Stamp, although rather deflated by his effort, was shamed enough to make another attempt. And, to his surprise – and considerable satisfaction – the door gave way, the rather inadequate lock splintering free of the frame. He peered inside.

'There's no-one here, ma'am,' he said, stepping into the room. 'I was not wrong – the man has cleared out.'

Sarah Tanner, followed by Norah, followed Stamp inside. The room was cold, the curtains drawn. She pulled them back, and looked about her. There would be some small clue; she was sure of it. Then she noticed the rug by the fire-place: it lay out of place, aligned with the hearth, but a good foot or more to the right of its usual location.

Carefully, she bent over and moved the rug to one side. There was a distinct rotten aroma that greeted her nostrils. At first, she thought it belonged to the rug itself, but then realised her mistake.

'Ma'am,' said Theobald Stamp, 'you must forgive me, but I am quite at a loss. Whatever are you doing?'

Mrs. Tanner, however, reached down and teased her fingers into a gap between the bare boards. In truth, she had a good idea of what she might find when she lifted up the wood, but the sight still revolted her.

It was a body; a woman's corpse, the features contorted and the neck badly bruised. It took her a moment to recognise the face; perhaps it was the incongruity of it all – the body interred beneath the dusty boards – or the rictus of her twisted mouth, that seemed to suggest terrible astonishment. But she recognised her all the same – it was the self-same woman whom she had seen almost a week before, in the gas-light outside the Lord Nelson public-house.

It was the Peeler's woman.

Before Sarah Tanner could say a word, Norah

Smallwood stood by her side and peered into the space. She turned quite pale.

'God help us,' said Norah.

'God help us, all right,' said Sarah Tanner. 'God help Miss Fulbrook. Good Lord, I've been such a fool.'

'No,' said Norah, 'you don't understand, missus. Lor! I can't fathom it, but that's her. I thought she was drowned. But that's his blessed aunt. That's Miss Ferntower.'

CHAPTER FORTY-FIVE

Theobald Stamp stepped closer to the exposed boards. Even in extreme circumstances there was something theatrical about his approach, his steps peculiarly measured, a handkerchief placed to his mouth. As he saw the body, he let out a violent, choking sob.

'Do you know her?' said Sarah Tanner to the actor.

'I told you,' repeated Norah Smallwood. 'It's her.'

Mrs. Tanner shook her head. 'No, it's not, I'd bet my life on that. Do you know the woman, Mr. Stamp?'

'Kate Evans, ma'am,' said Theobald Stamp. 'Formerly one of the company; a favourite of Mr. Smith's. Upon my oath, I did not imagine the man to be capable of this! A murderer! Did you have any inkling, ma'am? You said a woman's honour was at stake—'

'Not this woman,' replied Sarah Tanner, shaking her head.

'We must summon the police, at once,' said Stamp, stepping away from the body.

'You wait here, sir,' said Mrs. Tanner, 'in case Smith returns, or anyone should interfere. We will go and fetch a constable.'

'Are you sure?' said Stamp.

'Certain,' replied Sarah Tanner, tugging at Norah Smallwood's sleeve. 'It will not take long.'

Theobald Stamp watched, open-mouthed, still in a state of shock, as Sarah Tanner left the room. Norah Smallwood trailed after her, all but dragged down the stairs into Prince's Row.

'Are we going to get a copper?' asked Norah, breathless.

'Hang the police!'

'Missus, I don't understand . . . if that ain't Miss Ferntower in there, who is it?'

'An actress. A friend of Ferntower's. Lord! it should have been obvious – the veil, the two hotels! And the worst of it is, I let him use me as his dupe! What a performance! Look, Norah, there is not time. Find Ralph. He said he'd be working as pot-man at the Bottle of Hay, if nothing better turned up. I need him to do something for me. Tell him to go to the courts by St. Paul's – to Doctors' Commons – and ask after any allegations made under the name of Ferntower, made in the last few days.'

'Allegations?'

'Ferntower intends to marry Miss Fulbrook now, Norah, as soon as he can. He will not wait for banns, so he will need a licence. And a licence requires an allegation, a sworn oath. He will have to claim he has her guardian's consent. It will say what church they intend to use. Can you explain all that to Ralph?'

'I suppose,' said Norah Smallwood.

'Norah – it's important. Repeat what I just said.'

Norah Smallwood, in fits and starts, relayed the information back to her erstwhile employer, more or less correctly.

'Good. Tell him to say he is her father; that he fears there's been a fraud. And tell him to be careful. I'll meet him back at Calthorpe Street.'

'Where are you going?'

'To try and set things right. If I am not back by this evening, I will not be back at all.'

—

Several hours after the discovery in Prince's Row, Ralph Grundy paced nervously around Sarah Tanner's rooms in Calthorpe Street, whilst Norah Smallwood sat by the fire. Outside, the bells of a nearby church chimed six o'clock.

'Didn't she say how long she'd be?' said Ralph Grundy.

'It ain't my doing, is it?' replied Norah Smallwood. 'No, she didn't say nothing, I told you.'

Ralph Grundy tutted.

'What do you think she meant, "set things right"?' asked Norah, after a brief silence.

'I don't like thinking on it,' said Ralph Grundy.

A few minutes later footsteps were heard upon the stairs. Sarah Turner entered the room quite calmly and made only the most perfunctory attempt at a greeting.

'Where've you been, missus?' asked Ralph Grundy.

She waved her hand, dismissing the question. 'Never mind that, Ralph. Just tell me that you went to Doctors' Commons.'

'Aye,' said Ralph Grundy, 'I did. And I found him out, too – you weren't wrong, missus. He was there just this morning. I told 'em I was her father, like you said, and then I told 'em she was only thirteen, and him a Frenchman down on his luck. Then I says, "See the papers? Well, I should hope I can, with her mother just passed away and this scoundrel taking gross liberties . . ."'

'Ralph, please. I do not need the full drama. What did you find out?'

'Ah,' said Ralph Grundy, a little aggrieved to be halted in his tale, 'I got 'em to write us a copy. Cost me two bob, mind.'

'Show it to me then.'

Ralph Grundy nodded and hastily retrieved a piece of paper from his coat pocket. Sarah Tanner plucked it from his hand.

Faculty Office
28th April 1852

APPEARED PERSONALLY John Ferntower of the Parish of St. Paul's' Shadwell, in the County of Middlesex, a Batchelor of the age of twenty-one years and upwards, and prayed a Licence for the Solemnization of Matrimony in the Parish Church of St. Paul's, Shadwell, in the County of Middlesex, between him and Elizabeth Mary Fulbrook of the Parish of St. Stephen's, Holloway, a Spinster of the age of nineteen years, and made Oath that he believeth there is no impediment of Kindred or Alliance, or of any other lawful Cause, nor any Suit commenced in any Ecclesiastical Court, to bar or hinder the Proceeding of the said Matrimony, according to the Tenor of such Licence. And he further made Oath that the said John Ferntower and Elizabeth Mary Fulbrook, Spinster, have had their usual Places of Abode within the said Parishes of St. Paul's, Shadwell, and St. Stephen's respectively for the Space of Fifteen Days last past.

'They had a sworn oath from her guardian, too,' said Ralph Grundy.

'Well, he did not write it,' said Sarah Tanner, 'but at least we know the church.'

'What I don't understand, missus,' said the old man, 'is how come he's taking the trouble to get a licence and marry her by it. All it takes is someone to say it's a fraud – and he's done for.'

'Perhaps he does not think his father will prosecute, once the damage is done. I do not know. It will all be lawful unless a court says otherwise.'

'Missus, it ain't for me to say, but shouldn't we go to the church, then? We can still stop them, can't we?'

'They won't get married at night, Ralph. And if the licence was only granted this morning, it is unlikely he managed it this afternoon. In any case, we wait until tomorrow morning.'

'Are you planning something, missus?' said Ralph Grundy.

'I am expecting a letter in the post.'

Ralph Grundy frowned, a little frustrated by Sarah Tanner's guarded reply.

'You know what happened to his actual aunt, then?' said the old man.

'I have a good idea. He killed her all right.'

'Ain't you going to tell us?'

'Not yet. Not until I'm sure.'

CHAPTER FORTY-SIX

Pimlico, 28th April

Dear Mrs. Richards,

Forgive me, I will spare you any pleasantries. It is enough to say that all my worst fears have been realised. Your letter serves to confirm the worst – the most terrible – interpretation must be placed on the events of the day.

In short, the deed is already done. Mr. John Ferntower visited us this morning. He claimed that there was legal business requiring Miss Fulbrook's presence in London. I confess, I had a terrible head and did not feel well enough to travel by coach. I accepted his assurances that he would return Miss Fulbrook by noon. As I write, it has been *ten hours* since they left. At first I feared an accident but now I know the truth of the matter. I cannot tell you how heavy my heart is burdened with shame. That I should ever have trusted *that man* with Miss Fulbrook's happiness!

You say there is still something that may be done and that the police must not, on any account, be involved. Very well. *I* make no claim to be proficient in the arts of deception or familiar with the mind of a criminal. I put my faith in *you* one last time and once only. I will meet you at the church tomorrow at eleven, as you suggest. I pray we are not already too late.

Yours,
Lydia Payne

The letter arrived in the morning post. Sarah Tanner read it through carefully.

'What did you tell her, missus?'

'I wrote yesterday afternoon to say that Ferntower had deceived us; that I believed he wished to steal Miss Fulbrook away at the earliest opportunity.'

'You didn't mention no murder, then?'

'I thought that might unnerve her. Very well, at least now I know.'

Ralph Grundy nodded, glancing outside into the street.

'Is that yours, missus?'

Sarah Tanner looked through the window, as a rather respectable-looking carriage drew up on Calthorpe Street.

'Yes, that's mine,' she replied, rising to her feet.

'More arrangements you made yesterday?' said Ralph Grundy, full of curiosity.

'Quite.'

Ralph Grundy made to follow as Mrs. Tanner walked to the door, but she turned to face him, gently putting out her arm to stop him.

'No, Ralph, you stay here. I need someone to keep an eye on Norah.'

'Hold up, missus!' protested Ralph Grundy. 'I'm not the girl's nursemaid. And, besides, she ain't exactly at death's door.'

'I'm sorry, Ralph, but I don't need you, not today.'

'Who'll watch out for you, then?'

'I have someone, I won't be on my own.'

'Your gentleman friend, is it?' said Ralph Grundy.

'Arthur?' said Sarah Tanner, after a brief pause. 'Yes, that's it.'

'I expect an old man is no use to you, 'cepting on errands. He's useful enough then.'

'Ralph, I have no time for this. Please, I'd like you to wait for me, if you will. You've been a good friend; all being well, I'll see you when I get back.'

'All being well?'

Mrs. Tanner did not reply, but merely leant forward and placed a kiss upon the old man's cheek. Struck dumb, Ralph Grundy watched as his erstwhile employer quit the room.

'Has she gone?' said Norah Smallwood, who appeared from the rear of the apartment, moments later.

'Aye, she's gone,' muttered Ralph Grundy. 'I only hope she's planning on coming back.'

———

Some three-quarters of an hour after quitting her lodgings in Calthorpe Street, Sarah Tanner stood outside the church of St. Paul's, Shadwell. The church itself lay adjoining the broadest portion of the old Ratcliff Highway – the ill-famed haunt of sailors, better known for its low dance-halls and cheap publics than its religion – and, upon the southern side, separated only by a few narrow streets of slum houses, were the high walls and tobacco warehouses of the London Docks. It was a beautiful building, nonetheless, despite the contrast with its surroundings; a Roman design, topped by a tower and cupola, then

327

a pyramidal spire; front steps leading to tall wooden doors of double height, flanked upon either side by iron gas-lamps. And the lights were illuminated since, though it was long past day-break, there was a river-fog that hung about the nearby Thames, and immersed the low-lying regions about the docks in a faint brown mist.

As she stood upon the steps, a small man opened one of the church's doors, and slipped outside. He was a gentleman in his fifties, wearing spectacles, slightly hunched in his posture, with clothing that, though respectable-looking, appeared to have seen better days. He turned to Sarah Tanner and smiled a thin smile.

'Can I help you, ma'am?'

'I am looking for the parish clerk. I gather his name is Briggs.'

'You've found him, ma'am,' said the clerk, with some pride, perhaps little-used to being sought out by members of the fair sex. 'But won't you come inside? Such awful weather, is it not?'

Mrs. Tanner nodded and the clerk led her into the church. The building was empty and, at his behest, she took a seat on one of the nearest pews to the door.

'Now, ma'am, how can I oblige you? I assume you are the lady who sent word last night?'

'I confess, sir, it is a delicate business; you must forgive that I was so vague in my telegram. A young lady I have the honour to call a friend, a young lady by the name of Miss Fulbrook, has – well, there is no decent word for it – eloped with a young man of our acquaintance.'

'Really?' said the clerk. Mrs. Tanner watched him closely; the mention of Elizabeth Fulbrook's name struck home, she was sure of that. She wondered why John Ferntower had chosen the church. Was it only for its remote location, or was the man known to turn a blind eye to marriages made in undue haste?

'Of course, such things happen every day, but I have good reason to believe the wretched fellow – a young man by the name of Ferntower – has obtained a licence to marry, under the most false pretences. I also think he may intend to marry her here.'

The clerk coughed, nervously. 'In truth, ma'am, I believe I know something of the matter.'

'You do?'

'Yes,' said the clerk. 'I believe a young gentleman of that name talked to our Reverend Smythe yesterday evening. I cannot claim to have heard the whole conversation, but I gathered the young man was bound on an unexpected sea voyage, and wished to faciliate the joining of the bonds of holy matrimony sooner than he had anticipated. We are a sailors' church; it is not terribly uncommon.'

'And when is the wedding planned?'

'I believe tomorrow in the fore-noon was the earliest time to suit the Reverend's convenience.'

'Did Mr. Ferntower give an address?'

'Of course,' replied the clerk. 'I believe the Reverend is due to visit the gentleman this afternoon. There are matters to discuss regarding the service, and so forth.'

'And what might that address be?'

'Well, I can hardly say, ma'am. I'm sure a degree of discretion must be maintained in these matters.'

'I am sure a donation to the church might be considered an appropriate gesture of thanks, from the girl's friends. Say a guinea?'

The clerk smiled.

'Let me refer to my records, ma'am.'

———

As Sarah Tanner left the church, a cab drew up by the front steps. Lydia Payne stepped out, a definite look of anxiety upon her face.

'Dismiss the cab,' said Mrs. Tanner, without a word of greeting. 'I have a coach. He can take us the rest of the way. They are not yet married; we still have time to save her.'

'What? You have found them out? How?'

'An old friend of mine used to say "never trust the police or the parish", Miss Payne,' she replied, glancing back at the clerk who stood looking through the gap between the church doors. 'He wasn't far wrong.'

CHAPTER FORTY-SEVEN

The name of the road supplied by the curate was Peacock Buildings, although it displayed little of the colour of its namesake. Rather, the predominant shade was a rather sickly yellowy brown: the brown mud that pasted the cobbles; the dirty ochre of the London bricks which formed the walls of the huddled tene-ments; the brown paper and rags that seemed to have replaced glass in every other window; even the faint hint of brown fog that hung in the air.

At the very end of the thoroughfare, Sarah Tanner's carriage drew to a halt.

'It's too narrow,' said Mrs. Tanner, looking along the road with a sigh. 'So much for that. Drive on!'

'What a wretched place!' said Miss Payne, as the coach pulled off. 'What do you intend to do?'

'The first thing is to find a decent receiving-house.'

'Whatever for?'

'I need paper to write a little note.'

⬤

Less than half an hour later, Sarah Tanner's carriage returned to the Ratcliff Highway, a short distance from the narrow lane leading to Peacock Buildings.

'You have still not told me your plan, Mrs.

Richards,' said Lydia Payne, aggrieved. 'Miss Fulbrook has been kidnapped and you have spent your time in writing correspondence!'

'I intend to rescue Miss Fulbrook, Miss Payne – it is quite straightforward. I assume her doubts about her intended can only have magnified in such a place, even if he is not holding her against her will. A few home truths should suffice.'

'You do not think he is dangerous?'

'With any luck, he will not be there.'

Lydia Payne glanced down at the envelope Sarah Tanner held in her hand, an idea of its purpose entering her mind. 'The note?'

'An apology from the Reverend Smythe that he cannot visit the happy couple due to a sudden illness amongst his flock, but could Mr. Ferntower pay his respects at the church, between the hours of twelve and one? You see, I can fake a man's hand tolerably well.'

'You have many talents,' said Lydia Payne, in a tone that sounded not altogether approving. 'You think he will leave Miss Fulbrook behind?'

'I should think the fewer opportunities she has to question the whole affair, the better it will suit him. And she will hardly take herself out for a walk – not in these streets.'

'I still think I should accompany you – if she has any doubts about your sincerity, Miss Fulbrook will trust me.'

'No, there is no need for that. Besides, if I do not return within the hour – if there is some guard upon her person – you have an important task to perform, rest assured.'

'And what is that?'

'Summon the police; I will most likely be dead.'

With those words, Sarah Tanner bid the governess goodbye, leaving her quite speechless, and stepped down out of the carriage. In truth, Mrs. Tanner's dress was not extravagant, no more ostentatious than that of a decent upper servant, but nonetheless, in the back-streets of Shadwell, she attracted the gaze of those she passed by. Amongst them were a couple of small boys, who sat crouched in the gutter near the street corner, playing at tipcat with a rather rough-looking piece of wood. She crouched down beside them.

'Hello. Does either of you know Peacock Buildings?' she asked.

The children nodded, hesitant, a little wary.

'If I gave you a note to deliver to a gentleman there, would you do it for me? If I were to give you sixpence?'

'I'll do it, missus,' said the taller of the boys, the mention of currency gaining his full attention.

'But there is more to it,' continued Mrs. Tanner. 'You must give him the note and then hurry away. And if he asks who sent it, you say a gentleman gave it to you, near the church. For sixpence, remember. And hurry away – do not dawdle or chat.'

'Are you playing a game, missus?' said the younger of the boys.

'Yes, a game, with a friend of mine. Now tell me what you have to say, and we can play.'

'A gentleman, near the church,' repeated the older of the two.

'Good boy,' said Sarah Tanner, with a smile. 'Come with me, then, and we'll play our little game, and see who wins.'

———

Mrs. Tanner stood at the far end of Peacock Buildings, displaying an unmerited interest in the contents of the pawn-shop window situated upon the street corner.

The address which John Ferntower had given to the parish clerk was a two-pair back in a ramshackle-looking house that lay about half-way down the street. She watched the boy run down with the note and enter the house. A few seconds later, he returned with an assurance that *the gent took it, and he said about the church and all.* She gave the messenger his sixpence – to the boy's evident delight – and waited.

Some five minutes later, the figure of John Ferntower left the building and stepped on to the street. There was still a little fog in the air, but she kept her shawl wrapped tight around her face, and, to her satisfaction, felt sure she was unnoticed, since Ferntower promptly walked off in the opposite direction, in the direction of St. Paul's Church. Once she was confident that he was out of sight, she walked down the street herself, and quietly let herself into the house.

The interior shared some similarities with John Ferntower's lodgings in Prince's Row, in that it was equally neglected. But what had been merely shabby and threadbare upon the borders of Newport Market, had been turned rotten and derelict in the dank atmosphere of the riverside slums. There was no paper upon the walls, merely patches of damp; the rail of the stairs was rotten and soft to the touch; and an atmosphere of sulphurous decay seemed to have soaked into the very walls.

Sarah Tanner crept cautiously up the steps to the second floor. She saw no other tenants, although she could hear the distant sound of a baby crying. There was a sash-window upon the far end of the landing. In the light that shone through the murky panes, she carefully pulled a small pistol from her pocket, gingerly loading the barrel. With her free hand, she knocked upon the door to Ferntower's rooms.

No answer.

She tried the handle of the door. Finding it unlocked, she edged it open.

Inside, the room was pitch black, with thick cloth curtains drawn across the windows. It took her a moment to accustom her eyes to the darkness.

Too long, perhaps.

For as she stood there, a rough hand from behind the door grabbed her wrist, whilst another grabbed the pistol from her grip.

She knew the man in the instant he released her arm, and punched her full in the face, sending her reeling in a dizzy arc.

The Peeler.

CHAPTER FORTY-EIGHT

Sarah Tanner opened her eyes. She was down upon the floor, her back to the wall. Instinctively, she tried to move, but found her hands tied behind her.

'About time you woke up, my girl,' said a voice.

It was the Peeler; and beside him stood John Ferntower, holding her own pistol.

'Good afternoon, Miss Richards,' said Ferntower. 'I find it rather amusing that this is how it ends – just as we met. You threatened to kill me then, if you recall. If you like, you can consider this repayment in kind.'

The policeman stepped closer, crouching down in front of her, grabbing her bruised face in his hand with deliberate force. Sarah Tanner winced.

'It is her and all?!' exclaimed the Peeler. 'The one who sent me off chasing down Sardinia Street. I told you, girl, didn't I? Never tell lies; not round me, least-ways.'

The policeman smiled, letting go of Sarah Tanner's face, only to turn away and slap her cheek with the back of his hand.

'I told you, didn't I?' he said, cheerily.

Sarah Tanner coughed, the taste of her own blood filling her mouth.

'Was it all for the money, then?' she said, spitting out the words, turning to John Ferntower. 'Is that why you killed your aunt? Or was it just spite?'

'Really,' said John Ferntower, 'I don't know what you mean.'

'You were at the hotel, weren't you? The Brunswick, wasn't it? They said so at the inquest. I should have put two and two together then. That's when you killed her. Except everyone knew you hated her; that you had a grudge because of what she'd told your father. So you killed her and had your actress friend, Miss Evans, play her part; she just had to be "alive" a couple of days so that it could not be you who was to blame. Lord, you even got yourself arrested, just to be on the safe side. What did you do with the body?'

John Ferntower smiled. 'You are a terribly clever woman, aren't you, Miss Richards? My poor aunt, God rest her soul, poisoned my father against me, you see? It was Hawkes – Symes, call him what you will – who gave her the ammunition, I realise that now. I had to get rid of her, if I was to have any hope with Miss Fulbrook. As to the body, I put her in Miss Evans's luggage when she left the Brunswick and then – well, a friend took care of it.'

'You dumped her in the river,' said Sarah Tanner, looking at the policeman.

'You find all sorts of rubbish in the Thames, my girl,' said the policeman.

'And what about Georgie?'

'Georgie?'

'Phelps. The man you gutted in Leather Lane.'

'Him?' said the policeman. 'Poor lad. He gave me a right load of chaff. I had to shut him up.'

John Ferntower laughed. 'You know, Miss Richards, I've thought a good deal about that. An awkward coincidence, you see; I don't know why he picked the Hummums that night, but he did. If it had not happened, we might have avoided all of this. But then I suppose I'd never have had the pleasure of meeting you. You see, I knew George Phelps too. I rather lied to you on that score. We had some pleasant evenings round the baccarat table; Mr. Hawkes introduced us. I even brought him home to meet the family.'

'Wait! now I understand,' exclaimed Mrs. Tanner. 'George'd met your aunt! He knew it wasn't her at the Hummums.'

'Quite,' continued Ferntower. 'As you say, I thought it best for all concerned if "Miss Ferntower" left the Brunswick alive. I did not want Miss Evans scrutinised by the same staff who had actually seen my aunt. So we chose another hotel; a poor choice, as it turned out.'

'Your pal George was already sizing the crib. Said all sorts to our Katie,' added the policeman. 'Poked and pried through her room; got very curious. Might have said a good deal elsewhere, too. We couldn't have that. I had to put a stop to it.'

'And then you killed Miss Evans too. I suppose something went wrong there.'

'Ah,' said John Ferntower, as if caught out upon some trivial point, 'now I wondered what brought you here, today of all days. I see it was Miss Evans – you found her already? Why, you have a knack for stumbling across corpses, my dear.'

'Stamp told me she was a friend of yours.'

'Yes, well, I rather liked Kate.'

'Terrible shame,' added the Peeler, without much sorrow. 'Me and her were old pals, as it happens. Terrible.'

'Yes,' continued Ferntower, 'we made a good

338

arrangement with Miss Evans. Not a full share in the profits, mind you. Just a little boarding-house down by the coast; an annual stipend. But I'm afraid she got rather greedy.'

'She came back,' said Sarah Tanner. 'And she threatened to tell the truth. You tried to keep her quiet, but she wouldn't have it.'

John Ferntower shrugged. 'I took no pleasure in killing her, Miss Richards. And I'll take no pleasure in killing you, I assure you. In fact, I don't believe I could have done this without you; you were such a God-send. If only—'

'Hurry up and have done,' interjected the policeman.

John Ferntower smiled and crept close to his prisoner, placing the barrel of the pistol at her temple. Sarah Tanner shuddered.

'My colleague is quite right. Enough chatter. Now, which would you prefer, Miss Richards – or whatever your true name is – tell me, the bullet or the knife? Or even by hand? I have some expertise in that area. But then, you were so good as to bring the pistol; it only seems polite.'

'Just shoot her,' said the policeman, impatient.

'No,' said Ferntower, pulling back the gun a little, 'let the lady answer.'

'I'll see you both in hell, I swear on my mother's grave,' said Sarah Tanner, struggling against her bonds.

John Ferntower shook his head.

'I'm afraid you're only half right there,' he replied as, without another word, he cocked the pistol and swung it to his left, firing point-blank in the policeman's face. The retort of the gun, and the smell of burnt powder filled the room. The policeman's body tumbled backwards on to the bare floor, the top of his head burst open, ripe and red.

339

Sarah Tanner froze; then struggled harder.

John Ferntower chuckled, and reached inside his jacket, pulling out a small pocket-knife and then throwing it to one side. 'You won't escape, my dear. I took the precaution of emptying your pockets.'

'You killed him. You didn't even—'

'He was greedy too, Miss Richards. And witness to a murder. Besides, ten thousand a year split three ways is nothing at all, if you think about it.'

'And what about Miss Fulbrook?'

'She'll make me a beautiful wife, don't you think?' said Ferntower. 'And I do have a certain fondness for her. She is a charming young woman. So innocent; so trusting.'

'Someone will have heard the shot. You're already done for.'

'The rest of the building is derelict, Miss Richards. There's no-one to hear a thing. Now, do be quiet, there's a good woman.'

John Ferntower leant forward, his hands circling Sarah Tanner's throat. It was a slow, measured movement, almost ritualistic, and she could see in her assailant's eyes a thrill of satisfaction as he pressed into her skin.

It was a thrill that ended, as she wriggled in his grip, and with a desperate lunge, thrust the tip of a small stiletto blade into John Ferntower's neck.

Ferntower gave out a choking, suffocating gasp, clasping his hand to the wound. But the red fluid trickled through his fingers, an unstoppable crimson tide, coating his hand, then his sleeve. He shuffled backwards spasmodically, like a cornered animal, his feet skidding in the policeman's blood, his breath growing more hoarse and weaker with every second.

Sarah Tanner stood and watched. In truth, she felt nothing but a visceral revulsion; but nonetheless she stood and watched, as life slipped away from John Ferntower. She thought of Georgie Phelps and she stood there. Then, as Ferntower breathed his last, she picked up the delicate blade and wiped it on the hem of his jacket. With an unsteady hand, she tugged the back of her dress, and slid the knife back into the carefully constructed pocket that lay hidden between the whalebone stays – the self-same pocket which had enabled her, at the last, to recover the blade and free her bonds.

She glanced at the policeman's corpse, then turned to leave, opening the door, only to find it blocked by a man standing in the hall.

'My, my,' said Stephen Symes, surveying the room.

CHAPTER FORTY-NINE

Sarah Tanner climbed inside the waiting carriage.

'For pity's sake, where is the coachman?' she exclaimed.

'He said he had to relieve himself,' said Lydia Payne, stunned, gaping at Sarah Tanner's bruised and bloodied face. 'I'm sorry, I could not stop him.'

Mrs. Tanner leant out of the window. The coachman returned, the sound of him clambering on to the box-seat audible within the carriage.

'Drive!'

'Yes, ma'am.'

The whip cracked and the carriage jolted into action, its speed steadily increasing as it rattled along the Ratcliff Highway.

'What on earth happened to you?' demanded Miss Payne.

'Ferntower was there. Miss Fulbrook – I am afraid she is dead; he has killed her too.'

Lydia Payne shook her head. 'Miss Fulbrook? No, that is quite impossible.'

'Impossible?' said Sarah Tanner.

'I mean, I cannot believe it. He would not have killed her.'

Mrs. Tanner shrugged. 'No, I don't suppose he would. Not the golden goose.'

'Then why did you . . . ?'

'I was just curious, that's all.'

'Curious?'

'I had one last particle of doubt. But, do not worry, you've put paid to that, Miss Payne.'

Miss Payne's posture visibly stiffened. 'Whatever do you mean by that?'

'The man who killed George Phelps – my friend Georgie – do you remember, I told you the story at the Angel, did I not? – I saw him at Hillmarton Park last week, shaking hands with Mr. Ferntower. I assumed Mr. Ferntower knew him; that he had paid him to kill his sister. That he intended to sell his ward to Symes for a profit. I didn't stop to think who else was in the house.'

'You cannot be accusing me?'

'I expect you introduced him to Mr. Ferntower. As what, a cousin? Or an acquaintance? A respectable member of the constabulary? He had turned up un-expectedly. I suppose you had to say something. Kate Evans had paid him a visit, suggesting she get a bigger share, and he wasn't sure what to do about it. It was something like that, eh?'

'I think you must be quite mad!' protested Lydia Payne.

'I realised, when we found her body – Kate Evans. I assume you know Ferntower killed her? Possibly you suggested it? In any case, I realised that the blue devil's visit to Holloway made no sense – not if John Ferntower was behind it all. Why would he have gone to Hillmarton Park at all? Because there was someone else he went to see – and it was you.'

'And you consider this constitutes proof?' said Lydia Payne. 'That I conspired with these wretched people?'

'Please, Miss Payne – you are a good actress yourself – better than Miss Evans, I suspect – but not that good.

Although, I admit, it was clever how you and Ferntower played your parts – all the sniping at his character – how unworthy he was! – and so when even you came round to the idea of the marriage, Miss Fulbrook was convinced.'

'Ridiculous!' exclaimed Lydia Payne.

'I put it to the test. I wrote to you last night; I told you what I had planned, more or less. I could have gone straight to Shadwell, but I gave you time to warn them. I'm not a fool, Miss Payne, I know when someone's expecting me.'

Lydia Payne blanched.

'What happened?' she said at last, her face deathly pale. 'Tell me.'

'Ferntower killed your friend the Peeler; he objected to sharing, a selfish man to the last. I think he thought he could make the police believe I had done it.'

'And John?'

'Ah, *John*, is it?' said Sarah Tanner.

'Tell me.'

'He tried to murder me. I stabbed him in the neck. I watched him die. I won't say I enjoyed it; but I owed Georgie that much. They'll find him rotting in a few days, I expect.'

Lydia Payne shook her head. 'You're lying again.'

'Not this time.'

Miss Payne's face grew whiter still. Her hands, however, dipped into the small reticule she carried with her, and re-appeared holding a pistol.

'Don't imagine I won't use this,' said Lydia Payne. 'You're not the only one with a man's courage. I should kill you stone dead.'

'At least do me the courtesy of telling why you did it,' said Sarah Tanner, shifting uneasily in her seat.

'Don't be such a hypocrite!' exclaimed Lydia Payne.

'I have some idea of your past life, "Mrs. Richards". John told me about Mr. Symes and his associates. I did it for the money; to put an end to being nurse-maid to an ignorant slip of a girl for a pittance. I did it to have a life of my own – a good life.'

'I am sure Miss Fulbrook told me you had only been her governess for a couple of years. Was it so terrible?'

'I planned it out. Do you think it was an accident? Do you think you are the only female in London with any brains? I was one of the old man's reformatory girls; did you know that? No, I don't expect you did. Every year we were paraded before the governors. I made something of myself; quite a triumph for the Schools. He didn't remember me, of course, the old fool. You know, I rather believe he even grew quite fond of me.'

'But you became John Ferntower's lover instead? Was that part of your plan?'

'It served its purpose. You need not think I sent John down *the wrong path*, Miss Richards. He was already after Miss Fulbrook's money; I just provided some guidance.'

'And Symes put your nose out of joint; his plans rather clashed with yours.'

'More than that – he nearly ruined everything! John had given up hope; he could not see a way forward. If it had not been for you interfering, he might have abandoned our scheme entirely.'

'Even that first night I met him in St. Giles,' said Mrs. Tanner, 'he saw an opportunity to make use of me, did he not? To play me against Symes?'

'It does not matter now,' muttered Miss Payne. 'Tell me the truth,' she continued, raising the gun higher, 'did you really kill him?'

Sarah Tanner opened her mouth to speak. But as

she did so, the trap in the carriage roof, which had inched open wider and wider as the conversation progressed, revealed the sudden flash of a steel blade, which shot through the air in a blur, piercing Lydia Payne's hand. She groaned in agony, dropping the gun in an instant.

Stephen Symes peered through the trap.

'Yes, Miss Payne, I'm rather afraid she did.'

Lydia Payne gasped for breath, clutching her wounded hand.

'You remember Mr. Symes?' said Sarah Tanner. 'It pains me to admit it, but we came to a truce.'

'Help me, for pity's sake,' exclaimed Lydia Payne. 'I'm dying!'

'Not from that,' replied Sarah Tanner, looking at the wound. 'But I'm sure we can make other arrangements.'

'What do you mean by that?' gasped Lydia Payne, clutching her hand to her chest.

'Where is Miss Fulbrook?'

'Why should I tell you a thing?' said Lydia Payne. 'I thought you were dying.'

'Damn you both! In a lodging-house in the Minories. What do you mean "arrangements"?'

'You have two options, Miss Payne. The first is to confess to the police, explain how you kidnapped Elizabeth Fulbrook, how John Ferntower murdered his aunt. As to the second, I leave you in Mr. Symes's hands, to do with as he sees fit. I'm sure you can believe he has a vigorous imagination in such matters.'

'If I go to the police, I'll be hanged.'

'Perhaps, perhaps not. There is only you and Miss Fulbrook to tell the tale – we can concoct something plausible; my true part in it can be left out. And, as for Mr. *Hawkes*, I think you will find he has impeccable credentials; he might even volunteer something for your defence – an affidavit to say you were Ferntower's pawn. You might only get twenty-five years.'

'I won't do it,' said Lydia Payne. 'You can prove nothing.'

'Then you prefer the alternative?'

Lydia Payne shook her head and, without another word, jumped towards the coach door, turning the handle with her good hand, and scrambling out of the moving carriage. The coachman, seated upon the box beside Stephen Symes, instantly pulled up the horses, applying the brakes.

Lydia Payne lay crumpled in the road, her body crushed beneath the lumbering great wheels of a coal-man's waggon.

Symes leant down and smiled a grim smile.

'An option you neglected to mention?'

EPILOGUE

Sarah Tanner sat in the Regent Street drawing-room, a silver tea-service set before her, facing Her Majesty.

'So delightful of you to drop by, my dear,' said the old woman, tickling the back of the Pekinese that lay snoring in her lap.

'How could I refuse?' said Sarah Tanner.

'I confess, my dear, when you came to us, I thought it was a trick. I did not believe young Mr. Ferntower had the backbone for that sort of work.'

'Is that why Symes was content to let him shoot me?'

'Mr. Symes has his moods, my dear. You can forgive him, I am sure. Tell me, have you seen this morning's *Times*?'

'No, I have not.'

'They are calling it the "Shadwell Horror". Droll, is it not? And a report about a madwoman throwing herself under a waggon on the Ratcliff Highway. What a busy few days you have had, eh?'

'I have had enough excitement, I think,' said Sarah Tanner, taking a sip of tea.

'I could still have you killed, you know,' said Her Majesty, in a matter-of-fact tone tinged with amusement. 'I would be well within my rights.'

'If you meant that, you would have done it by now,' said Sarah Tanner.

'Ha!' exclaimed Her Majesty, a smile breaking out over her face. 'You have such spirit, my dear! It would be a shame to lose you, I swear it would! But do have a care, won't you? Don't presume on my good nature too often, eh?'

'I'll remember that,' said Sarah Tanner drily.

'And what will you do now, Miss Mills?'

'Mrs. Tanner. Those days are over.'

'Really? You might have fooled me, my dear. Still, what are your plans?'

Sarah Tanner paused, as if not quite certain herself. 'I'm going to re-open my coffee-shop.'

Her Majesty chortled. 'The very idea! Oh, it is so amusing, my dear, please do – yes, please do. But who is going to pay for it? I would offer, truly, but it would do offence to Mr. Symes's feelings.'

'I would hate that, I am sure. It is a friend.'

'Arthur DeSalle?'

'Perhaps. May I ask a question?'

'Of course, my dear.'

'What about Elizabeth Fulbrook?'

'Please, Miss Mills, you touch a nerve. I gather from Mr. Symes that the girl is so disconsolate over her wretched fiancé's deceit – not to mention his rather mysterious demise, that he has lost all hope of getting any satisfaction in that quarter.'

'I am very sorry to hear that.'

'Oh, I am quite sure of it,' replied Her Majesty.

❧

Sarah Tanner stood outside the remains of the Dining and Coffee Rooms and looked out along Leather Lane. There was something comforting in the daily business of the market; and, for the first time, she felt certain of her decision.

'How long do they reckon?' said Ralph Grundy, nodding towards the workmen scrambling through the rubble of the upper floor.

'Six weeks.'

'Make it twelve then, missus. And it'll cost a small fortune.'

'Are you still working at the Bottle of Hay, Ralph?'

'Aye, but it's hard work for an old man. I don't even get a decent breakfast. Listen, missus, tell us – who's paying for all this?'

'Never you mind.'

Ralph Grundy raised his eyebrows, but went off to inspect the workmen's progress.

Sarah Tanner, once he was gone, took an envelope from her pocket, and pulled out the letter inside.

Hillmarton Park, 3rd May

Dear Mrs. Richards,

I do not know how you found me in that wretched boarding-house; nor can I comprehend the dreadful events that took place in Shadwell. In truth, all certainty seems to have been stripped away from me in the past few days, and I find myself foundering. I have been glad to discover, at least, that you were wrong about my guardian.

I write simply to say this. I believe you have been the only true friend to me in this wretched affair and that you were duped by John Ferntower as readily as I. Moreover, even though I do not know the full circumstances, I am quite certain that you *saved* me.

You have my gratitude and I enclose a small token of my thanks.

Your respectfully,
Elizabeth Fulbrook

Sarah Tanner unfolded the piece of paper still within the envelope: a banker's draft for one hundred guineas.

'Here, missus,' said Ralph Grundy, looking in her direction, 'what's that you got there?'

'Nothing, Ralph,' said Mrs. Tanner, placing the note back in the envelope. 'Nothing at all.'

The sequel to *A Most Dangerous Woman*, the next
gripping mystery for Sarah Tanner

THE MESMERIST'S APPRENTICE

by

L. M. Jackson

Read on for an extract...

CHAPTER ONE

Norah Smallwood leant casually over the counter and glanced at her employer's newspaper. If there was one thing that perplexed her about the owner of the New Dining and Coffee Rooms, it was the general interest she took in the daily press. It made sense to collect the abandoned papers that accumulated in the coffee-house's little booths: that was a wise economy, since the fried fish stall on the corner of Baldwin's Gardens paid ready money for wrapping. But to read the tiny print in the meantime; to take any pleasure in the inky notices and reports of the *Morning Chronicle* or *Daily News* – well, that seemed quite unnatural in a woman. For her own part, although she had been taught to read, she found it something of a chore to attempt even the most straightforward of penny romances that were hawked around the market.

Every rule, however, has an exception. And although Norah felt a broad disdain for most forms of literature, she maintained an healthy interest in one branch of the art: the lively notices of public amusements that graced the front page of every newspaper. Thus, as her eyes alighted upon a particular advertisement, she paused in her rather desultory efforts at cleaning.

'Is that tomorrow?' she asked.

Sarah Tanner stopped reading and laid down the paper, rather pointedly. If the proprietress of the New Dining and Coffee Rooms had grown fond of Norah Smallwood – which was undoubtedly the case – she occasionally found her company a little too convivial. She preferred to treasure the rare quiet moments, when there were no customers at the counter and the occupants of the shop's little booths enjoyed their food and drink in solitary contemplation. In short, she slightly resented the interruption.

'What?'

'There,' said Norah, pointing. 'That's tomorrow, ain't it? What's it say?'

The item in question was a modest advertisement that lay half-way down the front page of the newspaper.

MESMERISM AND ITS ANALOGOUS PHENOMENA, PHYSICAL AND PSYCHICAL – Prof. FELTON will demonstrate the workings of the New Science at the Mechanics' Institution, Southampton Row, 28th April, commencing at eight o'clock. The lecture will examine the transference of health and incorporate a curious and interesting experiment. Gallery 3d.; reserved seats 1s. Members of the Institution admitted half-price. Private consultation from eleven until three o'clock.

'It says,' replied Mrs. Tanner, 'that anyone fool enough to part with threepence, to see some kitchen-maid faking a jig half-asleep, should go to Southampton Row tomorrow night.'

'Well, I'd go,' said Norah, doggedly ignoring the sarcasm, 'if I had threepence handy.'

'Then it's a good thing you don't. Besides, you're in a daze half the time as it is; it would look well if you came back magnetised. Now, unless I'm much mistaken,' said Mrs. Tanner, pointing, 'that table hasn't seen a dish-cloth all week – if it's not too much trouble?'

Norah Smallwood looked rather sullenly at her employer, and turned her back, muttering something that incorporated the words 'like a slave'. Sarah Tanner smiled a wry smile, and reached to pick up the paper once more. Her attention, however, was distracted by one of her customers who sat in the booth by the window. He was a young man – no, she thought to herself, not much more than a boy – in plain working clothes, with a thick head of brown curls and rather angular cheekbones. He was not from the market, she was sure of it. She did not know his face, nor did he wear the polished bluchers or colourful neckerchief which were the fashion amongst the coster-boys. There was nothing so unusual in that, but there was something odd in his manner. In particular, his food, a penny plate of hashed beef, was hardly touched, though it had sat upon the table for several minutes. Moreover, as he took up a mouthful on his fork, he seemed to masticate it with a curious thoughtfulness.

His eyes suddenly caught Sarah Tanner's as she looked at him.

'Here, missus,' he said, volubly enough for his voice to carry across the room, and the other diners to stare in his direction, 'this ain't up to much.'

Mrs. Tanner raised her eyebrows.

'I mean to say,' he continued, unabashed, 'you can pepper it up all you like, but you can't expect a fellow to eat it.'

'What you going on about?' demanded Norah, on her employer's behalf, with an indignant vehemence that caused a couple of the diners, both costers, to chuckle, doubtless anticipating an amusing *to-do*. Mrs. Tanner cast an admonitory glance in her direction.

'Are you saying there's something wrong with it?'

'Well, there ain't much right with it, missus,' insisted the boy. 'My belly's all twistin' up, and I ain't had more than a couple of morsels. What do you call it again?'

'Beef hash,' replied Mrs. Tanner calmly.

'Well, *you* might call it that,' said the boy, grimacing and spitting a mouthful of food back onto his plate, 'but I know a bit of horse-meat when I has it.'

'It's off a good leg of beef that we've been serving all morning, and no complaints.'

'That ain't my affair,' observed the boy. 'Maybe their gullets was so choked up, they didn't have half a chance.'

Mrs. Tanner looked over at her other customers. To her annoyance, if not surprise, the pair of costers who sat nearby suddenly seemed to contemplate their own plates with a degree of suspicion. She stepped out from behind the counter and walked over to the boy. He was no more than fifteen years old, despite his cocksure demeanour, and not particularly tall for his age.

'Hook it,' she said, firmly. 'Before I call a copper.'

'Here's a fine thing!' exclaimed the boy, seemingly affronted. 'Poison a fellow and chuck him out!'

'Look here, I don't know who you are,' she said, lowering her voice, 'but you won't get a penny from me for this cheap dodge, not if you drop down dead on the spot and half of London gets to hear about it. Now, hook it.'

'Dodge?' exclaimed the boy, deliberately loud. 'Now it ain't enough to poison a fellow but call him a liar an' all! Here – take your bleedin' penny for your hash and I hope it chokes you – if that horse-meat don't choke you first!'

And, before Mrs. Tanner could say a word, the boy stood up, pulled a penny from his waistcoat pocket, and shoved it into her hand, stalked from his seat to the door, and slammed it behind him.

'Must be wrong in the head,' said Norah, disdainfully.

Norah's employer shook her head, looking at the penny. 'I don't think so. Go and find Ralph – he's out the back.'

'What do you want him for?' asked Norah.

'Tell him he's in charge,' said Sarah Tanner, grabbing her shawl from the hook behind the counter. 'I'm just going out.'

Sarah Tanner stepped outside the shop and headed down Leather Lane, following in the boy's footsteps.

It was almost mid-day, and most of the costers' barrows were emptying, with the exception of a solitary vendor who seemed to have acquired two barrels of herring, whose aroma – a little too ripe for popular taste – filled the street. The market, however, was still crowded. For there were a host of lesser dealers upon the lane whose stock-in-trade were less perishable items. They filled the pavements around the barrows, occasionally interpolating their own little cart or some-times simply laying a cloth upon the ground. Dealers in 'fancy goods', 'plain goods' – and, if truth be told, goods that were no good to anyone – who sold every-thing from curtain-hooks to candles, patent remedies to pin-cushions. They always attracted a curious crowd and, in consequence, it was no easy matter to spot an individual amongst them.

Nonetheless, after a few minutes, when she had almost given up hope, she saw the self-same boy. He was loitering upon the edge of the market, near a small hand-barrow, propped upon the pavement so as to render it horizontal. The goods for sale were, as far as she could make out, of the 'fancy' kind – cheap jewellery, scarf-pins and brooches – not the sort to entice the average youth. But there were several interested parties already there, including a middle-aged gentleman of the shabby-genteel variety, bending over in earnest contempla-tion of the equally shabby wares, perhaps choosing an affordable gift for an elderly mother or long-suffering spouse.

She watched the boy edge forward. Instinctively, she stepped back behind the nearest barrow. For, in that instant, she had a good idea what would happen next.

There!

Even a seasoned police constable might have over-looked it. But she knew the movements of a practised pickpocket; and – if only for the briefest instant – she saw the glint of metal in his fingers, as a watch passed from one waistcoat pocket to another.

The boy then walked on briskly, but not so quickly as to attract attention. She followed, on the opposite side of the road, negotiating the various makeshift stalls. The boy slowed his steps to a casual sauntering pace and it was a simple matter to catch up with him. She waited for the right moment, dodging the crowd.

Then she reached out and grabbed hold of him.

'Eh!' the boy protested, instantly wriggling free. A look of angry indignation passed across his face; but it dissipated the second he saw his assailant.

'You! I thought you was a Peeler!'

'I'll fetch one if you like,' said Sarah Tanner.

'Well, you do that, missus. I ain't the party what's poisoning other parties, am I now?' he said, merrily. 'What do you want with us, anyhow?'

'You know there was nothing wrong with that meat. What are you playing at?'

'Playing?' said the boy. 'I ain't playing, darlin'. Straight as they come.'

'Is that so?'

'Just!' exclaimed the boy, visibly amused by the entire exchange.

'Then,' continued Mrs. Tanner, holding out her closed hand and opening it, 'what's this?'

The boy looked down and immediately put a hand to his own waistcoat pocket. For, before him, lay the very watch which had only recently passed into his own possession. His mouth fell open, then, after a second to two, he broke into uncontrollable laughter.

'That's a proper facer, that is!' he exclaimed, wiping his eyes. 'I thought you was playing the high and mighty, when you must be the best prig this side of Holborn – I didn't feel a bleedin' thing. Just! Well, I'm pleased to make your acquaintance, missus, honest I am.'

'I doubt there's much honest about you,' said Sarah Tanner warily. 'Do you want the watch back?'

'If you like,' shrugged the boy, 'it was only a lark.'

'Is that what you'll tell the magistrate?'

'What, are you going to give me in charge, then, is that it?' said the boy, with a chuckle. 'Nah, you keep it missus. I bet you've got an uncle or two who can give it a good home, eh?'

'I might do. I could get a good price on it. Let's say I give you half if you tell me what that business in my shop was all about.'

The boy merely smirked and shook his head.

'Pleasure, though, missus – charmed!'

And, with a cheerful nod, he raised a hand to his

cap and made to walk off. Sarah Tanner, without giving the matter much thought, grabbed hold of the boy's arm. But as he turned round, the youth took hold of her hand with his own, and looked her in the eye. All the good humour had drained from his face, to be replaced with a cold, malevolent stare.

'I'll keep away from your little shop, darlin', out of courtesy. But don't interfere with the Brass Band, 'cos we're not the boys to take it, see?'

And with those words, his cock-sure smile returned, and he darted into the crowd...